THE APARA CHRONICLES BOOK 5:

PHOENIX RISING

BY JEANNE RHODES-MOEN

DISCLAIMER:

Any similarities to actual persons living, dead, or otherwise is unintentional. I have used some actual place names from Asheville for realism.

Some characters occasionally utter words in other languages. See the last page of the book: Foreign Word List for definitions.

First published: 2024

E-Book ISBN **978-1-967683-01-7**

Print   ISBN **978-1-967683-00-0**

Cover design and book layout: Jeanne Rhodes-Moen

Published By:

Jeannius Designs
Asheville, NC 28805

www.Jeannius.com

Visit www.aparachronicles.com

DEDICATION AND THANKS

To Gillan, who has helped me rise from the ashes of life more than once in the years since we became friends.

And thanks to Nicky Rea, who has acted as my editor through this book series, encouraging me to see it through and mentoring me to push my limits and make it better.

BOOKS IN SERIES

HIDDEN IN BROAD DAYLIGHT (MARCH 2024)

IN YOUR DREAMS (MAY 2024)

PERSISTENCE OF VISION (AUGUST 2024)

GOING VIRAL (NOVEMBER 2024)

PHOENIX RISING (2025)

WORLDS COLLIDE (2025)

All books will be released during 2024-2025

ABOUT THE AUTHOR

Jeanne Rhodes-Moen was born in Washington D.C. in 1966. She grew up in Maryland, and attended Hood College, where she received a B.A. Psychology and a second B.A. in Math, Secondary Education.

In 1991, she married a Norwegian and moved to Norway, where she made jewelry based in their traditional filigree fused with her own imaginative style. Her first book, Silver Threads: Making Wire Filigree Jewelry, was published in 2006 by Kalmbach Books, and is currently available as Print-on-Demand and eBook on Amazon.

She and her two daughters moved to Asheville, NC, in 2005 after her husband passed from diabetic complications. Since then, she has done a combination of jewelry, lapidary, and jewelry photography.

More recently, she has been using her creative skills toward this series: The Apara Chronicles. A science fantasy book series; of which Hidden in Broad Daylight is the first installment.

Jeanne and her daughters all deal with ADHD, and she finds it has a positive effect on her creative abilities.

TABLE OF CONTENTS

MAD WORLD

The sun hangs low in a gray, partly cloudy sky, even though it is midday. Lissa stands on a rocky lake shore surrounded by tall, snow-capped mountains. It's cold, and the edges of the lake are iced over, with only the middle still fluid. There's a boat in dry storage on the ground nearby with the name "*Jotunheimen*" on the side. She reaches down and picks up a palm-sized, flat rock from a pile by her feet, and flings it far out into the unfrozen center of the deep lake, grunting with effort, and watching it skip several times before finally sinking into the water.

The last couple of years have been the worst of Lissa Pederson's life. That's saying something, considering Lissa is over 800 years old. As one of the higher echelon Apara leaders, Lissa has had to deal with more than she has in hundreds of years put together.

First, the race to stop an ominous set of mass premonitions that she and many other Apara were experiencing, only without the details to decode their message. When they finally solved the puzzle, they stopped most of the nuclear bombs being planted around the world, save one: Jerusalem. The Apara lost many of their own that day, and for a time, Lissa believed that toll included her twin brother, Peder.

Those losses were staggering and left the Apara reeling and short staffed. The race is on to rebuild their ranks to keep the world stable after Jerusalem's destruction. Unfortunately, they've run into two issues, not enough suitable transformees, and one they turned, went rogue.

It took about a year to stop Jason Templeton, and gain some headway in recouping their losses. Just when Lissa thought things were looking up, with their rogue in stasis under lock and key, Jason Templeton dealt them one last blow. He transformed a compatible genetic scientist to alter the transformation virus, albeit, not quite as he had hoped. It travelled the world, awakening abilities or heightened senses in many of their potentials without fully transforming them.

The Benefactors had to step in, sending a team of hybrid human-aliens to help with the outbreak. Just when that, too, settled down, a new, unforeseen threat literally blew up in their faces. A secret military operation in Israel discovered an Apara who survived the bomb by porting into an underground tomb. Their secret was out! At least partially, and the discovery led this new threat to Lissa's and Inspiration Inc.'s doorstep in the form of a terrorist attack which destroyed their Asheville center of operations, and nearly took the Asheville Apara with it!

Lissa throws more rocks into the lake, trying to release the stress and anger she has pent up inside since the latest nightmare event struck.

She hears Kari behind her saying, "Lissa, it's too cold to be out here! Come join me inside by the fire. I've got hot chocolate and *risgrøt* for you!"

She turns, even though she has the next stone primed and ready to heave, watching her partner coming from their house with a warm mug of hot chocolate in hand. She smelled it as soon as Kari brought it out of their home, but it was her words that broke Lissa's pensive mood. Lissa says "*Ja*" with an odd inhale to the word. "I'm just blowing off steam, *elskling*." She says and reaches for the mug of cocoa.

"I don't suppose you're ready to talk about it?" Kari inquires while gently rubbing her partner's back as they both look out over the large Nordic lake.

"I just need a little me time. I'll be fine. Besides, I'll be talking about it enough tomorrow at Conclave." Liz says, brushing off the looming cloud of stress that's been threatening to engulf her like a raging blizzard.

"Lissa, we've talked about this a thousand times! You can't keep going at this pace without a true recharge. Once you brief the Conclave, I want you to take a few days break! We can't do anything until we locate either Marc or the *Naqam* themselves." Kari's voice is awash with obvious concern, not only for her partner, but for what her faltering mental state could mean for the Apara and their mission.

Liz gently touches her partner of 600 plus years' cheek. "Kari, *hjerte mitt*! I will be fine! I've been through wars, plagues, natural disasters and Marc's constant moping about Collette and now Tess!" She smirks sarcastically. "I'll brief the Conclave and then I'll just need a couple of days to catch my breath." Lissa says, though her crystal blue eyes are shadowed with an exhaustion far deeper than the lake.

"You know this is different, Lissa! You've never had to deal with this much loss, both personal, and the losses to us all! We've been exposed! We were *attacked*! You were already feeling responsible for all the losses in Jerusalem, Apara and human, alike! Now, the virus, and the *Naqam*, too! You're running on fumes when we need you more than ever. I'll go to Sara and Sue if I must, but you cannot continue at this pace!" Kari says sternly, tugging on Liz's arm to come inside and get warm as the first flakes of a passing, Norwegian snow squall fall.

The two women walk arm in arm to the cabin, leaning into each other, and enter their home. As they go into the living room, Liz's twin brother looks up and gives her a lopsided smile, moving his legs off the sofa to make room for her in front of the fire. "*Hei*! Up for a game? I've been beating Kari for the last hour, I'm sure she wouldn't mind if you take over!" He says, motioning toward a game board that could be a Viking variant of chess.

Peder feels his sister's turbulent emotions as though she's thin ice on the lake, ready to crack under the next bit of pressure. His eyes flicker to Kari, making contact, and they both know something must be done to keep Liz from shattering psychologically.

CONCLAVE

Liz wakes, gets out of bed, and leaves Kari to sleep, as it's 4 am Norwegian time. From the back of a closet Liz takes out an ancient, wooden box carved with Viking motifs. She opens it and takes out a purple, tunic-like dress, and a gold necklace with a design engraved in a black stone with iridescent colors in it. The pendant is Liz's ID, given to her when she was first transformed by the Benefactors over 800 years ago.

Not everyone transformed was given such a marker, but those who were chosen as leaders, organizers, and decision makers were honored with these symbols of power. Hers has the Nordic runes ᚠ, Ansuz-Odin, and Kenaz-Torch, marking her as one with insight, inspiration, revelation, and creativity. The Asheville center, Inspiration, Inc, takes its name from these runes.

Liz was chosen and transformed by the Benefactors when she was only 16. Her first act was to transform her twin brother, Peder, as 'eternal life' without the other half of her soul would be unbearable.

She hasn't worn this ceremonial garb since the 1940s when the Conclave met to discuss the advent of the nuclear age. The full Conclave should have met post Jerusalem, but several of the longtime members were lost and everything was chaotic, so they met virtually instead.

Now, the Apara are facing something they've never faced before, an enemy of their own making; or at least made from one of their own. No one knows who the woman is the *Naqam* have in their clutches, but it was someone who survived the nuclear explosion by porting into a tomb beneath the city. While finding that one of their own survived Jerusalem should be a matter for celebration, the

Naqam have used this unknown woman's blood to transform compatible humans, and used these unsanctioned Apara transformees as a weapon against the Apara in Asheville. Such a threat is not to be taken lightly and could threaten the rest of the Apara as well.

She must face the remaining 'Elders', many of whom are far older than her, as well as the other leaders of Apara centers worldwide. While the discovery of the injured Apara woman was not Liz's fault, so much has happened on her watch, she cannot help but feel the weight of guilt on her shoulders.

After changing into her official garb, Liz ports out, reappearing in the geographic equivalent, in Sanctuary, of southern Pakistan, along the Indus River. Unlike its Earth equivalent, this version of the Indus Valley is still a fertile paradise. On Earth, it was once the location for a thriving, unusually modern, ancient city known as Mohenjo-daro. This was an early, experimental city where the Benefactors gathered some of the brightest humans, helping them build the city as part of their endeavor to educate and elevate these early human tribes.

Unfortunately, during the Benefactors' absence, the river receded, leaving the Indus Valley the desert wasteland it is today. This was not the case for the Sanctuary equivalent. While most Apara live relatively isolated around the world where they choose, Liz is now standing before one of the few Apara Cities in Sanctuary. It's small, by human standards, but is still a busy center of activity, with centers for scientific discovery, an Apara Museum, an enormous library containing books, scrolls, and tablets from all over the world, from ancient to modern times, and the Conclave Hall. Many of the oldest Apara, who are no longer active in the field have made this their home. The Conclave is a circular building made of metal and composite materials, but the exterior is covered in rich blue lapis lazuli found in the region. The blue is riddled with golden pyrite, making it look like a deep blue, starry sky.

The dome on top is fashioned from slabs of different types of quartz, cut and set into titanium frames to resemble a giant, faceted gem. When the sun is high and shines on the dome, the Conclave shall meet in the chamber below.

The sun's still low in the sky, but the facets sparkle as the sun glints off the different angles. Liz gasps in awe, having forgotten how beautiful the dome of The Conclave is. After taking a moment to admire it, she walks toward it.

In this city, known only as Daro, porting is discouraged. Residents and visitors alike are expected to walk through the city, as there are hundreds, and potentially thousands of Apara there daily, and random porting can lead to unexpected Apara collisions.

Liz passes through an archway made of blood-red carnelian, framed in a mosaic of turquoise and lapis. As she enters the building, she sees others wearing similar garb and necklaces in the rotunda. A kinetic art mobile made of various gem crystals hangs above the assembled delegates, sparkling as the sun filters in from above.

There's a table with exotic food from every culture represented, and benches to sit on. There's a multitude of languages being spoken aloud, but Liz perceives the mental hum of telepathic conversations, as well.

Sitting on an ornate bench is a darker skinned woman wearing exotic flowers woven into her long, braided, black hair.

Liz recognizes her as Ballari, one of the eldest of the Apara. She is of the original transformation; unkeyed, and without the need to feed on blood. Beside her is a young man, who looks to be just out of his teens. His name is Dev, and he is Ballari's adult son, transformed at her request. They sit and watch the others, not because they do not wish to socialize, but because many of the others do not wish to impose on the oldest of the old.

A woman Liz recognizes all too well approaches the pair and speaks with them. Their faces light up with joy at the interaction. Liz smiles, knowing only Sara would be so bold as to approach them as equals. While Sara may be obsessed with some modern cultural phenomena like Star Wars, she is over 4000 years old, and closer in age to these originals who no longer walk among most of the Apara. Liz once asked her why she does not pass on her medical duties to others and join the elders, only for Sara to laugh and say, "Because I would be so bored, even I might *die* of ennui!"

The room slowly fills as more Apara arrive, all wearing similar garb, and necklaces with a unique design on it. The design varies depending on the time and language spoken where and when they were transformed. The stones used originated from each person's birth area. Liz's pendant has a stone from a different part of Scandinavia, as national borders were not as they are now; hers is from what is now Finland. It is a form of labradorite known as Spectrolite and contains vivid rainbow flashes in a midnight-black feldspar base.

Liz meanders around the room, not engaging with many of the others. She's barely holding her anxiety in check in preparation for the briefing she must bring to the other leaders of the Apara. They have no *single* leader, but have a group of leaders who meet, as needed, when something affects them all, or threatens the entire world. As modern communications have improved, this group meets seldomly, but the advent of the *Naqam* warrants an in-person Conclave. While Liz is far from a true elder, age-wise, her experience gives her an unofficial status closer to theirs than many of the other center leaders.

As midday approaches, crystalline chimes ring out from the dome as the sun makes them expand–a call to Conclave–and the representatives ascend the stairs to the meeting area. All races and cultures, including some cultures which, technically, no longer exist, are represented. They file into a large room filled with colored light passing through quartz slabs–shades of purple, yellow, pink, and pure light are everywhere, diffused in brightness by a translucent ceiling between them and the dome.

The seating is something you might expect in any large representative forum, with comfortable seats set in consecutive semi-circles, with a place for the speaker facing the group. As one of the eldest of all Apara, Ballari is standing at a lapis-covered podium, waiting for all to be seated. She catches Liz's eye, motions for her to join her, and sit in a nearby chair until it's time to address the Conclave.

Liz walks down to the seat of honor, or as she feels, *perhaps dishonor*-and sits, controlling her heart rate, breathing, and other signs of anxiety. Once everyone settles and focuses on the podium, Ballari addresses the Conclave in her native Sanskrit. Everyone hears her in their own language through their necklaces, which translate the meaning into each person's language.

Ballari says, "Welcome, leaders and elders. I wish we were meeting under happier circumstances, but that has not been what recent times have provided us. As our new crisis is related to the destruction of Jerusalem, Lissa Pederson will address you, as she and her subordinate, Marc Girard, coordinated that effort, and were directly affected by the most recent events." She bows and steps back, waiting for Liz to take her place at the podium.

Liz approaches the podium and scans the crowd. Faces she's known for centuries stare back at her, plus some new ones tapped to replace those lost in Jerusalem. "My fellow Apara leaders, I bring you grave news. One of those presumed lost in Jerusalem survived by porting into an underground tomb, only to be discovered by an Israeli military intelligence team. We do not yet know who, other than the Apara is a woman. Unfortunately, our information suggesting they know of our existence and what we are, has been confirmed. My center in Asheville, North Carolina was recently invaded and destroyed by a team of unsanctioned Apara, transformed using a blood exchange from our missing sister. In addition, we believe my second in command, Marc Girard, was put into stasis and is in their custody. We have yet to sense any signs of life, but we believe he was on the roof when the building was destroyed. As we have found no remains, we assume they took him back to Israel." She pauses as rumblings among those in the chamber increase to the point where her voice will not carry, nor translate, as there is too much being said simultaneously.

As the cacophony reaches a peak, Ballari picks up a gnarled and carved, sandalwood staff and bangs it on the stone floor until the voices and echoes are replaced by silence.

"A source has informed us the *Naqam*, as their organization is called, believes we *caused* the nuclear devastation, and have thus set their sights on us as their enemy. At this point in time, we believe they are unaware of the global nature of our kind, and believe my center was responsible, specifically Marc and myself. However, who they do or do not blame is not the most critical issue. There are now an unknown number of unsanctioned Apara working for a hostile military organization. My source informed me they've all been conditioned to be loyal to the *Naqam*. They were meant to be among us, if suitable, but my information says that suitability is not considered by the *Naqam*, only compatibility." Liz explains.

The Māori representative stands silently, waiting to be recognized. Liz acknowledges her. She asks, "How did they know who was compatible? Surely this was not just a random effort to transform people!"

"In fact, it started out that way, but they eventually gained access to one of my people through a pre-transformation acquaintance. Many of our newest Apara were still using standard cell phones, and her acquaintance used technology to clone and access her phone's memory. They learned of the Roulette Virus, how it brings out abilities in compatible people, and used this knowledge to find, abduct, and transform compatible individuals in their region against their will. That's who attacked my center. Their attack was twofold. Again, through my novice Apara—they captured and compelled her to access the database, providing them with a list of compatible individuals in their region. We can only assume they are expanding their Apara forces with those on the list. What they will do once they've transformed them is anyone's guess. We assume we are still targets, but there is also the possibility they could use *their* Apara for covert actions against other nations or come after other centers if they realize Inspiration Inc. is but one of an international network." Liz explains.

Despite increasing murmurs, she continues, "Currently, they are focused on my center alone. I and my people are actively searching for their base in an attempt to deal with the group and recover both Marc and our unknown Apara woman. Hopefully, we can put a stop to them before they discover just how many of us there are in the world. Right now, they feel they can handle us, but if they discover we number over 20,000, worldwide, they will likely expose us rather than fight us directly, which would put all our lives and missions in jeopardy. Considering this, I felt it necessary to call this Conclave and inform you of the potential danger, but request that you leave the problem to us for now." Liz scans the room visually, as well as psychically to gauge reactions to the news.

A Russian delegate, Ivan Popov stands, and once acknowledged, asks, "When you say 'deal with them', what do you plan to do? It will be difficult to redact so many minds, plus the possible complications of rogue, conditioned Apara."

Liz nods, replying, "All options are on the table. We don't know enough, at this point, about their numbers, or how far knowledge of our existence has spread. Our source, an American military soldier, has told us all he could, but he was not completely in their confidence."

Ivan blurts out, "Do you mean to tell us that the American military *knows* about us, too?"

Liz looks pensive. "Not that we are aware of. He was conscripted by the Israelis when he discovered the body of the Apara woman after a cave-in. He had a prior romantic relationship with one of the new transformees in my center, so used that connection to gain access to her and the information they needed. The *Naqam* left both the soldier and my Apara novice to die in the explosion.

In the aftermath, our source has cooperated willingly and completely and is under *my* protection."

One of the Elders stands; a one-time warrior of a long-gone tribe. After clearing his throat, he speaks in a language few would understand without their necklaces, but the sentiment comes across loud and clear. "The only way you can *ensure* an end to the threat is to utterly *decimate* it."

There are murmurs in the chamber; some of shock and others of agreement. For some of the younger generations, the concept of killing humans is beyond the pale, even in a case like this. Liz nods and says, "Yes, it is one of our options, though I would rather not take those lives, but I know it may be necessary; I am ready to take that task upon my shoulders."

Satisfied that Liz will do what's necessary, the warrior elder sits, arms crossed, but mollified. Murmurs continue in the hall until Ballari strikes the floor with her staff once again, then nods to Liz to continue.

"I'll be setting up an information feed to keep all of you in the loop, but for now, we will take care of this. I would ask for those of you in the Middle East keep an eye out for anything that could reveal where their base may be. Use your local contacts. We believe my second, Marc Girard, must be in stasis, as none of us has sensed him, including his partner. We hope, when he regains consciousness, that may change. However, you should know they've developed technology which can counteract our abilities. I will send what details we have through the feed. Sara and the hybrids are researching what little we know about them, but most of the technology was damaged or destroyed when our center was. Our source filled us in on a few items, including an anti-path implant he was given before approaching my novice Apara."

Again, murmurs fill the chamber, but Liz stops Ballari from banging her staff again, sending out a wideband path for **QUIET**, silencing the crowd, some of them stare at Liz in shock at her telepathic outburst. "Now that I have your attention again—if you have any information that can help us find the *Naqam* and retrieve our people, please let us know. If not, please follow the feed. We will keep you informed, but we must focus on this, and constant inquiries for updates will only distract us, and please! Do not take any action yourselves. The element of surprise will be necessary when we deal with them. If any of you take it upon yourselves to get involved, it could ruin our chances of getting all of them, or rescuing our people intact."

Ballari rises to the podium as Liz steps back and takes her seat again. Ballari speaks, "I implore you to take what Lissa says seriously. The sooner this is resolved, the sooner we can undertake a new search and rescue mission."

Questioning looks and surprised murmurs erupt, but before anyone can ask, Ballari continues, "If one of us survived by porting into underground chambers, others may have done so as well, but as long as the *Naqam* are active, they may be watching, or searching for others themselves. We must do our due diligence, and attempt to find and recover *all* Apara who survived."

The tone of the crowd changes to one of agreement, as most of those in the crowd knew people lost in Jerusalem. The possibility of finding even a few of their friends and family ignites a small spark of hope.

Ballari continues with a few other bits of business that should be addressed while they are gathered, including final lists of the missing, those presumed dead, and updated tallies of new transformees, including any problems among them. When business is concluded, they are dismissed and return to the lower chamber, where a feast with delicacies from all over awaits them. Most of the Apara eat and discuss the events of the day, but Liz feels anxious, knowing some blame her for letting an unknown enemy sneak up on her and destroy her center, possibly endangering them all. While most do not share that view, it resonates with her own self-condemnation, and she surreptitiously slips away.

As she exits the carnelian inlaid archway, she senses a familiar energy waiting just outside. "Liz, you know *it is not* your fault!" Sara says, putting a small, warm hand on her arm.

"*Logically,* I *know* that, but I'm not the only one in that chamber that sees it that way." Liz sighs, and the two women walk along a winding pathway through a sculpted garden and down toward the river.

Sara says, "There will always be those who find it necessary to blame others, and yet, they are usually the first ones to deny fault when it is theirs. Liz, I know you don't want to hear this, but you must take a step back and catch your breath. Now that you've informed the Conclave, can you please do that?"

"Not with Marc still out there and the *Naqam* still a serious threat!" Liz admits as she sits on a stone bench facing the lotus strewn flowing river.

"Then delegate! But you're heading for a crash of catastrophic proportions." Sara holds up one hand to silence Liz's words. "Yes, Kari and I have been talking, but I have been concerned for your wellbeing for some time. We need you, but not a broken you. Delegate, and take a break, or I will have to exercise my authority, and make you do it! Do yourself a favor and take care of yourself for once. Trust me, you must do this before you crash and burn." Sara puts one hand on Lissa's shoulder, and stares her in the eye until she senses that her words have hit their target, then she vanishes, leaving Lissa to ponder her next moves.

RISING FROM THE RUBBLE

It's been two weeks since the explosion that destroyed Inspiration Inc's offices in south Asheville. The *Naqam's* plan was to blow up the building with the 'vampires' inside and extract their bodies without a fight, returning them to Israel for interrogation and eventual trials for crimes against humanity, once revived.

Thanks to Callie, a new Apara with a big talent, the ability to create physical portals, all the Apara working there were rescued before the explosives detonated, with one exception, Marc Girard.

While they await signs of life from Marc, Liz moves forward with plans to build a new office building in Asheville. Technically, it will be two buildings, one on human Earth, and an identical one in Sanctuary, tying them together with their portal technology. This will allow them to disconnect from the human-world building should they be attacked again, and to prevent any unauthorized Apara from porting in. Should they try, they would find themselves in a vacant building. The new building will be less isolated, so it will be more difficult for such a group to attack without warning. Their new location is on the west end of downtown Asheville, overlooking the French Broad River and West Asheville. The lot has been empty for several years while the city contemplated a use for it. With a little finagling, Lissa secured the property, outbidding yet another proposed hotel, as well as an apartment complex. The new location will take four months to build in human reality, but much less time in Sanctuary because of the technology the Benefactors gave the Apara.

In the meantime, Liz has her hands full with crisis management. She spends a fair amount of time convincing several potentials they recently hired to stay on. Some will temporarily be placed at their

Hendersonville satellite office, but the lost mission ones will work from home until their building is completed. Because of the peculiarities of Lost Mission Potentials, Liz feels they need to be where Tess, Kari, and Sue can properly evaluate them.

Officially, the cause of the explosion was declared a fractured gas line under the building. The explosives and timers used by the *Naqam*, were a new type that left no residues, and destroyed the timing mechanism. However, Liz has Apara working in the local government and emergency services who made certain the real cause won't become known. The last thing the Apara need is for a terrorist attack to become public knowledge. Should it be, people would question why Israeli militants would blow up a company in Asheville, which will bring unwanted scrutiny of their activities, and no doubt dozens of conspiracy theories. The goal of the Apara is to exist in plain sight without drawing unwelcome attention to themselves or their activities, while protecting humanity, mostly from itself.

There's one other Apara Liz has on her mind tonight besides Marc, his partner, Tess. Tess has become part of Liz's core family consisting of her brother, Peder, her partner, Kari, and some of her closest transformees and their partners, like Marc and Tess.

Tess has been on a psychological roller coaster ride ever since she found out about Marc's true nature. It turned her life upside down from that day because she knew, but he couldn't make her forget what he was. They didn't think she was compatible, so she became one of the only humans to work side-by-side with the Apara, specifically with Marc, trapping her in limbo between the two realities.

It turned out she was compatible after all, as she became Apara the night of the Jerusalem bomb. They lost nearly 3000 of their people trying to stop the horrors of that night, and nearly lost Marc as well. Thanks to the bond he and Tess share, he was able to port home by using her mind as a beacon, while many others could not escape the firestorm. To keep Marc alive, Tess cut her own wrist and fed him, and accidentally got his blood in her open wound, starting a rather unexpected transformation.

Since then, her life has been a series of trials. Her psychic skills are very formidable, as the Benefactors tinkered with her DNA in utero. Between their strength, a lack of subconscious training, and confidence issues, she has struggled to control them.

She recently overcame some of those rough seas, only to lose Marc when the *Naqam* destroyed the building, and she was forced to leave him behind to escape through Callie's portal. At first, she was distraught, but eventually, she came out of it resolved to fight, literally, to get him back. Liz worries about her, knowing that if they don't find Marc soon, Tess could slip backwards psychologically.

Liz has operatives doing searches for any information about the *Naqam*, but so far, little has panned out. Charlie, a human once involved with the now-Apara, Amy, lived in the *Naqam's* underground base, but he is unable to tell them *where* it is.

They're stuck for the moment. Neither Liz nor Tess have sensed Marc, though Tess is certain she'd have felt it if he had died rather than just gone into stasis.

At first, Liz set up a command center at Medical, in Sanctuary, but found it too distracting and moved her operations to her home; a home she shares with her partner, Kari, and her brother, Peder. Peder has lived with them ever since he was catastrophically injured in Jerusalem.

She's sitting in her living room, going over some of the recently hired potentials, as well as a few more they planned to hire before their offices were destroyed. She needs these new potentials, especially the three Lost Mission ones, to stay on her 'hook' until the new offices can be completed, so they can evaluate, and bring them into the Apara's fold.

The current file open on her tablet is for a young woman, twenty-four years old, born in North Dakota, who now lives near Greenville, SC. Her name is Phoenix Ashlyn Johnsen. Liz notes Phoenix's parents are of Scandinavian heritage, and wonders if she speaks any of the Scandi-languages.

As she's reviewing her information, including the evaluations Tess and Sue have done, her brother, Peder, comes into the room with two bottles of Norwegian beer, *Ringnes Pilsner*, one of the oldest beers brewed in Norway. He also has a tray of traditional Norwegian 'bread food'; open-faced rolls with things like salami, cucumber, *gravlaks*, scrambled eggs, or other toppings. He slides it in front of Liz on the table.

"Lissa, du må spise noe!" He says in Norwegian

"Javel?" She barks at him, stressed by all that's happened.

He settles in a nearby chair, and says, "I know you won't waste away, but you can't focus well when you don't eat properly." He says, concerned for his sister's somber and stressed mood.

Liz relents and puts her tablet down, grabbing a roll with scrambled eggs and dill, and another with gravlaks, thanking him in their native Norwegian, *"Takk for maten."*

"What has you so engrossed?" He asks as he takes one of the salami and cucumber rolls for himself.

"Just going over the people we have lined up to join us, but no office to hire them for!" She blurts out, frustrated.

"Are you worried they might lose interest?" He asks, opening her beer and pouring it into a tall glass.

"That's part of it. We really need every high-grade potential we can recruit." She sighs.

"You know how Charlie said they turned potentials they found through the viral outbreak; do you think they realize that all the humans we hire are potentials?" Peder asks.

"I *sure* hope not! Though that is a *distinct* possibility, especially since Amy worked here as a human first, before being turned. Liz admits with a weary expression and a sigh. "Are you thinking they may target *our* human employees?"

"I don't know, but now that they know about us, every potential we bring in could be at risk. While Jason is no longer an issue, we may need to protect them from an even greater threat." He suggests taking a long pull on his bottle.

Liz leans back on the sofa and stretches, yawning. "Speaking of potentials…." She trails off, preparing to breach a sensitive subject with Peder, "Perhaps it's time you jump on that train and see if anyone suits you." She gives him a lopsided grin.

"You know I don't feel comfortable turning anyone, not since I turned Halfdan." He admits.

"Are you *ever* going to get over your guilt about *him*? There was a one in four chance that anyone we turned back then would have psychological issues. Granted, some were worse than others, but you had *no way* of knowing that he would go *berserker* once turned." Liz reminds him.

"I know, but after he tore through Inga's family farm just outside the village, killing everyone there, I haven't dared take that risk again!" He explains, waves of guilt emanate from him.

"Peder! That's just an *excuse* and you *know* it! Today's potentials are a different matter. Some of these…" She taps her tablet. "Lost Mission ones aren't fully prepped, but if they weren't suitable, they never would have been chosen and tagged. I'd really like you to consider finding someone. We need to pair up responsible Apara with more potentials to train them and keep them out of trouble." She pauses and puts one hand on her brother's arm. "I know you've had no desire to be alone since you spent all that time in and out of consciousness in Sanctuary after the bomb, but seriously, isn't it about time you considered going back to your place? At least with a partner, you wouldn't be alone. You're always welcome here, but honestly, Kari and I… don't take this wrong, but we could use a little *us* time."

"Ah, *sorry*. You've literally been in my life since our births over 800 years ago! I sometimes forget that just because I'm your twin, doesn't mean I can't get in the way." He grins mischievously.

"Please don't see it as me *trying* to get rid of you, but I'm just under so much stress recently, and it's starting to wear on Kari and me. I'm not *asking* you to move out tomorrow, but I would ask you to be *open* to possibilities, *please*?" She nudges him in the leg.

"I'll try to keep an open mind." He says.

"Maybe an open *heart*, as well?" She eyes him questioningly.

"We'll *see*...." He temporizes.

"That's all I'm asking!" She finishes her last sandwich and waves him off so she can get back to her work before Kari comes home. Kari usually demands Liz puts her work aside, so they can have some quality time together.

BECOMING A BADASS

Tess has been at home since Marc's capture, but it's getting to her. She can smell his scent everywhere, and it only makes her more frustrated that they haven't been able to find him.

In a huff, she puts on her shoes and a clean t-shirt, ports out, and arrives in the lobby of one of the dormitory-style buildings near medical. She bounds up the stairs to the third floor, to number 36 and knocks. A minute passes, and the door opens.

"Hey, girl! *Good* to see ya! Come on in! How're you doing?" Amy says, making her friend feel welcome. She's been concerned about Tess and is happy for a chance to catch up and find out how she's holding up.

Tess shrugs, "As okay as I can be, under the circumstances. There's still nothing on Marc. Depending on how injured he was, it could take him a while just to come out of stasis." She says, attempting to reassure herself as to why she hasn't sensed him at all.

"Yeah, and if what Charlie told us is true, I'm sure they'll use some of that same tech they used on me to keep him from reaching out to *anyone*." Amy suggests.

Amy grabs some chips and dip and a box of chocolates, and they sit at a small kitchen table in Amy's one-bedroom apartment.

"So, how do you like your new abode?" Tess grins, looking around at this relatively small space.

"Eh, I've lived in worse while stationed abroad! In one barracks, they had about ten bunk beds, well, five by two, in a room like this! The gal above mine had IBS and used to fart half the night!" She laughs thinking about it.

"Oh, *God*! That must have been *awful*!" Tess grimaces at the thought.

"Yeah, especially when the mess fixed burritos! Beans and bunk beds don't mix!" Amy jokes, trying to elicit a laugh from Tess.

"No, I guess they wouldn't!" Tess laughs hard for the first time since Marc was taken. When she stops, Tess looks more serious. "Amy, I've been thinking. I hate being all alone at the house, aside from Mabel, and we've got a *perfectly* good apartment connected to the house from when I first started dealing with my psychic abilities and had to move to a shielded place. Do you think... maybe you'd be interested in moving in there? I'd like the company."

"That would be *awesome*! We can be buds like when we first started at Inspiration, Inc! Besides, the guy upstairs gets up at 1 am every morning and exercises before porting to a center in Europe! Drives me nuts!" Amy jokes.

"Well, that's all settled, then. *Besides*, it will make the favor I have to ask of you easier." She gives her a sheepish grin.

Amy raises an eyebrow questioningly, implying 'go on'.

"I *know* you've been teaching me self-defense and stuff but *damn it!* I feel so helpless just waiting for any news about Marc. I want to help get him back, but I need some *real* training! Like *hand-to-hand,* or I'm afraid Liz won't let me in on the *action*." Tess sits back in the kitchen chair, brooding. "I just can't sit here helplessly and wait!"

Amy puts her hand on Tess's reassuringly. "I told you from day one, I'd teach you! If you *want* to learn more *advanced* hand-to-hand, and other combat techniques, I'm *all* in! Even how to *shoot!*"

"*Thanks!* I'm not terribly fond of guns, but under the circumstances, I guess I'll have to get over that." She sighs. She's been mostly passive in the Apara world, doing evaluations, or coming up with ideas for others to act upon. Now, it's time for her to jump in with both feet.

With Marc missing and unable to act on her behalf, she must take the initiative and fight in whatever way necessary. After she fought with Jason in Hot Springs, she realized she doesn't need to *stay* on the sidelines anymore. She's strong enough, physically, to be in on the action, and that's where she must be if it means getting Marc back. Having gone through the Apara rite of passage of 'dying', going into stasis, and coming back, she's less afraid of acting.

The next day, Amy moves into Tess's old apartment, still furnished from when she moved to Sanctuary. "Thanks again, Tess! After that attack, they moved me into the dorms so fast my head spun! Since I'm a known Apara, even if they think they blew me up, Liz doesn't want me to risk living outside Sanctuary, but those dorms, while utilitarian, don't feel like home." Amy confesses.

"Well, as far as I'm concerned, you're welcome to use it as long as you want." Tess says with a grin.

"Or at least until we get Marc back." Amy laughs. "I don't know how he'll feel about me staying here."

"Well, for now, this apartment is yours. When we get Marc back, we'll see what happens. Maybe they'll have new Sanctuary-homes built by then and you can get your own place, or maybe Dave will pop the partner question? But, if anyone's welcome to use this, it's my *best* friend!" Tess gives Amy a hug.

Despite Tess's brave face and willingness to fight for Marc, Amy senses her fear he may never come home. Amy hugs her tighter and says, "We're *gonna* get him back and kick some *ass* in the process!" She pulls away and looks Tess in the eye. She can tell Tess wants to cry but is trying to be strong. "Hey, girl, you *need* to let that all out tonight, cause *tomorrow*, I need you focused when we begin your training, *okay*?"

With that, the dam bursts and Tess lets out all the pain and fear she's held inside until she's totally cried out.

"Feel better?" Amy asks when the tears subside.

"Guess so, but I *really* do worry he won't come home, and then what?" Tess sniffles as she speaks.

"Everyone's trying to find him. And tomorrow, we're gonna make you ready for whatever may come." She hugs her again, then stands. Tess curls up on the sofa and Amy takes a quilt lying on a bench nearby and drapes it over Tess. "Rest, girl. I'm here if you need me."

Amy lets Liz know what's happening, and that she'll get to her 'other' work after a workout with Tess in the morning. Tess spends the night, passed out on her old sofa. In the morning, Amy comes out with two hot coffees and waves one under Tess's nose, waking her. "I know it doesn't do anything for us, but I still can't start the day without it." She chuckles and Tess sits up.

Thanks to her Apara metabolism, any signs of her unburdening cry the night before have long since faded. Even so, she feels exhausted, and gladly accepts the cup almost ritualistically, giving a slight toast with it to her friend.

Amy settles in a nearby chair. "So, is there anywhere around here we can practice?" Amy asks, thinking of some of the artwork and fragile items in the main house, and the smallness of the apartment.

"There's a basement under the main house. Some of my stuff is down there from when I first moved here, but I think we can rearrange it and make room. We should make sure we don't mess up Marc's wine cellar. He's been getting some from his family in Bordeaux for a long time and stashes it down there. Says he likes the taste, but sometimes, I think he misses the ability to get *drunk*." Tess says, laughing.

"Go get something comfortable on; something you can move easily in." Amy suggests and follows her back to the primary residence. Tess points the way to the basement and Amy goes on down. It's a full basement, finished but very basic. Amy moves Tess's boxes to the right, so they protect Marc's precious wine collection. By the time Tess comes downstairs in shorts and a t-shirt, with her long hair braided tightly in a French braid, Amy has moved and consolidated everything, leaving them a large space to work in.

"So, will this work for you?" Tess asks, as she steps off the last step and onto the cool, linoleum floor.

"*Yup!* This'll do nicely! I would've normally said to get some mats down here, but if you're fighting for real, there's not gonna be any mats to break your fall, plus, you'll heal quickly enough!"

They begin with some of their old self-defense warm-ups, stretching, and some basic practice blocking strikes. After about an hour of this, Amy plops onto the hard floor and motions for Tess to join her.

"Human combat training is a combination of defending yourself from your enemy and getting your hits in to subdue them in any way possible. With Apara, the focus will be more on getting your hits in, than self-defense because we heal so quickly. Since we've both been through the whole 'first stasis thing', we know there's a *damn* good chance we'll come back. Dave's been coaching me on what can hurt or even *kill* us. We can recover from *almost* anything, including *dismemberment*." She grimaces and shakes her head at the concept, but severe damage to the brain can be fatal, because it holds all you are in it. There's apparently some redundancy thanks to our Benefactor's tinkering, but the thing you absolutely gotta protect most is your head! Gunshots, knives, swords, drowning, strangulation, and so on, we'll recover from even some damage to the brain, but if more than 40% is damaged or destroyed, the chance of survival and full recovery drops dramatically. Naturally, extreme fire and vaporization by nuclear explosion are also fatal."

Tess's eyes go wide, and she lets out a long breath, "So the old mythology of a stake through the heart and beheading?"

You can recover from both, though the beheading requires that both your body and head can be *reconnected*, and I've heard Sara gets *crotchety* when she has to deal with that kinda thing!" Amy grins.

Tess snidely says, "I think that's *normal* for Sara!" and laughs.

"We're gonna start with bare-handed combat, which is closest to your self-defense training. The most important thing is to anticipate where your attacker or enemy is coming from and what they're likely to do. I'm betting, with your people reading skills, you'll be *good* at that." She says and stands, reaching a hand down to Tess, and yanking her upright. You stand over there and I'll come at you. I want you to anticipate my plan of attack. *Ready*?"

Tess stands back and nods, getting into a defensive position as she's done many times before. Amy rushes her, slides down to the ground and on her side, knocking Tess's legs out from under her with little effort. Tess falls down face first, bloodying her lip.

"*Shit!*" She yells and pulls herself back up. Her lip is already healing, but she licks the blood off as if it's too precious to waste.

"Don't worry, girl! You'll get it! Use *all* your skills to anticipate, not just your eyes." Amy suggests as she sets up for a new attack. This time, she runs at Tess and leaps arms first into a flying tackle, but Tess shifts mostly out of her way, only getting grazed by the tackle, losing her balance, and falling on her ass. She bursts out laughing.

Amy lands from her lunge and rolls, ending up back on her feet in a sprinting position, allowing her to attack again almost immediately, which she does. Tess rolls out of the way, banging her head on a support pillar, as she couldn't stand fast enough. Again, Amy rolls and lands, ready to pounce. Tess stands, one leg behind the other, knees bent, and her arms ready to grab, deflect, punch, or whatever is called for as Amy comes at her again, but this time, Amy ports out and hits her from behind. Tess goes down with Amy on top of her, pinning her down.

"No fair!" Tess blurts out!

"*Hey*, all's *fair* in war, especially when you're *fighting* for *love!*" She gets off Tess and helps her sit up. "Tell me what *you* did *wrong*."

Tess scowls. "*Me?* You *cheated!* You ported out and hit me out of the blue."

"Yes, I *did*. Now, can't you feel when someone's porting?" Amy inquires with one eyebrow raised.

"Well, yeah, when they're porting *in*, but I've never really paid attention to when they port out." Tess replies, pondering the possibilities.

"I want you to close your eyes and stand up when I port out. It's more subtle, but if you're aware of what to watch for, you can catch the subtle ripples of energy a second or so before I port out, and more strongly, when I port in. Not only must you sense my pending port, but try to predict my re-entry location." Amy explains.

The first couple of tries, Amy ports out and back again before Tess can stand, so she tags her from different directions. "*Focus!* If it helps, think of it as opening a door, and you can feel the air movement from that action, except it's *energy*. Let's try again."

This time, Tess *can* feel it. She stands as Amy ports out. Since Tess is standing, she doesn't tag her, but asks, "Did you feel me port in as well?"

"Yeah, *that's* the easy part." Tess quips in frustration.

"This time, stand when you feel me port out, turn in the direction you feel me porting in from, and go into a defensive position." Amy ports out and Tess immediately stands and turns thirty degrees to her right and blocks a blow from Amy as she ports back in.

"*Very Good!*" Amy says. They repeat the exercise multiple times. In the end, Tess can anticipate Amy porting out and where she'll come back in.

The two sit, out of breath, but Tess has made progress. "You'll be fighting *both* humans and Apara. You can't think human all the time or they'll *get* you. Let's break for lunch and then we'll work some more."

They take a break and then head back to the basement. "Tess, you blocked me when I attacked, but when dealing with the real thing, you *can't* hold back, cause they sure as *hell* won't!" Amy says bluntly.

"I don't want to hurt you, you're my friend." Tess says.

"I know, but right now, I need you to give it *everything* you've got! Pretend I'm some *fanatical*, mercenary Apara, and I'm gonna do my best to kill you or at least put you in stasis. You *must* defend yourself and get in some blows, or you're just holding them off until you're too exhausted and they win! Don't *worry* about hurting me. I'll heal." She gives her a wide, cheesy grin, and immediately lunges. The two spar for a while and Tess goes on the offensive, but is still holding back.

Amy stops and leans against a support pillar. "You're *still* hesitating and holding back! Pretend that if *you* don't *stop* me, I'm gonna murder a group of helpless humans, and you've got to stop me, 'cause you're the *only* one that can!"

They square off again, and Tess puts more effort in this time. At one point, Tess winds up to punch Amy, but she moves away too quickly for Tess to connect. Nonetheless, Amy is flung across the room as though Tess connected; she is out like a light.

"What the *hell?*" Tess says and lopes over to Amy. She's breathing and her heart's beating, but she's unconscious. Tess grabs her phone and dials Sara for help. When Sara ports in, Tess motions anxiously toward Amy sprawled out on the floor.

"What the *hell* did you do?" Sara demands, taking out a scanner. "Her psychic readings are all *frazzled.*" She says as she interprets the readings.

"I'm not sure. I didn't think I connected. She's teaching me combat techniques, and she kept dodging my blows. I got frustrated and put my all into it. I swear I didn't hit her, but she flew across the room as though I *did.*" Tess rambles out. "Is she going to be alright?"

"Should be, I'm just trying to get an idea why her energy patterns look like she's been hit with the psychic equivalent of Han Solo's blaster on stun!" Sara says as she checks Amy's other vitals.

"I'm not sure his *had* a stun setting." Tess remarks.

"You *know* what I *mean!*" She says annoyed.

Amy stirs and groans. "*Oh, damn!* What hit me?" She asks, grasping her head in pain.

"Head hurts?" Sara asks and Amy nods. She takes an infuser out of her bag and infuses Amy with an Apara analgesic.

Amy glances at Tess. "You sure got me *that* time! Didn't know you could punch that hard."

"But that's just it! I don't think I did!" Tess looks deep in thought as she replays their sparring in her mind. "I was annoyed that you dodged me again! I was determined to hit you, and suddenly, you went *flying!*"

"Hm... could it have been your PK?" Amy wonders aloud.

"I honestly don't know. I wasn't *trying* to use it. I know, I *know*, I should be trying to use *all* my tools in my Apara toolbox, but it doesn't seem *fair* to use PK." Tess mumbles.

Sara looks at Tess quizzically, scanning her, and Tess's hands are psychically 'hot' with energy. "Wait here." She gives Tess a concerned glance, then ports out, returning five minutes later with Isanda in tow. "Check her energy. Is that what I think it is?" Sara inquires.

Instead of using any scanners or tools, Isanda approaches Tess and moves her hands over Tess's arms and hands with a couple of inches to spare. As she gets to her hands, her energy-sensitive hair makes a strange, squirmy flutter. She stares at Tess and then Sara. "Indeed, it is." Isanda says and continues checking both Tess's energy and Amy's.

"What is it, Sara?" Tess asks, shifting herself into a more comfortable position.

"Remember when we found out you were, as you called it, 'a *fucking* science experiment'?" Sara looks at Tess with mild amusement. "*That* was a trait they were trying to give you. Your PK translated into an energy blast that physically knocked Amy across the room, but also worked like a psychic taser, knocking her out." Sara sounds a bit flabbergasted by this development.

"How'd I do *that*?" Tess asks.

Isanda says, "You did it *intuitively*, but now that you have manifested this trait, I will help you *harness* it. We cannot have you getting frustrated and knocking people out as you pass them." She says, eyes sparkling with yellow glints of humor.

Amy, still somewhat stunned and weak, lets out a whistle. "*Girl*, if you can get that talent up and running, combined with my training, you'll be like a locomotive running through a Delorean!"

Sara's deep in thought, then says, "That she *could*, and as no one else shares this talent, there would be little defense against it. I wonder what it would do to *humans*?" Sara ponders.

"I'm not sure I want to know!" Tess blurts out.

Amy gives her a sympathetic look, then turns to the others. "Give us a sec?" Isanda and Sara move off to the other side of the room, discussing this latest development.

Amy plops down on the floor beside Tess. "Girl, I know you don't wanna hear *this*, but if you're gonna get Marc back, you have to be ready to not only give your all, but *potentially kill* the enemy." She says bluntly.

Tess stares back with a look of horror. "I don't *want* to *kill* anyone! I just want *Marc back*!" She says with a huff.

"I get it, but these guys aren't playing around. From what Charlie told me, they're all seriously militant. If they think they can kill you, they will try, and if they think you're gonna rescue Marc, they may try to kill him *before* you can get to him. They could also use you as leverage to make him talk or do things for them. I know it goes against everything you believe, but you'll have to get over your squeamishness." Amy says sympathetically.

Tess sits there, pondering this distasteful possibility. "The night I found out about Marc; *well*, the *second* time, I was worried about him killing me if he couldn't make me forget. He told me killing is abhorrent to him, and that he'd *never* hurt me or anyone he feeds on, but sometimes, the only way to deal with the bad guys is to 'take them out'. I guess this is what he meant?"

"Yeah, I'd say that's about right. Your enemy *will not stop* or play nice just because you look like a weak *woman*, especially once they realize you *aren't* so weak! You must go at them with all you've got 'cause they're not gonna pull their punches." She sighs. "I think we've done more than enough for today, and we both have other duties. We'll train more tomorrow, and I suspect those two have plans for you as well!"

"*That's* what *worries* me!" Tess sighs, watching Sara and Isanda converse in some ancient language.

***

For the next couple of weeks, both Tess and Amy's Apara duties are cut down so they can train. They work on bare handed combat, combat with knives, and using 'found objects' as improvised weapons. Last, Amy teaches Tess to use guns and other weapons. Tess is a natural at targeting because she used to do archery, which uses similar mental calculations such as siting your target and gauging things like movement you may have to compensate for.

Isanda works with Tess as well, teaching her how to wind up the energy and lash it out at a target. The energy is not visible to humans, though some Apara may see a kind of shimmering disturbance in the air *if* they are *looking* for it. This makes it a potent offensive weapon, as it's hard to dodge something you can't see coming. Isanda teaches her the important lesson of not using all her reserves at once, and how to replenish her energy from her environment, even siphoning it from her enemies if they are not blocking her psychically.

Toward the end of the two weeks, Amy brings in her local team so Tess can learn to fight against others she doesn't know, as well as going up against multiple targets. In the end, with few exceptions, she's able to get through her opponents, leaving most of them knocked out or, at least, dazed, and in mental and physical pain with few injuries herself.

After a grueling session that left Dave and five of Amy's best guys incapacitated, Amy says, "I think I've taught you about all I can, girl! *Hell*, I may have a few tricks to learn from you now!" She chuckles.

"Now, if we can only find Marc." Tess says, exhausted.

"We will. One of my teams from that region is out there in the desert using Sara's masking agent, driving around like some tourist group to see if they can find any sign of the base. As you said, if he were *truly* gone, you'd *feel* that!" Amy pats her on her arm.

"Yeah, I've got to believe he's still alive. It's been nearly a month now, and *nothing*! You know, I don't get why the Hybrids don't do anything about all of this! I mean, we're a hair's breadth from being exposed!" Tess complains.

"I wish they would, and I'm not sure why they don't, but you *could* ask Isanda." Amy suggests.

"I think I will! She says, stomping upstairs and jumping in the shower. She puts on clean clothes, and ports to Medical.

A QUEST FOR ANSWERS

Tess ports in outside Sara's office, but she's not there. She waits, but grows impatient, and starts to pace the hallway. After about thirty-five minutes, Sara shows up, taken aback by the anger in Tess's aura. She's been working up quite an internal rage since realizing that the Hybrids could probably find and rescue Marc without all this torturous waiting.

"What's got you all worked up?" Sara asks as she waves Tess into her office.

"I've got a few questions I'd like to ask Isanda!" She raises her voice in urgency.

Sara looks at her aura, her usual bluish-purple is tinged with red flames, and says, "She's working with Dee right now on her genetic PK, but I'll ask her to come see you." She ports out.

A few minutes later, Sara and Isanda return and motion for Tess to follow them to a larger room. The three of them sit at a small table. Isanda tilts her head at Tess and her hair flutters at Tess's crackling emotional energy. She flinches as she senses Tess's anger growing.

"What is it you wish to ask me, young one?" Isanda exudes waves of calming energy to bring Tess down from the peak of her rage.

"I want to *know* why you all, with all your technology, can't go find and rescue Marc, and *stop* these people?" Her voice is just short of a yell.

Ever calm but not condescending, Isanda replies. "That *is* complex, Tessa Waterford. Some of it is rules and some of it is practical. Our Benefactors *prefer* that you and your people do as much as you can on your own. The virus was an exception because you needed more advanced genetic technology to prevent a global crisis. There exist *other, more practical* considerations. If, as you say, they have created other Apara, even if we cloak our ship, they may be able to see us just as you or I can see it when cloaked. Our ship is a *medical* craft and has no weapons or defenses. Should they target us, it could lead to a very different and more *damaging* exposure. We would be seen as hostile invaders, which would damage any hope of making official contact for at least two hundred years and would disrupt your society at this stage of its development." She reaches over and grabs a pitcher and three cups, pouring some of her tea-like concoction Tess had once before. Tess nods and accepts it, taking small sips at first, but then drinking it down. It takes the edge off her anger and helps bring her more rational mind to the forefront once again.

"I guess that *could* be an issue." Tess says, her anger losing steam.

"We are *not* warriors. We are *scientists*, technicians, and teachers. If it were to go badly, we would be unable to defend ourselves, and our technology could fall into hostile hands. We *are* working on a few things that will help, including an antidote for the deuterium compound they've created. Unfortunately, there is no *inoculation* against it, only something that will help disperse it more rapidly. Our mothership is scanning for the electromagnetic field they are cloaking themselves with, but it is difficult. While the radiation has receded, the nuclear blast altered iron molecules in the region, and that is causing interference and false field readings. As you, perhaps, now understand, we are not sitting completely idle, but we *are* limited in what we *can* do." Isanda explains, her hair fluttering gently as Tess calms down, and her eyes show green and silver flecks on dark, blue-green irises, indicating sadness and regret that she cannot do more.

SENSELESS

Deep down in the lowest level of the *Naqam* base, there are two people kept in a cooled room. A woman lies on a hospital bed, with gray, metallic bands around her ankles, wrists, and neck. She's unconscious and breathing slowly. There is an IV with a bag of blood slowly dripping down into her arm.

The other body is a man, and for all intents and purposes, he appears dead, yet he, too has the suppressor bands on all 4 appendages, and his neck. Instead of a bed, he's floating in a sensory deprivation tank with electrodes attached to his body. There are fading bruises everywhere, and his eyes are sunken in. He too, has an IV with blood slowly seeping into his arm, where his body absorbs it despite the lack of heartbeat, breathing, or signs of brain activity.

Marc Girard has been in stasis for over a month as the damages from falling off the roof were severe. Before the explosives went off, he'd just crawled through a rather contorted crawl space to a small hatch on the roof of Inspiration, Inc. As he emerged and looked down from the roof to the parking lot, he felt a sharp pain in his leg, followed by a loss of bodily control, and all his non-human senses and abilities went dead. He fell from the top of the building, unable to do anything to avoid crashing into the parking lot below; he couldn't port, right himself to land on his feet, or even telepathically or physically scream for help. Everything went black, and stasis was instantaneous when he hit the asphalt.

The rogue, Israeli Apara retrieved his broken body just before the building exploded and took him back to their base in Israel, where he has been ever since. The scientists have been studying the healing process and are giddy with excitement over what they've observed. Uri, a government agent, is there to check on the scientists' work. He stops to talk to a female doctor, "So, Dr. Zelkind, have you made any interesting discoveries?"

"Oh, yes! We've taken tissue samples and scans every hour. It's an amazing, regenerative process they go through when their bodies die. Though it isn't truly death, as their cells do not deteriorate or decompose. We've been rationing blood to him to control the rate of regeneration. If we could only find the parts of his DNA that do this, we could make humans live practically forever!" She says, excitedly.

"Hm, or have armies that rise again after battle and live to fight another day!" Uri ponders aloud.

"Yes, I suppose that could be advantageous." Zelkind answers absentmindedly, as she looks at the latest slides of tissue samples taken from Marc.

"I don't suppose there's any way we can transfer this condition to non-compatibles, can we?" Uri leans over her shoulder to look at her notes.

"If there is, it's beyond us. There are unrecognizable components in their DNA that could take years to understand." She says.

"*Pity* there are not that many compatible individuals in Israel. Certainly not enough for any kind of fighting force, albeit, their increased strength and abilities do compensate for the small number of potential soldiers, but our targets share those abilities. We may have to go outside our borders to procure more subjects." He says and walks briskly out of the lab.

About an hour later, Marc's body makes a sudden, small, convulsive movement, sending ripples throughout the water in the chamber. This water is *not* ordinary water, but a variant of the deuterium solution. They have adjusted the formula to keep Apara senses dull and somewhat scrambled, but not strong enough to short circuit their neurons like the darts do. Alarms on the monitoring sensors go off as Marc's heart begins to beat lethargically; his lungs fill slowly and shallowly with air, and slow, low-amplitude brain waves appear on the previously flat-lined EEG.

Dr. Zelkind checks her latest subject visually and notes that nearly all the heavy bruising and signs of external damage have faded.

"Increase his IV by 30%", she orders, and a tech complies. "Hold it after three deciliters, however. We don't want him to regain too much strength yet." She goes from monitor to monitor, noting the new activity with glee. An hour later, she looks through the view port in the sensory deprivation chamber again, notes that his eyes show he's in REM-sleep, and marks it on the EEG.

It takes another 8 hours for Marc to reach consciousness, and when he does, he discovers he's in total darkness, there's no sound as there's something over his ears, and his body feels numb. He reaches out psychically to Tess, Liz, Kari, or anyone who might hear him, and may be able to find him, but when he does, there's an electric shock on his right wrist that arcs through the water to the other bands, nearly causing him to seize.

He hears an odd banging sound on his tank: someone opens the chamber, and light flares, stabbing at his long-disused eyes. Marc can hear a faint, female voice through whatever's covering his ears, echoing slightly through the lapping water.

"He's coming to. Prepare to increase the power output on the bands and drain the tank."

He's disoriented and wonders if perhaps he's in Medical, but his eyes slowly blink open again as they become acclimated to the bright light above him.

It's a light like they use in surgery; stunningly bright and on a hinged arm so they can move it where they need it. He hears a new sound as someone removes the covers over his ears—the water draining, and as it does, his skin regains sensation, including remaining soreness, though he can't remember why he hurts. With sensation returning, he shivers, as it's cold in the room, and they kept the water at body temperature to create the sensory deprivation effect.

Someone grabs his arm and checks for a pulse, saying, "Pulse is increasing. It's nearing 40 beats per minute. Respiration is shallow but steady. Brainwaves are increasing in intensity, amplitude, and type." The voice says.

Marc is aware of everything around him now, though he's far too weak to attempt to move. The chamber he's in opens fully, and he hears chains jingling as they're attached to a metal grating under him, now that he's no longer floating. He feels a sudden, upward jerk, and hears a motor as he's lifted from the chamber and left, naked, on the metal grate, in 55-degree temperatures while damp. They leave him that way until he air-dries. He's still too weak to do anything but lie there and shiver. He fades in and out of awareness, but eventually feels the platform move again and hands on his body as he's placed on some kind of examination table and partially covered by a light sheet.

He feels hands running over his body, squeezing places on his arms, legs, and ribs like they're checking for breaks. He hears, "I'd say all the broken bones have knitted and healed, but we'll do an x-ray while he's still docile." He feels hands on his face and sees the face of a woman in her thirties with short, dark hair. She was once attractive, but has a nasty scar across her jaw that looks like it has been both cut and burned. Marc stares at her face and instinctively reaches out and tries to touch her mind, but a shock hits him in one of the bands on his wrists.

"Tsk, tsk! No attempting to use your powers or you'll be *instantly* punished." She says in a heavy Israeli accent. "You can hear me, yes?" She asks and watches as Marc closes his eyes and makes a very subtle nod of his head. His vocal cords feel paralyzed, too weak from disuse to function. After she finishes examining him, she tells a tall, male assistant, "Get a jumpsuit on him and move him over to the other bed. Be sure to lock his bands down magnetically."

After a while, Marc finds his vocal cords can make small grunts and groans. He tries to speak but no words will form, like there's a short between his brain and his tongue. Exhausted, he sleeps again. When he wakes, he feels more normal, though his psychic senses are completely shut down. As his eyes open, he hears a rather surly voice. "You are Marc Girard, of Inspiration, Incorporated, yes?"

Marc groans and slowly turns his head toward the voice. There's an almost comically serious, uniformed man staring expectantly at him, waiting for his answer.

Marc summons what strength he can and answers, "Yes, where... am... I? What *happened*?"

"You may address me as Uri. You are in a secret base, Mr. Girard, and yes, we *know* exactly *what* you are!" The somewhat neurotic man stands and walks around the hospital bed, circling it like a melodramatic shark. "Did you *hear* me? I *know* what you are."

Marc stares at him, not saying anything in case this is some sort of trick to get him to expose the Apara. The man walks over to a small refrigerator and pulls out a bag of blood. "If you wish to be fed, you *will* cooperate, *Girard*! As I said, we *know* exactly what *you* and all your associates at Inspiration, Inc. *are*. Well, *were*...." He trails off, twisting the truth as psychological warfare. "You *see*, we *blew up* the entire building. It was a *very* powerful explosive that burned hot, so there was practically nothing left other than rubble." He gloats, implying that everyone there had gone up with it, and were destroyed in the explosion and subsequent fire.

Uri notes Marc's upset, and Marc extends his telepathic senses again, trying to touch Tess's mind, to confirm if she's alive or if what this Uri says is true, but this time, two of the bands zap him.

"It'll only get worse, spreading to all five bands should you continue to try your powers. The bands themselves are inhibitors. I'm afraid you won't be able to use any of your *vampire* tricks down here."

Marc glares at him, unsure what to believe. He has no way of confirming or refuting what Uri has told him, but this man clearly *knows* what Marc is. "Why... why am... I *here*?" He asks, struggling to squeeze out each word.

"Because, Mr. Girard, we know you and your group of supernatural mercenaries were *behind* the destruction of Jerusalem. We've been gathering evidence, and we will try you for crimes against the State and humanity." Uri says smugly.

Marc shakes his head, but it makes him more disoriented. "*Didn't bomb* Jerusalem. Was trying to *stop* it!" He forces out.

Uri stares at him with darkly humorous disbelief. "Do you really expect me to *believe* that? He laughs ironically. "We *found* one of your people, barely alive, in a tomb beneath the ruins of Jerusalem. With her, was a very damaged cell phone. We recovered enough to discover frequent calls to you and a Lissa Pedersen, also of Inspiration, Inc! We have *video* of your people appearing out of thin air and disappearing, *especially* near ground zero. We know about your *Benefactors*. Who are they? Islamic extremists? Some of the Antisemitic groups in America? The Russians, perhaps?"

Marc answers and coughs from using his voice too much, too soon. "The *Benefactors* aren't your concern. They... did *not hire* us to bomb you!" He pauses to catch his breath. "There were several other bombs being assembled worldwide... by... by a group of terrorists. They wished to decentralize society and send the world back... (coughs) to a more agrarian structure by destroying major cities." Marc wheezes and coughs again, but this time, can taste his own blood as it sputters up from one of his lungs. There's shooting pain on his right side, like a rib is impaling his lung. He coughs hard enough that some blood splatters on the sheet they've covered him with.

"I do *not* believe you." He says coldly, devoutly hanging on to the conspiracy theory crafted to make these *demons,* as he thinks of them, into an enemy he can blame for all the destruction and suffering of his people. He turns and snaps his fingers. "*Zelkind!* He does not appear as *healed* as you believe. See to him so he will be well enough to *interrogate* thoroughly." He snarls and angrily walks off.

Dr. Zelkind approaches, and despite working for Uri, her touch is that of a healer, gently probing until she finds a piece of rib that has snapped, and prodding him in his right lung. "I'll need to treat this. I'll have to make an incision and reposition the offending bit of bone. I don't have any anesthetics that work on your kind, so it *will* be painful." She says, donning a mask, gloves, and taking out a scalpel.

Marc lets out a raspy, wet breath, then says, "I will *try* to control the pain. If you *remove* the broken piece, it will grow back." He explains.

Zelkind carefully makes a small incision above the broken fragment, reaches in with her gloved fingers, separating muscle tissue to get at it. She carefully pulls it out. Marc isn't screaming in pain, but he must make a significant effort to get through it. "I'll be right back and sew that up."

"Not necessary, Doctor. It will heal on its own, though it will heal *faster* if I can feed." He says.

Torn between helping him but not letting him get too strong, she squeezes some of the blood from the bag into a paper cup, perhaps a deciliter, and approaches him. "I will give it to you, but if you attempt to bite me, they will shoot you again."

"I will *not* bite the hand that feeds me, Doctor. I *promise*." He says with a weak smile.

She edges over to him, noting his bonds are all securely connected to the bed by powerful magnets. She tips the cup so he can drink it, and he does. She's both fascinated to watch this, and his eventual healing, and a little queasy watching someone literally drink blood.

"Thank you." Marc mutters, and slowly blinks his eyes, slipping into a healing slumber, allowing his body to use the energy he needed for consciousness to heal his rib.

DIGITAL DAMAGE

As part of Ty's revamp of the computer system, the Apara potential servers were relocated to Sanctuary, with portal linked communication between there and their building in South Asheville. Thus, when the building blew up, none of their stored data was lost, only the terminal computers. However, Val made a discovery while setting up a new link with the New York offices, something that was interrupted because of Val's vision, and the aftermath of the attack.

"Ty, can you come here? We have a *problem*." Val bellows to her partner, who joins her promptly.

"What *now*?" He asks, frustrated that the New York linkage may be delayed yet again. So far, the new system is only linked to the Asheville and Los Angeles offices, with New York next in line. Atlanta, Chicago, and other hub centers around the world will be set up, with all other, smaller centers linking through the hubs. The system was originally begun because of Jason's creative hacking skills. Even though he is no longer a threat, they continue with this plan as a safety measure against any future hacking.

"You're not going to believe this, but I think there's a *virus* on the main server." She says, pointing to some unusual activity in the logs. "This is the night *before* the explosion, see?"

"*Merda!*" He curses in Italian and skims the tracer logs. He soon discovers something made a file of encrypted data, and the log lists it as being copied to the USB flash drive via their terminal in Asheville. "Didn't that Charlie fellow say they wanted a list of Israeli potentials?"

"Yeah, but there are only a relative handful, perhaps forty-five, max. Here's the Israeli generated search file, but this file here, is *something else.* It's encrypted, but I can see there are *hundreds* of entries in it, I just don't know whose files are in there."

"We must let Liz know. Can you run decryption programs on that file? And what of the virus? Can you find it and quarantine it? Is it still active?" He asks, running his fingers through his curly black hair anxiously.

"I'm still trying to locate it. If you look at the recent logs, it appears something's going on that shouldn't be, but the virus must be a trojan, masquerading as some other type of file. You know what this means, don't you?" She asks.

"*All* too well, *Amore*, all too well." He says and whips out his cell phone, calling the Los Angeles Center. Ty says, "Mateo? This is Ty Russo. We think we've found something quirky on the server here, possibly a virus from when they accessed files before blowing our center." There's a pause, and then he continues. "Yeah, I'm cutting the inter-world connection until we figure this out, but I need you to have Sirene go through the logs on your end, line-by-line, and see if there's any sign your system's infected. We believe the virus is *still* on our main server but is posing as some other type of file. As soon as we know more, I'll pass it on to Sirene, but if there's any sign your local network is infected, *shut down all access* to your peripheral centers and kill your main server until further notice, *okay*?" Again, a pause. "Great, just let us know if she finds anything in the logs." Ty hangs up and returns to Val.

"You *forgot* to remind them to check their *routers!*" She references the time she helped him figure out how Jason was getting into their system.

Ty sighs and sends a text to both Mateo and Sirene to double check the routers, as well. "We have to let Kari, Tess, and anyone else who's been accessing this server from their homes in Sanctuary know. All we need is to find out they've created a damn, backdoor to the system, and are harvesting potentials even now!"

"There, I've sent out a system maintenance message that anyone who logs in should get, including what little we know so far. You should get Liz and Kari out here right away. They need to know about this ASAP." Val suggests, gently taking his hand to ease his frustration.

"I'll call Liz." He walks away again and calls her while he shuts down the linkage for the L.A. Center. He calls New York to inform them there will be *yet* another delay.

Liz and Kari port in a few minutes later, looking more than stressed. "Okay, what *exactly* did you find?" Kari demands, as the database is *her* jurisdiction.

Val slides over, and Kari pulls up a chair to sit with her at the large monitor. "I found some unusual activity while adding in the programming for the New York link. If I had to guess, when that guy, what was his name? *Elias*? Used a flash drive to get the list of potentials in and near Israel, a virus was transferred *back* to our server covertly. No doubt an adaptive, AI, smart virus that isn't limited to a specific OS. It looks like it accessed *around* 360 potential entries and created this file. Unfortunately, it's *encrypted* with something our software doesn't recognize right off, so it's going to take time to decrypt the list, so we know who's on it." Val explains.

Liz slips into her native Norwegian and lets out a string of curses. *"Fy faen! Jævla drittsekker!* So, you're telling us we're *back* to where we were with *Jason*, only *worse*? These guys are a covert military group who think we're terrorists! *Faen!* Can this get *any* worse?"

Ty says, "We still know little, but I'd say that's a good possibility. We've cut the links to L.A., and let New York know of the delay. If anyone else logs in, they'll get a maintenance message about the situation, and I'll add a virus scanner they can use to check their computers. Sirene, out in L.A., is checking their system to see if it's infected. If it isn't by now, then we'll assume it's programmed only to infect the database itself and not to spread to other machines."

"Fyttirakkern! Keep me in the loop. As soon as you know *anything* more, call me, any time of the day or night! I've got to send out a general alert to all centers to keep tabs on their local potentials." Liz says and turns to Kari. "Get tech to produce as many of

the GPS tracker implants as they can and get them out to all centers so they can tag... *Hell!* They can't even access the database to find their local lists, can they?" Liz fumes.

Ty is silent, thinking. "I can pull a copy of the database from the last backup *prior* to the attack and set up a simple search-by-region interface. I'll send you access instructions later today, so you can send it out to all the centers. It'll take me a few hours to set up the clean database, basic security, and set up a VPN and remote access interface." He rambles off as he goes over to a shelf of SSD drives connected to a separate computer. He skims the catalog list and pulls the appropriate SSD. "Got it, will get to work on it right away. It won't include any new entries since the attack." He reminds them.

"Tess and Sue have both been pretty tied up, but I'll find out if they have any new ones on their personal systems." Kari says. She's remarkably calm compared to Liz, but that's one thing that makes them a good couple, when Liz gets stressed out, Kari goes calm and rational.

Liz ports out without even a goodbye, leaving Kari to sit with Val as she works on the breach.

COMMUNICATION

A few days later, After Marc's rib has fully regrown, Dr. Zelkind declares they're done with him for the moment and approaches him with two large guards armed with both dart guns and assault rifles. She sighs and says, "I'm transferring you to another location where you won't be locked down. Don't try anything, or they'll tranq you again, and if that fails...." She trails off, but the implication is clear.

"I have no desire to be tranqed or shot, Doctor." He says and she pushes a button that releases the magnetic field holding the bands in place. Marc sits up slowly so as not to startle the armed guards and provoke them into action. The bands are still on his wrists, ankles, and neck, fully neutralizing his Apara abilities, and he still feels weak as they've only fed him minimally to prevent him from regaining full strength and attempting to escape. As he stands, he glances at the other Apara in the room, the one they've kept unconscious, and recognizes her as Alyona Koslov out of their center in Vladivostok.

The two guards flank him on either side, with Dr Zelkind following behind. They get to a room with a transparent sliding door with a small opening in it for communication, and a digital lock. Dr. Zelkind moves ahead of Marc and the guards, and punches in a code, careful not to let anyone see it. The door slides open, and she walks inside, followed by Marc, and the men. The door slides shut. There's a peculiar tinge to the lighting in the room that makes Marc feel odd.

The guards stand by the door, weapons ready, as Zelkind uses a unique key to remove the bands, placing them in a bag. "There, that should be more comfortable; but again, don't try anything! The only reason I'm removing them is that they're redundant in here. The room itself has the same properties. None of your powers will work in here." She explains. The door slides open as she leaves the cell, followed by the guards, but they stay outside the room, flanking the transparent door. Zelkind turns around. "Just in case you're wondering if you might be able to break through this door, it's two-inch thick, transparent aluminum. I doubt you could break through it even at full strength."

Marc looks around the cell and finds inset drawers in the wall with a couple more of the obnoxious, orange jumpsuits they put him in. In a nook in the corner, there's a walled off area with a shower and toilet. He goes in, strips off the stale jumpsuit and showers, changing into a clean one and dumping the old one in a pull-out compartment marked 'laundry'. When he closes it, he can hear it go down the shoot.

He lies on the narrow bed provided him, but his mind is going in several directions at once, so he paces around the cell. He thinks, *If Tess and the others were really dead, wouldn't I have felt it, even limited by their technology?* At the thought of losing Tess, his heart clenches with dread.

He tries, but to no avail, to reach out and sense anything from *any* of his closest Apara contacts, like Tess and Liz. He tries reaching out to other Apara who aren't connected with Inspiration Inc, like his friend Li, and gets nothing, hoping that the tech may be responsible for his lack of connection to Tess, Liz, and others, and not whether they are alive or dead.

Marc is left alone to finish healing, given regular food twice a day, and minimal supplies of blood; just enough to complete his healing. A few days later, he's lying on the bed, thinking about Tess when the door slides open and an armed guard slips inside, followed by Uri, holding a single band made of a metal frame, containing a liquid in a tube inside of it. The guard motions for Marc to sit up. Uri approaches him, eyeing him warily, and slips this new band on Marc's upper arm. As Uri closes it and locks it in place, Marc feels something pierce his skin, and he looks up questioningly at Uri. Uri paces back and forth slowly, circling Marc like a shark. "That, Mr. Girard, is *incentive* to tell the truth. I *will* have the truth out of you about your people and your involvement in all of this, and if I don't get it, that will infuse various amounts of the compound we hit you with before, though we've altered it slightly to make your nerves burn with pain without knocking you out." He gloats over Marc, believing he has the upper hand. Uri pulls up a chair and sits opposite Marc, a remote-control device in his hand. "*This* will trigger an infusion. At first, only a drop or two, but the *more* you *lie* to me, the more will be *infused*."

"I *have* been telling you the truth! But you don't *believe* me, so where's my incentive to talk to you if you're just going to *torture* me?" Marc asks, touches of his usually absent, French accent slipping through.

"So, you still *insist* you and your people were there to *stop* the bomb, yes?" Uri asks, leading the conversation.

"Yes!" Marc replies.

"Then tell me, how did you *know* about the bomb if you weren't working with the *bombers*? We found no chatter or any kind of indication that this was going to happen, and yet, you, a creature living half a world away, somehow knew it was going to happen?" He asks, his voice drips with disdain for even having to tolerate this demonic creature in a man's guise.

Marc sighs, and then replies, "You obviously know we have various psychic abilities, right?"

"Yes, go on." Uri says impatiently.

"Most of our abilities are based on the ones humans have latently. Not all of us are equally adept in all psychic abilities. One of my *stronger* skills is precognition." He pauses, checking to see if Uri is following him.

Uri stares at him, running his finger lightly over the trigger button for his torture device. Mark takes that as a signal to continue. "Those of us with that ability *saw* this coming. At first, we only knew it would be catastrophic, a horrible loss of life, and it would be somewhere in *this* region. We monitored the same things you did, and there were no signs of couriers or communications, and yet, our people adept in pattern recognition saw evidence of *coordinated* movements. My job was to coordinate and parse through all the premonitions and info that came in to me from others like me, and make sense of it. Unfortunately, it wasn't until your bomb was imminent that the puzzle pieces fell into place. Whether or not you believe it, there were bombs being built in multiple major cities worldwide, and they were *supposed* to be on a timer. All the visions fell into one of two categories; one was centralized here, and the other was worldwide devastation, *including* here."

"So, you're claiming you *sacrificed* Jerusalem to save the world?" Uri's finger gets twitchy, and Marc, despite his empathy being cut off, can read Uri's body language just fine, and knows the man's impatient, and looking for an excuse to push the button.

"*No*, sometimes, more than one outcome is seen, but only one can *actually* happen. The contents of the premonitions were disjointed and unclear. We sent our people here intending to find and disarm the bomb. We thought we could do it—thought it could be *stopped.* One of my people found the bomb, but what none of us foresaw, was that it was rigged to trigger if any changes were made once armed. The proximity trigger started a fifteen second countdown, and the bomb blew, taking a lot of my people, as well as yours, with it. So, you see, in the end, there was no future where we could *stop this bomb.* We could only stop the other bombs around the world because they were *incomplete.* This one was the only one that was *completed* and *armed.*" Marc explains, gauging whether Uri believes him.

Uri narrows his eyes as he tries to discern whether or not Marc is lying. "Exactly *how* were these supposed terrorists coordinating?"

"In the 1970s, the Russians, and even Americans, were experimenting with extra sensory warfare. I believe someone by the same name as you, one of your fellow countrymen, took part in the CIA's Stargate Program, *Uri Geller*?" Marc asks, waiting for a reaction.

"*Yes*, I am *aware* of his involvement." Uri says curtly.

"The Russians got further than anyone was aware, using Extremely Low Frequencies (ELF), but the equipment necessary at that time was too cumbersome, and some even had side effects, including minor strokes. After the Soviet Union fell in the 1990s, much of their old tech and weaponry got sold on the weapons/tech black market. We believe someone got a hold of this older tech, modernized, and miniaturized it. They created micro-implants that were surgically implanted in the skull itself, near an ear. No one could detect it because they didn't know to look for it. As you obviously have deduced, our own telepathy works on a frequency; and the one in the implants were just slightly off our own. We were picking up on it, but not clearly enough. It was like a telepathic itch, and some of us picked up on the communications unconsciously, *triggering* our premonitions." Marc explains and watches Uri's finger twitch but withdraw from the trigger. "I'm uncertain I believe you, but I will do some research. Tell me, just *how many* people did *you* lose, and just how many like you *are* there in the world? Are they all in one region or are they *everywhere*?"

Marc looks down and away from him, debating what he should say. "I cannot reveal that to you or anyone outside of my people."

Anger flares on Uri's face and he's about to push the trigger when there's a distant boom, the main power fails, and emergency lighting comes on. Uri swears furiously in Hebrew, then tells his men, "*Watch him!*" Uri uses a hidden release to open the transparent door and yells something in Hebrew down the hall.

While Uri is out, the two men have their guns aimed at him. He can feel what else is without power, whatever technology they're using to dampen his abilities. He tries to port home, but still can't, so reaches out telepathically, and feels Tess's mind, relief flooding his soul. **Tess! Are you alright? Did everyone else get out of the building in time?** He paths lightning fast.

MARC? Oh, my God! You're alive! Where are you? We're trying to find you!

Don't know! Just answer me, is everyone alright? Marc paths rapidly, not knowing when the power and dampening field might return.

Yes! Callie portaled us out just in time! She tries to sense where in the world he is, but before she can, the connection drops, and she loses him again.

Back in the cell, the power has returned, along with the ability dampener, but Marc's relieved that Uri lied about everyone being killed, and it fills him with resolve to resist.

Uri returns to the door and orders the guards to come out and stand outside, glaring at Marc. "We *will* continue this later, but I must attend to other matters just now!"

Uri does not return that day, but Dr. Zelkind comes in later in the evening with food and blood. She examines his ribs to make sure everything has healed properly. "*Truly* remarkable!" She exclaims, as she can feel the entire length of the rib has grown back into place. Naturally, the guards are there, ready to strike, so Marc doesn't resist. "How are you feeling?"

Marc looks at her in frustration and rolls his eyes. "*How* do you *think* I feel? I've been *shot*, fallen off a building, experimented on, starved, and cut off from all my extra senses, and my people! Uri *says* they're all *dead*, including my *partner!*" He stares at her, making her feel uncomfortable.

She looks away and clears her throat. "Uri does *not* see you as a *person*, only as some sort of demon."

Which makes Marc shake his head and roll his eyes. "I'm *not* a demon. As you've discovered, a virus changes people like me. It's all about *genetics!* As a scientist, you *must* understand there is nothing truly *supernatural or demonic* about me or the others like me!"

"Yes, I have thought this myself, but *Uri* is the head of this facility and project. I need to take a blood sample." She says, changing the subject, pulling out a syringe, and finding a vein in his arm to draw from.

Mark pauses, noticing Dr. Zelkind is much more at ease with him than Uri is. "Are you afraid of *me*?" He asks, suspecting he knows the answer.

"Not really. If you get out of hand, they'll stop you." She nods her head at the two large men with weapons at the ready.

"Do you see me as a *person*?" He asks, calmly.

She pulls out the syringe, capping it and putting it into a biohazard box. "I'm *not* sure how I see you. You are *clearly* a rational, thinking being, though I cannot say if you have a *soul* or not. *Some* say your kind are but shells once you change, but I have not seen that with any of the others they've transformed."

"May I ask *how many* you've changed?" He inquires cautiously.

She glances at him briefly before answering, uncertain she should tell him such information, but decides the intel isn't critical. "As of today, we've transformed eleven, though one of them is having a long transformation with side effects." She says cryptically.

"Side effects?" He thinks, *Merde, if they got a lost missioner, that'll be rough!*

"Yes, one of the young women is changing over more slowly than the others and has been wreaking havoc with our electrical systems." She comments casually, thinking he will tell no one because he will never leave here.

"Ah, is *that* what caused the power outage?" He asks, watching her reaction.

She tenses up, uncertain she should have volunteered that information after all, but answers him truthfully. "Yes, she's having seizures, and her transformation has lasted over twice as long as the others so far." She faces him, realizing he may know what to do for the woman. "Have you seen this before, *perhaps*?"

"Yes, it usually goes hand in hand with some potent abilities. Her body is fighting it more than most. Had she been with my people, we'd give her a special immunosuppressant, but human ones will not work, and I don't know anything about making it." He explains.

"Oh, that is problematic," Zelkind says.

Marc pauses, thinking *the poor woman must be going through hell*; he decides she is more important than staying silent. "There is an alternative, but it may seem drastic. By now, the virus has spread through a lot of her cells. If you *stop* her heart, she will go into *stasis*, like I was after the fall. That will shut everything down *except* the transformation, *including* her immune system."

"And she'll be alright after that?" Dr. Zelkind asks, showing genuine concern for her patient.

"Yes, if you do it quickly and painlessly so you avoid any trauma, she'll be fine." Marc confirms.

"Thank you, I appreciate your help." She says, and measures out blood for him, giving him extra, still not a full amount, but more, as a reward.

He takes it, notices the increase, and nods to her. "It's appreciated." She leaves the cell, returning to her latest transformation patient. She arrives in time to witness a fever seizure as the woman's temperature spikes to 106 F. She grabs a crash cart, amps it up, and shocks the woman, stopping her heart. When she flat lines, another doctor comes running in with Uri in tow.

"What the H*ell's* going on? How could she *die*?" Uri demands.

"I spoke to your prisoner. He's seen this before. He told me that his people have immuno-suppressants that help, but human ones will not. Alternately, he suggested stopping her heart will force her into stasis, and her transformation will proceed, unimpeded." She explains, standing firm about her actions.

"And *what* if she doesn't revive? She wasn't fully *transformed*! Why do you believe *he* would tell you the *truth*?" Uri demands, as the other doctor checks the patient's vitals, finding everything flat-lined.

"He has no reason to lie about this, and the woman was suffering. In fact, after observing your earlier interrogation, I suspect he *may* be telling the truth about *other* things as well." She insists.

"Stick to medical concerns, *Doctor*! She'd better revive, or you've just *cost* us a soldier in this war!" He sneers and leaves, the other doctor following nervously behind him.

Two days later, the transformee wakes up, fully transformed, though upset about what they have done to her. Zelkind has doubts about the ethics of what they're doing, if, in fact, what Marc told Uri is true.

HOPE

Tess frantically searches for any trace of Marc's mind after being cut off mid-thought. She'd been running Ty's virus utility on her laptop when she heard Marc's telepathic shout.

Amy feels Tess's excitement from her apartment and runs in through the back door to check on her. "You *heard* from him? Is he alright?" Amy blurts out as she barges into Tess's living room, excitedly.

"He didn't say, but he *felt* alright, stressed, but relieved. He asked if we all got out of the building in time, so he *knows* they blew it up." Tess elucidates.

"Do you know where he is?" Amy asks, sitting down by Tess, eager to have something to work with.

Tess frowns and shakes her head. "No, he didn't know, and the contact didn't last long enough for me to get a feel for his location. I've got to tell Liz. Maybe, now that we know he's alive... at least there's *hope*."

"You've always *had* hope, girl, but *now* you've got *evidence*." Amy suggests with a lopsided grin.

Tess gets an odd expression. "*Do* I? What if it was just wishful thinking? Maybe I only imagined hearing him?" Tess wonders. "It only lasted about a minute, and it *felt* like him, but I've been hoping to hear from him *so* badly!"

Amy knows Tess too well and can sense her teetering on her belief. She reaches out telepathically to Liz, and seconds later, Liz is there with them. Tess is so absorbed in her own deliberation; Liz's sudden appearance catches her off guard and startles her. "*Liz!*" She says, not sure what to say next because she doesn't dare get her hopes up, in case it was just wishful thinking, and her imagination.

"Amy says you heard from Marc." She asks eagerly.

"I *think* I did, but now I'm wondering if it was *wishful* thinking." She says, making eye contact with Liz, searching for confirmation.

"*Open* your mind to me and I'll review the memory." Liz suggests.

Tess relaxes and feels Liz slip into her mind. The brief interaction with Marc replays, and as Liz slips back out, she looks relieved. "That *was* Marc! He's *alive!*"

Almost afraid to believe it, she asks, "Are you *absolutely* sure?"

"*Positive!* I've known him a long time, and that *was* him, *not* your imagination!" Liz reaches out and hugs Tess, rocking her gently. "We're *going* to get him back, I *promise!*"

"You know I want to be part of the rescue, right?" Tess asks.

Liz looks at Tess and then glances at Amy, who nods, reassuring Liz telepathically Tess can join *any* rescue mission.

Amy speaks up, knowing it will do good for Tess to hear this as well. "She's *ready!* With this new, energy-burst ability she's got, she's as good to go as *any* of my guys! If we can figure out where he is, we can make plans."

Liz glances back at Tess. "All right, consider yourself *part* of the team. He didn't give you any idea where he is, did he?"

"No, he was more concerned with whether we all escaped the explosion. I got the impression they told him we were *dead.*" Tess says as Liz joins them around the coffee table.

"*Yes*, I can imagine they might. Losing all of us, especially you, would be very demoralizing; so, it's good he knows we're all well. I want you to continue trying to feel him and reach him. Maybe something you picked up unconsciously will surface later regarding his location. Often, in brief paths like that, there's a lot of wordless information that comes through with the rest, but it takes time to process." She reassures Tess.

Amy speaks up. "Liz, while you're here, what's the status of the database breach?"

Liz slouches back into the armchair and sighs in exasperation. "Not good. Ty and Val are on it. We've confirmed that the virus did *not* transfer to the L.A. office, thankfully, so your computers are probably clean." Liz says, noticing Ty's custom virus scanner ticking away on Tess's laptop nearby.

Tess looks up and asks, "Does that mean I can go back to perusing the new lost mission finds? It'll take my mind off things while we wait."

"Give it a couple of days. For now, they're backing up the server, isolating that drive, and restoring it from the last backup before the attack. It'll take him a little time to get it up, running, and secure. The virus was on the flash drive they used to copy the results you found, Amy." Liz explains.

"*Damn*! If only I'd been more wary, and less overconfident about handling Charlie, then maybe none of this would've happened." Amy admits.

"It's *not* your fault. There's no way you could have known what we were dealing with, even *with* your precognitive hunches. You had no reason to believe Charlie would have technology to neutralize us or that others like us would be his backup. *Hell*! I didn't even see that as a possibility!" Liz admits, getting up and patting Amy on the shoulder reassuringly. "I need to get back to Kari. We were trying to have a little quality time tonight. We've been trying for a while, but something always gets in the way." She smiles weakly and ports out.

RECONNAISSANCE

Amy hangs around with Tess for a while and makes her put her laptop away. They watch the latest Marvel movie and de-stress after the excitement. One movie soon becomes a three-movie marathon, after which, Amy says, "I'm crash'n, girl. You should get some sleep, too! We'll run some practice scenarios tomorrow. I'll even drag Dave in to help!" She yawns and heads to her apartment.

Tess cleans up after their marathon, putting dishes in the kitchen, and feeding a very hungry Mabel. She leans down and pats the cat's head, yawns, and lethargically climbs the stairs to go to bed. As she lies down, part of her can *almost* feel Marc lying there, as though it were only yesterday, and he was home with her. She still gets an occasional whiff of him in the house. She curls up around his pillow, imagining it's him, and falls asleep.

At first, she dreams of Marc calling out to her. She can hear his voice but can't see him anywhere. She searches all over the house, but there's nothing. She looks out the window, and instead of the clearing in a semi-wooded area with the river flowing past their home, she sees a desert, with barren mountains and wind whipped clouds of sand blowing around.

In the distance, she sees a figure beckoning. It's Marc! She wants to go to him but the window's closed. She steps back from it, contemplating what to do, and feels an odd sensation, like she's slowly spinning back and forth in bed, then there's that all too familiar roar, a flash of light, and she's out of body, making Mabel stand at the foot of her bed and hiss at her vehemently.

She thinks, *here we go again!* As her astral body drifts through the ceiling and roof. She sees the regular surroundings of the house, but feels a tug, and the world flashes into a multicolored-warp speed view as she traverses the worlds. When she finally stops, she's looking down over the ruins of a city, twisted girders and rubble, though some areas appear cleared.

She feels that tug again, floating upward and over some mountains to the desert she saw in her dream. She doesn't see Marc, but she heads for where he was in her dream. She gets to the spot, and the only thing there is a dilapidated, old building, barely larger than one of the dormitory rooms at Medical.

She drifts closer and feels a very uncomfortable sensation. The closer she gets, the more it feels like sparks are passing through her entire astral body. Not exactly painful, but very disconcerting and annoying, like she's being continuously zapped by static electricity. As she gets to ground level, however, it lessens.

Usually, she's had little control over where she travels while out of body, but *this* time is different. Ever since she arrived over Jerusalem, she's been able to follow the tug on her soul. Now, she floats just outside an apparently abandoned building that should be condemned.

She thinks, "*Let's see what's inside.*" She floats toward it and through the outer wall. She mentally shivers as she goes through the walls, as it's more difficult than usual, like it takes more effort to phase through them. Once inside, she mentally examines the problematic walls and discovers they are not made of half-rotten wood, but steel and... *is that lead?* She thinks. Tentatively, she explores it by putting her astral hand back through it, and it's like trying to push an apple through a mesh strainer with the skin still on it. Possible, but only with extreme effort. The first time, she'd had some momentum, but now, going slowly, she feels the density of the lead-filled, steel-clad walls retarding her progress.

She thinks, *something tells me this isn't what it appears to be.* She phases through an inner door and faces a large elevator shaft in the middle of the room with a keypad, hand scanner, and other security measures. She passes into it and follows the shaft down.

As she drops further underground, she senses Marc. It's weak, like when he was unconscious after coming out of stasis, but he's *nearby.* She imagines him as a glowing beacon, and soon, she feels his astral warmth and glow and follows it. She arrives in a plain, white room, very spartan. Marc is lying on the bed in an orange jumpsuit.

She paths him, but he can't hear her. Frustrated, she explores the room to see if she can figure out why. She feels a variation of the same prickly energy field she passed through earlier. She relaxes, opening her mind's eye. Despite the white walls, she perceives them as though they have a black glow like a black-light aura. She drifts back to Marc and sees his energy is hemmed in by that same, black-light glow. She wonders, *some kind of suppression field like we used in Hot Springs*? She floats near Marc, pondering the situation. She unconsciously drifts closer to him without realizing it. As she briefly passes through his legs, he sits bolt upright in bed and utters, "*Tess*?"

When she realizes he felt her, she knows what she must do. As much as she hates it when people walk through her while she's in astral form, she has to merge with Marc. Only then can she bypass the dampening field and reach him. She watches him looking around for her, confused and wondering if he was only dreaming.

He settles again, and she consciously moves closer to him. She forces her astral self to overlap his physical body. He looks startled but doesn't move. The closer she gets to overlaying him, the more she can feel him. *I feel his soul!* She thinks, *or at least his inner core that would be his astral body, if he could travel, as I can.*

Marc, can you hear me? she paths. She feels him react to her question with surprise.

Tess? How are you getting through to me? I can't reach out to you anymore, not since the power came back on, and with it, their ability suppressor. He replies. He pictures her giving him a lopsided grin in his mind.

Do you remember when I visited you in Medical after Jason broke your neck?

You mean when you went astral those first times? He feels a glimmer of hope.

Yup! That's it! I'm here, with you, in astral form. But this time, you couldn't sense me until I passed through you a few minutes ago.

That WAS you? I was sure I sensed you! He paths, elated to feel her presence.

Neither their EM shield outside, nor this field in here, works against astral travel. I can feel the energy from both, it doesn't stop me, but it's unpleasant. I'm IN your body with you, which is why you can hear me! The field only affects your efforts to reach out, not hear what's within! She paths excitedly. *I know where you are now! We'll come for you soon, somehow!* but her mental voice fades in his mind, and he feels her sudden absence as she's mentally yanked back into her body, faster than warp speed. When she opens her eyes, Mable is sitting on her chest, licking her face desperately.

"*Mabel!* You silly cat!" She says aloud and pets her head roughly before tossing her off the bed. She tries to enter that state again, and go back to Marc, but can't.

Instead, she sends out a path to Amy and Liz. *I found him!*

MOMENTUM

Time has been standing still for Tess since the explosion and Marc's capture, *except* when working with Amy on training, and now, in the last couple of days since hearing from Marc and then visiting him astrally. Now that she knows he's alive and *where* he's being held, they can pick up momentum and come up with a plan of attack. They've called a planning session meeting at Tess's home, where Tess, Liz, Amy, Dave, and Charlie are present.

Liz clears her throat and begins, "Let's get started, everyone! Good news! We've finally got something concrete to work with. Tess, our Benefactors' cloaked mother ship, has been in orbit over the Middle East monitoring the region's EM fluctuations for any signs of the base. We've correlated their data with your subjective, astral experience with Marc, and found an anomaly that coincides with the power loss you reported. Their sensors show that for one minute, and thirty-two seconds, a roughly two-kilometer diameter area lost the EM signature it's had since we began monitoring. They tuned it to match the background EM field of the region, but when it failed, the internal signature of the base became visible. It matches your estimated location for Marc." Liz confirms with a sigh of relief.

"So, that means it *wasn't* my imagination!" Tess asks excitedly.

"*Indeed*! Now we need to come up with a viable rescue plan, as well as what to *do* with the base." Liz says, less enthusiastically.

"What do you mean?" Tess asks.

"They *know* about us now, and there's no way to wipe their memories. They'll keep coming after us or outright *expose* us. We *can't* let that happen." Liz explains.

"You're talking about *destroying* the underground base with *everyone* in it, aren't you?" Amy asks Liz.

"Unless we can come up with a better plan, that's what we'll have to do." Liz tells them unenthusiastically. "I don't *want to kill* anyone, but sometimes in my 800 plus years, it's been *necessary*. I fear this one may be one of those times."

Charlie clears his throat, unsure if they'll even want his input. "The people they've transformed, won't they survive?"

"It depends on what we do." She nods to him as an acknowledgment for his input.

"Except for Elias, who volunteered, all the others they changed into beings like you they took by force and changed *against* their will. Yes, some of them took part in the attack, but Uri's people made sure they were *compliant*, if you know what I mean." Charlie continues.

"We'll take that into consideration, but right now, recovering *Marc* is our primary goal. Marc and the other Apara prisoner, if she's still alive." Liz amends.

"She was when I was there. They keep her knocked out and use her blood to transform others. I heard rumors she tried to escape before they had the suppressor technology perfected, and they had to shoot her. After that, they kept her unconscious and barely alive." He explains.

"Do you know *where* she's kept?" Amy asks, giving him a reassuring look.

"Most likely in the lowest levels of the center; it's the highest security level. I heard it's rigged to incinerate the entire level, but I don't know if that's true. I know it used to be a top-secret center for weapons development, including bio-warfare." Charlie explains, feeling more comfortable speaking despite being surrounded by a group of vampires.

"Thanks, Charlie," Amy says. "That makes sense. Most biohazard places have such a room where it can be burned hot to kill any potential bugs that might otherwise escape." She shivers. "I just can't imagine being in there when they burn it."

They brainstorm for a couple of hours, breaking for food. The Apara converse in the dining room, but Charlie sits alone in a chair in the living room. Amy notices, fills an extra plate with food, and joins him.

"Hey, brought you some food." She says.

He accepts it, saying, "Thanks. I wasn't sure it would be a good idea to go in there when they're all hungry." He gives her a weak grin, trying to pass it off as a joke, but she can sense he's still uncertain what his fate will be when all is said and done.

"*No one* is going to hurt you. You're *helping* us." Amy says, giving him a platonic nudge to his knee.

"For *now*, Amy, but what about when my usefulness is over? I *know* too much! I know how things work! *Hell*! Uri left me to die because he considered me a liability! How do I know I won't end up on the *menu* here?" He says, refusing to make eye contact.

"*Stop that*! I've already told them you're too *tough* to eat!" She suppresses a grin when he looks up in shock at her comment.

Realizing she's joking, he relaxes. "You know, I volunteered to become like you, but they told me I didn't have the necessary genes, and they needed me as I am, in order to get to you."

"Yeah, I know you're not compatible. I checked that myself once I was transformed, but you'd already hopped a transport to the Holy Land! You know that was a real *dumbass* move, dude! Made me feel like I didn't matter." She admits.

"Of course you *matter*! Though, as I told you before, there's *someone else* now, assuming she hasn't become a liability as well." He says, worried about Janna.

"I'll mention her to Liz. If we can, we'll get her out, but the two of you have to keep our secret. That's non-negotiable!" Amy says as she stands, slapping him on the upper back like a fellow soldier might. Dave glares at Charlie from the dining room.

They spend the rest of the night devising a plan. They'll still need to think through the details but will attempt a rescue in five days' time.

Everyone but Amy leaves, who stays and helps Tess clean up. She can sense an optimism in Tess she hasn't felt in a while. "Charlie's afraid we're gonna *eat* him." She comments, trying to make conversation.

Tess stares at her in disbelief. "Well, you could always tell him that would be like eating a *pet!*" She gives a sarcastic grin, then says. "I'm *kidding!* I remember kind of feeling like that, surrounded by Apara while I was still, well, *mostly* human!"

"*Mostly?*" Amy raises an eyebrow in question.

"Yeah, you *know*, I was stuck between humanity and Apara. Still physically human, but had all those crazy, new abilities, my attitudes changed once I found out all of this exists, and what they do. Marc and everyone tried to make me part of their world, but I still *felt* like a curiosity or even a pet, at least until Marc's emotional baggage got lost." She quips with a big smile. "I'm sure we can *find* a place for Charlie in our world, but I suspect, like me, he'll end up living in limbo."

"He wants us to rescue his *girlfriend* from the base. I said we'd try. I just hope she hasn't gone over to the dark side, or that may not be an option." Amy says, grabs a pile of clean dishes, and puts them up on a shelf. She tries to put stuff on the next one but has to stand on her toes. "You know, it's too bad becoming Apara didn't make me *taller!*" She laughs.

The two of them finish up, and Amy heads back to her apartment. Tess has a hard time sleeping with everything running through her head, but when she finally does, she dreams of Marc being home with her once again.

HEADS UP!

As the day nears, Liz ports in to visit Tess at her home. "Ready for tomorrow?" Liz asks.

"I guess so, though I'm nervous, but after all of Amy's training, I *should* be ready." Tess admits.

Liz laughs lightly, "Amy's been keeping me up to date on your training, and you've impressed her. She asked me if it's possible for others to learn your energy-blast skill, but I had to disappoint her, at least for now." Liz sits down with Tess at the coffee table. "But your combat training *isn't* why I'm here."

"Oh? Is everything okay?" Tess asks, suddenly worried something's wrong.

"Oh, yes, but I think it would be advantageous if we could give Marc a *heads-up*." She suggests leaning forward with an expectant expression.

"Liz, you know I don't have a handle on all this astral stuff. The only time I've done it halfway consciously was when I worked with the others to track Jason's hangout down near Lake Lure, and Astral is the only way to get through to him." Tess says, frustrated by her lack of mastery over this very useful skill.

"Yes, I realize that. Sue thinks she can help you with her therascape ability. She's been working on her gifts with some long-termers and thinks she can guide you into an out-of-body state. Sara told me Isanda has a few suggestions, too." Liz explains.

"I can try. I just can't promise anything. Besides, I want to make sure he's still okay." She admits with a shrug. "But since we're going tomorrow, we'd better do it soon."

Liz says, "Whenever you're ready. I just need to give Sue and Isanda at least thirty minutes' heads-up."

Tess nods and says, "I'll go get ready and do some relaxation stuff. Give me about an hour and I should be ready."

Liz ports out to plan with the others, and an hour later, Liz, Sue, Isanda, and Sara arrive. Isanda's carrying a flask of liquid in one hand, and Sara, as per usual, has her tablet and scanner at the ready. Liz says, "Sara wants to document everything since there are no other Apara with this skill. She told me there were stories of someone back in the ninth-century, but that person is no longer with us, and it wasn't exactly something she could study as she can today." Liz nods to Sara and then continues. "Where do you usually have your out-of-body jaunts?"

"Aside from the first time in the tub, and when Annie hijacked me, I've always been in bed. Hmm..., I *should* feed Mabel and put her somewhere first. She's the one who broke me out of my last one, and I couldn't get back in the mindset again." Tess explains as she heads toward the kitchen, grabbing a can of cat food, and Mabel from the top tier of her cat tree, Mabel resists, digging into the upholstery. She takes Mabel into the downstairs bathroom, puts her food in there, and locks her in. Returning to the others, she says, "She's not thrilled about being locked in there, but it's better than her pouncing on me again while we do this." They all ascend the stairs to the bedroom.

Liz asks, "Is there anything in particular you've done prior to your astrals?"

"No, not really. Last time, I really wanted to have more time with Marc after his path and curled up with his pillow. I can still smell him on it." She says wistfully.

Liz gently lays her hand on Tess's arm. "We're *going* to get him *back*, I'm sure of it."

Tess sits on the bed, but before she can lie down, Isanda hands her the small flask of liquid. In her usual soft voice, she says, "Drink this. It is a variation of the tea from the Benefactors' world, with something extra." Tess takes it, looking up skeptically.

"Something *extra*?" Tess asks.

"Yes, I believe you call it psiamp. It should boost your abilities slightly and help Susan Burns link with you, though I understand the two of you often work in tandem." She cocks her head to one side, waiting for her to drink it.

Tess looks skeptical. "I don't know... every time I take that stuff, I get more than I bargain for." she hesitates.

"It is a carefully measured micro-dose. You react strongly to psiamp because of your genetic alterations. I compensated for your sensitivity when I mixed this. Please, drink it all." Isanda encourages her.

Tess rolls her eyes, but downs the drink, and lies down, making herself as comfortable as possible. Sue pulls up a comfortable chair and drinks a flask she'd gotten before they ported in. Isanda extends her long, delicate fingers, sensing Tess's energy. She closes her eyes, making minute alterations to its flow. "There, that *should* help." Isanda says and backs away. Sara looks on eagerly, monitoring everything with vibrant curiosity.

Tess grows sleepy, the room blurs out, and she falls asleep. In her mind, she hears Sue calling her. *Tess, your body's asleep, but your mind needs to wake up. The two must become detached, independent from each other. Your body is becoming heavy and grounded, while your mind is becoming vibrantly aware and light. Do you feel it?*

Tess feels that familiar duality that often preludes her astral journeys. She can feel her body, the bed underneath her, and the surrounding air vividly. Her body is heavy and immovable; paralyzed in slumber, while her thoughts race. *Yes*, Tess answers telepathically.

Sue's mental narration continues, *shift your focus from your body and the here and now; focus on Marc, what he feels like, and where he is. Reach out and let him pull you to him like a magnet.*

Smoke swirls in Tess's dream mind and she flashes back on the view from the window, desert and all. She knows Marc's there, yet can't see him waving at her in the distance. She experiences the familiar roar and flash of light as her astral body separates from her physical one, and she knows she's aloft when she can no longer feel herself breathing. She floats upwards, seeing everyone in the room. She notices a shimmering tendril of energy, almost smoke like, between herself and Sue. Isanda glows compared to the others, with sparks of energy in her fluttering hair.

Suddenly, her heart clenches and she swears she hears Marc scream mentally. No sooner does she focus on him than she's there, descending toward the base, passing more rapidly through the EM shield and the lead-lined shack, only feeling slightly slowed by the barriers as her momentum toward Marc spurs her on. She feels that same clenching sensation in her chest, but it shifts to pain, and her mind travels down to Marc as though she's ported, nearly instantaneously!

When she arrives, she lets out a mental gasp of alarm. Uri is interrogating Marc again, and this time, he's resorting to torture. She must focus, but can hear him ask, "How *many* of your people are there? *Where* are they? What are their *ultimate* goals? Do you plan to *destroy* more cities? Farm humans for sustenance? TELL ME!" He shouts. When Marc doesn't comply, he pushes a button on a device and Marc spasms in pain, arching his back like he's having some kind of electroshock convulsion. Tess feels his pain and the burning in his nerves as the modified deuterium compound makes his nerves fire all at once.

Tess lets out a mental *NO! STOP!* Followed by a reply in her head from Sue.

What is it? What's wrong? Sue demands.

Sue? Tess asks, disoriented by the feedback she's getting from Marc, as Uri tortures him.

Yes, they have me acting as a relay. What's wrong? She paths, trying to cut through the turmoil she senses from her friend.

Some man's torturing him! Asking him questions about us, but Marc won't answer him. Whatever he's doing is causing him terrifically horrible pain... like his nerves are on fire! Tess paths through the residual echoes of Marc's anguish.

Sue relays this information verbally to the others in Tess's bedroom. Liz paces the room, anxiety for her onetime charge, friend, and Apara brother rises as she feels helpless to stop this travesty.

Sara suggests, "Tell Tess to diminish his pain, as she would if she were physically there. Let him know we're coming, and the torture may be easier to bear."

Sue relays the message, and senses Tess steeling herself to do what she must. Tess drifts closer to Marc, planning to 'touch' his mind by interfacing with his physical body again and soothing the pain. She reaches him, and a tendril of her astral-self connects with his arm right as Uri pushes the button again impatiently. His pain feeds back into her and makes her want to flee back to her own body, but she persists.

She's able to ease his pain somewhat, making it almost bearable for him. This only infuriates Uri, so he ups the dosage. This time, the pain courses through him like a tidal wave, making it nearly unbearable for them both. Tess must pull back, distance herself, but she doesn't want to let go of Marc in his time of need. Torn, she does what she must and pulls away to regroup; rethinking her angle of attack, but when she does, she can't fully disconnect from Marc. It's as though their energies are fused together in a convulsive contraction.

Frantically, she tries again, wishing she could just port him back with her. She mentally tugs, but it's like trying to win a tug of war with a tree. Unexpectedly, the resistance stops, there's a lesser flash of light that makes her mentally glance away, and *the* pain stops. When her astral senses recover, she can't believe what she sees—Marc's astral body is there before her, looking almost solid, as they are on the same plane of existence.

If a soul could tremble, that's how she'd describe Marc, trembling and nearly in shock, unaware of what's just happened to him. She drifts closer, tentatively reaching out her soul to him, touching him and pathing, *Marc! It's okay! I'm here!*

His awareness comes to a sudden, sharp focus, and he realizes Tess is floating right in front of him. He briefly wonders if he's passed out from the torture and is dreaming of her. *Tess?* He paths questioningly. *How are you here? How can he not see you?* He believes she must be here physically if he can see her.

Calm down! I'll explain. She paths, but thinks, *if I can figure it out myself!*

But I can see you! It's like you're right here, in front of me! He paths as he grows increasingly frantic to understand what's happening.

Marc, I'm out of body again, and so, it seems, are you! She says, carefully wording it so it doesn't freak him out.

She fails miserably, as he emanates fear and confusion. *But I can't do that! Am I dead for real this time?* He asks, his awareness shifting his view to his body, which is passed out on his bed, with Uri cursing up a storm, and checking that Marc has a pulse and is breathing.

I know that, but I think I accidentally PULLED you out. You were in so much pain, and it fed into me as I tried to help you through it. I panicked, pulled away, and POOF! Here you are! She looks down at his body. *Your body is still breathing. I can tell.*

Tess is disconcerted as a woman rushes through her, heads straight for Uri, and Marc's limp body, and passes through Tess on the way. If she could be nauseous in her astral body, that's how she'd describe the sensation. The woman checks on Marc, noting he is alive, but his heartbeat is rapid and irregular, and she notes signs of his muscles spasming as the deuterium concoction still courses through his system. The two watch what happens next, unnoticed by either of the humans in the room.

The woman, Dr. Zelkind, berates Uri. "I *know* you're the *head* of this project, but you're risking *everything* torturing him! He's *clearly* not going to tell you anything if you don't give him a chance! We don't know whether they are truly immortal or not, but his heart is *not* beating normally."

"Be very careful, *Zelkind!* I can have you removed from the project... *permanently!*" He says, eyebrows raised, and eyes menacing.

"You are forgetting who you're talking to! You may be "in charge" of the base, but I was assigned here by my uncle in *Mossad!* If something happens to me, what do you think will *happen* to you?" She glares at him.

Uri's taken aback as he's reminded that while he outranks her in one way, her familial status trumps his rank without question. "But we *must* know how much of a danger they are to us! They're *parasites*! They feed on people like us!" He rebuts.

She looks annoyed and asks, "Is that how you see all of them? Including our own?"

"They, at least, are *useful* parasites." He nods and crosses his arms over his chest. Tess notes how much he's acting like a frightened child who must overcompensate with bravado, as he faces something he doesn't understand.

Zelkind loses her patience. "*Leave!* Let me attend to him! His and the others' conditions are *my* responsibility." She stands her ground, seething, until he turns and leaves without saying another word. She removes the torture device attached to Marc's upper arm, then leaves the room and returns with a small flask and syringe, filling the latter with its contents and injecting it into Marc's carotid artery. She watches his body, shivering, and trembling from the torturous compound, but as the injected fluid makes its way through his system, the unconscious contractions in his muscles become less intense and less frequent, until they fade completely.

She knows he's in no condition to escape, so leaves his cell again, leaving the door open, but returns after a minute with a full bag of blood and an IV rack. She straightens out his body on the bed, as the seizures have contorted his position; she slips the fine IV needle at the end of the tube into his arm and starts the drip. She feels his forehead, and he's cold with sweat.

Marc and Tess watch from the Astral plane, unseen by Zelkind, but as Marc's body normalizes, he's drawn back to it.

Tess! I... I think.... He paths, but she stops him.

I know! Tomorrow! Marc! We're coming tomorrow! Remember and be ready! She paths as she watches him drift toward his body, overlay it, and sink into it again.

Once alone again in the Astral world, Tess feels a nagging tug on her mind, but it's not a tug to return. It's Sue calling her name repeatedly, trying to get an update. Tess paths an offhanded, *Be there shortly!* to Sue without further elucidation, and lingers long enough to see Marc cough and open his eyes as Dr. Zelkind looks on. With that, exhaustion overtakes her; she feels like she's not just warping home, but falling, and landing with a thud, sitting up straight in bed as everyone stares at her.

"Message delivered. Give me a few minutes to clear my head, and I'll tell you everything." She falls back against her pillow and sobs as flashbacks of his pain cascade through to her waking memory.

COUNTDOWN

The big day arrives. Tess had trouble sleeping, her mind sifting through possibilities, but she must get up, as the rest of the team will arrive soon to go through the battle plan one last time. She showers and gets ready. She slips through a large pantry off the kitchen, into a walk-in freezer, and pulls out a box of Marc's eclairs to thaw. She sighs and reminds herself, *We are getting Marc out today! We must! The pain he went through last night was something no one should ever have to endure, except for the man who put him through it!* She thinks snidely

She takes the box with her, as well as a large freezer bag of multicolored macarons, and puts them on the kitchen counter to thaw. She takes out a couple of serving trays to lay them on and fixes some coffee and hot water for tea. She pulls out a canister of Liz's favorite, Sassafras tea. Kari brought it over for such meetings, as it is a tonic for Liz's nerves.

It's difficult for her to focus; torn between the pain from her jaunt and subsequent communion with Marc, and their plan to rescue him from his tormentors later today. She's anxious about the looming battle and using lethal force.

She puts plates, mugs, and glasses on the dining room table, so everyone can help themselves before they settle in on their last planning session. She sets serving thermoses with coffee and hot water out, as well as various tea bags. Lastly, she brings out Marc's baked goods on trays, having warmed or thawed them. Liz said she didn't have to do anything except be at the meeting, but Tess feels that having some of Marc's baked goods is appropriate, like having him with them in spirit as they finalize their plans.

She sits in Marc's favorite chair in the living room, burning off some of her anxiety, and clears her head for the mission. This is only the second mission for her since becoming Apara. Until now, she's always been in the background where she'd be safe. She was supposed to stay in the background for the last one too, but she couldn't let Jason escape if she could do anything about it. She knew if she didn't try, he'd escape, and even though she failed, and ended up in stasis at the bottom of an old mine shaft, she's determined to give her all in this mission; she must! She can't picture her life without Marc in it, especially not the preternaturally long one she'll have as an Apara.

She cuts short her meditation and grounding as she feels the first of the team port in. Liz arrives with a Latina woman Tess doesn't know and who has not previously been at their meetings. Moments later, Amy bursts in the back door, having felt Liz's imminent arrival. With that, Amy paths her hand-selected security team, including Dave, to port in. Dave grudgingly drags Charlie with him upon Amy's request.

Liz looks around her and says, "Looks like that's everyone. I don't think any of you know Teresa Mendoza. She's new to us but has a talent we *need*. Teresa is one of the Lost Missioners from Atlanta who was infected with the Roulette virus. She can create electromagnetic pulses that disable power systems, vehicles, or anything that relies on electrical energy. She's been working hard to get a grasp on her abilities, so I wasn't sure until now if she'd be ready for this mission, but she is, and her role is vital."

Everyone settles around the table. Charlie spends about an hour going over everything he knows about the layout of the subterranean base, either from first-hand experience or from what he'd heard while there. There are seven levels to the base that he knows of. The bottom most is where they kept the original subject, and likely where they have Marc, which Tess confirms from her astral travels.

Charlie shares his memories of the base with Amy, while Dave stands by, somewhat jealous of the mental intimacy the former lovers are sharing, but Amy will be able to further share the layout with the others, making it easier to navigate the facility.

Amy's next, and despite her diminutive stature, her team clearly respects her unconditionally based on their rapt attention. "Alright, everyone, we've been over this multiple times, but from what Liz tells me, Teresa is going to solve one problem for us. With her EMP talent, she should be able to knock out their generators, taking down the EM shield, and with it, the field in Marc's cell. Now, we know that when the field went down, he was able to communicate, but we have to assume that, for some reason, he was still unable to port out, or he'd have rescued himself when the power failed. Perhaps, he was just too weak, but we know they've developed technology that can neutralize our talents. They likely have redundant measures in place to prevent escape. This means once we're in, we may be subject to whatever measures are in place. So be prepared to go full hand-to-hand and fight your way in and out, if necessary." She glances at everyone in the meeting, lingering on Tess, knowing she can do this, but she's still concerned that this is her first, official, combat situation. "And even if you can port, we need to take down or disable as many of them as possible. *No one* except those we need to rescue can be allowed to escape.

Liz clears her throat. "We have several goals. The primary is to rescue Marc. They are also holding one other Apara prisoner, the woman Charlie discovered in the ancient tomb. We *must* recover her as well. We don't know what state she's in, so she may not be able to leave under her own power. If we're able to port out, and she's incapacitated, whoever finds her should port her straight to Medical. We'll manage without one of your team if they can't get back to the base, Amy. I also need one of them to accompany Teresa. She doesn't have any battle training, so someone must protect her. We hope she'll be able to take out the primary power source from the surface, but if they have multiple generators, and her EMP doesn't reach them all, she'll have to go into the base to get to them. If we find any potentials who are still human or newly turned, we'll attempt to rescue them, but unfortunately, they are *not* a priority. We promised Charlie we'll try to get one woman out. She's a medic in the Army that got conscripted with him. Her name is Janna Baker, and you'll find a photo of her on your combat communicators. Charlie and Dave will head for the living quarters where she and Charlie were kept to see if she's there, but in case she isn't, the rest of you are to familiarize yourselves with her appearance, and watch for her." Liz pauses and takes a long sip of her tea. "Last, while I'm *loath* to do this, we have *no* choice. The *Naqam* are a danger to us all. They know of us, and have a list of some of our potentials, though we don't yet know who is on their list. We'll have to destroy the base with their leader and operatives inside it; not just to protect ourselves, but the *over 300 potentials* on that list. Other than Elias, their first transformee, and the one who forced Amy to give them access to the database, the others were all conscripted civilians they'd found because of the Roulette virus and its side-effects. We also assume they've abducted and transformed the local ones they got from our server. Once the base is destroyed, our IT people will hunt down and destroy any information about us which may have been backed up or transferred to other agencies. As I don't wish to force any of you to do this, the final part, the *destruction* of the base, is on me."

There's murmuring among the security team members, who aren't sure they should let Liz take on that mission, but she stares them into silence. "I've been Apara over 800 years, and I know how this part of the job can affect people. I've had to do things like this before, including during wars. This is *my decision* and my *duty*. The rest of you do your part, and hopefully we'll meet our goals, putting an end to the *Naqam*, once and for all.

Amy rises. "Just a last couple of things. We have special combat suits for everyone. Sara has been prepping them at Medical. They should withstand their deuterium darts, but if they don't, they contain antidotes that will automatically be injected into your system to counteract the compound. If hit, get out of sight. It may take a few minutes for the antidote to fully neutralize the compound. Tess, you're with me. We started here together, and

I'm going to see you through this." She nods to Tess and paths, *I know you can do this, but you're too important to this mission not to have a backup... besides, what are buds for?*

"Tess will be using her fighting skills and her PK energy blasts. Her primary goal will be to take out any unfriendly Apara as they are subject, as all of you know, to her blasts. It won't kill them, but her blasts will knock them on their asses and out cold, so we can deal with any human soldiers, and rescue our people." Amy takes a deep breath. "With that, do anything you all need to today, and get some rest before our assault. Our goal is to hit them at 0300 hours, or 3 am their time, so meet up at Medical at 1800 hours or 6 pm eastern to suit up and prepare. There's seven hours difference from Eastern US time, so we'll leave medical a little before 2000 hours or 8 pm eastern." Amy uses military time out of habit, but knows Tess and Teresa may not be used to it.

With that, they talk among themselves before departing, leaving Tess alone to prepare herself.

IT'S A GO!

Everyone meets at Medical and suits up. Knowing they'll likely have to deal with soldiers shooting at them once they enter the compound, they're all armed, including Tess. Amy senses her unease with the concept of shooting a *real* person; a target or a dummy is one thing, even an Apara, who would easily survive, but the idea of shooting a human, even in self-defense or war, makes Tess question whether she can do it. Amy lays her hand on her shoulder, and says, "It's *just* in case. Stick with your energy blasts and hand-to-hand as much as possible. I've *got* your back, but if I'm unavailable, you may need *that*." She says, nodding at the semi-automatic handgun she trained Tess to use.

"I know, but I've always hated these things and swore never to own one, even when I was afraid of Colton coming after me. I *get* it! If I want to rescue Marc and keep *myself* out of their hands, I may *have* to shoot someone. Don't be surprised if I aim for their *legs* rather than their *hearts*!" Tess exclaims, and Amy pats her on the back with a grin.

"Got it, girl!" She says and checks with her team.

At 7:50 pm their time, they port in near the base. Their new combat suits are made from genetically engineered silk, spun by silkworms infused with benefactor-tweaked, spider DNA, creating a lightweight, flexible, and projectile-proof material. Besides protecting them from deuterium darts, they also contain a compound that will deflect most motion, energy, and heat sensors, making them fade into the background as they approach the shack, the entry to the base. Liz, Teresa, and one of Amy's team, a Chinese woman, ironically named Fang, approach the shack. The others hang back about a mile away so Teresa can do her thing. Besides her EMP, Teresa can sense electrical hot spots. She's learned to use local energy to increase the strength of her EMP, but it takes a few minutes to build up. The three of them walk around until Teresa finds a hot spot indicating a generator below her feet. Liz and Fang stand back but remain vigilant as she works.

At first, the sand beneath her feet glows dully, then sparkles as it starts to dance with small, electric charges arcing in the sand. It contains an altered version of magnetite that the bomb blast deposited, and electricity arcs between the particles randomly. As Teresa focuses, the arcs become less random, and become glowing feeds of energy that make the sand glow from within as they travel to her feet, where she absorbs them. Slowly, she takes on a glow, herself. The glow slowly pulses, then builds up speed until the sand goes briefly dark as the last of the energy internalizes in her body.

Suddenly, it flares brightly and travels out in a growing sphere. Moments later, the EM shield fades, and the generator below her feet fails. The team successfully ports into the main building where the elevator is. Liz paths them, *I'll be here, preparing to destroy the base. Good luck, everyone! Remember, we need to take down as many of them as possible, so engage, disable, and move on. Port only when necessary!*

With that, the teams port out except for Teresa and Fang, who wait with Liz unless needed.

TEAM ONE: CHARLIE AND DAVE.

Dave taps into Charlie's mind for the coordinates of Charlie and Janna's dwelling. Porting straight there is the best option for getting her out quickly. Unfortunately, she's *not* there. Her things are, but the room is empty, and it looks like she may not have been there for some time due to the remains of a moldy sandwich on a nearby table. They hear the voices of several human soldiers in the common room stumbling around in the dark. Teresa's EMP took out the backup system, as well, at least on *this* level, which was closest to the surface.

Dave, who has no trouble seeing in the dark, turns to Charlie who has a light on his combat helmet. "Feel like a little *brawl*?" He asks with a mischievous grin. Despite his public display of dislike for Charlie, as Amy's ex-lover, he's come to respect the man as a fellow soldier.

Charlie lets out a low chuckle, "You bet! Can't stand most of those arrogant jerks!"

Dave ports them in and the two make relatively quick work of the men in the living quarters. When the power and backup power went out, they were unable to open the lock on the sliding door and were trapped. One of the soldiers gets in a good punch to Charlie's jaw, his head lamp making him an easier target, but Dave comes up behind the guy, putting him in a choke hold until he passes out.

Once the soldiers are all incapacitated, Dave turns to Charlie. "Where *else* could she be?"

Charlie looks concerned. "I really don't know. She clearly hasn't been there for a few days or that sandwich would have been tossed, so I'm worried." He admits.

Dave slaps him on the shoulder and says, "Let's join the attack and see if we can find her. They port out and begin looking. They go down another level, the main power is still out, but about half of the emergency lights are on, though some are flickering. There are a fair number of unconscious bodies on the floor. Dave senses his crew fighting on this and the next level down, and the two run to join them.

TEAM 2: AMY AND TESS

They port out but linger in the membrane as they search for other Apara minds. They ignore the ones they know, and home in on one nearby in fatigues. They port in and the enemy Apara immediately rushes toward them, porting out, and reappearing behind Amy and Tess, thinking to surprise them, but Tess is ready; she *trained* for this, and turns to face him, flies into a kick Amy taught her, and unleashes one of her PK energy blasts simultaneously, hitting the enemy, and knocking him back about 8 feet, leaving him unconscious.

"Got him, girl! Good going!" Amy exclaims in a whisper, proud of her student and friend. Amy approaches the unconscious Apara and infuses him with a dose of cent-opal dust to prevent the man from porting out once he comes to.

Tess blurts out, "I *got* him! I *really* did it!"

"Yes, but if you don't keep your voice down, you're gonna attract more attention than you *can handle!*" Amy suggests. They head down the dimly lit hall, occasionally engaging human soldiers along the way, and easily trouncing them. They run into a larger group, and at one point, Tess is dealing with three large guys. She's holding her own, but then another comes in carrying an assault rifle, at which point Amy ports away from her own battle, slides in behind the armed soldier, and shoots, bringing him down before he can fire at Tess. She paths, **there are *too many, girl,* you're gonna need to try your full, peripheral blast!**

But they're human! I don't know what it will do to them! She paths in reply, still fighting with two of the three opponents. The other is lying on the floor in pain after Tess kneed him in the groin when he tried a frontal assault.

I know, but they're not gonna get outta here alive, anyway! She reminds her.

Tess thinks, *Maybe it'll do them a small favor by knocking them out, so they don't feel it when it happens.* She's still fighting, but she pulls energy from around her, including the men she's fighting with. She and Amy hear others approaching from down the hall. The two men she's fighting lose steam and drop to the ground as though pulled down by increasing gravity. At least a dozen new soldiers are approaching. Tess watches them, holding on until they get closer, and then releases a burst not unlike Teresa's EMP, only with raw, telekinetic energy radiating in all directions. Amy puts her own mental shields up, but her suit protects her from the psychic pulse that leaves everyone else in the hallway out-for-the-count.

"Come on! We've got to work our way to Marc. Have you tried pathing him yet?" Amy asks.

"Been kinda busy, but I'll try now." She says, finding a place where she can shield her body while she reaches out, just in case new soldiers arrive.

She paths, *Marc! Can you hear me?*

It takes a couple of seconds, but he replies. *Tess? Are you here? In the middle of this?* She senses his fear she might get hurt, or worse, like getting captured by Uri and his people.

Tess paths back, *I'm here! With Amy, Liz, and others. We're here to rescue you!* As occupied with this mission as she is, she can't help but think of that last line as a reference to the original Star Wars, when Luke rescues Leia, and the irony of her rescuing Marc. Tess thinks, *I've really been spending too much time with Sara! I've got Star Wars on the brain!*

You're NOT a combat Apara! What's Liz thinking? Marc exclaims telepathically.

I am now! She paths forcefully. *Can you port out or do we need to come get you?*

He paths, *I still can't port. Not sure why. Everything else works except that and PK. Where are you?*

She can hear distant footsteps running her way, but paths rapidly, *still about three floors up from you. Can you get out of your cell?*

No, I have an emergency code I lifted from a guard's mind when the power failed, but it didn't work. Marc paths, using his returning physical strength to force the door open, but can't.

Tess peeks out from where she's hiding when she hears Amy say "*Damn!*" under her breath, as over a dozen soldiers head their way, and at least one of them is Apara. She paths, *We'll work our way to you! Be ready!* She breaks the connection to focus on her oncoming foes.

"I don't suppose you're up for another peripheral, are you?" Amy asks with a sardonic grin.

Tess is out of breath, but joins Amy in a battle-ready stance. *Not until enough of them get close enough I can recharge. Amy, at least one of them isn't human!* Tess paths, as pathing is quicker than speech.

I noticed. I feel the anger rolling off them. I think it's the woman they're flanking. She's broadcasting anger and hatred louder than the rest of them! The lead soldiers arrive and engage the two Apara women, and Tess siphons energy from them, but it's slower this time, like she needs to fill a well she's drained dry. *This is taking too long! The rest are gonna be on top of us soon!* She paths.

Amy pulls something out of a pocket in her suit and throws it, pathing to Tess, *Get back and shield your eyes!*

The two women close their eyes and port a few feet back as a loud noise and brilliant light flashes and disorients the soldiers, allowing them to knock out several before they can get their senses back, but the enemy Apara woman and about half the soldiers are still standing and recovering quickly. Amy engages the Apara woman as she lunges straight at her. She rolls backwards, flipping the Apara woman in the process while she rolls into her ready position. Tess looks on, torn between who to attack first. She gets a flash from the mind of the Apara woman. She has a knife-like device, but it's more than that, it's filled with the deuterium compound, designed to penetrate armor and skin, releasing the compound into the system. She knows she's going to use it on Amy, but the other soldiers are heading toward her. She closes her eyes and acts instinctively. With this many bodies near her, she quickly recharges before the attacking soldiers can falter from the drain. Tess focuses on the woman charging Amy and the men charging her, and a double blast rips out from Tess, one peripheral, hitting the human men, and a focused pulse stopping the woman just short of reaching Amy, but her arm falls and the knife tears through Amy's suit, piercing her skin. Amy howls in pain as the compound hits her nervous system. The antidote deploys, but Amy is down until it works. Amy yells through the pain as she can't path.

"Tess, drag me out of sight! You'll have to go on without me, and I'll catch up as soon as the antidote works!"

Tess doesn't want to leave her friend but knows what's at stake. She drags Amy over to a supply closet, twisting the doorknob and breaking the lock. She puts her inside, saying, "Don't you dare get caught or be in here when they blow this place!"

Amy gives her a grin through the pain, and hands her the cent-opal infuser. "Go save Marc! You've *got* this, girl! Path Dave and tell him where I am. I'll be *fine*." She says and winces

Tess nods and closes the door on Amy to hide her, then quickly infuses the unconscious Apara woman. She paths Dave. ***Amy's down! Watch out for deuterium filled daggers! They cut through the suits!*** She paths Amy's location and ports down the hall, past the multitude of bodies they've left in their wake. Tess wonders if they're alive or not, but won't let herself check, as she'd rather not know if her blasts have killed the humans or not.

MARC

Marc tries to get his cell door open, but can't. What Dr. Zelkind told him is true, the two-inch-thick, transparent aluminum is too hard to crack and the lock too solid to break. He paces back and forth, reaching out to Tess. He can feel her, but she's ignoring him and focused on the fight. He can sense when she's fighting and worries about her. He hears familiar footsteps and opens his eyes as Dr. Zelkind approaches. She fits a physical key into a lock on the outside of the cell, releasing the door and sliding it open.

"I'd say your people are here to get you. If you want out, I need your help first!" She insists.

"My *help*?" He asks skeptically, as he slips out of the cell and follows her down a hallway.

"I want you to take the two latest transformees out with you, including the one you helped me with." She says. "They didn't ask for this. It's too late for the others, Uri had them conditioned for the cause, but he hasn't done that with them yet." She says, but Marc senses some doubt in her mind.

They get to two cells, one contains a man who looks to be in his mid-fifties, and the other, a woman with dark hair who's pacing her cell angrily. The woman tenses up as she realizes someone's standing outside the cells, as though maybe she could fight her way out, given the chance.

"The man was seventy-four when transformed. He appears to be getting physically younger, but Uri's waiting to see how young he becomes before bothering with conditioning. And this is the woman you helped." Zelkind explains. She turns to the two, recently turned Apara. "The base is under attack. They're here to rescue this man. We're going to get you two out of here."

Marc looks at her questioningly. "*Why* are you helping us?" He asks.

"I don't agree with what Uri is doing, and quite frankly, I find your explanation more likely than his paranoid delusions. He's a *zealot*. Not only is he a former soldier and an agent, but his religious beliefs make you demons in his mind. Demons, he feels he must destroy for his God." She explains, justifying her betrayal of the project and Uri.

Marc chews on his lower lip in thought. "I could get them both out much faster if I could port out. My abilities, aside from porting and PK have returned. Can you do *anything* to restore them?"

She hesitates, but says, "Yes, and if you *promise* to take me with you, I will."

Marc senses the woman's sincerity, and knows he has to trust her. "Deal. What do you need to do?"

Zelkind digs into a deep pocket on her lab-coat and pulls out a small packet. She unfolds the trifold packet and takes out a pair of gloves and a scalpel. "Turn around. There's a device implanted near your spine that specifically blocks porting and PK. It's self-contained so won't go down in the event of a power failure."

Marc nods and turns around. "Just be quick. I still have one more thing to do before I can leave."

She touches his back, sliding her fingers along his spine until she finds a small lump. "I have no way to numb this, so brace yourself." She says, making a quick, yet precise incision large enough to reach two fingers of her gloved hand in, pulling out the blood-covered device, and throwing it down the hallway. "I'll stitch you up but will have to do this for each of them as well." She says and pulls out a suture kit.

"Never mind that. I'll heal shortly. I can port them out now." He says.

She puts a hand on his chest to stop him and turns to the two people in the cells. "I'm going to release you, but I need to do to you what I just did to him so you can get out of here." She turns to Marc. "Besides preventing you from teleporting, they're rigged to explode if you leave the base without them being *disarmed*. They're powerful enough to sever your spine if not put you back into... what did you call it? Stasis?"

"Yes, that's our term. Hurry, Doctor. We must get moving." He says, and she releases the other two and removes their anti-port implants, as Marc numbs their pain.

"All done, we can go." She tells them.

"One last thing; the woman like me, the one you found in the tomb. I need to take her *with* me." Marc says.

Zelkind nods, understanding his need to save her as well. "I'll take you to her, but you'll have to carry or teleport her out. She's been under a long time, and it will take too long to revive her." The four of them head down the hallway, through another sliding door, and into the room Marc first awoke in. Alyona Koslov is still lying there, unconscious. Marc has known her for a couple of centuries, and had even sought comfort with her a few times, but mostly, she's his friend, and he can't leave her behind.

Zelkind undoes all the monitor wires and the metallic bonds. She explains, "I have to cut out her device too, and then I'm going to give her this to bring her out of the induced coma, but it will take time, and she'll be disoriented." She removes the device, and injects the woman with a syringe of yellow liquid. She moves away and allows Marc to pick her up.

"I'm guessing neither of them knows how to port?" He nods at the two novice Apara.

"No, Uri saves that for last, when he feels he can trust them." She says.

Marc shakes his head, realizing he's going to have to port himself and four others out. He reaches out to Tess telepathically. *Tess! Where are you now? I'm free, but not alone! Have others to take with us.*

With others of our team. Some of the last of those on this base are trying to get away down a passage near here, and we've got orders to disable everyone we can. Marc... Liz is going to destroy the base. She says, still feeling guilty about that part.

He paths. *Got it. Is it safe to port to you with civilians?*

Should be. Dave just ported in with Amy, one of them got to her, but she'll be fine... and... long story... her ex, Charlie, so don't attack him when you see him! He's with us! We were just debating if we should pursue the last of them or just let the destruction of the base do it. She explains.

Marc tells the others with him. "I have to be in physical contact with all of you for this to work." Zelkind and the two new Apara put their hands on Marc and the five of them disappear, reappearing near Tess.

Marc spots Tess, lays Alyona down gently on the ground, and runs and embraces her. He looks her in the eye and paths, *I wasn't sure I'd ever see you again, love! Let's get out of here, all of us.*

The hallway is dusky; lights flicker in the smoke and dust filled passage. Dave has Amy in hand, as she's still not recovered enough to port by herself. Marc picks up Alyona motions for some of the security team to take the two novice Apara and Dr. Zelkind. They all port out and directly to Medical, where Sara, Annie, and other medical personnel are ready to deal with their needs.

Amy, still weak, tells Dave: "Tell everyone else to get out, and give Liz the all clear."

Dave paths Liz, letting her know once everyone's accounted for, and their goals met, except for one. He and Charlie didn't find Janna. Liz acknowledges the message and sends Fang and Teresa back to rendezvous with the others at Medical.

Liz enters the elevator and flips switches on a device. The power is still out, so the elevator won't go down on its own. She opens an access panel to the elevator cables. She's already disabled the emergency brakes on the system telekinetically, and pulls out what looks like a penlight, aiming it at the primary cable holding the elevator aloft. She pushes a button, and a laser cutter slices effortlessly through the titanium and steel cable. Just before it breaks, she ports out, knowing her job is done.

The elevator crashes down and explodes with tremendous force before hitting the bottom, collapsing the base, and killing or trapping anyone in it below ground. The device contains additional cent-opal dust and shards that will further disable any remaining enemy Apara caught in the explosion. After long discussion, they've decided that the conditioned Apara are unlikely to be redeemable, and the compound will weaken them, and prevent them from porting out should they survive the collapse.

She ports to Medical and seeks Charlie out. He's sitting on a bench, while Annie, now working as a full-fledged, Apara medic, is treating several minor wounds he received, as well as attempting to reduce the swelling where the soldier hit him in the face. Liz stands behind Annie and says, "Charlie, I'm sorry we *couldn't* find her."

"I know. She wasn't in our room, so I don't know where she could have been, and we checked the brig, she wasn't there either. I just hope she didn't suffer much...." He says, understanding why Liz had to bring the base down.

An unknown woman walks in their direction, looking shellshocked and hesitant. She looks like she's about to cry when she says, "Ch... *Charlie*? Is that you?"

Charlie turns around, pulling away from Annie's small, healing hands, and gasps. He stands up, upending Annie's tray of medical supplies, and stumbles over to the dark-haired woman Dr. Zelkind had Marc rescue. "*Janna!*" He exclaims.

"Charlie, stay back!" She mutters with her hand over her mouth.

He stops, taken aback by her apparent rejection. "Why? What's wrong?"

"You're not going to believe this!" She trails off, and pulls her hand away from her mouth, "They tested everyone on base and I was *compatible!*" Her involuntarily extended fangs show him she is now like Amy and the others. She cringes, and Sara comes up with a bag of blood, realizing the problem.

"Sit child. Your reunion will wait until you've fed." She seats the trembling woman in a chair and helps her with the bag of blood.

Amy, still weak, comes over and rubs Charlie's shoulder. "I'm *sorry*. I didn't expect that." She says.

He slowly approaches Janna, crouches down, and watches her feed hungrily. "It's okay, Janna. I *know* you're still you, just as Amy is still Amy." He glances back at Amy and gives her a melancholy smile, then reaches over, and extends a hand to Janna. She drops the empty blood bag and takes his hand. He stands, pulling her up into an embrace, not worrying about whether she might sink her fangs into him or not. She's safe, and that's all that matters.

Marc carries Alyona over to a waiting gurney with some of Sara's people ready to take her to be treated. As he lays her down on it, she stirs and looks up. "Marc?" She whispers. "*Where...?*"

"*Hush*, save your energy. You're *safe* now. We'll talk when you're better and I'll fill you in on everything." He reaches down and squeezes her hand reassuringly as Tess comes up behind him.

They wheel her away to a room and Tess asks, "Who's that?"

"Alyona Koslov, she's the woman they found in the tomb, as well as an old friend." Marc says.

Tess puts her arm around Marc's waist and pulls him closer, leaning her head on his shoulder, beyond exhausted by the physical, psychic, and emotional energy spent. Sara motions for Marc to follow her for an examination. As he pulls away to follow her, Tess grabs his arm, and he turns back to her. "When you've gotten Sara's blessing, let's go home. I think I may sleep for a week, but I'll sleep well, knowing you're with me." She grins. He nods, smiles, and follows Sara.

Tess senses a subtle, crackling energy behind her, and knows it can only be one person. She turns around, Isanda is there, flecks of turquoise blue and near metallic gold in her dynamic eyes. Tess touches her mind as she often had as a child and feels Isanda's satisfaction and pride in her role in her mission. "You did very well, young one. Come with me."

Tess follows her to her lab and sits, as Isanda motions to a reclining chair. She feels Isanda standing behind her, examining her energy and mind, putting things back into balance.

"You did very well, but you need to rest for several days. Your mind and body, while capable of more, are not used to this much power running through you. Don't be surprised if your abilities and sensitivities are unstable for a few days. They *will* normalize."

"I'm so wiped out I don't think resting will be a problem." Tess says, yawning dramatically.

"Go, young one. Sara will be done with Marc Girard shortly." She gives Tess a rare smile and there are glints of bright yellow in her eyes. "Sara wishes him to spend the night at Medical, but he refuses to spend another night away from you. Go, be well."

Tess returns to the triage area to wait for Marc, who comes out a few minutes later; Sara following in his wake, still taking readings, and looking quite perturbed.

"I *will come back* tomorrow!" Marc snaps, his only desire is spending time with Tess and sleeping.

"I need to make sure there's no lasting damage!" Sara gripes at him, but he ignores her, something Sara's unaccustomed to.

He enfolds Tess in his arms, finally feeling like it's all real, and the nightmare is finally over.

AFTERMATH

Once everyone's checked over in Medical and debriefed, most go their separate ways. Sara fits Janna and the other new Apara, Heath Smyth, a British citizen who emigrated to Israel about 20 years earlier, with Cent-opal bracelets until someone can teach them to control their abilities. They're given quarters in the dorms near Medical.

Despite Janna's transformation, Charlie refuses to leave her side, choosing to share her quarters. He's been living in the dorms anyway since the explosion, as he knows about them, and is presumed dead in the human world. Liz approves the arrangement, but makes sure Janna knows to feed regularly, so she won't lose control, and attack Charlie. She realizes this may solve the problem of his knowing about them but being incompatible. While they won't have centuries together, he'll have an incentive to protect their secret because he'll be *protecting Janna*.

Amy decides this is a good night to stay with Dave, considering Marc will be back home with Tess. She ports in and grabs a few things, pathing Tess, **Will be with Dave tonight if you need me for anything!** She sends a mental, knowing grin, and breaks the connection before Tess can path back.

Liz follows Tess and Marc home to make sure he's all right. "Are you sure I can't convince you to stay the night in Medical? Sara's quite insistent." She inquires, worried about her former charge.

"I'm *fine!* Tess and I need to get caught up." He glances at Tess, amazement in his eyes. "I leave you for a few weeks, come back, and you've gone all Amazon warrior on me!" He teases.

"I had to get you back. I *couldn't* just stand back and hope the others would do it for me. Besides, it felt *good* to kick their asses!" She grins, but then her grin falters as she remembers that those same people she'd fought and incapacitated were very likely dead tonight, and if not, would be when their air, food, and water run out.

He senses what's upsetting her, pulls her in for a hug, and rocks her gently.

Liz, sensing Marc's concern for Tess, paths him, *she did great, really! And this new skill she's got, if she can master it, and teach it, it could make an enormous difference.*

Marc replies, *I get that, but right now, I just want to be in the here and now, not in the maybes and possibilities of tomorrow. Give us a couple of days to recover and we'll talk about it all then.*

Liz nods and ports out, leaving the two partners to each other.

Tess and Marc talk for a while, but are so exhausted they fall asleep within an hour after getting home, entwined in each other's arms, with Mabel sleeping at the foot of the bed.

***

Liz ports home, finding Kari and Peder up late, playing *Hnefatafl*, an old, Viking strategy game that predates chess, but uses a similar board. Kari sighs in relief when Liz ports in, and extends her hand to her exhausted partner, pulling her down on the sofa next to her.

"I know you rescued Marc and others, but what about the *Naqam*? Are they gone for good?" Kari asks her partner as she gently rubs her back to relieve the tension she feels empathically.

"We destroyed the base, but nothing is certain. We incapacitated all but four they'd turned, and we rescued the two most recent. That means two are unaccounted for. There's a good chance, with that much concrete and steel dropping on them, that any Apara caught in the collapse either won't survive, or will be in indefinite stasis, meaning they'll only recover if someone digs them out and gets them somewhere they can heal properly. Still, it bothers me that two are *completely unaccounted* for, plus, according to Charlie, no one saw any sign of their leader, Uri Jabarin. Charlie didn't know his last name, but our new guest, Dr. Hannah Zelkind filled us in, so we have that now."

"You're saying there's a chance this *isn't* over yet?" Kari asks; concern dripping from her words.

"There's no doubt we've dealt them a serious blow, but no, I can't be certain. In the meantime, we've got our IT people at Google and social media outlets creating intelligent algorithms that will search for certain keywords, terms, and names that will trigger red flags. If the tagged info turns out to be about us, it'll get deleted from whatever server or computer it's on, and we'll deal with the memories of those who posted it. Our Benefactors are putting up a cloaked, monitoring satellite which will monitor for any changes near the collapsed base. Once the dust settles, I'm considering sending a team in to port into any air pockets to see if they can locate Jabarin. He's the biggest danger. Dr. Zelkind is being more than cooperative, and she's given us what information she can about the man. He's a zealot and obsessive. So, if he did survive, he won't let his crusade against us wane; he'll pop up again and wage a literal, holy war on us." Liz explains as she slumps back against the back of the sofa and leans against Kari in exhaustion.

Peder scowls, and then asks, "So, other than that, do we just wait and see what happens? What do we do if he resurfaces and outs us to the world?"

"I don't think he will, *kjære broren min*. Now that we destroyed his project, if he even survived, it'll be *personal* for him. If he outs us, he'll lose his shot at holy vengeance."

"Shouldn't we let the others know? Especially the ones they know about, like Marc and Amy?" Kari asks.

"Not for now. Let them have their hard-won victory. It'll take time for the *Naqam* to regroup if anyone survived. In the meantime, we need to resurrect our center from the ashes. I spoke to our construction team, and the new building will be finished about two to three weeks earlier than originally planned. I've got several potentials waiting to hear from us about jobs, especially in the new departments we're setting up." She yawns, flashing her family a sly grin. "So, which one of you is losing? I'll play the winner a game before I pass out."

REBUILDING

Three days later, Liz knocks on Peder's bedroom door. He's been living with Liz and Kari since he left Medical after the Jerusalem bomb. Peder opens the door telekinetically, and Liz enters, carrying her tablet. "Peder, I've got a *favor* to ask." She says, as she shoves some clothes out of a nearby chair and sits.

"*Javel*?" He asks, looking up from his adventure videogame based on warriors trying to earn enough points to enter Valhalla. When he realizes this is more than just a sisterly visit, he pauses his game and gives her his full attention. "What's up?"

"I've been keeping an eye on a few of our Lost Mission potentials via social media; the ones we were in the process of hiring when all hell broke loose. One of them is growing impatient with the delay." She hands him the tablet with the woman's file open. "Phoenix was born in North Dakota but grew up here in Asheville. She had an internship with a publishing company in Charlotte that closed a couple years back. She's now in Greenville (SC) but lost her job in early January. She was working at a print shop. You were out the day of her interview, so I don't think you met her. If we can't bring her in soon, she's going to start looking for work elsewhere. With her experience in the field, I was planning to put her in your division when we get it up and running, but by then, she may be working elsewhere." Liz explains.

"Yes, she certainly has the skills we need for book production, as well as a promising profile as a potential. It would be a shame to let her slip through our fingers." He says, absentmindedly scanning her file.

"I'm glad you *agree*! I spoke to her earlier today and asked if she'd be interested in getting a head start on a work-from-home basis while our building's under construction and she looks for a place to live. Since it's *your* department, I'd like you to help her set up, and have regular meetings with her until she gets in the swing of things." Liz suggests, hoping her brother will take on a project that will get him out of the house, and possibly more.

"I suppose I can do that, since it's going to be *my* department. Does she have the hardware and software to work from home?" He asks.

Liz suppresses a grin, hoping Peder doesn't realize she's taking a page from Sara's book that Peder may find this young woman of interest beyond her work skills. "She has some, though she could use a duplex laser printer for printing out proof-reading copies. You'll have to see what programs she has." She suggests.

"Okay, have Kari set up a time for me to go down there, and I'll get her started. I know we've got a few projects waiting in the wings from before the shit hit the fan, so if she's already got experience, we can get those going and keep her in our scope at the same time." Peder says, picks up his game controller, resumes, and slips back into his game as if he'd never paused it.

Liz leaves his room grinning to herself, careful not to let him see her expression or sense her reaction, or he may realize she's got an ulterior motive for connecting him with Phoenix.

PHOENIX

Phoenix Ashlyn Johnsen is a striking young woman. She's tall and willowy, with facial features typical of the Scandinavian gene pool, but her hair is a natural, fiery ginger with the complexion to match. Her eyes are soul-piercing, ice blue. At first glance, she looks like a woman who might be physically frail, but she's quite strong and disciplined from years of dancing.

She has a degree in publishing and marketing, with a minor in English Lit, and has loved books her whole life. As a child, she couldn't get enough of them. When she wasn't dancing, she was reading; as she got to her teens, reading led to writing, and she self-published some of her short stories on one of the major platforms with some success. She has a strong passion for both and for life.

For years, Phoenix has had one literary dirty pleasure. She loves vampire novels, especially the more erotic kind. She doesn't know why, but she loves them and prefers the ones where they really aren't evil monsters, but misunderstood immortals. However, between school, dance projects, and work, she put them aside to focus on the real world, until something unusual happened after Christmas.

While originally from North Dakota, most of her family now lives in the Southeast. This Christmas, she went to her mother's place in Athens, Georgia. It was a big get-together with family from all over the South. It's a yearly family event that everyone tries to make, come hell or high water; in this year's case, despite a highly contagious, but relatively mild virus going around. Two of her cousins from the Atlanta area were there, feeling fatigued, with low-grade fevers, but didn't feel bad enough to miss the big, annual, shindig. They just took something to keep the aches and fever down and hung out with everyone.

A few days later, nearly everyone in the family had the bug. It was mild: just lethargy, aches, and a low-grade fever; it was that way for everyone, *except* Phoenix. She came down with something quite different. At first, it was similar, but the aches soon turned to burning pin-fire pains in all her joints. She felt like she could barely even get up out of bed, and her fever rose. By the third day, her fever hit 104.8, her mom threatened to drive all the way from Athens to Greenville, and take her to urgent care personally, if she didn't go there herself. She called one of her friends, found one of the old masks from one of the more recent viral outbreaks, and had her friend Randy drive her to the Urgent care about twenty minutes away.

The wait was long, as many people were coming down with this bug. While most cases were mild, a lot of people head for Urgent Care as soon as something that *might* be a new strain of COVID, Avian flu, or RSV pops up. Phoenix was there for two and a half hours, popping acetaminophen and ibuprofen to keep her fever down, but it just stayed where it was, 104.8 F and didn't drop.

When she was finally called in to the examination room, she took three steps, stumbled, and passed out. She was taken to the emergency room in Greenville and put into isolation. Since they hadn't seen any reactions like this to the current virus, they assumed she had something else and decided to err on the side of caution. Her friend, Randy, told the paramedics what she'd been taking and that it hadn't brought down her fever, so they tried cooling her with ice packs, and even a cool bath to bring it down.

Her temperature rose and hit a high of 106.4. Her organs shut down, and at 3:49 am, they called brain death. She never regained consciousness before her apparent death. They took her body to the morgue with isolation protocols, in case this was some new virus. They isolated her friend Randy until they could determine what the virus might be. They notified CDC, and they sent in specialists to do viral testing and an autopsy. The hospital woke her mother up in the middle of the night, informed her that her daughter had died, and she hopped in the car and drove to Greenville.

They had barely begun the autopsy and made the first incision when her eyes flew open, and she screamed in pain. They returned her to the hospital for further testing, but her fever was gone, she no longer had any pain in her joints, and her organs were all functioning normally. She felt weak, but fine. When her tests came back, it showed she had the same, normally mild virus that had been going around since mid-December and that she was slightly anemic. The doctors declared she had an unusual reaction to the virus and told her to take some iron supplements and get some rest.

They released her from the hospital and her mother stayed with her for a few days to make sure she was better. She was fatigued and always hungry, especially for iron and protein-rich foods, even with taking an iron supplement. After about a week, she finally felt well enough that her mother went home.

She hadn't felt well enough to go out with friends for New Year's Eve, so got together with a couple of friends one night and went to a local bar a few days later. She and her friends were knocking back beers, but it wasn't affecting her, so she left early. She walked to her car, which was in a parking deck a few blocks away, but never made it there.

Someone grabbed her from behind and pulled her into an alley. The masked assailant held her at knifepoint and demanded her purse, cell phone, and any other valuables. She complied but realized that there were irreplaceable family photos in her wallet, and begged for them, grabbing at the purse straps in desperation. The robber ripped the purse away, stabbed her in the abdomen, and she fell to the ground, bleeding, and sobbing. After a few minutes, she knew she was near death, and everything went black.

She woke up the next afternoon to light shining down into the alley from above and the sounds of cars, trucks, horns, and people just out of sight. She was disoriented and brought her hands up to rub her eyes, only to see them covered in her own, dried blood.

Memories flooded her mind, and she reached down to where she'd been stabbed. While covered with blood, there was no gaping wound, only a slightly raised line where it had sliced into her flesh. She was weak, but pulled herself upright, and looked. Sure enough, there was a faint, raised, red line with just a hint of scabbing on her abdomen, and blood everywhere. Her purse and cell were gone, as were her car keys. She had to get home, but if she went out like this, blood soaked, and yet without a wound, they'd wonder if she were the assailant, and not the victim.

She fumbled around the alley unsteadily and found a discarded coat. It smelled horrible, and was likely abandoned by some homeless person, but it would cover up the worst of the blood. She knew she wasn't far from her car, if the mugger hadn't taken it. The parking garage was right around the corner, so she made a mad dash for it, took the elevator up to the fifth floor, and was relieved to find her car still there. The missing keys were not a problem. She kept a spare duct taped behind her novelty, Norwegian flag plate on the front of her car, and a spare apartment key hidden at home. She stuck her fingers under the plate, pulled it loose, got in the car, and sat there, halfway stunned and very confused. She rolled down her window, tossed out the putrid jacket, and started the car. Luckily, she was there on a flat rate pass from Saturday night and the deck was free on Sundays, so she could leave without paying anything, which was a relief since her purse and all her money and cards were stolen.

She got home, went straight to the bathroom and looked at her stomach. She wiped away the dried blood and could see that she wasn't imagining it. The wound was there but nearly healed. She showered and changed clothes, glad to be clean. After a lot of contemplation, she reported that her phone and purse had been stolen to the police and that she'd been knocked out, but was otherwise unharmed. She gave them what description she could but left out the whole stabbing her to death part.

Again, she was craving red meat, spinach, dark chocolate, and even liver. She didn't know what was wrong with her, but she was confused and distraught. She called out of work for the next few days from lethargy. When she went back to work, however, she was fired for being out too much.

She didn't understand what was happening to her, and didn't think she could confide in her doctor. Who would *believe* her? It wasn't until she was flipping channels on a streaming TV app on her smart TV, and one of the horror channels was showing a vampire movie that it hit her. She'd died and come back twice in less than a month, and both times craved red meat and such. Not that she believed she was becoming a vampire *for real*; after all, she didn't have any *fangs* and no trouble being in the sunlight, or eating regular food, but it nagged at her.

Having no job to go to, and vampires on the brain, she fell into her old habit of reading vampire stories and erotica. Perhaps some part of her felt akin to the mythical monsters after what had happened to her, or perhaps her subconscious was trying to tell her something, but she couldn't read enough about them.

She needed to find another job, even if she felt like just hiding in her own little world, where it was safe. She thought about relocating and getting a fresh start. She'd seen an article about a company in Asheville starting an independent publishing division and contacted them with her resume. She got a reply later the same day, along with an application, which was a very pleasant surprise. Inspiration Inc. hired her, but before she could find a place in Asheville, and move there to start her new position, a gas explosion destroyed their building.

She got really depressed after that, and even dabbled in a little self-pitying, self-cutting on her arms. Phoenix didn't intend to commit suicide but did it more out of frustration for her situation. When she did, however, the wounds healed within a couple of hours, bringing her condition to the forefront of her mind once again.

A couple of days after the explosion in South Asheville, the woman who hired her, Liz Pedersen, contacted her, informing her they were going to rebuild and that she still wanted to hire her, but it would take time. They agreed she'd continue to apply for unemployment while she could, and that they'd stay in touch.

***

That was several weeks ago, and Phoenix is wondering if she should just find something else to do. She hasn't had any more brushes with death but still tests her self-healing ability now and then to make sure it's all real.

She posts on Facebook she might have to find a different 'new job' rather than wait for the one in Asheville. She can't really move up there until she knows for a fact that she'll be working, as rent is a lot higher there than she is paying now, but she has to survive.

The next morning, Liz Pedersen, head of Inspiration, Inc., calls her and makes a deal with her to start as a work-from-home employee, as most of the others who worked for them *prior* to the explosion are currently doing. The next day, she gets calls from Kari Andersen, setting up a visit from Peder Pedersen, Liz's brother, to get her started. In addition, they offer her a *bonus* to help her pay for relocating to the Asheville area.

She finally feels like things are about to get better, but more than she could ever imagine is yet to come.

ORIENTATION

Despite being able to teleport wherever they need to go, some Apara still *enjoy* driving. Peder, however, is *not* one of them. There are days he'd still rather ride a horse than drive a car. Unfortunately, with situations like today, where he's going to Greenville, South Carolina, about an hour and fifteen minutes from Asheville, he doesn't have much choice but to drive. There would be too many questions about how he traveled over 60 miles without a car.

Luckily, Liz and Kari do have one outside their portal home near Asheville. He heads out, stopping at a storage facility they have, where they've been storing equipment for the new offices, and grabs a few things their new employee will need, including a color, duplex laser printer for proof-reading printouts, a company tablet, and a case of printer paper.

The drive takes longer than expected, as he hits traffic, but pulls up outside of Phoenix's place, almost half an hour late. He leaves everything in the car to make certain he has the right place. He rings the doorbell and hears a female voice yell, "Just a sec!"

When Phoenix opens the door and sees Peder, she gives him a charming smile. "Peter, right?" She asks.

"Actually, it's Peder. I'm Norwegian." He says, still a bit focused on her brilliant smile.

"Really? So's my dad's family! I was born in North Dakota, where *'Uff Da'* is as common as 'y'all' is down here! Come on in." She motions him in, but he pauses.

"I need to grab a few things from the car, but I wanted to make sure I have the right place first." He grins.

"Can I give you a hand with anything?" She asks. Her voice is a pleasant, sunny tone that really hits a chord with Peder.

"You can grab the box of paper and the tablet if that's not too heavy for you." He suggests.

She chuckles. "I may look like a twig that could crack in a light breeze, but I guarantee you, I'm a lot *stronger* than I look!" She grins, and walks with a spring in her step, out to the car.

"All right, then!" Peder says and pulls the box of printer paper out, handing it to her, and puts the tablet for her on top. "Got it?"

"*Sure!* No problem!" She says, turns, and carries it back with nearly as much spring in her step as she had unladen.

Peder reaches into his car, gets a shoulder bag with his laptop, tablet, a few odds and ends, including cables, and slings it over his shoulder, then picks up the 40-pound printer, and surreptitiously uses his PK to close and lock the car door once he's certain no one's looking. He carries it into the first-floor apartment, asking, "Where should I put this?"

"In the room to the right of the front door. That's where my computer stuff is. Are you *thirsty*? Have you *eaten*?" She yells from the kitchen in an upbeat tone.

"I'm fine for now." He yells back as he unpacks the new printer from its box.

Phoenix comes in carrying a tray with a pitcher of purplish-blue liquid, two glasses, as well as some flatbread, and to Peder's surprise, a chunk of '*brunost*', or as it's called in America, 'Ski Queen' cheese. She even has a Norwegian-style cheese knife, or *ostehøvel*, as it's called. *Brunost* is a brown-colored cheese made from caramelized goat's whey and heavy cream. It tastes like a cross between caramel and peanut butter. It's about as Norwegian as you can get, and it's been a while since Peder has gone out of his way to get any. It wasn't invented until the mid-1800s, so it wasn't part of Peder's upbringing, but he enjoys it when he has it. Phoenix notices his expression, and says, "Well, you said you're

Norwegian! My mom keeps sending me care packages with stuff like this." She puts it down on a small stand in her computer room and runs back to the kitchen to get a couple of small plates.

When she comes back, Peder has poured himself some of the drink and turns to her, asking, "*Blåbær saft*? Um, blueberry, right? I used to pick lots of those in Norway as a child. The forest floor was covered with them." He takes a sip, savoring the all-to-familiar flavor.

"Yeah, my parents went over to visit my dad's family in Mo i Rana last fall, and brought back all sorts of stuff for me, including the drink mix, a big bottle of Piffi spice, and several packets of Norwegian soups and stuff. Mom got the cheese on a day trip into Atlanta at an international grocery store." She says as she makes room on her desk for the printer. "So, where in Norway are you from?" She asks to keep the conversation going, glad there's something other than just work to talk about.

"A small community near Langesund, along the southeastern coast." He rambles off, knowing that the actual village he lived in no longer exists, but Langesund is close to the original settlement.

"Cool! Other end of the country compared to dad's family." She remarks.

"And your mother?" He asks, curious about her red hair and complexion.

"Oh, her grandparents came over from Ireland after World War II. I think they wanted to get as far from Germany and Germans as possible." She comments, as she connects the printer to her computer, sits down, and installs the software drivers for it.

"I guess that's where you got your red hair? It's not as common today as it... as it once was." He says, catching himself before he could say, 'in my day, when a lot of Northmen had red hair.'

He takes his time getting her set up and able to log into a central server Ty and Val set up for work until the new offices are ready. He goes over the software she has and finds she's got most of what she needs. They go through book templates they currently have, but she knows how to set up her own, which is an advantage.

As he's working with her, he finds his mood improving, like her own energy is, somehow, contagious, and oddly healing. He realizes he feels better than he has in a while.

1:30 pm rolls around and she asks, "Are you hungry? I *am*."

He pauses, not usually bothering with lunch lately since he's not doing 'social eating' with their human potentials daily. However, he says, "Eat if you need to."

She flashes him a bright smile. "Would you like anything? I've got ham and roast beef for sandwiches." She says as she stands to go to the kitchen.

"If you want to, anything's fine, but you don't have to go out of your way." He says, not wanting to be a bother.

"No problem. Back in a few." She says in a chipper tone.

He stands, stretches, and walks around the room, noting her book shelves. There are quite a few books on publishing and graphic design, but there are also books on dance, theater, Art History, Scandinavia, and gardening. He moves on from her non-fiction shelves and finds a few popular novels, including some mysteries, a bunch of Stephen King books, and then some books that elicit a smirk. She has a substantial collection of books about vampires, ranging from the more common Anne Rice and Charmaine Harris books to paranormal romance and gaming. He thinks, *Sue said she's noticed a pattern where many potentials have an interest in, if not a fascination with, vampires. What was it she said? 'Potentials often build on some of their subconscious conditioning, which may come out as dreams about or a fascination with vampires, even if the fictional ones are mostly bullshit!'*

He hears her returning and turns around to face the door. She comes in with a plate full of diagonally cut sandwiches, mostly ham, roast beef, and a few Jarlsberg on rye. "Here we go! Help yourself." She says, putting down the large plate on the same stand as she'd put the *brunost* and flatbread earlier. "Looks like we've still got a bit of the blueberry drink, but if you want something else, like coffee or soda, I'll see what I've got." She chirps.

"This'll be fine." He says, but before moving over to grab food, he comments, "You've got quite an eclectic book collection. I hope you don't mind, but I needed to stretch and checked out your shelves." He smiles, trying to avoid appearing too nosey.

"No problem; mom's always said you can learn a lot about a person from their bookshelves! You should see my other shelves! I've got a lot of classics and poetry in there from my English Lit studies. These..." And she motions to the ones in her computer room, "are more the things I read for fun or need to reference, like the computer books or dance ones.

Peder notices a pair of ballet toe-shoes, well used, in a glass display box on one shelf. "You've studied ballet?" He inquires, becoming more curious about this multifaceted, young woman they'll be bringing into Inspiration, Inc, and hopefully, as a new Apara someday.

"Oh, yeah! Several years of it, but I eventually moved on to more modern dance, ballroom, and even some historical styles. *Aren't* you going to eat?" She asks, sitting down with a plateful, mostly rare, roast beef.

He smiles, taking a little of this and that and sitting again. He notices she has an open book, pages down, on the other side of her computer. "Is that your current book?" He asks, knowing its topic just by the style of cover and writing on it.

"Yeah, it's a series I really like. It's been sold as e-books, but they recently added a print-on-demand option, and I just had to order the series! Call me old-fashioned, but I still love the feel of a physical book in my hands." She says before taking several bites of her roast beef.

"What's it about?" He asks, curious as to her reaction.

"Oh, probably nothing you'd be interested in. It's about a woman who ends up being a vampire psychologist." She blushes slightly.

Thinking about Sue, he nearly chokes on his food, saying, "Wait, is she a vampire who's a psychologist or a psychologist that treats vampires?" He asks with a lopsided grin.

"In this book, she's human, more or less, but she gets involved with a man who's a vampire and ends up doing therapy for *dysfunctional* vampires. It's a fun series." She comments offhandedly.

"I noticed that quite a few of your fiction books are in that *genre*." He says without implying anything specific.

She looks slightly flustered but answers him. "Yeah, it's silly really, not like such creatures exist! I've just had a fascination with them for a long time. I kind of grew out of it for a while. Had so much on my plate that I, well, didn't exactly lose interest but...." She trails off.

"It became less of a *focus* for a while?" He suggests trying to read her emotional overtones as they discuss the subject.

"Yeah, *that's* it. I'd kind of stopped reading them for the last two or three years, until recently." He notices the tone of her voice and emotions shift to a more somber, almost frightened overtone.

"So, what jump-started your interest again?" He asks.

"I hope you don't mind, but I'd rather not get into it right now. Let's just say that my life took an odd shift a couple of months back, and I can kind of relate to them." She sighs and then changes the subject. "So, do you need any more sandwiches? How about some coffee?" She inquires, hoping to divert the conversation away from the mystery of her altered biology.

"No, I'm fine." He says, sensing this is not a subject she's ready to discuss with a stranger. However, he makes a mental note to mention it to Liz when he gets home again.

They work the rest of the afternoon, with Peder giving her a test book to set up using an existing template. She starts it while he's there so he can observe and see how she does. They wrap up for the day, agreeing she should finish it on her own and send him a PDF of the finished book. They agree he will come down to Greenville to meet with her Tuesdays and Fridays, while otherwise communicating remotely.

Shortly after he leaves her home, he feels the *absence* of her energy. He pushes the nagging feeling that this is important out of his mind. He gets on the road and drives back through the mountains, across the NC line, to Asheville, all the while fighting that same feeling every time it pokes out its figurative head.

He arrives back at Liz's portal-home, the facade that leads to her and Kari's Sanctuary dwelling, in Biltmore Forest, south of town. He goes in, and his sister, Liz, is staring expectantly at him.

"*What*?" Peder asks defensively.

"*Well*? How'd it go? Think she might make the *cut*?" Liz asks, curious to hear his impressions and gauge his reaction.

He puts his bag down on a table and plops down in a chair nearby. "I suspect she'll be a good one for us. She has a great attitude and intelligence. *Oh!* And she's got the whole vampire fascination thing going on we sometimes see." He grins, thinking about her bookshelves.

"Hm, a sign that her subconscious is trying to prepare her.... That *is* a good sign!" Liz comments, noticing some odd, emotional ripples coming from Peder.

"Yeah, though, there was something... she said she'd stopped reading her vampire books a while back, but something happened recently that made her take them up again. Unfortunately, she didn't want to talk about it, and while I could read a lot of her other surface thoughts, she kept those under wraps." He recounts, thinking about the dynamic mind he'd otherwise sensed.

"Perhaps she has a touch of precognition? Maybe you can get her to talk about it more next time?" She asks, taking a sip of her usual sassafras tea.

"I'll see what I can do, but she was adamant about not discussing it, for now. It may take a while before she'll open up to me about it. She's got a thing for the vampire romance books, though, so, whoever you pair her up with should be able to use that to their advantage." He suggests yawning.

"I'm *sure* that will be an option." She grins but hides it surreptitiously with a sip of tea. She hopes Peder may connect with this young woman. Tess suggested the pairing after Phoenix's interview. She and Kari have been working on that aspect of her people-reading skills to help find compatible people for partnerships. Whether platonic, familial, or romantic, it's always best to pair a new Apara with a dedicated partner to help them learn, adapt, and occasionally, be kept out of trouble.

"Where's Kari?" Peder asks, not used to seeing Liz alone lately.

"She's over visiting Tess and Marc, making sure he's doing well, but also helping Tess catch up with some of the backlog of Lost Missioners. Sue's been so busy with Alyona and the two new Apara they force turned, she's not had any time to work with Tess in the last few days.

"So, feel up to a game of *Hnefatafl*?" He asks with a lopsided grin, noticing the game is still out and set up.

Liz chuckles and sits up, sliding the board over to where they can play, saying, "Only if you're ready to *lose* badly!"

They play a few games until Kari ports back in with a tablet full of files from Tess's research, eager to fill Liz in on the latest, promising potentials. Peder excuses himself and heads to his room, intending to play his own games, but ends up distracted by thoughts of Phoenix he just can't shake.

***

About two and a half weeks later, they're working at Phoenix's house on the first, full book she's doing an original layout on, going over the final version together to look for anything she may have missed, but it's ready for final proofing. She asks, "Do you mind if we stop a little early today? I want to see a new movie that's out today at 5:40 and I need to get through rush hour traffic to get there." She explains with a hopeful look in her eye.

"Sure, I think we're done for now. I'll pass this on to my proofer to get a fresh look for errors, so there isn't much you can do until that's done." He says, smiling. "What are you going to see?"

She looks a tad embarrassed, but says, "It's an adaptation of the Night Huntress books by Jeaniene Frost. It's the first one, *Halfway to the Grave*. You've probably never heard of it before."

"I'm not familiar with the story, but I saw you have several books by that author on your shelf." He says with a raised eyebrow. "What's it about? I mean, I assume it's something vampire related, since it's in that section of your shelves, *right*?"

"You've got me! It's a fun series. A woman is a vampire hunter. She, herself is half-vampire, but she ends up partnering with one 'good guy' vampire to go after bad ones." She summarizes it as succinctly as she can.

"Hm, would you like some company? Or is this something you'd rather see alone? I'm not feeling like making the trek over the mountain during rush hour." He suggests, curious to see if this might give him some insight into Phoenix outside of work.

She looks a bit surprised. "You're welcome, if you want to. It's probably more geared toward women, but who knows! You might *just* like it!" She says, warming to the idea of doing something besides setting up books with Peder. "Let me grab another ticket online, get ready, and we can head out." She suggests.

While she's out, he paths Liz, *I'll be late tonight, so I'll catch up with you and Kari whenever I get home.*

He can sense a hint of curious surprise from his sister. *Oh? What's up? Everything all right?*

Yes! Of course, it is. I've just got an opportunity to get some insight into Phoenix. She's going to, of all things, a vampire movie tonight. So, I'm going to tag along and try to get a read on some of her reactions and emotions connected to it. Besides, you know how traffic gets on 26 on Friday afternoons. Anything to avoid that mess. He paths, including a mental eyeroll.

Sounds good! She paths and he picks up on amused overtones in her thoughts.

Lissa! It's not like that! This isn't a date! I just think observing her thoughts and emotions, if I can, while she's watching such a movie could tell us a bit about how she might react when it comes time to bring her in. That's all! He paths, annoyed at his sister's half-pathed implications, but on some level, is also acutely aware that there's some kind of connection forming between Phoenix and himself. He writes it off to just a good, working relationship, while suppressing some emotions he's not willing to confront now.

We'll talk when you get home. Liz paths, but in person, she's smiling slyly, hoping Peder might *finally* find someone.

Phoenix comes back with dramatic make-up on, wearing black, faux-leather pants, a tight, red, spaghetti string top, and a black leather jacket. In addition, she has a belt with a knife holster and a plastic, silvery dagger. Her hair is down, rather than in her usual ponytail, parted to one side. "I'm *ready!*" She says, excited to see the premiere.

Peder looks at her with a lopsided grin. "Is this how you usually dress for the movies?" He asks, amused.

She looks at him like he's being obtuse, and goes over to her shelves, pulling out one book from the series, and tossing it to him. "No, *silly!* I'm *cosplaying!* I'm dressing as Cat, the main character, and I bet at least half the other women and girls there will be as well! I'm sure some guys will dress as Bones, the Master Vampire she gets hooked up with in the series.

Peder suppresses his grin but can't suppress the twinkle of amusement in his eyes. "All right! Would you like me to drive?" He asks, even though he doesn't like driving more than necessary, especially not in heavy traffic.

"Do you know how to get to the Camelot Theater?" She asks.

"No, but there's always Google Maps." He suggests.

She shakes her head and rolls her eyes. "Don't worry about it. I know some shortcuts, so I'll drive!" She says, slipping on some high boots with high heels and grabbing her car keys.

Peder follows her out, noting how her mannerisms have changed now that she's in costume, almost like she's stepping into this character. They get in her car, and he asks, "So, you say this character is *half*-vampire? How's that *possible*?"

"Well, in that universe, newly turned male vampires can still father children, but only for a short time. So, one got her mother pregnant right after he became one of them, and then took off, leaving her mom pregnant with a half-human, half-vampire child that she's got to raise alone! Her mom *hates* vampires." She rambles off with typical fandom enthusiasm.

"Sounds like you have these books practically memorized." He remarks, enjoying watching her excitement.

"Yeah, read them a few times, plus have the audiobooks so I can listen when I work." She glances over and sees his bemusement. "I *know* what you're thinking! I'm *obsessed* or something. I'm not, but I love this series and have been waiting for them to do a movie for several years. Besides, sometimes, it's just *fun* to dress up, be someone else for a night, and forget who you really are." She says and he gets a twinge of yet another melancholy overtone from her, like she wants to forget something about herself, but he can't get a handle on what.

Phoenix drives and they make various small talk, and when she gets to the Camelot Theater, there's already a long line of fans waiting to get in. She sighs. "And that is the other reason I wanted to get here a little early, but I guess not early *enough*! Oh, I got you a ticket next to me. By some miracle, there was still an open seat there."

"Let me know what I owe you for the ticket." He says.

"Tell you *what*, you can get the popcorn! That should just about even out." She grins at him and goes through the parking lot to find a spot, finding one of the last ones, far from the theater. "Maybe I should've skipped the *spiked* heels? We've got a bit of a walk." She winces.

"I don't mind." He chuckles.

"You know, it's too bad your hair isn't curly, your eyes brown, and could do a kind of commoner Brit/Aussie dialect, or you could have played Bones to my Cat!" She jokes.

He looks at her, faking shock. "*Me?* Play a *vampire*? Wouldn't I need *fangs* for that?" He jokes.

She rolls her eyes and says, "Well, if anyone asks if you're supposed to be Bones, just say yes for the fun of it? *Please*?" She gives him parody-like, puppy-dog eyes, and he lets out a laugh.

"As long as no one expects me to act like the character, I guess." He comments as they near the line and some others in line are staring at them.

Someone from up ahead yells, "Great Cat! But your Bones could use a little work! He's not *pale* enough to be a *vampire!*" and they look at the guy who yelled it, decked out in full costume, complete with white powder to make him look pale, and a set of prosthetic fangs.

Peder has to work hard not to completely lose it and laugh hysterically, thinking, *if these guys only knew!*

They get in, grab popcorn and drinks from the concessions stand, and go in. The movie theater is packed, with only an odd, empty seat now and then. They're about halfway back and get settled in.

When the lights go out and the movie starts, Peder eavesdrops on her mind and emotions. Again, he gets the impression that Phoenix really relates to the main character, especially when they explain how she's half-vampire herself, which confuses him. *In reality, you're Apara or you're not.* Naturally, he feels her reaction to the relationship between Bones and Cat, and almost a longing, but also regret or disappointment, like she could never have that. He thinks, *Naturally, it doesn't work that way, but I wonder how she'd feel if she knew that she'll at least get a semblance of her fantasy? Not sure who we can match her up with, but then again, Lissa is always shuffling people around to different centers these days for just that reason.*

The movie wraps up and the fan-filled theater erupts in enthusiastic applause and cheers. They enter the lobby, and Phoenix just enthusiastically stops to chat with other fans about what was right, and what they should have done differently in the movie to be truer to the book. Peder stands in the background, observing. Some guy comes up to him and suggests, "Hey, dude! *Next* time, put more effort into your cosplay!"

Peder is tempted to show the annoying wannabe his fangs, but ignores him, thinking, *Lissa would not be amused if she ever found out.*

The theater makes an announcement, asking everyone who's already seen their showing to please leave the building and theater parking because they're having capacity issues.

They leave, and Phoenix has extra spring in her step, still on an adrenaline rush from the movie. They get to her car and start driving. She glances at Peder and asks, "*So*, what did you *think*? I realize you're not a *fan* or anything, but did you *enjoy* it?"

"*Yes*, it was quite interesting." He says, thinking more of the insights gained than the plot of the film. "It's just not quite the take on vampires I'm used to."

"Oh, I *know*! The traditional stories of the evil vampire seducing, turning women, and killing people and so on. I prefer to think that maybe, just, maybe, some of them could even be good guys! Maybe even heroes." She suggests. "You probably think that's *silly*. Or, more likely, that *I am* for being into all of this?"

"No, you're *not* silly at all. Many people are fascinated by this genre the last couple of decades. Frankly, I *agree*! They are far more likely to be good guys than bad guys. "If they wish to stay *hidden* from society, they would have to follow certain rules for *feeding*, or interactions with humans, wouldn't they?" He asks, testing the waters to see if she naturally leans toward Apara style ethics.

"Yeah, I guess you're right. If they want to live in the human world, they'd have to find a way to blend in and not draw attention to themselves. *Killing* people for blood certainly would draw attention, wouldn't it?" She asks, as the idea rings a bell in her mind, somehow making sense and almost seeming factual. She catches herself and thinks, *Don't go there! Vampires don't really exist! Whatever happened to me has to have a logical explanation! Just wish I could get some answers, but if I tell anyone, they'll either think I'm crazy or dissect me to find out why I can come back from the dead and heal rapidly. I wouldn't want to deal with either of those possibilities! No way!*

"Who knows! Maybe you're right, and they could be *heroes*, protecting people without them knowing it, because they can't let anyone know what they are. Maybe it's a way they can *repay* the humans for being their food source?" He watches her reaction. *If her subconscious pre-conditioning is starting to surface, these concepts should seem logical to her.*

"Hm, interesting angle. I kind of *like* that! But you'd still have to deal with them being affected by stuff like daylight, holy water, not showing any reflections, and so on! I mean, if they can't go out in daylight, someone *might* get suspicious!" She argues.

Peder chuckles. "Here's a thought for you. What if vampires *do* exist, except, instead of being the *undead*, they're as alive as you and I are. Maybe a *virus changes* them genetically. Maybe all the *metaphysical* and *religious* stuff is bunk. Then they could be right in front of you, in broad daylight, and you'd never know they were anything *other* than human." He suggests, watching her reaction.

"*Okay*, I could see that, but if they aren't *dead*, why would they need to drink *blood*?" She asks, thinking she has him stumped.

"Because their bodies can't make it from raw materials. They need whole, human blood they can convert, making them dependent on humans. So, as a way of paying humans back, they're protectors of some kind." He lays out the puzzle pieces in front of her.

"I *guess* that's plausible, but how would they *protect* humans? Would they run around like Superman or Wonder Woman and stop crime? Cause then we'd know they were out there. Maybe we wouldn't know what they are, but we'd know they were superhumans of some kind like mutants or metahumans like in the DC universe! If they want to hide, they couldn't do anything overtly." She insists.

"*True*, but perhaps they have special abilities, like seeing the future, and can stop bad things from happening." He suggests as a plausible answer.

She chuckles, "Then why do bad things *still* happen? If they can see the future, why don't they stop *all* the bad stuff? School shootings, robberies, plane crashes, or give a heads up when some natural disaster is coming?"

"Maybe they do, but I don't think they would be omniscient. I think they would do their best but could never stop everything bad. You'd have to have so many of them out there, probably almost as many vampires as humans to stop *all* the bad stuff." He says.

"Interesting concept! Maybe *you* should start writing your own vampire series!" She says. "I'd read it!"

"I've got too much to do as it is; but, maybe someday, someone will." He says as she's getting off the main road to go to her place.

"Almost back to my place. Thanks for keeping me company. I sure hope my fan-girlishness didn't make you think any less of me!" She says as they turn into her parking spot, next to his car.

"*Not* at all. I have several friends who are, shall we say, into super-accurate, historic recreations. Everyone needs interests, as well as ways to just blow off steam and have fun." He says, gets out of the car, and unlocks his own. "Have a good weekend, Phoenix. I'll see you on Tuesday." He gets in his car and heads back to Asheville, thinking, *At least I've planted the main idea behind us in her mind now. She may not remember it all consciously, but at least, when it comes time for... for SOME-ONE to turn her, it should make it easier for her to accept.*

He uses his cell to pull up a Norwegian radio station on his car stereo, tries to clear his mind, and make sense of everything. He knows Liz will give him the proverbial third degree when he gets home, and part of him knows that he'd better have his thoughts, ideas, and emotions in check, or his sister will have plenty to interrogate him about.

LOOSE ENDS

Now that the battle is over, things are slowly settling into normality, but there are still a few loose ends, including two humans who know about the Apara who *cannot* be turned. Charlie's situation solved itself. He's chosen to stay with Janna, be part of her life, and the Apara's world, willingly.

Amy did some digging, and they officially reported Charlie lost in the cave-in when they discovered Alyona in the ancient tomb. He was told that they had transferred him to the Israelis as a US liaison, but as far as his official service record goes, he was killed in the cave-in, body never recovered; meaning, even if he wanted to go back to his old life, he can't, not without being declared a deserter for faking his death. Once he understood what the Apara were all about, he offered his services. Janna's return only solidified his commitment.

Dr. Hannah Zelkind is in a similar bind. When they found Alyona's body in the tomb, Uri, who was assigned to watch over the reconstruction, contacted Mossad to send experts. Hannah's uncle, an upper-level agent, had her picked up from a refugee and orphan center she was working at in Tel Aviv and choppered her in to work with Uri, and a few other, conscripted doctors and scientists. She did not choose to be part of the project but was commanded to be part of it as her uncle's eyes and ears.

After hearing Marc's version of events, and seeing his reactions while being tortured, she had doubts she was on the right side, and omitted things from her reports to her uncle, and even fed him some misinformation from time to time. When the Apara rescue team came, she knew her only option was to go with them. She'd already deduced that they'd have to destroy the base to protect themselves and their people, so her only options were to die with the rest of them or extend an olive branch through Marc; help rescue the two newly turned 'vampires' and beg to be taken with them.

After things settle down, she, Sara, and Liz meet to decide what will happen to her.

Liz regards the woman, uncertain what to make of her. She'd clearly been part of the operation, but at the same time, she did not get the vibe of someone intending them any harm. Marc put in a good word for her, explaining that she defended him when Uri tortured him, and had been otherwise kind to him under the circumstances.

Liz lets out a long sigh. Sara is sitting with Dr. Zelkind on the other side of the table, giving off protective vibes. "Dr. Zelkind, I'm afraid you've put us in a little bit of a bind. You clearly know *a lot* about us, both in general as well as medically. Such knowledge would be dangerous if someone got it out of you."

"Yes, I *realize* that. As I've already told Sara and the others I've spoken to, I have no intention of *betraying* those secrets. I feel horrible about how your people were treated now that I know what *really* happened the night of the bomb." She explains somberly.

"Be that as it may, we can't be 100% certain there aren't others out there that Uri Jabarin and his people told about us. Getting hold of you, and getting that information out of you, in any way they can, would likely be a priority if anyone knows or finds out you're alive. I realize that, in the end, you chose to help Marc and the others, and Sara's support of you weighs strongly in your favor, but I'm still not sure *what* to do with you." Liz says, concerned.

"I understand. You must weigh the risks vs. the benefits of keeping me around and alive." Dr. Hannah Zelkind acknowledges.

"Dr. Zelkind, we have *no intention* of killing you. That's *not* our way unless absolutely necessary, as it was when we destroyed the base. Too much was at stake. I know you don't understand the totality of what we are or what we do, and *have been doing* for thousands of years, but everything we *do* is for the *benefit* of humanity." Liz says, tapping her pen on the table.

"If you're not weighing whether to kill me, what exactly are my options?" Dr. Zelkind asks.

"There are only two options. One is that you stay here with us, preferably in *this* reality, and don't return to your version of Earth. You'll have everything you could need here with us: Food, shelter, entertainment, for example. Sara has even requested that we let you work with her and some other—associates of hers regarding the weapons created to use against us, so we can make certain they're never a threat to us again." She explains. "And the other option is, while we can sublimate knowledge of short-term or recent memories, we can't do that with all your knowledge about us. However, some of Sara's associates have technology which *can* do that, but it would mean you would end up with amnesia for the entire period of your association with the *Naqam*, and that could be difficult for you to cope with." Liz explains, but gives her time to weigh the options herself.

Liz expects her to take a few minutes, but she immediately responds. "There's only one viable option. If I go back, I'll face endless questions from Mossad, especially my uncle, who sent me to work there. If I can't provide answers, they will find other means to extract them. Being the only survivor of the base will also put my loyalty in question. I'm dead to them already, and it's *best* I stay that way." She pauses and glances at Sara. "I'd also welcome the chance to work with Sara and any of your people. I'd love to understand more about the Apara, even if it's only for my own knowledge and understanding." She says bravely.

Liz is satisfied with her answer and nods. "Very well I'm sure Sara will find you lodging in the dorms at Medical for now, Dr. Zelkind."

"Ma'am, please, Dr. Zelkind is my past, please call me Hannah." She says.

"Very well, Hannah. Welcome to our world." Liz says, standing, shaking her hand, and pathing to Sara. *She's your responsibility! We've been making a habit of taking in stray humans lately, haven't we?* Liz leaves the room and leaves Hannah in Sara's capable hands.

"Before I tell you what you need to know, Marc asked me to give you a thank you gift." Sara says.

"*Oh?* That *isn't necessary.* I only did what was right." Hannah says humbly.

"Still, I made him a promise. If I may, what is the source of the scarring on your jaw?" Sara asks politely, knowing such disfigurements can be sensitive subjects.

"I was working at a volunteer evacuation center outside of Jerusalem the night of the bomb. We were far enough away to avoid the blast itself, and upwind from the radiation cloud, but the concussive blast caused damage to the center. I was caught when the roof caved in, which cut my face. Then an electrical fire began. I tried to rescue some children trapped behind the fire line and this is the result." She explains, remembered pain and horror in her eyes and mind.

Sara nods curtly. "Then you do *certainly deserve* this gift, Hannah. Close your eyes." She says, and when Hannah does, she feels Sara's small, warm hand on her cheek over the scars. "Above all else in my very long life, I've been a healer. I know I can't heal the pain in your memories from that night, but at least I can start you on a healing path." She removes her hand and pulls out a mirror from her bag, holding it in front of Hannah. "Open your eyes."

Hannah does, and lets out a gasp, tentatively putting her fingers up to her face to feel for the once prevalent scars, only finding smooth, healed flesh. "Oh! *Thank you!*" She says, and cries tears of joy. Sara lets her cry for a few minutes, giving her tissues to dry the tears.

When she's finally calm again, Sara smiles and says, "Hannah, *about* my associates—I think my friend Isanda would very much like to meet you, but I need to prepare you as she's not quite... like the rest of us. Are you a Star Wars fan?" She chuckles and helps Hannah up, the two women leave the room and walk down the hall, with Sara explaining their origin story and the entire purpose of the Apara.

TOGETHER AGAIN

Marc and Tess sleep for a couple of days, as Sara dosed the blood bags with a sedative. She knew both would need time to recover. Marc, from his captivity and torture, and Tess from her physical and psychic exertion in the fight to save Marc from the *Naqam*.

Liz put extra dry cat food out before she left the partners to their healing slumber, but eventually, Mabel runs out and demands more by crawling up above Tess's head on the pillow and licking her face furiously with her rough, wet tongue, eventually rousing Tess.

"*Mabel*! You *ornery* cat! Can't I get any sleep without you begging for food or cuddles?" She snaps, groggily. She rolls over toward her nightstand and picks up her phone. It's on silent but still has power, as their new, Apara phones contain technology which makes them only require charging about once a month. She squints as her eyes are full of sleep-sand but rubs them clean and looks at the date and time, plopping her phone back onto the nightstand, rolling her eyes, and leaning back into her pillow. *Two days? I guess I know who's behind that!* She thinks and turns toward Marc. She smiles as she studies his face. It's been weeks since she'd woken to him beside her, and she nearly cries with joy over his recovery. She notices stress lines in his face that weren't there before. She knows it's a result of his captivity, the torture he endured, and knows the *physical* marks will fade.

After working with Sue, she also knows the *deeper, invisible* scars will take time, or at least they would for her, had she been in his situation. She knows Marc has lived through many human life-times but doesn't know how much strife he may have lived through before they met, just that he lived through the horror of Jerusalem, Jason breaking his neck, and now this. As much as she adores him, she thinks, *we sure have been to hell and back since meeting, both of us! But as they say, for better or for worse....*

As Tess isn't paying attention to Mabel, the cantankerous feline decides it's time to deal with the *other* hand that feeds her literally. She begins licking Marc's hand on the bed, but when he doesn't respond, she bites down on his thumb hard.

"*Mabel!*" Tess shouts at her. "*Bad* kitty!" Mabel tears out of the bed and stares at Tess from the floor, tail twitching!

In the meantime, Marc wakes enough to pull back his hand in pain and open his eyes. "What the hell?" He says as he absent-mindedly rubs his thumb, feeling the tiny puncture wounds where Mabel bit down. The pain quickly subsides, the welts heal, and he stretches, yawns, and rolls to face Tess. He opens his eyes fully, sees her face, and smiles. "Ah, *Love!* I've missed you!" He says and caresses her cheek lovingly with his hand. "I wasn't sure I'd *ever* see you again." He pulls her toward him, touching her forehead with his own. "*So* sleepy!" he remarks, yawning again.

"You can thank *Sara* for that! She dosed the blood, *again!*" Tess says, reaching around Marc's back and hugging him.

Eventually, he pulls back, and slowly sits up, looking pensive. "They said they blew up the building. How *bad* was it? Was anyone besides me *hurt*?" He asks.

Long story, but we all got out *just* in time. The only other injuries were from debris slipping through Callie's closing portal. A few people got cuts and bruises, but they healed quickly. Amy went through worse, but that was before we were trapped. They shot her, putting her in stasis. From what she and Charlie said, they left them in the basement with the explosives hoping to kill both of them and make *Charlie* a scapegoat in case any evidence of the bombs was found." She explains. "We're building a new center downtown."

Marc sighs and smirks. "I still can't get over your transformation to *Wonder Tess!*" He chides her. "I'm not sure I *ever* expected that from you. But I'm glad you did it. Knowing that if anything ever happens to me, permanently, you'll be able to take care of yourself. That puts my mind at ease." He studies her face, almost like he's looking for physical reflections of her internal changes.

"I *hope* nothing ever happens to you! All those weeks we didn't know if you were alive or dead, I *had* to distract myself from thinking you were gone for good. I couldn't picture life *without* you—especially not *centuries* or longer." She leans over to kiss him. "Don't you *ever, fucking* get *captured* again! *Hear* me?" She snipes sarcastically at him, knowing it wasn't something he did intentionally.

"Or *what*? You'll beat me up with your Kung-Fu and PK blasters?" He grins wickedly.

"*Something* like that!" She sighs and sinks against him and the headboard, just happy to feel him there with her again.

After a few more days of recovery and reunion time, Tess slowly gets back to the Lost Mission project, though Marc needs a bit more time to get back on track. He finds it hard to focus, and Sara explains that some of that is residual damage from the deuterium compound. It, too, will heal, but until it does, he should rest and not stress as much as possible.

REELING HER IN

Weeks pass, and Peder and Phoenix continue working together, often doing things together on Friday evenings, after work, like going out for pizza or a movie. Peder swears to himself that he's going to keep it platonic, and that this is a way to keep her on the hook until they can get her into their new location and match her up with someone to transform her. He gets psychological murmurs of unease whenever he thinks of someone *else* turning her, but he stuffs those feelings down in a mental lockbox and hides the proverbial key.

Work on the new building in downtown Asheville is moving at an accelerated pace, and the time when they can ease Phoenix into the fold is sneaking up on them both. When Peder finds out that the new building will be ready by mid-June, he realizes Phoenix has mentioned nothing about moving. He's gotten used to commuting down to Greenville twice a week but looks forward to when she'll be in the Asheville area. He looks at local apartments available online and finds one near Liz's portal home. He pops by the apartment complex office and asks to see it. He's pretty sure it would meet Phoenix's needs, so uses his mental influence to get the apartment manager to hold it, temporarily, while he speaks with Phoenix about it.

He gets in his car and calls her. Once she answers, he says, "Hi, I noticed you haven't mentioned moving up here yet. I'm not sure if Liz told you or not, but our new building will be ready in just about a month."

She's quiet for a few seconds. "So *soon*? I thought it wouldn't be done until July sometime. I haven't started looking yet!"

"I realize you've been busy with all the work we've dumped on you, and I hope you don't mind, but I may have found an apartment that would suit you, about fifteen minutes' drive from work. It's about the same size as yours, and near just about anything you could need, even a movie theater!" He says, hoping he's not overstepping things.

"Is it affordable?" She asks, tentatively, knowing her place in South Carolina is on the lower-end, rent-wise.

"Yes, it should be, and if it's a problem, I'm sure Liz has a little wiggle room in the budget for your salary. You've certainly proved your value to us with your work, so far! I think I may even get her to budget your first month's rent in as part of your moving incentive package." He suggests sweetening the pot.

"Have you looked at it, or did you just see it online? I've seen more than a couple of places in the past that post a model apartment and when you get there, the one that's available is a dump." She says, skeptically.

He chuckles lightly. "Yes, in fact, I'm outside the rental office. They're holding it until I get your answer. I even took pictures." He sends them to her in a text.

"Hold on, let me look!" She says and flips through the pictures.

"That is nice! Are you sure the rent's okay? Is the neighborhood good?"

"Yes. It's not too far from where my sister's place is. It's just off the main road to town, so it's a straight shot downtown and then hang a left to get to work." He says enticingly.

They discuss it a little more, including the details like rent, deposit, and so on. "I'll have to call my landlady ASAP and tell her I'm moving sooner than expected. She's pretty easy-going, though. Can you tell them I'll take it and I can drive up tomorrow to sign any papers?" She gets an odd feeling, like she's taking a major step in her life, and not just a move for a job.

"I'll do that right away!" He says with a sigh of relief. Not only would she be moving to town, but she would be a lot shorter drive in the meantime. They hang up and he informs the manager that the apartment is now taken. He's tempted to haggle rental price as well, but knows he shouldn't abuse his abilities like that. It was one thing to get the manager to hold it or give them first option, another to use it to gain economically, or to help someone else do so.

In the next couple of weeks, he stays after work time on Tuesdays and Fridays and even makes some extra trips to help her pack. He thinks, *what are friends for?* When moving day comes, he's there to help her load, and she drives up in her car while he drives the van. Once they've unloaded everything, they're standing in her new apartment, surrounded by tall stacks of boxes ready to unpack.

He says, "Liz said not to worry about work for the next couple of days. Get unpacked and settled in. That's the most important thing."

"*Really*? Tell her I appreciate that! Y'all have been *so* wonderful and so welcoming! I don't know many companies that go out of their way to help a new employee move and help me get started with work from home and everything!" She says and gives him a hug.

The energy behind her embrace sends a shock through him, and he can't ignore that her feelings for him have grown beyond platonic friendship. When she pulls back out of the hug, she says, "Sorry, that was probably inappropriate."

He lets out the breath he's been holding and says, "Not at all. We do our best to be there for our employees as a thank you for all you do for us." He grins, but his stomach sinks as his inner conflict strikes at his heart and mind, like an emotional viper.

"Kind of like your idea of vampires, huh? You guys are dependent on me, so you help me in return?" She gives him an amused look.

He fights not to react to her reference, and merely says, "*Something* like that." Now, he knows what he must do, and his sister will never let him back out of it. He'll tell Liz that *he wants* to be the one to turn Phoenix, and that *he* will take her as a partner when the time comes –if *she* agrees.

He tells Phoenix he's meeting his sister out by the main road, and says his goodbyes, but finds some dark corner outside and ports out, reappearing in Sanctuary, a short distance from Liz's home. He needs to work up the courage to do what he must. He hates admitting when his sister's right, but it is time for him to settle down with someone.

He's been alone for way too long, just kind of tagging along as his sister's twin, and Kari's figurative brother-in-law. He knows she's the right one, but telling Liz is going to be like eating crow, painful.

After about half an hour, he ports the rest of the way home. Liz and Kari are cuddled up listening to music and talking on the sofa, but as soon as Peder ports in, Liz can tell something's changed. She telekinetically stops the music player and gives him a sidelong look. "*Spill*, brother dear!" She commands, suspecting what he's going to tell her.

He sits in a chair nearby, steeling himself to make a commitment he won't be able to back out of. "Lissa, I want to be the one to bring Phoenix over when it's time." He rambles out quickly, as if he could lose momentum mid-sentence if he dares slow down.

Liz glances at Kari. "You *win* the bet, *love!*" She smiles at Kari.

"*Bet*? What *bet*?" Peder asks, feeling like he's been left out of a joke.

"Kari and I had a bet." Liz grins widely. "I said you'd never admit you wanted to turn her until after we all moved into the new building, and she said you'd crack *before* then! *So* close! But Kari wins!"

"Wait, you both *assumed* I'd turn her?" Peder asks, dumbfounded by Liz and Kari's blatant assumption.

Liz's expression softens, and she leans forward to address him. "We suspected." She admits, "Though it was Tess who suggested you two would make a *nice* couple. She and Kari have been working on divining good match-ups. It'll make it a lot easier with the higher influx of potential transformees, if we know who's likely to be a good fit ahead of time."

Peder looks awkward, like he just got the punchline of a joke that's been going around for months, and he's it! "That's why you *assigned* me to her?" He says, feeling manipulated.

"In part. You were a natural choice anyway since she'll be in your department. I've even got your offices next to each other on the new floor plan! I've been hoping you'd let yourself see that it's time, and she's a good fit for you." She says, reaching across the coffee table to put her hand, reassuringly, on his.

"You're getting *almost* as manipulative as Sara, you know that, don't *you*?" He quips, feigning irritation, but knows she's right.

"Any idea when she'll be ready to bring over?" Kari interrupts their sibling moment.

"No, though I get the feeling she'd like to take things further than just friendship soon, but I'd rather get to where I can tell her about myself first." He explains, thinking, *I'd rather keep things honest, so she doesn't think I just want to sleep with her to turn her. Besides, I could give her one of her fantasies.* "I'd say give me a few weeks to work up to it."

"Don't wait *too* long. She's a Lost Missioner, and we can use all the highly skilled Apara we can turn. Plus, if you *drag* it out too long, she could get frustrated and lose interest." Kari reminds him.

"I'll make sure *that* doesn't happen. I just need to find the right way to tell her and the right time. Now, if you two will *excuse* me, I'm beat." He says and stalks off to bed. He doesn't sleep much, as his mind keeps coming back to the inevitable questions: *Where do I go from here with her? And how can I do this without hurting her or freaking her out in the process?*

A New Beginning

Their new, four-story building is finished, and Inspiration, Inc. is officially reopening. The building is larger than the old one to compensate for the influx of new potentials, as they both expand their business front and find new people to bring into the fold.

Phoenix arrives early for her first official day at the new office. Kari grins when Phoenix enters the lobby. "*Phoenix*! So nice to see you again! *Welcome!*" She stands up and extends her hand to the young woman. Phoenix has dressed in a lightweight summer dress, her hair neatly up in a bun like when she did ballet. She shakes Kari's hand enthusiastically. "Kari, *right*? Not great with names, at least not when I've only actually met someone in person once or twice."

"Well, you got it on the first try, and even *pronounced* it correctly!" She says, smiling. "Liz has you in an office on the fourth floor, *next to Peder*, since you two work together so *well*."

Phoenix feels a nervous twinge of excitement at being able to see him every workday and having an office next to him. She ponders what excuses she can make to go to his office several times a day. She replies, "Well, I've heard Peder mention you and Liz enough. I'd better get it right." She smiles, then says, "Next to Peder's office? Cool! I've really enjoyed working with him for the last months, both in person and remotely. He's a *great* guy!" She admits, trying to be positive while keeping an air of professionalism in her manner.

"I *know* he'll be glad to work with you, too, and not driving all that distance will make him happy. I'm amazed he went down there as often as he did. He *must* have enjoyed working with you, too. Normally, he hates driving with a passion." Kari says, emphasizing that perhaps there was more to his willingness to commute to her place twice a week than just work obligations.

Phoenix blushes and says, "*Oh!* I didn't realize that. I *knew* he hated rush-hour traffic, but he never complained about making the trip twice a week. I mean, he's the one that *suggested* Tuesdays and Fridays." And her heart flutters a jot, thinking maybe he's feeling something, too. She knows she must be careful, however, as he *is* her boss, and if she's misreading things, it could go very badly; the whole move and everything will end up being for naught if she has to leave the job because she can't face him after such embarrassment, or if things don't work out between them.

"If you'll just have a seat for a minute, I think Liz wants to escort you upstairs and show you your office personally, but you're a little early, and she's meeting with one of the other employees just now." Kari smiles and motions to the seating area in the lobby.

Phoenix sits, relieved to finally be at Inspiration Inc., as working in the office feels more real to her than working from home, but also a bit of emotional anxiety, specifically about what may or may not happen with Peder. Of course, Peder's sister running the company doesn't make her any *less* nervous. She thinks, *If things go wrong, I may have to do more than switch departments, I might have to leave altogether.*

After a few minutes, Liz and another woman come out of her office. The woman walks off, and Liz grins as she sees Phoenix. "Phoenix! I'm so *glad* you can join us here in our new locale. Peder has been telling me so many good things about you." She says enthusiastically.

"Wow, glad to hear it. I've really enjoyed working with him so much over the last months. Kari says my office will be next to his?" Phoenix asks.

"Yes, I thought you two could continue working on book projects together and seeing as how you have more experience in the field than most of our other new hires for that department, I'd like you to be the go-to-person whenever Peder isn't here, so putting your office next to his makes that easy for everyone." She explains.

"*Wow!* I didn't expect that!" She says, a bit surprised by how much confidence they're showing her by giving her that position, even unofficially.

"Well, you are part of *our* family now, and from everything Peder's told me, you've certainly *got* what it takes!" She says with a double meaning, knowing Phoenix will soon, literally, be part of her extended Apara family, as Peder's partner. "Come on, let me show you around and take you up to your office."

Liz gives her a tour, pointing out the lunchroom and explaining, "If you ever forget your lunch or just get hungry while working, there's always a selection of open-faced rolls with various toppings in the fridge. We fix them fresh, every morning. We'd much rather have you well-fed and focused, than hungry and distracted from your work." She explains.

Liz takes her through the different departments, including web design. She met Marc before, at her interview, where Liz, Kari, Tess, and Marc were present. She explains that the second floor is for expansion space for all departments, while the third works largely with their new job placement services, and charity fundraising services. Finally, they get to the fourth floor and the elevator opens. They step out and Phoenix sees a familiar face that Liz flags down.

"Tess, you *remember* Phoenix, right?" Liz asks, knowing she knows who Phoenix is.

"Oh, *yes!* Hi, welcome. I heard you're going to be up here with us on the fourth floor. Glad you can *join* us!" Tess says with a friendly smile.

"Tess is our *Human* Resources person, and while she works with the job placement services, she also works on recruiting for our own company. Her office is three down from yours, on the left." Liz points out. "There's a smaller lunch or break room at the end of the hall if you need it."

Phoenix looks all around her at the hallway. It's filled with pleasant colors, wall decorations, plants, and other things that make it feel homier than many offices. She thinks, *this is certainly an improvement over that grimy, print shop I worked in before. Smells a hell of a lot better too!*

Liz guides her down the hallway toward Phoenix's new office and gets to Peder's open door. He looks up and says, *"Damn!* You're *early.* I planned to be downstairs to greet you when you got here." He comes over and gives her a hug. "I hear you're my new *neighbor."* He grins.

"So, it seems! I *promise* not to throw any wild office parties." She jokes.

"At least *invite* me if you do." He suggests, with a twinkle in his eye. He turns to Liz and raises an eyebrow, pathing, ***Here goes everything!***

"Let's move on to your office. Feel free to personalize it. We want our employees to feel comfortable. Plus, we find it makes our clients feel more at ease when it's not a harsh, sterile environment." Liz explains and shows her in. Her office is larger than she'd expected, with more than enough room for her desk, bookshelves, and a comfortable meeting area for meeting with clients. There's a window spanning the entire end of her office, so she takes in the view. From the fourth floor, she has an amazing view of the mountains to the west and notices puffy, white, cumulous clouds casting shadows on the mountains that may lead to darker thunderheads later in the day, as a typical, afternoon, summer storm.

"This is great! Far more than I ever *expected.* I thought I'd be lucky to get a cubical in a shared space somewhere." She admits with a grin and awe in her eyes.

"Well, that's the advantage of building from scratch, isn't it? We built with extra capacity, so we have offices for *most* people, rather than cubicles." Liz says and joins Phoenix by the window. "The fourth floor does provide a wonderful view, doesn't it." She smiles and turns to Phoenix. "You have such a unique name, and quite appropriate for us in this time. Like your name, Inspiration, Inc. has risen from the literal ashes to reopen, and we're glad you can be a part of it!"

"I'm happy to be here, too." She says, but thinks, *Kind of ironic, but I guess my name also reflects whatever has happened to me. Considering I've risen from the literal dead twice. I wish I could tell someone about this, but that's just NOT an option.*

"I'll leave you with Peder to get settled in. He'll show you all the ropes with the on-site system, backups, and routines." She smiles, glancing at Peder, pathing, **Good luck! You've chosen well, brother!**

Liz leaves Phoenix in her brother's hands and heads back downstairs to her office.

Phoenix blurts out, "Hey, sorry if I spoiled your plans. I was so anxious about my first day here, meeting everyone, and stuff, I had a hell of a time sleeping. So, instead of just lying in bed, staring at my ceiling, I got an early start, went out, got breakfast on the drive up here, and *still* got here early!"

He pats her on the back, rubbing her back gently. "It's fine. I'm just glad you're finally here! So, what do you think of our new place?"

"It's *awesome*! I love the homey feel. It's friendly, and welcoming, as are the people, at least so far!" She says, moving around, looking at the shelves, her desk, and so on. She gets over to the sofa in her meeting area and plops down on it, bouncing a little, as the springs in the new furniture are quite firm.

Peder holds up one finger and says, "I'll be *right* back." He trots out the door and into his office, returning with a wrapped gift box for her. "Just call it a welcome to the *family* gift."

"You didn't need to do that!" She says, feeling moved by his gesture. She opens the box and finds various things for her office, including office supplies, a few knickknacks, and an antique-looking wooden box with ballet shoes painted on it. "This is so nice of you! *Thanks*!"

"Open the box!" He nudges her encouragingly. She gives him an odd look, then opens the antique box to find something wrapped in red silk. She opens the red silk and finds a Blu-ray of the movie they'd gone to see so many months ago about her favorite vampire couple, *Cat and Bones*. She squeals, exclaiming, "This isn't *even* supposed to come out until next week! How'd you *get* it?"

He gives her a smug grin. "Got a friend in the industry. I had to promise you wouldn't *brag* about getting it early to anyone but wanted to have it for you today."

She leans over and gives him an honest, full, bear hug. "I *love* it! *All* of it! Thank you so much!" She pauses and gets a sly grin, saying, "Come over tonight and watch it *with* me?" She thinks, *I shouldn't push it, but maybe it'll inspire him.*

He chuckles. "I *think* I can swing that, but now, we've got to get down to business!" He boots up her computer. "I need to go over the in-house routines and security with you." He says and motions for her to come over to her desk and sit down. They spend the day getting her up to speed so she can get back to the project she's been working on at home.

AN OVERDUE CELEBRATION

It's mid-July; Ty is working on the server, planning out the linkages to several major centers, such as Chicago, London, Moscow, Beijing, and Sydney, now that they've vanquished the *Naqam*. Ty adds extra security measures to prevent future incidents like the one in Asheville by adding extra steps before anything can be transferred to or from a USB device connected to Earth-side terminals.

Ironically, he's been having some issues with the one center he shouldn't, their own. Having the *actual* offices in Sanctuary with an identical, portal shell building in Asheville has been causing some interworld-connection issues. The new security features he's installed are randomly causing issues with some of their in-house computers, and USB flash drives, causing them to lock down.

This particularly plagues Phoenix since she brought files in on a flash drive after her home internet went down for two days. A nasty storm tore through the region, frying much of the cable internet south of town. She could still work on things at home she'd already downloaded, but couldn't save them directly to the work server, so she brought them in, and manually updated the project files on the server. As soon as she opened one of them, her computer locked down, and it took Ty and Val half a day to get it unlocked.

While her computer was down, she used a spare computer in Tess's office. Unfortunately, it's happened two more times since then, and Ty is busy determining why his new security patch is making her computer believe there is still an unrecognized, USB drive connected. The work server is also off site, in Sanctuary, so if something happens to their new locale, their projects won't be lost. Somewhere in the coding is a glitch in the inter-world bridge that makes the security for the potential database server also active on the work server. He's been unable to trace it so far and is *very annoyed.*

Val enters the room, and he senses she wants to talk to him about something but knows it may be a bad time. He looks up and gives her a forced smile through his irritation. "What's up, *Amore mia?*" He says, moderating his tone.

"It's *mom.*" She sighs.

He pauses his work, asking, "Is she *alright*? She hasn't taken a turn for the *worse*, has she?" He's suddenly concerned that the trinaline Sara's been slipping into her insulin may be becoming less effective.

"*No!* She's *fine.* She's just *nagging* me again." Val says, sitting down in a swiveling office chair next to Ty.

"Ah, the *wedding*?" He asks.

"Of *course!* We planned to do it in March when the weather was nice and her flowering trees were blooming, but with our center being attacked, we had to postpone it. She's *feeling* good physically, but I get the impression she's worried she won't live to see it happen." Val says, rubbing his back with one hand, noticing the tension in his muscles. "Server still not *listening* to you?" She asks, referring to it lately in a more personified manner, since it often has a mind of its own.

"Yeah, I just can't trace the issue plaguing Phoenix's machine!" He explains.

"Maybe you should take a break and think about something else. Get a fresh start?" She suggests standing so she can massage the knots out of his shoulders.

"Hm, that feels good." He leans into her ministrations. "I'm guessing that's *your* way of suggesting we talk more about your *mom* and the *wedding*?" He snickers.

"It means a lot to her. I know it's *hot* right now, in the middle of summer, but I thought we could just do a small gathering at her place. The weather's supposed to be *truly nice* this weekend...." She trails off.

He chuckles. "Kinda short notice for a *wedding*, isn't it?"

"I've *already* got the dress, and it's not like our friends need to *fly* in! They can just *port* in!" She quips.

"Yeah, *right!* Explain how a bunch of people show up at her place out in Silverwood *without* cars." He banters sarcastically.

"*Okay*, so I didn't think about *that* part, but if we only invite our friends here, your friends Vince and Dee, Sara and Annie and a few others, we should be able to swing it. *Hell*, if they don't want to drive in from their portal homes, can't they carpool, and use that gadget that lets you port the whole car?" She asks, working on a particularly tight knot below his right shoulder blade.

He grunts as she digs her slender, yet strong fingers into the knot. "Okay, *okay!* I relent! If it's not too much of a burden for your mom, then we'll do it *this* weekend! I'll holler at my friend who was a priest before he was turned. He can officiate."

"*Thank you!*" She reaches her arms around him from behind and hugs him. "By the way, mom's *the one* that suggested this weekend. She said something about the Cherokee gods blessing us with a cool and sunny spell *just right* for a wedding!" She laughs and lets go of him.

He says, "Well *then*, who am *I* to balk at what the Cherokee gods *ordain!*" He gives her a broad, toothy grin. "Go on! Let everyone know. I'll holler at Vince and give him and Dee an invite. He *loves* weddings!"

Val leaves the room with a spring in her step, pathing to their friends at the center, *Hey everyone! Wedding's this weekend at my mom's in Silverwood, outside of Charlotte! Please come!*

She gets a mélange of telepathic replies, varying from non-articulated thoughts of congratulations to full sentences of the same. She calls her mom, Gavina. "Mom, it's a go! We're on for the weekend!"

Val hears an audible gasp of excitement from her mother. "*Finally!* My neighbor said he'll help me set everything up on my end, and I've got to start planning out the food for the reception afterwards!" She says with glee.

"You *don't* have to go out of your way, please, I don't want you to *overexert* yourself." Val says.

"*Nonsense!* This is what I've been *waiting* for! To see my *only, living offspring* finally get married. Hm, now, I realize it's up to you two to find someone to officiate, but I do have one *request*?" Gavina says.

"Of course, mom! What is it?" Val asks, knowing this wedding is more for her mom than for herself and Ty.

"I still have your grandparent's wedding blanket and vase. I'd like to include that in the ceremony. Recently, it's come to mean more to me to honor our heritage and Cherokee ways. I know Ty's not *one* of us, but if we could include those minor aspects, I'd be thrilled." She explains.

Val feels a tad melancholy as she ponders the irony of her mom referring to Ty as 'not one of us', considering Val has left humanity and become *one* of the Apara, while her mom is still very human. "Of course, mom. Ty has a friend who can officiate on short notice. I'll make sure Ty passes along your wishes. I've got to get back to work now, but I'll call you tonight so we can figure out the specifics, and I'll let you know how many people to expect!" Val says, saying goodbye.

She thinks about other, non-Apara friends she should invite, like Tish, Jess, and Mel. Her mood shifts to sadness when she thinks about Jamella not being there. They used to joke about doing a double wedding to confuse the hell out of people with identical dresses and veils since they looked so much alike. Her friend could be a bit of a fluff-head, but she misses her and still feels horrible that she died because Jason mistook Jamella for herself.

***

Peder is working in his office when Phoenix comes in with a question about her latest project.

"Got a sec?" She asks from his doorway.

He looks up and grins, saying, "Always! Come on in."

She enters, and they discuss an issue with a large table in the book, and whether to run it over two pages.

Once in agreement, she says, "Great, I just wanted to double-check with you first." She gets up, but he stops her from leaving the room.

"Phoenix, are you *doing* anything this Sunday?" He asks.

"No, not really. I was going to finish unpacking the rest of my books, so I can bring some of my computer and publishing books in here for reference." She quips, leaning against his door frame.

"I don't know if you've heard, but Val and Ty are *getting married* this weekend outside of Charlotte." He says.

"*Really*? I knew they were together, but didn't know they were making it official." She replies, smiling.

"Yeah, it's more for her mother's sake. Anyway, almost everyone going are already couples, Liz and Kari, Marc and Tess, and so on. Want to be my 'plus one' on Sunday, so I don't stick out like a sore thumb?" He asks.

"*Sure*! Why not. I've certainly seen *enough* of them this week, alone, to consider them friends." She says, exasperated.

"Still having trouble with your computer?" He gives her a concerned glance.

She lets out a huff of disbelief. "Oh, *yeah*! It's locked up on me three times this week! Something about extra security that's supposed to only work on their accounting server, but has been affecting the work server, and any computers that connect to it, or at least *mine*! It's driving me bonkers! Thank God Tess has that spare in her office. She's been a *lifesaver* this week!"

"I'll have a chat with Ty about that, okay?" He reassures her.

"Thanks, I don't want to *nag* them, but I'd like to get back to my office. Tess has that divider up between the backup and the rest of her office, but it's still *her* office, and not *mine*, if you get my drift?" She sighs.

"Yeah, I do, I *really* do. I've been staying with my sister for quite a while. I was injured almost two years ago and moved in with Liz during my recovery. I really should move out again soon. I mean, she *is* family, but it isn't *my* home, it's Liz and Kari's." He reflects.

"Sounds like maybe you should have rented my place instead of passing it on to me." She suggests.

"No, we needed to get you moved up here quickly, besides, I have a home, I just don't want to be alone there right now. It's not a rush for me, though I suspect Liz and Kari are tired of my "haunting" their place." He jokes.

"How badly were you injured?" She asks, trying to scan him visually for any obvious signs.

"Oh, I'm healed *now*. Mostly, I don't want to be alone after all that. I don't want to get into the gory details, but I was in a horrific... *accident*. It's taken me a long time to recover, but I'm getting there." He says, realizing that if things work out, he and Phoenix can move into his old home soon, as partners, solving two problems at once.

"I'm glad you got better!" She gives him a lopsided smile. "I've got to get back to work! The deadline for this project is next Friday and I'm behind as it is. Let me know when you want to head out Sunday." She heads back to her office to use her machine while it's currently unlocked. She makes sure she saves frequently, just in case she needs to swap to Tess's backup machine again.

***

Sunday morning comes and Peder picks Phoenix up at her apartment. She comes out in a floral, summer dress with light, lacy sleeves, and her hair and makeup are done. Peder is taken aback by her transformation. She was pleasant looking before, reminding him a tad of Inga, a girl from his youth, but now, she's *stunning*. She slides in the car and says, "Okay! Let's *go*! Val said traffic can get kind of bad out that way, so we shouldn't dawdle." She notices Peder is staring at her, and unusually quiet. "Peder? Are you *in* there?"

He shakes his head and blushes, realizing he just spaced out, admiring her appearance. "Yeah, *sorry*! You look *very* nice!" He says, turning to face the road, as he puts it in drive, and heads back out onto Hendersonville Road.

"I hope you don't mind, but I did a playlist on my phone with music for the drive. Do you mind if I connect it to your radio?" She asks.

"Sure, go right ahead. What kind of music is it?" He asks, curious about what she likes.

"Don't worry! Nothing *too* crazy. I thought I'd start with something relaxing. Ever heard of Secret Garden?" She asks.

"*Yes*! As a matter of fact, I was at Eurovision the year they won for Norway!" He admits, chuckling.

"You couldn't have been! I read they won in 1995! You weren't even born then!" She inquires.

Peder realizes his mistake and improvises. "*Sorry!* It was another band about ten years ago I saw, but I have seen Secret Garden perform in Kristiansand, where Rolf Loveland is from." He thinks, *Damn it! Must be more careful!*

Phoenix looks at him askance, and asks, "Huh, do you get back to Norway often?"

"Yes, fairly often, though I don't do much actual travelling these days." He explains as they pull onto the main highway.

"Since your accident?" She wonders.

"*Exactly*! I just haven't had the energy to do anything for a while, but I'm doing a *lot* better now!" He says. She puts her music on and they listen, occasionally chatting along the way.

THE BIG DAY

Val and Ty arrive at her mother's place the day before the wedding and are amazed by the floral fantasyland her mother has created for Val's big day. Her rock garden is filled with blooming red and pink roses, fragrant gardenias, and other summer flowers. The altar, where they will hold the ceremony, is a trellised archway, overgrown with climbing red, pink, and white roses in bloom. Her mother even has a manmade waterfall that flows through the garden and into a koi pond. There are folding chairs for all the guests, and a walkway down the middle for Val to march down. They're inspecting the garden when Gavina comes out in a huff. "Well, you two could've *at least* come in and said hello *first*!" She says, hands on hips, but when Val turns around to face her, she's smiling and her arms are extended for a hug. Val runs over and gives her mother a big embrace, careful not to hug her too hard.

"Mom! It's *wonderful*! You must have been working on this forever!" She exclaims.

"Yes, but my *neighbor* helped! We've been spending a bit of time together lately. He put up the trellis this spring, helped me finish my waterfall, and got it working. I've kept something nice growing the whole time since you two *missed* our March dates!" She eyes Val, doing her best to give her a guilt trip.

"I *know*, and I'm *really* sorry about that, but it couldn't be avoided." Val reminds her mom as the two women walk back toward the garden and Ty.

"Gavina, you've done an amazing job here! This will be a wedding neither of us will *ever* forget." He smiles at the small woman and paths Val. **Your mother looks quite healthy. I think working in the garden has helped as much as the trinaline!**

I'm sure it has! I just hope she doesn't give up and go downhill after this. This is what's kept her going.

Ty sends his partner a mental embrace. *We'll just have to find something else to keep her going. Did I hear her say something about a neighbor?*

True! Maybe it's a bit more than just neighborly friendship. Val paths.

Gavina comes up and puts one hand on each of their arms. "Stop gawking and come along! I've got a big dinner waiting for you two." She eyes Ty. "*Now* you're going to get *real* Cherokee food!" She smirks.

They follow Gavina, and she's set the table with her best dishes. She motions for them to take a seat and heads into her kitchen. Val follows her instead and enters the kitchen where steaming pots are on the stove and serving dishes are being filled. "Let me help you carry those in." She tells her mom.

"You *should* be with Ty. I'll bring them out." She chastises.

"Don't be *silly*, Mom! You're going to work yourself to *death!*" She says before she realizes it and can feel Gavina's reaction is one of a jarring reminder.

She stands still for a minute, not saying anything, eyes closed while she waits for her heart to settle down. "*Perhaps* you're right, my little Valkyrie! Take the stew... *STOP! Use* the potholders or you'll *burn* yourself!" Gavina says as she sees Val reach for the steaming pot of venison stew made with vegetables from her garden. Val nearly made a major error. As an Apara, her skin tolerates higher and lower temperatures than humans without getting burns or frostbite, and even if she burned, it would heal rapidly. She thinks, *Damn! I need to remember to think and act human around Mom... well, Mom and the other humans who are coming!*

Val takes the stew out and Gavina follows closely behind with freshly made ramp bread. She dried some ramps, a garlicky plant found in the region, to use for special meals. They're wild, spring plants, so are not in season in July. She goes back before Val can stop her and comes back with corn on the cob and butter. One more trip in, along with Val for pan-fried potatoes with ramps, and fresh green beans. Last, she brings out three glasses of beer. Ty smells it carefully and takes a cautious sip. A look of surprise in his eyes. "Do I taste walnuts in this?" He inquires curiously.

"Why *yes*! It's a Native brew made with walnuts and other good things! You have *quite* a sensitive pallet!" Gavina replies with surprise.

They all eat and talk through dinner. By the time they're done, it's nearly 10 PM. Ty clears the table and does the dishes so Val and her mom can take some time to relax. When he comes back out, they talk for a while. Gavina reminds them both they still need to come back with a trailer to get the rest of Val's things, including all the *kid's* toys and clothes. By the time Midnight rolls around, Val and Ty are ready for bed, but Gavina stops them.

"*Not* tonight! Val, you take *my* bed, and Ty can have the guest room!" Gavina insists.

Ty stifles a chuckle as Val gets annoyed. Her mom insists on following the wedding tradition of the groom not seeing the bride before the ceremony, on the wedding day. Val whines, "*Mom!* We *live* together! What *difference* does it make?"

"Humor me, Valyri, *please*! I want Ty to see you in all your glory, for the first time as you come down the aisle!" She insists, and Val rolls her eyes, but nods in compliance.

"Let me at least get my things from the bedroom." She sulks, tromps off, collects her suitcase, and *drags* it to her mother's bed-room, feigning weakness as she drags the 'heavy' suitcase. She comes back out and asks, "Where are *you* going to sleep?"

"I've got things to make for tomorrow, and when I sleep, I'll be just fine on the sofa for tonight." She says with a sharp nod. "Go on! Get your beauty sleep!"

Val growls in irritation but goes in and closes the door. She paths Ty, *I'll port over in a little while!*

No, stay there! I think your mom's radar would know, Amore! I'll see you at the altar! He paths with a mental embrace.

***

The next day, at noon, Ty is waiting at the altar in a fine, dark blue suit. His friend, Benedetto, or Ben, an Apara who was once both a priest and a scientist in Italy, is presiding. There are about twenty-eight other Apara attending, as well as a handful of Val's human friends, a few of her mother's neighbors, and a handful of relatives who carpooled in from Cherokee, NC. The weather is perfect; mid-70s, sunny, with puffy, white clouds, and a light breeze. Soft music is playing, intermingled with the sound of cicadas buzzing lightly in the background. The scene is saturated with red, white, and pink flowers, and the scent of gardenias and roses permeates the air.

The music shifts and all eyes turn to the path strewn with white rose petals. Val and her mother appear. At first glance, Val's dress looks like a traditional, white wedding dress. The lines are simple, with less lace, but along the train, are white hawk feathers sewn onto the satiny fabric. There's no veil, but a crown woven of smaller gardenia blossoms and white daisies. Her bouquet is a combination of the most perfect red roses and gardenias Gavina could find in her garden, and she's wearing her mother's necklace with turquoise and the small hawk's feather in silver. Gavina is wearing a simple, pale blue dress with Cherokee symbols on it, and is escorting her daughter down the aisle to the altar.

Ty is in awe of how beautiful Val looks and paths her, *this was worth the wait!*

Her smile broadens slightly as she hears his words and feels his emotions in her mind. Val can hear other, soft murmurs from the guests, and listens in on random thoughts. She nearly loses her composure when she senses the jealousy from her friend, and former coworker, Jess, whose boyfriend nagged her into eloping to Vegas when she'd always wanted something more traditional. She feels Tish's joy, as though Val is her own daughter walking down the aisle. Mel is thinking about Jamella and how she hopes she's looking on from Heaven.

When they reach the altar, Gavina nods to Ty with a wide grin, and Val steps up on the dais to join him. They face each other and take each other's hands.

Ben speaks with a slight, Italian accent similar to Ty's. "We are here to join Valyri and Titus in the lifelong bonds of *eternal* partnership. Equal, yet different; individuals, yet one. Out of a world of billions, they have found each other and made each other whole. They've written their own vows, which they will now speak."

Val begins, "I saw you coming a mile away, and knew you were the one for me. There was no detouring from my path, I only had to wait for thee."

"Your bright and shining soul drew me as a beacon in a storm, easing my mind and healing my soul. I will share this path with you as long as I live, Valyri." Ty replies and places a braided, gold band on her finger.

"Where you go, so will I. We'll walk this path together, wherever it may lead." She smiles and places a matching band on his.

Gavina steps forward, holding a large, white blanket. She ceremoniously steps up upon the dais and stands next to the priest. "Valyri, Ty, please face your family and friends so that they may see your love for each other." Ty and Valyri face the crowd and stand side by side. The priest helps her place the blanket across their backs and drapes it over their shoulders.

Gavina says, "Whatever sorrows, failings, shame, or weakness was in your lives before now, are now part of the past. May your life together be full of happiness, peace, and fulfillment!" She steps back down and picks up an unusual vase. It's covered in native American patterning and has two spouts at the top, one on each side. "Drink now, together, and *spill* not, for then you shall have a strong bond and mutual understanding that can see you through anything life may bring."

Val rolls her eyes and they each take hold of the vase. Ty must stoop down to be at the same level as Val, but they drink the water from the vase simultaneously, without losing a drop, then they hand it back to Gavina. They turn to face each other, still wrapped in the white blanket. The priest speaks.

"As two become one, yet the one is greater than the two alone. I join you, forever more. You may seal this joining with a kiss."

The couple kisses and cheers erupt from those in attendance. The priest takes the blanket and the two step down, walking back down the path. Instead of rice, there are more rose petals tossed in the air by those along the path.

The crowd stands and mingles while tables are brought out and set up; the folding chairs are moved to the tables. A longer table is along the edge of the scene, covered in a white tablecloth. Gavina asks, "Could I get some volunteers to help me bring out the food for the reception?"

Several people, including Tish, Peder, and Phoenix follow her and help bring out platters of finger food, and last, a homemade wedding cake with actual gardenia blossoms adorning it, as they are edible flowers. Gavina used the smaller, tender flowers to decorate the cake. In addition, there are sugar-crystalized gardenia petals pressed into the sides of the cake, making it glitter in the daylight. The petals themselves are as sweet as the flowers are fragrant. Once the food is placed on the table and everyone settles down, Val and Ty return, having spent some time getting their photos done, something Gavina insisted upon. The long skirt and train of Val's dress has been removed to show a simpler, white skirt. They go up to the table and cut the first slice of the cake together, placing it on a plate. Instead of feeding each other cake, they walk over and place it in front of Gavina. Val says, "Mom, without you, this day could *never* have happened. I love *you!*"

Gavina tears up, but takes a bite of the cake, and the reception begins. Val and Ty meander through the tables, talking to everyone and noting that one table has Jess, Mel, Tish, and Ty's friends Vince and Dee. Val paths, **Alas! If they only knew!** She sends a knowing, mental chuckle at the thought of all the Apara, or vampires, as humans would call them, mingling with a handful of humans at a wedding reception.

Amore! You have a very wicked sense of humor! They do not know and never shall! Ty paths in return.

***

Peder and Phoenix settle in with Tess, Marc, Liz, and Kari at a table, and all are busy eating and chatting. Phoenix leans back in her chair, watching the newly married couple from afar, hoping that someday, she may be as happy with someone as they apparently are with each other.

She spaces out, wondering, *Could Peder be the one? I like him a lot, but it almost seems like he wants to keep things platonic.* She sighs softly, uncertain what to make of him. *One minute, he's with me, and there's a spark of something more. Other times, it's like he's holding back.*

Peder picks up on her thoughts and sends her a subconscious, tele-pathic message. *Wait for me. When you're truly ready, we'll be together.*

While she doesn't hear it consciously, she reacts and shifts in her seat, notably relaxing. Liz notices the one-sided telepathic in-teraction and paths her brother. *So, when are you going to take things further?* she paths.

He regards her with a slightly perturbed expression. *When I feel she's ready to accept me for who and what I am. I don't want to push it, only to reveal what I am, and have her feel used or uncertain of my intensions.* He replies telepathically.

As you will, but don't take too long! She's clearly interested, but I fear you must give her a reason to hang on, and wait for you, or you could lose her! Liz paths, almost scolding her brother for his romantic lethargy.

The reception lasts a couple of hours, and as it winds down, Val and Ty ascend the dais again. Ty has a wine glass and spoon in his hand and clinks the glass to get everyone's attention. "As I understand it, there is yet one tradition left to discharge. If I could ask any unattached young ladies to gather below us here, it's time for Val to cast forth her bouquet!" He says, grinning widely.

Several of the Apara women join in the festivities even though they have partners, otherwise, there would be almost no one to play out this part of the show. Tess turns to Phoenix and says, "*Come on!* You should be up there for sure!" She extends her hand, and Phoenix takes it, following her up to the area below the dais. Val's friend Mel is also there, as well as a couple of her other hu-man friends who made the trip.

Val looks out over the celebration and gasps, as she sees something no one else does. On each side of her mom, shadowy figures become sharper and clearer, and there are smiles on their faces. It's her dad, and sister, Kyra, both passed on, but there to witness her joining with Ty. She struggles not to tear up and wishes her mom could see them—right beside her, yet farther away than any distance on Earth. Her sis-ter waves enthusiastically, just before the two fade away.

Val forces herself to focus on the gathering crowd of women waiting for her to toss her bouquet. She forces a smile as she holds back the happy tears from seeing her family 'together', even briefly, then turns around and faces the archway. Ty counts, "One... two...*THREE!*" and Val tosses her beautiful rose and gardenia bouquet over her shoulder. It heads straight out but the path curves slightly, barely passing above Mel's fingertips, and practically lands, stems down, in Phoenix's hands. Tess turns around and gives her a congratulatory hug, staring at Peder over Phoenix's shoulder with a sly grin.

Peder paths, *Tess! That's NOT what your PK is for and you know it!* He glowers at his ex-telekinesis student.

Tess grins at him, pathing, *To paraphrase, all's fair... in love!*

Peder shakes his head, feeling like the women in his 'family' are all conspiring and playing matchmaker. He's already decided to turn Phoenix, but he doesn't want to rush it. He rushed turning his friend, Halvdan, all those years ago, thinking it would be great to have his best friend with him for centuries to come! He'd also planned to turn a woman he cared for, Inga, the youngest daughter of a farmer near their village.

Things did not go well with Halvdan's turning, however. He had trouble controlling his strength and his hunger. He accidentally killed a woman he'd had a relationship with. This threw him into a deep depression, and eventually, he came to resent and blame Peder for turning him. He let his anger overtake him, and ported to the farm where Inga lived, killing everyone there, saving her for last. He drained her slowly in retaliation for Peder's changing him and ruining his life.

In that one turning, Peder lost his best friend and the woman he wanted to take as a partner and wife, along with her entire family. Halvdan torched the farm, then returned to do the same to their village, and fled into the forest.

Peder and Lissa hunted him down. Halvdan was beyond redemption, and the only thing they could do was end his misery. After putting him into a deep sleep, they took an ax to his head, then used their combined PK to disperse his body into the sea so he could not come back to life.

This is why Peder has *never* turned anyone since, nor taken a true partner. Part of him has been afraid of a repeat, as though it was his blood that maddened Halvdan's mind and soul, and part of him felt, somehow, that he should remain alone, as punishment.

But now, fate and the future are nudging him to take a leap of faith and turn and take a partner. Peder just wants to do it right. He *wants* to make sure she *understands* what he is, and what she *will* become. Last, he *wants her* to *want him*, even knowing all of this. He hopes Phoenix's unconscious fixation with her vampire literature may bode well for her to be that *one* person who can accept him, say yes, and really mean it.

Peder's train of thought derails as he hears her lope back to the table, out of breath, bouquet in hand. "I *caught* it! I *actually* caught it! I've tried at various friends' weddings but never caught it before now!" She sits down with a thud, smiles widely, and her eyes glitter with joy as she leans forward and inhales the aroma of roses and gardenias.

Liz leans across the table and jokes, "Uh oh, brother dear! You know what *this* means!"

Peder glares at his sister, lips pursed and eyes narrowed, and paths, **Let it be! I will do this in my own time!**

The reception winds down and people leave. Peder and Phoenix drive back to Asheville, talking occasionally, but eventually, Phoenix falls asleep in the passenger's seat, and Peder gets lost running dozens of scenarios through his mind about how he can break it all to Phoenix without frightening her, or even losing her.

Going, Going, Gone

Monday rolls around and Liz ports in to work early, at 6 am. She intentionally ignored anything business-related unless it was an emergency on Sunday, because of Val and Ty's wedding. There's been so much stress on her shoulders since before Jerusalem, she wanted to put it all aside and enjoy the wedding.

She boots up her computer and tablet, and fixes herself a fresh cup of hot, sassafras tea. She brought back a few of the sugar-crystallized gardenia pedals from the reception, drops three of them into her tea, and stirs it around, allowing the sugar and the flavor to suffuse her tea, sweetening it, and adding to the sassafras flavoring.

While everything is starting up, she takes the day's tray of open-faced sandwiches she and Kari made this morning into the lunchroom, snagging a couple for herself, sliding them onto a paper plate, and heading back to her office. Ignoring all business for a day and attending the wedding, even if it was mostly for show, helped her relax.

She returns to her office and a rapid pinging from her computer immediately sets her nerves on edge. She puts the plate down next to her tea, and slides into her chair, pulling up the application that governs various search algorithms they use to keep abreast of world trends and happenings. She hasn't heard this tone before, so has to go through it until she finds out which algorithm is trying to get her attention. When she finds it, her face blanches, she closes her eyes, and her stomach sinks. It's the algorithm Peder set up when Jason kidnapped Dee. This algorithm matches any known potentials against missing persons reports. She hovers the cursor over the hopping icon for a second and then clicks. The summary pops up, showing not one, but *six* missing potentials, all in different parts of the world. Three in the Middle East, including one in Israel. One in California; one in China and one in Luxemburg. If an Apara's blood could run cold, hers would be ice water.

She knows Val and Ty are not bothering with a honeymoon. The wedding was the important thing, done primarily for her mother's benefit. She hates to pull them in early, but her built-in warning system is nagging her horribly.

She sends a text to Ty, thinking it would be the least intrusive way of reaching them if they're awake. Ty responds with:

> **I'm up, but am letting Val sleep. She and her mom were up half the night. We're still in Silverwood.**

Liz texts back:

> **We have a problem. Did you and Val ever make any headway on that encrypted list of potentials they stole?**

Ty:

> **No. We haven't broken the code they used, and once their base was destroyed, it got put on the back burner! Why?**

Liz:

> **Came in early. An alert from an algorithm matching missing persons with known potentials of any age popped up. Had it been just one, I wouldn't be so concerned, as accidents and things happen, but there were six.**

Ty:

> ***Merda!* I'll head in shortly. Val will join us later if need be.**

A few minutes later, Ty ports directly into Liz's office. "Are they all in one area or spread out?" He asks.

Liz answers, concern clearly visible in her eyes. "All over, though three were in the Middle East with one in Israel." She says.

He drops onto the sofa in her office and runs his fingers through his hair anxiously. "We ran every decryption software program we have on it and nothing cracked it. I think we're going to need some external help. Someone who knows about such codes." He sits there quietly, thinking; then his eyes light up. "I know just the person! Vince ran decryption in World Wars I and II for us. He's also a bit of a puzzle buff. He just might crack this." He says, shaking his tablet with the encoded list in front of him

Lissa looks at Ty with a sideways glance, thinking, *there's definitely more to Vince than he seems! I just don't know what, but I'll figure it out!* "Your *friend* Vince is a quite the jack of all trades, *isn't he?* Well, whatever you do, hurry. I have a terrible feeling about this!" Liz says, as her precognitive senses start to itch with worry.

"I'll talk to him and then head back to Silverwood, in case you need me, but there's nothing I can do other than hand this off to him." He says and vanishes with the tablet in hand.

PUZZLING

Ty paths Vince. **Are you decent, my old friend?**

Of course! What's up? Vince paths in reply.

Ty ports in, finding Vince in his artist loft, tinkering with some kind of makeshift machine. "What in the world is coming out of that brilliant mind of yours now?" Ty asks.

"*Ah*! Titus, I'm just tinkering with something I made a century or two ago. Not much point in it now, as humans have invented something else to do the job! It was supposed to be an automatic coin counter. But the need for that has come and gone with modern tech." Vince sets it aside and gives Ty his full attention, noticing his stress levels. "Something is wrong, *perhaps*?"

"*Very* likely, and I'm out of ideas on my end. Do you still tinker with codes and anagrams?" Ty asks, sitting on a nearby stool.

"Yes, occasionally. Ever since they made that *horrid* little fiction book and film about me and the Illuminati, I've been looking into some of what they *attributed* to me!" He laughs. "I figure, if they're going to attribute it to me, maybe I should learn a thing or two about it! Particularly some of the antiquated, religious-based ciphers, and such."

"Well, maybe you can make heads or tails of this, *then*? When they attacked us in Asheville, the *Naqam* used some kind of virus to scrape entries from our potential database. They didn't get them all, but got a bunch of random ones, besides the ones they specifically made Amy pull up, and put on the drive from Israel and the surrounding areas." Ty explains.

"Aren't the *Naqam* no more? Didn't we *destroy* their underground base?" Vince asks, confused as to the urgency.

"Yes, we did. However, at least two of the enemy Apara are unaccounted for. We assumed they got taken out in the collapse, but neither they nor the head of the unit, Uri Jabarin, were seen during the fighting. Liz pulled me out of Charlotte this morning because an automated search algorithm matched six missing persons' reports with known potentials worldwide." Ty explains urgently.

"I see…. Perhaps you think the two rogue Apara and their human leader escaped before the collapse?" Vince says, as he skims the encoded lines in the file.

"That's the working supposition, yes. And if they did and escaped with that list… Leonardo, old friend, you're by far the most brilliant man I know, and with your background in decryption in the World Wars, and your penchant for puzzles and anagrams, we *need* you on this! Nothing we ran, software-wise could break the codes, but we need to know if the six missing are coincidence or…." Ty says, but Vince interrupts him impatiently.

"Or if their names are right there, in this list?" Vince asks, rhetorically.

"*Yes*! If they are, that means the *Naqam* are literally coming back with a vengeance, *pun intended*." He says, as he notices Vince react to the pun on their Hebrew name, as it means 'vengeance'.

"*Indeed*! And that would be terrible! Fine, leave that with me and I will work on it today. I make no promises, but I will give it my all. Dee is away at Medical today working on her genetic PK abilities, so I should have nothing to distract me, at least until *she* comes home!" He gives his old friend a knowing glance. "Go on! Go back to your beautiful bride and I will alert you as soon as I have anything!"

"Thank you! I owe you for this!" Ty says and gives a slight bow of respect to his old friend and master painter, inventor, and sculptor.

"No, dear friend! It is *my* honor! Had you not asked me to help in Atlanta, I might never have found my *Dee*!" Vince says, bowing in return.

Ty vanishes and goes back to let Val know what's going on, as well as pathing to Liz that Vince will work on it. Liz says not to say anything until they know more, or there may be panic. There are still some Apara who are very uneasy after the attack on their South Asheville center. That the human, militant threat may not have been vanquished will send new ripples of anxiety through their people.

***

It takes Vince three days, but he finds the key to the decryption and paths Ty. *I've done it, Vecchio Amico! May I port in?* He asks, politely.

Of course! You broke the code? Ty paths back.

Vince appears in his home, tablet in hand, as well as a roll of paper full of scribbles. "*Yes*! It was a *challenge*, and I must admit that the research I did because of that *infernal* movie made a difference." He says with a huff.

"Don't just stand there!" Ty says, clearing off the dining room table. "*Show* me what you've got."

"I've translated the first few lines manually but can give you the formula to decipher the rest." He says, rolling out the four-foot-long scroll of handmade paper with scribblings, symbols, and equations on it. "I should have realized it right off, considering where the group is from, but then I had to factor in that this list of names was originally in English!" He rambles.

"Vince, *please*, *get* to the *point*! We need to decode this as quickly as possible! Liz told me another five potentials have gone missing since Monday, according to the algorithm. Liz is about to pull her hair out over this." Ty says urgently.

"Very well, my friend! The key is in a Hebrew cipher, Gematria! But to find it, you must find the *keyword*! There are different types: Jewish, English, and Simple. I thought it might be the first one but then realized that since the original files are in English, that would be more likely. A number is assigned to each letter. Normally, you could just use a Gematria calculator for it; however, they used all three forms to create the key. Once I figured out what it was, I cracked it!" He continues to ramble as though Ty should be as fascinated as he is.

"*What* did you *find*?" Ty asks, growing impatient.

"The keyword is obvious when you consider what we are to them...." Vince trails off, waiting for Ty to put it together.

"*Vampire*?" Ty asks.

"*Correct*! However, the actual number we needed is the three versions, added together, and then each number in the sum is added together! Vampire in the Jewish version is 885; in English, it's 504, and in simple, it is 84. Add these together and you get 1473!" He explains, excitedly as if he'd just found a treasure. "1+4+7+3 is 15. Then you take 1+5, which gives you 6. Now, Gematria doesn't work so well when going from a number to a letter as multiple letters may use the same number. It turns out that it gives us the correct key for what we used to call an enigma machine, a gadget used in World War II for sending and decoding coded messages. I became quite adept at using that tool during the war. The catch is, that every 777 characters, the key number increases by one. I entered the formula into the tablet that should convert the list back to English for you. *Oh!* One last thing, the lines are written *backwards*! Right to left instead of left to right. You should be able to code that in, correct?" Vince says, ending with a hopeful grin.

"Old friend, I do believe you just shorted out my brain with that explanation, but I'll create an algorithm using your formula. You said you decoded a few entries?" Ty asks.

"Yes, just the first eleven lines. That's how I realized the key code goes up one every 777. It is a number which is thought to have power. Something about someone seeing a lightning bolt zigzag and thinking it was writing 777. I've included the mathematical formula for a series with a period of 777. So, if you can program it, it should automatically count 777 characters and then increase the key number by one. Then you'll need to reverse the order, line by line." He says, almost out of breath. He taps on the tablet and brings up a text document. "Here are the first eleven listings."

Sure enough, the formula yields a list of names, ages, dates of birth, current locations, and any identifying number they may have such as a social security number.

"You *truly* are a genius, Vince!" Ty says but turns back to look behind him as Val comes down the hall from the bedroom, half asleep.

"Ty? Do we have *company*?" She yawns.

"Yes, *Amore*. It's just my friend, Vince. I asked him to look at the encrypted list of potentials and he cracked the code!" He says, extending a hand to her, and pulling her against him.

"He did? *How*?" She asks.

"Don't get him started on *that* again!" He chuckles knowing how long-winded his friend can get about things he's excited about." He hands her the list of the first eleven names and her mouth drops open.

"That's incredible! Do you have some kind of super-computer or massive algorithm database?" She asks Vince.

He laughs, saying, "Only the *big one* in my head!"

"You did all this manually? You really must be some kind of genius." She says and looks at him closely. She has the oddest feeling she's seen him before, and not just at their wedding. There is something familiar about him, especially that beard and his distinctive blue eyes. She ponders this, as he continues to chuckle at her compliment. Suddenly, her eyes grow wide, and she says, "Excuse me." She jogs off to their home library.

For once, she's thankful for Ty's obsession with organizing books, and she quickly finds her art history texts. She grabs the one for the Renaissance period and flips through it, passing the page she wants, but because of her improved senses and processing, realizes it and backtracks. There, in her book, is a portrait with those same eyes, and an article she'd clipped out and saved suggesting a portrait of Jesus this artist had done, was, in actuality, a self-portrait, showing he had blue eyes and blondish hair. The face in the painting is older than the man in her living room, and his beard and hair are longer and less well-kept, but those *eyes*! They are *unmistakable*! She thinks, *It's him! That's Leonardo DaVinci!* She bookmarks her place with her finger and stomps back out into the living room, a tad nervous now that she knows his *secret* identity. She comes up next to Ty, and stares, wide-eyed and silent, at Vince, who looks down at the book Val has in her hand, and laughs.

"I see your partner is as *brilliant* as you have told me, Titus! It seems my *secret* is out! At least, as far as *she* goes!" He says, his laugh becoming a full, belly laugh. As his laughter lessens, it's still sparkling in his eyes.

"You're *really* him? I mean, Leonardo DaVinci?" Val asks, wide-eyed.

"Indeed, my lady!" He says with a flourished bow. "But *please*, it must be our secret! I do not wish to live in the limelight, even among the Apara. So, please, only call me Vince." He insists.

"Yes, sir..., *Vince*." She says, still feeling star-struck at meeting an artistic legend.

Ty turns back to Vince, saying, "Thank you, again. I must go make the algorithm, decrypt the rest of the file, and get it to Liz as soon as possible." He reaches out and the two men do a Spartan handshake, where each grips the forearm of the other. Vince nods politely to Val before porting out.

Val turns to Ty, eyes narrowed, lips pursed and *swats* him on the arm. "Why *didn't* you tell me?" She utters in annoyance.

"Because he *prefers* to remain known only as Vince Leonard; just another of the Apara. *Now*, I must get this programmed, so I can get the list to Liz. We're up to eleven, worldwide, reported missing *this* week. I'd say it's a given that it's the *Naqam*, but we need to know all the names on the list so we can protect those that have not *yet* been taken!" He explains and they work together on an algorithm that will decode the mystery list.

URGENCY

It's not yet sunrise in Asheville, but Ty and Val have been working for hours since they are six hours ahead in Sanctuary Central European Time (SCET). Liz is asleep at home with Kari, even though they are also in SCET, as their sleep schedule is for Asheville time. Her cell phone buzzes, but she's exhausted and sleeps through the first round. It stops and starts buzzing again. She raises her hand and her cell flies from the nightstand and into her grip. Still lying down, she maneuvers it down to her ear and answers. "*Javel*?" She utters on autopilot.

"*Liz!* It's Ty! I need to see you ASAP! It's *urgent*!" He insists.

"Ty?" She looks at her phone and it's 5:13 am, Asheville time. She mumbles under her breath. "*Hva i helvete driver han med?*" Then continues into the phone, "Ty, this *better* be good! I only got to sleep around two hours ago." She says groggily and yawns.

"It is, Liz, *it is*! Vince cracked the code, and it's worse than we imagined." Ty insists.

That wakes Liz up, and Kari with her. "*Well? Tell me!*" Liz demands, suddenly feeling an anxious, crawling sensation down her neck.

"You *need* to see the list in person, but all the people on your list, are within the first 30 on this one, and Liz, *Phoenix* is number 33." Ty says gravely.

There's silence on Liz's end of the phone for a couple of seconds, followed by a stream of curses in Norwegian, "*Faen i helvete! Jævla drittsekker!* Ty, Kari and I are up and getting ready. Meet us *here* in ten minutes. I've got to wake Peder. He *needs* to know about Phoenix." Liz pulls on yesterday's clothes and senses Kari's concern for her, as well as for Peder, Phoenix, and all the other *at-risk* potentials. She turns to

Kari. "Call Amy and tell her to send people to watch Phoenix, and if possible, get her GPS tagged *immediately!*"

Kari doesn't reply, but finishes getting dressed, and sets things in motion.

Liz practically runs down the hall to Peder's door, banging loudly on it. "*Peder! Bror! Wake up!*"

Peder comes to the door in his underwear, sandy, blonde hair shaggy, and unkept. "*What* is it?" He says, irritated that his sleep has been disturbed.

"*Pull* yourself together, Peder! Phoenix is in *danger!*" Liz says bluntly.

Peder is instantly alert, and his irritation shifts to anxiety. "What's *wrong*? Has something *happened*?" He prompts.

Kari ports in behind Liz. "She's *fine* for the moment! Amy and Dave ported right over to watch her and are setting up sensors. Sara's on her way to tag her while she sleeps. Amy will set up a rotating watch, and tech is getting a port filter ready, so only *known* people can port in or out." She explains.

Peder is giving off frantic, emotional waves. "What in *all of Valhalla* is going on? Why is *she* in *danger*?"

Val and Ty port in with printouts of the generated lists as well as electronic copies on their tablets.

Peder ducks back into his room, snagging a tee-shirt and jeans he had lying over a chair, and comes back out. "Will someone *please* tell me what's *going on*? *Why* is Phoenix in *danger*?"

Liz puts her hand on Peder's shoulder, gently nudging him to sit down in a chair in the living room. "Remember the algorithm you set up after Jason shot Niall?"

"Yes, what does that have to do with Phoenix?" Peder says, attempting to maintain a modicum of calm.

"When Ty relocated the server, all those auto-alerts were consolidated and alerts are sent to my computer. When I got to the office Monday, the alert for missing potentials was going off. It wasn't just *one* person, but *six*! Now, it's up to *eleven*. They're disappearing from all over the world." Liz explains.

"But *what's* that have to do with *Phoenix*?" Peder asks as he feels his heart sink and his stomach knot.

Ty interrupts. "Liz, I just checked, we're up to *sixteen* now."

"*Utrolig!*" She says, shaking her head and closing her eyes.

Ty continues. "My friend, Vince, has expertise in codes and decryption. We sent him the list we found on the server after the explosion and he was able to decrypt it." He hands printouts to Liz, Kari, and Peder. "All sixteen known missing are in the first *thirty* on the list, and if you turn the page...."

Peder does, looks up, distraught, and says, "Phoenix is number *thirty-three*?" His voice cracks under stress.

"Yes, and if they're going in *order*...." Val says, without saying the rest.

"Then Phoenix is in *imminent* danger!" Peder says, doing his best to control his gut reaction to port to her apartment and drag her back to Liz's to keep her safe.

Liz looks at her brother, feeling his pain and indecision. "Peder, speed things up; as in immediately, not a week, not even a few days. I know you want to ease her in, but that's not an option now. I've pathed Tess and told her what's up. She'll meet you at the office shortly so you two can discuss your options on how to break it to her, so you can turn her as soon as possible, preferably today!" Liz pauses and looks above and to the left as she gets a message from Sara that they've tagged Phoenix. "Okay, Sara's GPS tagged her with Benefactor-grade tech, so if they take her, we'll be able to find her."

Peder looks shell-shocked. He hates having to rush it, but he'd rather have her a little freaked out, but safe than lose her to the *Naqam*. "I'm heading to the office to wait for Tess." He says and ports out.

Liz sighs in exasperation, "Well, that's *one* person. Now, we must figure out what to do with the *rest*! Are any of the others in the pipeline for transformation?"

Val says, "We haven't cross-referenced the list with our potentials yet. When we saw *Phoenix* on the list, we figured that was a priority."

"*Indeed*! I hate to lose *any* of our potentials, but now that my brother has set his sights on someone after over *800 years*, losing her would be soul-crushing for him. I just hope she takes things well. Anyway, Kari, I suspect we'll need to mobilize most of Amy's trainees worldwide. Did tech ever make that large batch of GPS tags we talked about before we took out their base?"

"Yes, I've got them in storage at work." She replies, gently reaching over and rubbing Liz's back to ease her tension.

"Good. Val, Ty, I *assume* you have this list on your tablets or on your computers, but can you sort it by location?" Liz inquires, feeling her pulse pound in her head from stress.

"Yes, I just have to alter the sort parameters." Ty says and taps on his tablet until it sorts out geographically and generates a series of region-specific lists to send out to other centers.

"Get Amy to mobilize her people as soon as Phoenix's place is secure, and she's safe at Inspiration, Inc. Until then, I want Amy and Dave on guard at Phoenix's place and keep an eye on her while she travels to work." Liz sighs as she studies the list of potentials. We highlighted the missing ones in yellow. "I see there are gaps between the missing potentials. Someone needs to check on these others before going on to the rest of them. Assuming the *Naqam* are abducting and turning our potentials for their own purposes, it's vital we know how many are likely in their hands. Get our social media guys to do checks on these people and have Amy's team check each of the ones not yet reported missing in the first thirty. They apparently started disappearing this Sunday or Monday, meaning there's a good chance they've already transformed some of them." Liz pauses, closing her eyes and massaging her temples. She knows Kari is worried about her, and paths, *I'm fine, just not enough sleep and too much stress, kjære. I'm going to leave you to coordinate with Amy and her teams, but get people checked and tagged even if they must do it in broad daylight!*

Kari gives Liz a lingering caress on her back before porting out.

They continue brainstorming, but when done, everyone has left except for Liz. Sara ports in.

"What are you doing here, Sara?" Liz asks, exhausted.

"Kari's concerned about you. You may be *nearly* indestructible, but you are *still* subject to stress." She says, scanning Liz with her tablet and a scanner. "*Huh*! If I didn't see it myself, I wouldn't *believe* it! You, my friend, are dealing with *hypertension*! Your blood pressure is *elevated*! Granted, even if you *could* have a stroke or hemorrhage, it would only send you into stasis and *force* you to get some *rest*!" She says with her hands on her hips. She reaches into her bag and pulls out an infuser with pale, green liquid in it.

Liz flinches back, afraid Sara's going to sedate her, and take her out of this crisis by force. Sara stares her down. "*No*, I'm not going to *knock you out*! I'm going to give you a *vasodilator*. It will *lower* your blood pressure a little, and bring down your tension level, and headaches."

Liz sighs and shakes her head, but extends her arm to Sara, allowing her to dose her with the infuser. After a few seconds, her muscles relax, and the pounding in her head ceases. She feels better and can think more clearly. Sara pulls out several ampules of the same compound. "You can dose yourself if you have another episode. No more than half an ampule every twelve hours or you will end up passing out!" She puts the infuser and ampules on the table and ports out.

RUSH JOB

Peder paces his office frantically while waiting for Tess He knows he must convince Phoenix to let him change her as soon as possible, or risk losing her to the *Naqam*, a fate he dreads. He hates rushing things, as he had with turning his best friend, Halvdan, which ended badly.

He wants to tell Phoenix the truth and prepare her before their relationship goes any further, but he'll have to do what would have taken a few weeks, in a day or two. He can't *risk waiting* any longer, but he must find a way to do it without frightening her or harming her psychologically. He pauses, closes his eyes, reaches out to touch her mind, and relaxes when he feels her slumbering consciousness.

Peder hears footsteps in the hallway and sticks his head out the door, startling Tess. "*Geez*, Peder! I didn't think you'd be here yet." She says, heart pounding.

"I came as soon as Liz filled me in. Preferably, I need to turn her today, but I'm *not* ready! *Hell*, I know *she* isn't!" Peder rambles out, anxious vibes radiating from him like pinging sonar.

"Sit down and take a few deep breaths. We'll figure this out *together*, okay?" Tess follows him into his office, and they settle on his sofa. "I *know* it's personal, but just how far have things gone between you two?" Tess inquires.

"Not *that* far. I didn't want to *rush* her. In fact, I want her to *know about me* before anything intimate happens." He blurts out.

"How do you think she feels about you?" Tess asks.

"I know she cares about me, but you know that or you wouldn't have used your PK to send that bouquet into her waiting hands!" He says, glaring.

"*True*, just making sure we're on the same page. From what I sense, she likes you plenty, probably even *loves* you. She certainly *thinks* about you a lot! I kept picking up on her while she was using my spare computer recently. *Thankfully, I think* Val and Ty got that glitch fixed! Phoenix's mind leaks and it got distracting, and I had to *ambush* Marc when we got home!" She grins.

"*Tess, how* can I break this to her? It's not something I can blurt out without either scaring her to death or frightening her into running away!" He sighs and sinks into the sofa.

"Didn't you tell me she's got a *thing* for vampire romance books?" Tess asks with a lop-sided smirk.

"Yeah, but this is *real*, not one of her *fictitious* romance novels." Peder shakes his head, uncertain what to do.

"No, but you can take advantage of those leanings. What if we can find a non-threatening way to show her what you are?" Tess suggests.

He grumbles. "Tess, I'm pretty sure she'll run screaming away and *never* speak to me again!"

"Are you *sure*? If she's that caught up in those stories, I bet she'll be *mighty* tempted to explore the possibilities, especially if it's someone she *cares* about and *trusts*...." Tess draws the last part out. "She *trusts* you, you know that, right? As well as care about you."

"But if I just blurt it out and tell her, 'Oh, by the way, I'm like the guys you daydream about from your books!' And drop my *fangs* into place, won't she *freak*?" He says, sarcasm dripping from every word.

"Probably, if you do it *that* way. Or she'll think you're *nuts*!" Tess grins at him.

"Gee, thanks." He says.

Tess leans back and ponders. "*Well*, you *could* always try a variation on how I found out about *Marc*." She suggests, her head cocked to one side.

"Tess, you really *freaked* out when you saw him in the alley. We *all* know how that went!" He reminds her.

"True, but *hear me out*. I saw him feeding on a stranger. I didn't know if she was alive or not. What if she caught you feeding on *someone* who *volunteers*?" She suggests as an idea culminates in her mind.

"Kind of hard when none of the humans here know what I am, so...." He says in frustration.

"The person you feed on doesn't have to be *human*! She just needs to *believe* they're human, *willing*, and *not afraid* of you. *Hell*, you can feed from *me!*" She suggests.

"Maybe we'd better clear that with *Marc*! He can be awfully possessive of you!" He snickers.

"I can make those decisions for *myself*. No one says there must be *any* sexual overtones! Just that you're hungry and need to feed." She suggests.

"That's all fine and dandy, but how are we going to get her to walk in on us while I'm feeding on you?" He asks, distracted by the thought they may come for Phoenix while she's driving to work.

Tess gets an amused expression. "Excuse me while I make a quick call!" She picks up her cell and calls Ty.

"Hey, Ty, it's Tess. I'm with Peder and we're brainstorming how to break things to Phoenix now that we know she's on their wish list. Did you solve the lockdown issue on Phoenix's computer, or has it just been *behaving* for the moment?" She inquires. "Hm, you found the issue, *damn*! Don't suppose you could *fake* it?" She pauses. "Yes, *fake* the *lockdown!* I need to get her working back in my office, because I've got an idea how we can break the whole 'vampire' thing to her. Uh-huh, yes! That would do it! You're a *prince*!" She says and hangs up.

Tess looks smugly satisfied with her idea, while Peder looks uncertain. She fills him in on her plan. "Ty's going to simulate a new lockdown on her machine, and we'll put on a little show for her. If I'm right, seeing me willingly let you feed on me *should* make a difference!" She explains.

"I still think she'll freak out and run away." He complains.

"I believe her curiosity may kick in when she sees I'm willing." Tess explains, but Peder is still skeptical. The two of them discuss plans and contingencies, and Tess admits they're going to have to play it by ear, but she thinks it's their best option.

Peder senses Phoenix's arrival outside and breathes a sigh of relief, knowing if she's inside the building, she's *safe*. Tess returns to her office so Phoenix doesn't witness them conspiring.

Peder composes himself, hides his anxiety, and reviews what he must do. He's startled as Phoenix pops her head into his office and yawns. "Morning, Peder!" She says, in a drowsy tone.

"Morning. *Tired*?" He asks.

"Yeah, I had *weird* dreams and kept waking up thinking people were lurking outside my apartment." She says, leaning against his door frame.

"*Lurking?*" He asks, curious if she may have picked up on Sara GPS tagging her or the others securing her place.

"It's nothing, really! Probably just watched the DVD you gave me too many times. I put it on before bed again. In fact, I fell asleep with it on." She laughs. "Probably just the power of suggestion."

"Ah, dreamed about *vampires*?" He asks, knowing she'll be doing more than dreaming about them by day's end, she'll be coming face-to-face with their reality on a very personal level.

"Yeah..." She yawns, "but I don't mind dreaming about stuff like *that*! It's *not* real, so I can *indulge* in the fantasy, you know? It's the realistic, stressful dreams like being back in school and taking an exam I haven't studied for, or dealing with real people I'd rather *avoid*, that I can't stand! Anyway, I should get started. Deadline day! I've got to have the WNC Photography and Folklore book done by tonight, so I can print it for final proofing by the client Monday." She smirks and slips into her office next door.

Peder sits back and paths Tess, *She's in her office. She's got a deadline on a book project today.*

Tess paths back, *Good! All the better to push her to use my machine! I'll let her get started, then go downstairs to 'see Marc'. While I'm out, Ty'll pull the plug on her machine. I've told Liz to expect us for a 'meeting' after that, and we'll monitor her reactions from there.*

I suppose we can use the excuse that I need to feed before the meeting, so I won't be tempted to go for anyone's throat? He paths with overtones of amusement at his pun.

That would certainly be a good excuse! I'll give her about an hour and then set things in motion. Tess paths.

Peder sits anxiously in his office, uncertain how everything will play out. He knows he must turn her as soon as possible. The only other option is to take her to Sanctuary as *protective custody*, which he's pretty sure she wouldn't react well to.

An hour passes, Tess heads toward the elevator, but stops at Phoenix's open door to say hello. "Morning, Phoenix. We made it to Friday! Got any fun plans for the weekend?" Tess asks cheerily.

"Nah, I've been so focused on getting this book done, I haven't really thought too much about it! I may see a movie tomorrow afternoon. It's so hot this week after that cool spell last weekend, and the movie theater's always good and cold." She gives Tess a friendly smile.

"Sounds like a plan. I'm running down to see Marc before a meeting with Liz later. Do you need anything from downstairs?" Tess inquires casually.

"No, I'm fine. I've got to dig into this project and get it finished, then I can breathe easier. I probably should've skipped the wedding and worked on it instead; then I had that mess with my computer this week, so I'm running behind. I've got to focus! So, I'll talk to you later, okay?" Phoenix says apologetically.

Tess nods and heads downstairs, pathing to Ty that he can pull the plug any time. He waits a couple of minutes for Tess to get clear, then triggers a lockdown on Phoenix's computer that visually resembles the earlier error.

Phoenix is focusing on adjusting some photo sizes when the screen goes gray, and a square pops up saying

**Your computer has been put into emergency
lockdown mode due to a security issue.
Please contact the system administrator for assistance.**

She stares at the screen in stunned silence before reacting. She realizes she hasn't saved in a while and slams her hand down on her desk. "You've *got* to be kidding me!" She blurts out and her stress level rises.

She stomps over to Peder's office to blow off some steam before hollering for Val or Ty, but he's not there. Being unable to vent makes her more anxious. She picks up the office phone and dials Ty's extension, telling him about the lockdown. He says he's *'unable'* to unlock it from there, so he'll send Val up to help her.

Phoenix sits there, staring at the accursed lock-screen, drumming her fingers on her right hand from stress and annoyance. She hears footsteps coming down the hall and Val sticks her head in the door. "I hear you need a data doctor?" She asks.

Phoenix rolls back from the desk in a huff and motions toward the grayed-out lock screen. Val grabs another chair from nearby and settles in front of the computer. She works on it for about half an hour, then says, "I can't find anything. Oh, *wait!* That's *odd.*" She feigns discovering something curious.

"*What*?" Phoenix scoots her chair closer.

"It's not the USB thing, this time, it's flagging a *possible* virus." She says, and runs a first level antivirus, gets an all clear, then restarts the machine. It appears to be working, but as soon as Phoenix opens one of her files again, it locks down.

Val says, "I'll have to download new antivirus files and run a more advanced scan. It may be hiding as a trojan that the basic scan can't detect. Sorry, but this could take a while."

"*ARG!*" She exclaims. "*Never* fails! This crap always hits when I've got a freaking deadline!" She rants. "See what you can do, but I can't wait around all day. I'm going to use Tess's backup machine!" She grabs the humongous folder of corrections and stomps off down the hall to Tess's office. She's about to knock on her door frame when she notices Tess's office is empty. She shakes her head, thinking, *She went downstairs to see Marc. Oh well, I'm sure she won't mind if I use it. It wasn't an issue last week and I need to get this done today!*

She settles behind the free-standing wall divider between the spare machine and the main office and puts her papers down with a smack on the desk. She boots up the computer, logs in with her server password, and pulls up her document. It takes time to back-track and find where she last made a correction, since she hadn't saved recently. Once she finds the spot, she continues her corrections, becoming hyper-focused on her work.

She hears voices coming closer from the hall and realizes it's Tess and Peder. She's in the middle of a more complex correction, so doesn't want to stop in the middle of it to tell Tess she needs her machine again. She hears them approach the office and Tess says, "Well, come on in and shut the door! We don't want an audience, do we?" She asks.

"Absolutely *not!* I'm just glad you're okay with this. I should have dealt with it last night, and now, I don't have time to go out before our big meeting with Liz and the client." Peder says.

Phoenix quietly stops what she's doing, wondering what they're talking about. She listens in, staying immobile, so they won't realize she's there. She thinks, *Oh, please don't let this be what it sounds like*, wondering if it's something sexual.

"Let's get this over with! Let me sit down. Last time I got light-headed." Tess says and moves over to the sofa.

Peder joins her. "Are you sure you're okay with this? I really hate to ask...." He says.

"It's no big deal! I know you won't hurt me, and it's better than having you literally going for the client's *throat!* I trust you, just don't take too much! Marc and I have plans this weekend, and I don't want to be too weak to enjoy them." She says, laughing lightly.

Phoenix thinks, *Going for the client's throat?* She gets a sinking feeling and thinks, *No, that's impossible!* She cautiously turns her head and peers silently through the small gap between the divider panels.

Peder says, "I won't take much. Just enough to take the edge off, so I don't get tempted during our meeting, so your weekend plans are safe!" He knows Phoenix is watching, opens his mouth, and lets down his fangs. He senses her mentally flinch as she watches and hears her heart race as he gently bites down on Tess's wrist, making sure Phoenix can see his fangs sink into her flesh, and blood trickle up before he puts his lips down and drinks. Tess closes her eyes, but is completely relaxed, as though a vampire feeding on her is no big deal.

Phoenix watches, enraptured as she witnesses something she's fantasized about. Her stomach knots up and her mouth goes dry as she comprehends the ramifications of this revelation. She thinks, *Oh Hell! He's really a vampire! And I... no... shit... I'm in love with a God-damn vampire!* She feels turbulent emotions erupt and run the gamut from fear to envy that Tess knows what it feels like to be fed upon, something her fantasies have played with for years.

Part of her longs to experience it herself, but she stops herself before she can mentally indulge. *Damn it! This is not one of my freaking books! I don't know what's real or not! Obviously, he's some kind of vampire, but that's all I know! Shit!* She holds her breath as she watches, so they won't know she's there.

Peder senses Phoenix's mixed reactions and resists the temptation to break out of the charade and comfort her. He withdraws his fangs from Tess's wrist, so Phoenix can see his fangs again, as well as the wounds. He sits back, takes a deep breath, and says, "Thanks! I really do appreciate this. I'll just heal those right up so no one sees the punctures." He places his hand over her wrist and when he pulls it away, the skin is as unblemished as it was before he bit her.

"No problem, really. I know you wouldn't ask if it wasn't important. We should get down to that meeting or Liz will have both our heads!" She chuckles and gets up, slowly, feigning a touch of weakness.

Peder steadies her and helps her up. "I didn't take much, so you should be over the worst in a few minutes. Do you need to sit for a few?"

"Nah, I think it was just a slight, low blood pressure reaction more than anything." She says.

The two leave the office, closing the door behind them.

Phoenix gasps for breath after holding it so long, turns back around toward her computer, and slumps into the chair. She thinks, *This can't be real! How can he be a vampire? I mean, if he were, wouldn't he have burst into flames at the wedding? But I saw it all! I know I've daydreamed about stuff like this for years, but now that I know it's REAL, I'm not so sure I want it!*

After a few seconds, her mind argues with itself. *Damn! If I don't want it, why do I envy Tess? Why do I want him even more than I did? Why the fuck did this have to happen now?* She thinks as she looks at her computer screen, which has gone dark from inactivity. *How am I going to focus on work when....* Suddenly, she hears someone turning the doorknob. It startles her enough that she bumps her chair into the divider panel behind her.

"*Hello*? Is someone in here?" Tess asks.

Phoenix's heart is in her throat, but she stands and composes herself. "Just me! Computer's down *again* and I've got to get my project done *today*! Sorry I didn't ask, but you and Peder had just gotten in the elevator when I came out of my office. I figured it would be okay, and I can't afford to lose any more time than I already have."

"Oh, *yeah*, perfectly fine! I was just in here a few minutes ago, going over some things with... Peder before the meeting and didn't see you here, so...." Tess says, faking a little anxiety in her voice.

"Nah, I came in after that. I've been in here alone since I saw you get in the elevator with him." She says.

"Well, I'm being scatterbrained today and forgot my tablet, so I just need to grab it and head back. Go ahead and use the computer. I'll be in and out all day." She says, feigning a forced smile. She picks up her tablet and heads out again.

Phoenix leans on her desk with her forehead leaning on the palms of her hands. "I've got to focus!" She says aloud, as though saying it has the power to make it happen. She tries to put Peder's condition on the back burner and focus, thinking she'll deal with it after she gets the book done.

This works for about half an hour, until her mind flashes back to him sinking his teeth into Tess's arm, sending tingles down her spine, and even further down where it's potentially more distracting. She thinks, *Stop it! Damn it! That's NOT going to happen! It can't, because if I let it happen, I'm not sure there will be any turning back.*

She attempts to ignore the unspoken truth that eventually, if things continue between them, she knows what will happen; she knows she won't be able to walk away. She smashes her hand on the table to bring herself back to reality and focus. She gets a couple of chapters done, but it takes all her focus and energy. She repeatedly gets distracted and makes mistakes she must correct and loses track of time.

BIDING TIME

Peder is in Liz's office with Tess, Liz and Kari. He and Tess are both try-ing to sense what's going on in Phoenix's mind and with her emotions as she comes to grips with what Peder is and what it means.

After a while, Peder sits up straight and opens his eyes, and Tess fol-lows suit. He says, "I suppose the fact that she hasn't run out of the build-ing, hopped in her car, and driven out of state is a good sign?" He sighs.

Liz chuckles lightly. "Yes, brother dearest! It means she's try-ing to process things rationally and not letting her fear of what you are overtake her."

Peder makes eye contact with his sister. "And yet, I do sense fear from her, though I can't quite articulate what she's most afraid of." He admits.

Tess clears her throat. "That should be obvious! She's more afraid of herself and her own judgement than she is of you! She's confused as to what is and isn't real. I caught her thinking about how you didn't self-immolate at the wedding, out in the sun, so she under-stands that, while you're obviously some kind of vampire, you aren't necessarily what the mythological and book ones are."

"She kept trying to push it out of her mind, though. Do you think she's trying to ignore the truth?" Peder asks.

"No. I think the one thing that's causing trouble right now, though it may also be one reason she hasn't run; she's got a dead-line. She's trying to focus and can't, but that's stressing her out more than what you are, because she wants to do a good job and not be late on this project." Tess elucidates.

Peder weighs Tess's analysis, but says, "I sense some fear of me, though it's less than I expected."

"As I thought, seeing me let you feed from me, and how I trusted you, is diffusing some of her fear that you're a monster. She's spent a lot of time with you, and you've never done anything to hurt her. That counts for a lot!" Tess explains reassuringly.

"So, what next? Do I just wait and see if she confronts me or what?" He inquires.

Kari chimes in. "She's unlikely to do that. I think she's still worried about how you might react to her knowing. She's also worried she may make poor choices if you two deal with it face to face. She'll retreat rather than confront, I think. Not because she's afraid of you, but she..." Tess closes her eyes and reaches out a tendril to Phoenix's mind. "She's afraid she'll let her fantasies influence her decisions about you and any relationship you two have."

Liz puts a gentle hand on her brother's shoulder. "Peder, it's going to be fine in the long run. She'll come around, that much I'm certain of. It may just, well...." Liz trails off, looking at Tess, as she can't quite articulate what she needs to say.

Tess nods at Liz, understanding what she wants to convey. "You'll need to turn her as soon as possible, but if worse comes to worst, you may have to just haze her mind and turn her without giving her any choice and pick up the pieces afterward. It might piss her off for a while, but she does love... yes, *love* you. I think part of her wants to give in and let you feed from her or even turn her. She's just uncertain that she'll be making the *rational* choice."

"I'd rather *not* turn her against her will. I want her to choose to be with me and be at peace with that choice." Peder says, feeling somewhat disheartened.

"Tess is right. She loves you. She'll forgive you even if you force the issue. You can always tell her I *ordered* you to do it." Liz says, concerned about Peder's resolve.

Tess says, "Tell you what, it's been about an hour since I left her. I'll grab some sandwiches from the kitchen and take them up to her. Maybe if she gets some food and sees I'm fine, she'll relax a tad." She grabs her tablet and leaves. Peder stays downstairs; not sure he can face Phoenix yet for fear she'll turn and run.

Tess grabs a couple of paper plates and piles several open-faced sandwiches on them to take upstairs. She reaches out mentally to Phoenix and senses exhaustion. She gets to her office door and opens it, putting her tablet and the food on her desk and walking around the divider to find Phoenix with her head down on her desk, keyboard shoved out of the way. "Phoenix? Are you okay?"

Phoenix startles and sits up. She's been crying and takes a rapid breath in to clear her nose. "Yeah, sorry. I'm so tired. Tried to rest my eyes for a few and must have dozed off. I'll deduct that time from my hours or make it up later."

She looks up at Tess, unsure if she can trust her now that she may be under Peder's influence. She's considered that as a reason Tess wasn't afraid of him. Maybe she was under his control somehow, like in some of her stories. But when she looks in Tess's eyes, she can't sense anything amiss.

"Don't worry about it! I think we've all had days like that. How's the book coming?" Tess asks.

"I'm having a lot of trouble focusing, so, it's going slowly." She admits, realizing she's only done about one third of what she normally could have done in the same time.

"Maybe eating will help. I brought some sandwiches for both of us. Take a break and have lunch with me." She insists and Phoenix drags her chair over to Tess's desk. She settles in with a paper plate and a sandwich. She tries to eat it, but her stomach is in knots. She must force herself to swallow it and tries to hide her internal distress.

"Did Peder come upstairs too?" She asks, timidly.

"No, he and Liz are still working. I'm going down again when I'm done, but my blood sugar was crashing." She smiles and takes a bite of a sandwich with homemade wild red raspberry jam on it.

Phoenix nearly chokes, *thinking, blood sugar or blood loss?* But she finishes the sandwich, knowing she can't eat another without feeling like it might try to escape and take the first one with it! "You know what? I think I'm going to stretch my legs. See if that wakes me up. If I don't get back before you head back to your meeting, thanks for lunch."

"Not a problem. I'm not going to eat this many, but I'll put the rest in the mini-fridge over there in case you get hungry later. Are you sure you're okay? Is there anything I can do?" Tess inquires, trying to look confused, and concerned about Phoenix's mental state.

"I'll be fine. I just have a lot on my mind, and it's been distracting me." She says and leaves the office. She hastens down the hall to a small door marked roof, goes through it and up a short flight of stairs and comes out into a rooftop garden. There's a solid wall around the whole thing, so there's no risk of falling off the roof. There's a dome over that with glass panels. The room is sunny, but climate controlled, which is nice since it's 95 degrees today. She walks around and finds a little elevated pond filled with fish swimming around in it. The walls of it are stone, with a wide ledge for sitting on. She sits there, staring down into the water, watching fish swim back and forth, finding it calms her mind.

She first visited their roof garden atrium when her computer locked up the prior week. She found the location oddly calming; almost mentally healing. She dips her fingertips into the water, watching the ripples it forms, and the fish react, believing she's going to feed them. A couple of big, orange goldfish with puffy cheeks come up and try to nibble her fingertips. She's feeling more centered but hears footsteps. She turns around and Peder is there, looking concerned. Her heart skips a couple of beats and speeds up as she realizes it's him.

"Hey, Phoenix." He says, coming toward her. "Tess says you aren't feeling well. Figured you might have come up here. Are you okay?"

She forces herself not to step back as he approaches, knowing that would make him suspicious. She fakes a smile. "Yeah, feeling better now that I've been up here for a few, but I should really get back to work. Deadlines and all, you know!" She stands to leave, but as she passes him, he gently grabs her by her upper arm.

"How about this, let's go grab a bite to eat after work. We can celebrate your project's completion." He suggests and feels her reaction when he says the word 'bite'.

"Not tonight, Peder. I'm brewing on a headache and I really just want to get home. I'm going to work late just to finish this thing, so I can't really justify going out to dinner, you know?" She says.

"Come on! You've got to eat! You could take a break and we could go grab some garlic sesame noodles down by Pack Square." He suggests giving her his most charming smile.

She thinks, *Garlic?* Then says, "Thanks, but I'm not up to it today; maybe some other time." She forces a smile, but he gives her a concerned glance and reaches out and gently brushes her face with his hand, making her flinch unconsciously.

"Have I done something to upset you?" He asks, making eye contact.

She fights the urge to withdraw from him, but also finds she wants him to touch her more. "No, it's not you, it's *me*. I'm just having a *really* off day." She smiles weakly and walks out past him, back to Tess's office. Tess has left, and she settles in to work on the project again. She makes some headway but is distracted and misses things.

She pauses her work, considering her options. She thinks, *Maybe I can transfer to one of the other departments? Distance myself from him? But he'd wonder why, and I'd feel like crap doing it.*

Phoenix decides she's going to go home when she's done, throw some stuff in a duffle bag, and head to the beach for the weekend. Then she can think through everything without dealing with Peder firsthand. She thinks, *I've got to focus, 'cause at this rate, it'll be midnight before I'm done, and I won't be in any shape to drive four or five hours to the beach!*

***

The others are observing her from afar telempathically. Tess picks up on her thoughts of heading to the beach and realizes they can't let her do that. She'd be too hard to protect out in the open, and they don't know how imminent an abduction attempt by the *Naqam* may be.

Liz looks at Peder and says, "You can't let her leave here without you tonight. For all we know, they could be ready to snatch her today!"

"Yeah, and I've got to get her where she can't avoid me or run away. She knows now, so I just need her to understand I won't hurt her." He says.

Tess puts her hand on Peder's shoulder. "I think she gets that. I'm not even sure she'd see you turning her as *hurting* her. What you need to do is convince her it's okay to give herself permission to want it. Sue and I have been talking with Sara. It seems the reason for the fascination with vampire stories, and, as I can attest to first hand, the irrational desire to have someone bite me, is all part of the subconscious preparation they gave us to make it desirable to become Apara. Granted, neither Phoenix nor I had the full dose of subliminals, but both we, and Sue had that odd fascination with being bitten. It will nudge her in the right direction, believe me! It certainly did me!" Tess smirks.

They continue finalizing a plan. One way or another, Peder will confront her tonight about what he is and what he wants.

***

When Phoenix gets back to Tess's office, she calls Val to ask about her computer, but she's told there's no way it will be up and running for her today, so she continues in Tess's office. She hears footsteps and voices in the hallway once again; one is Tess, but the other is also female, and Phoenix realizes it's Liz. They enter the office.

"Let me find those files, Liz. I knew I'd forgotten something when I came down for the meeting." Tess says and roots through a drawer in her desk. While Phoenix is distracted by that, Liz reaches into her mind and puts her into a state similar to when they feed on someone. Once Phoenix is oblivious to her surroundings, she stands behind her, placing her hands on Phoenix's shoulders. She reaches into her mind as though it were one of those Chinese puzzle squares and pushes the thoughts of Peder and what he is into a far corner, while she brings her work up to the top and forces it into sharp focus.

Liz tells Tess, "She should focus and work until she's done. Best she finishes it tonight, because she's not going to be in any condition to work on it this weekend, is she?"

"No, and depending on how her transformation goes, it may take several days before she's up to much of anything. You're worried about Peder, aren't you?" Tess senses her unease.

"This must go well! He's held off turning anyone or even taking a regular partner for over 800 years because of something that happened to the one person he turned. It's a long story, but if things get rough, I'm worried he won't handle it well." Liz says as she moves back over toward Tess's desk. Phoenix is still in that mental limbo state.

"You don't think he'll chicken out, do you?" Tess asks.

Liz is pensive, then says, "I doubt it. He knows her safety is at stake if he puts this off. I just hope he can convince her to let him turn her willingly. On the off chance he doesn't do it though, I will. She must be brought in ASAP." Liz glances back toward Phoenix and releases her mind. Phoenix immediately dives into her work, focusing like she has nothing else on her mind.

Liz paths Tess, *As soon as she's done, the compulsion will break and the rest will come back to her. That's when Peder will have to step in.*

Tess nods and picks up a folder from her desk. "Here it is, Liz! The files you need. I'll catch you on Monday." Tess says, completing the excuse for Liz coming to her office.

"Thanks." Liz says and leaves, while Tess packs her things.

She gets Phoenix's attention, though she can feel the girl's mind straining to go back to her hyper focus. "I'm heading out early but use the computer as long as you need to. If you're the last one out, remember to turn off the hallway lights. See you Monday!"

"Yeah, I'll probably be here for a while, but at least my focus finally kicked in. Have a good weekend." Phoenix says absentmindedly.

"You, too, Phoenix. You, too." Tess says and leaves the room.

Unavoidable

Thanks to Liz's tinkering, she slips into hyper focus, completely forgetting her dilemma with Peder. She works several hours, never stopping to eat. She finishes and saves it to the server, feeling like she's run a mental marathon. She glances at the time on her computer. "8:45? It can't be that late!" She mumbles.

She heads to the window and peeks out the blinds; it's dark and the streetlights are on. She watches streams of car headlights driving into town on the primary thoroughfare, Patton Avenue, no doubt heading to downtown bars and clubs for a little Friday evening fun.

Well, at least I got it done before midnight, but I really should get out of here! She thinks and grabs her stuff to leave. Phoenix feels dizzy and sits down again as the memories of what she saw earlier that day, between Peder and Tess, come flooding back into her consciousness. She's disoriented, like someone edited in a new paragraph in the summary of her day. She thinks, *How the hell did I forget about that?* Remaining waves of memories and turbulent emotions cascade in, overwhelming her. She must put some distance between herself and Peder, so she can process it all. She grabs her things and opens the office door but hears light classical music by Grieg playing. She looks down the hall toward the sound and realizes Peder is still there. Her heart sinks thinking about what he is and what that means for any future relationship.

Oh, Crap! I've got to sneak out without him noticing. I've got to get past his door without being seen or heard! She thinks. She slips off her shoes and slips them into her canvas bag, then silently closes Tess's door, gingerly tiptoeing down the hallway toward the elevator, but stops as she approaches Peder's office. She edges closer, peers through the gap between the door and the frame on the hinged side and is relieved to see he's sitting with his back toward the door, proofreading one of the other projects. She's unsure how acute his hearing may be, so silently pads past his door, holding her breath, and when she gets a couple more doors further down, speeds up her pace toward the elevator. She makes it there and pushes the button several times, wondering why it's taking so long when everyone but she and Peder have gone home.

When the elevator arrives, it opens with a ping. She sighs with relief and slips through the sliding doors, not realizing Peder heard the elevator. She hears "Phoenix! *Hold* the elevator!" She gasps, pretending not to hear him, and lets the doors slide close, but they move sluggishly, only to be stopped by a hand breaking the sensor beam. Peder steps in, pretending to be out of breath. "Didn't you hear me asking you to wait up?" He senses her unease and fear. It almost physically hurts him, but he knows he must go through with this, for her own safety.

"Sorry, I'm tired! I've been working for several hours straight and was kind of oblivious. I'm heading home." She doesn't back away from him, as that would be an obvious indication something was off.

"Are you sure you're in any shape to drive? Maybe you should let me drive you home." He puts a hand gently on her arm.

She flinches unconsciously, thinking, *Shit! He's going to know something's up if I can't control my reactions.* "No! *Really*, it's all right Peder. I'll be fine." She snaps.

"You clearly *haven't* eaten! How about that rain check on a meal, my treat?" He smiles and edges closer to her, invading her expanded space, and she feels uneasy and afraid.

"That's *not* necessary. I just want to go home and sleep. Really, I'm f... fine." She says with a shiver. His nearness makes her both afraid and yet disturbingly tempted.

He tilts his head to one side, one eyebrow raised. "You *know*, you've been acting kind of odd today, almost like you're *trying* to avoid me?" He gives her a sad look, knowing she fears him.

Not sure what to say to convince him otherwise, she stammers out, "*Please*, it's been a *hell* of a rough day, that's all!" She's on the verge of a breakdown and tears, as her heart and her mind war over her future. She thinks *Why the hell is it taking so long to get to the first floor?* Noting that they should have been there by now.

He closes the gap, forcing her to make eye contact with him. "If I didn't know any better...." The elevator *shutters* to a rocky stop, throwing Phoenix off balance. Peder grabs her by her shoulders and lowers her to the floor. He crouches in front of her, watching her, knowing she's terrified, but he must follow through so she can't deny the reality of what he is. "As I was *saying*, you're acting like you're afraid I might... *bite*." A tip of one fang shows behind his subtle, questioning smile.

Phoenix lunges away from him and ends up in one corner of the elevator, nearest the doors. No place to run. "P... *please*, Peder, don't!" She pleads.

He plops down next to her, back against the wall of the elevator, and lets out an audible sigh. "*Calm* down! I should've resisted my flare for the dramatic." He twists to look at her, gently runs his hand along her cheek, looks her in the eye, and wishes his touch didn't make her flinch. "Yes, I *know* what you saw. I knew you were there the *whole* time. I want you to know what I am, Phoenix. Even more importantly, I *need* you to understand that I'm *not* going to hurt you." He backs off a touch.

She looks up at him, uncertainty in her eyes. "Wh... what *are* you? *Really!*" Fear permeates her trembling voice.

He smiles gently, without the fangs. He speaks in a soft, calm voice, asking, "What do you *think* I am? What do I *appear to be*?"

She has trouble saying it at first, but swallows hard, and forces the words out. "You... you appear to be a vam... vampire, but that's not possible! They don't *really* exist. They're *just* in stories!" She insists, trying to convince herself more than answer him.

He chuckles sympathetically. "Perhaps not like in your stories or movies, but *we exist.* I've wanted to tell you for some time, but it's difficult to tell someone I care about, I'm not human." He cocks his head to one side, waiting for her reply.

Phoenix doesn't say anything at first, but stares at him like she's trying to discern some hidden truth. "I've *seen* you in the daylight, and I *know* you like garlic. You're *not* cold to the touch. *How* can you be a *vampire?*" She hopes he'll tell her it's all an elaborate prank.

He gently takes her hand in his, hoping to calm her. "You saw my fangs come down when I fed from Tess. Watch now." He opens his mouth to reveal normal, human teeth. His fangs come down into place from above, like cat claws extending from their sheaths. She gasps. "Go on, feel them, they're real. I *promise* I won't bite your fingers!" He gives her such an innocent puppy dog look as she giggles nervously.

Slowly, she reaches over and tentatively feels one of his fangs, noting the contours, and that they are *not* prosthetics or some kind of trickery. She looks up, making eye contact, then looks away again, anxiously. "So, they're retractable, huh?" She's so dumbstruck by it all, she can't figure out anything better to say.

He smiles and says, "Yeah, it'd be pretty hard to blend in if I have to go around like this *all* the time!" He retracts them as quickly as they came down. "As to the other things, mythology often *starts* with a grain of truth and takes on a life of its own that bears little semblance to the original truth. Take my hand. As you yourself said, I'm warm to the touch." He moves her hand over his heart. My heart beats, as yours does. I'm as *alive* as you are." He lets her hand go, tapping her chin to get her to make eye contact. "Sunlight doesn't hurt me, but we typically feed at night, when darkness gives us cover. During the day, we come across as normal humans." He blurts out, "Look up!" He points to the mirrored elevator ceiling. "I've *even* got a reflection!" He smirks.

After staring at his reflection for several seconds, she realizes looking up and exposing her throat might not be the smartest move and quickly looks back down to face him. "So, other than the fangs and drinking blood, what *else* is true?" She asks, cautiously letting her curiosity venture out.

He relaxes and gives her a grin. "My life span is virtually unlimited. My body repairs itself quickly and perfectly. If I'm hurt badly, I'll 'die' by human standards, but as soon as the damage is healed, I'm *back*!" He says with a fangless grin.

"You'd better hope no one tries to *cremate* you!" She jokes. "I'm almost afraid to ask how old you are."

"Yeah, that part may be a little tough to swallow, but I'm over 800 years old." He gives her a sheepish grin as he waits for her to react.

She gasps and rolls her eyes. "*UGH!* When I fall for an older man, I aim for the Guinness record!" She quips sarcastically.

He thinks, relieved, *She's joking! That's an excellent sign!"* That's *part* of why I wanted you to know." He engulfs both of her hands with his. Phoenix, it's been a *long* time since I've felt this way about anyone, and I know you've been feeling it too. It isn't fair to take this any further without you *knowing* the truth." He pauses, waiting for her reaction.

"So, that's why you haven't... well, you know, made any moves when you've visited?" She stammers out.

"I figured it would be worse if we get intimate and *then* you found out! Besides, I know you care about me, but I want that care to be honest before we get in any deeper." He senses her emotions are a tumult of warring feelings: fear, curiosity, uncertainty, and love.

She relaxes a little, sighs, and looks him in the eye. "Peder, I do care. I'm just not sure how to deal with all of this! Since you're being honest with me, I'll admit part of me *is tempted* and curious, and part of me says run away! *Well,* if I weren't *trapped* in a *damn* elevator, that is!" She admits and looks down at their hands, suddenly insecure again.

"I know about that *temptation*. One perk of being what I am is I have certain psychic skills, *including* telepathy." He pauses as she looks at him and blushes, mouth hanging open. "I *wasn't trying* to listen in on your private thoughts, but sometimes, when you're working, you fantasize you're one of your book characters, and when you do, your mind leaks!" He chuckles and puts one hand on her knee to reassure her. Phoenix's blush deepens, and her expression is somewhere between distraught and embarrassed that he's seen her inner fantasies. "That's one reason I let myself get so close to you. I hoped that your desire to experience that, even as a fantasy, might help you accept me for *what* I am."

Highly embarrassed, she gasps, "Oh, *God*! If I'd known you could read minds...."

"Yeah, I know, you'd have kept your thoughts from wandering to things happening between us outside of your 'other' fantasies, right?" He watches her reaction as she nods, blushing a deep crimson. She's halfway worried the blood rushing to her cheeks will tempt him. He strokes her face gently, along her jawline. Besides, now that you know, I could give you some of your *fantasies*. I felt that *need* from you, too. Especially as you watched me feed from Tess; that need to know what it feels like to be *bitten* like the women in your books, and in your fantasies. I felt your frustration because you believed it could never happen, right?" He pauses.

A tear rolls down one cheek. "I'm not sure it's a good idea for me to go there!" She mutters, realizing his abilities give him an immense advantage over her.

He cocks his head to one side and gives her a charming smile. "My dear Phoenix, there's nothing wrong with letting yourself indulge in what you want occasionally! You *know* I won't hurt you!" He reaches up and gently rubs her tears away with his fingertips.

She looks up at him, a mixture of fear and longing in her eyes, and thinks *it's not you I'm worried about, it's my resolve!* Her fear, longing, and curiosity war for dominance within her, but curiosity wins a small skirmish, and she asks, "If I let you *bite* me, what are the *consequences*? Will I become *like* you? Or be 'yours' like in some stories?" She asks, quietly, but curiously.

He laughs lightly, knowing she's been reading too many vampire romance novels. "No! Honestly, a little blood loss is all, but there's a compound released when I bite that helps your blood regenerate quickly!"

"So, biting me won't make me into a vampire, or biting me three times or whatever?" She searches his expression, trying to determine if he's being honest with her.

He twists his mouth into a suppressed grin, trying to keep from laughing out loud. "Do the math! If everyone I bit became a vampire, and everyone they bit, and so on, even since I was turned, there'd be no more humans *left* on the planet!"

As she considers that, she relaxes a tad. "And you're certain it doesn't make a person your slave, or bound to you, or some kind of half-vampire or something?"

"No, *thank goodness*! That's *all* I need is a few thousand *minions* to keep out of trouble!" He blurts out with biting sarcasm, then his expression shifts to a more serious one. "However, we already share a bond. I know you've felt it, and the more we're together, the stronger it will get, just like any couple! If I were to feed from you, at least regularly, that may add to it; and the more *often* I feed from you, the stronger that emotional and psychic bond will become." He explains.

Curiosity wins another skirmish, and she dares to ask, "How does one *become* like you? What *changed* you into, *oh, God*! A vampire?"

"It isn't too different from one of the mythological ways. The process involves one of us feeding from a human and then giving blood back to the human within a short period. There's a virus that causes the transformation, but it must be sensitized to a transformee's DNA by feeding on them first, and then giving them blood, and there's one other thing. The human must be *genetically compatible*."

She looks confused by this new tidbit of vampire lore. "Compatible?" She closes her eyes and waits for the other shoe to drop.

"The virus will only work on a minute percentage of people, even with blood exchange. They must carry a certain genetic sequence the virus locks onto. If it's not there, we can't transform them." He senses her anxiety rising as she debates asking what she knows needs answered.

She swallows anxiously, her breathing becoming more rapid. "Am I... compatible?" She asks quietly, afraid to look him in the eye, but even more afraid of the answer.

He gently cups her chin and turns her head to look at him. "Phoenix, I'm not going to lie to you; yes, *you are*."

Her stomach drops, and even though she dreads his likely answer, she asks, "Do you *plan* to turn me into a *vampire*?" She's trembling, and he wants to reach out and hold her to still her anxiety, but resists, taking her hand instead, and caressing it. "I *want* to, but I'd prefer you be willing." He says, fudging the truth. He wants it to be her choice, but he will do it without her permission if he must, if it means saving her from the *Naqam*. He catches her eye and holds her gaze.

"Are you saying it's up to me? You'd never do it *without* my permission?" She asks.

He pauses, figuring out what to say. "There's one exception. If, for some reason, your life hangs in the balance and you're unable to choose, then I'd assume you'd want to live, even if it means being like me." He says truthfully but shadowed with vagueness.

"I sure hope that doesn't become an issue!" She blurts out.

"Same here, but I don't want to *lose* you, and if it's a matter of turning you or losing you forever, I know what *I'll* choose! However, I hope that you'll eventually join me, willingly, and allow me to share this gift with you." He admits.

Phoenix feels a rush of heat in her body as she flashes on images and imagined sensations of him feeding on her, giving her his blood, and turning her like in her books and fantasies. Before, she would have indulged in such vivid imaginings, wallowed in them, but now that it can happen, and even worse, he may hear her thoughts, she cuts them off before they can go any further. She's overwhelmed and afraid she'll give in more than anything else. "Oh, boy! This is *too* much for me right now! I feel like my head's about to explode!" She leans back into the corner of the elevator, breathing rapidly.

Peder stands and extends a hand down to her, giving her a lopsided smile. "How about we get you some food and continue this discussion somewhere more comfortable?"

She looks up at him like he's an idiot. "Uh, I think you've *forgotten* something! We're stuck in an elevator and no one's around to get us out! We'll have to call Liz or Marc or the fire department!" She stops chattering and stares off in thought. Her eyes refocus a few seconds later and she stares him in the eye. "Is Liz *really* your twin sister?"

He chuckles, thinking, *She's quick!* "Yes, she *is*." He says without elucidating, waiting to see if she follows her thoughts to their logical conclusion.

She lets out a long breath, asking, "She's *like you*, too?"

"Yes, she is. In fact, she *transformed* me." He explains, still waiting for her to take his hand. She does so absent-mindedly. He pulls her up, and she stumbles against him briefly, feeling the warmth of his torso.

He chews on his lower lip, sheepishly, and then says, "By the way, the elevator isn't *really* stuck."

She looks at him, traces of anger and betrayal emanating from her as she realizes the elevator was part of the whole drama he'd created. "What the *Hell* do you mean? It's not *really* stuck!"

He pauses, thinking about how to phrase things. "It's another of those *perks* I mentioned. Have you ever heard of telekinesis?

Her eyes widen. "You mean moving stuff with your mind?"

He nods. "It's one of my stronger abilities. I tried to approach you in the garden, but you were determined to get away from me. I needed to get you somewhere where you couldn't make excuses and run away; somewhere you'd have to face me and hear me out. At first, I slowed down the elevator, so I'd have more time, but when I realized, you weren't going to cooperate, I flipped the circuit breakers telekinetically. Watch! "He closes his eyes. The elevator lurches less violently and continues down at normal speed.

She sighs and says, "I guess if I run away when the doors open, you won't have any trouble catching me?" She asks sarcastically.

He gives her a slow but friendly grin. "Won't even get winded! Even if you get away, we share a psychic connection. I can find you even if you flee the state or the country!" He says, gently rubbing her arm with his hand.

"And how did *that* happen?" She's annoyed, wondering if he did something funky to her.

The elevator opens and they walk out onto a completely deserted, and mostly dark ground floor. They step out and stop while the elevator closes again. "The connection? How does it happen with any two people who become close? My telepathy boosts it, but it happens with regular couples, too. Couples finish each other's sentences or know when something's wrong with their partner all the time!"

She sounds annoyed but knows what he says is true. Occasionally, she still knows when something's wrong with her ex-boyfriend, even though she hates the guy for running off with her best friend a couple of years earlier. She gives a derisive snort. "I guess you're also *physically* stronger than normal, too? How do I know you won't just turn me even if I say no?"

A glimpse of frustration sneaks into his expression because she's fighting so hard to avoid what her heart tells her. "*Because* it's important that *you* decide this for yourself and accept it. It'll be easier on both of us if you do. You'll adjust better, and I won't have to put up with you holding a grudge for the next century!" He grins.

She consciously slows her breathing, swallows, tries to understand what's really going on in his head. She wishes she had a touch of telepathy to even the field. "Out of curiosity, is there some rule that says you've got to have my permission or you *can't* do it?"

He gives her a light laugh; not mocking, but sympathetic. "No, not at all. I could cloud your mind and do it right now without you putting up a fight. Like so...." He catches her gaze. She stops all resistance and tips her head back. She feels him move closer, but rather than bite her, he kisses her throat over the pulsing artery. "*See*? The reason I don't is that you *need to* accept it. If I turn you, we'll be together for a long time, and I *know* how *stubborn* you are! I don't want you to hate me for years to come!" He opens the front door for her, and she slips out. The night air is sultry and oppressive, and it makes her feel sluggish.

She turns around and looks at him, "I guess I see your point, but I'm still feeling kind of pressured!" She fumbles with her purse to find her keys.

"How would you feel if I were human and wanted to make love to you? Or asked you to marry me?" He argues.

She glances at him as they walk. "The problem is, I suspect being turned into a *vampire* is a lot more permanent than your average human relationship! I'm assuming there's no cure?" She's distracted and bumps into a light post as they walk to her car.

He takes her by the arms and turns her toward him, taking inventory of her to make sure she hasn't injured herself. "No, there's no cure, but I don't know anyone that's really wanted to be 'cured'" But he thinks, *Except for Halvdan,* but doesn't want to frighten her by telling her about him. "You know, you *aren't* in any shape to drive. So, hand over the keys." He gives her a 'hand it over' gesture.

She rolls her eyes, but realizes he's right, and reluctantly hands over her car keys. He chuckles when he sees her keychain. It's a plastic bauble with a picture of lips with fangs, and the words "Bite Me!" on it. He grins and asks her, "So, is this an open invitation?"

She glares at him intensely, saying, "*Absolutely* not! Just because I'm *into vampires* doesn't mean I'm going to let you have your wicked way with me!" But she thinks, *Who the Hell am I kidding? I may talk brave, but part of me wants... NO! Can't go down that path!*

He turns her to face him. "I told you, it's *your* choice. I don't want to force this on you, though, I'll do my best to tempt you, as any human male might! In the end, you must do what feels right. You must be able to accept it and live with your decision. I'm asking you to hear me out, and I hope you'll let me be there for you... with you, because you want to be there, too, not just because I want you!"

DRIVING TOWARD DESTINY

He unlocks the car and holds the passenger door open for her. Getting into the car with him feels symbolic. It's more than a door; it's a path she's not sure she'll ever be able to return from. After a moment's hesitation, she gets in and straps herself in.

He starts the car. As he's backing out of her parking space, he asks, "How about Chinese? I know a great place for carry out that's open late. It's a bit of a detour, but worth it. We can eat and talk more at your place."

She's distracted, feeling like handing over her keys and leaving the driving to him is symbolic surrender. She answers absentmindedly, "Sure, you know I like Chinese food." She pauses, then asks, "So, if you get out of line, does the whole 'rescinding your invitation' thing work?" She glances at him anxiously while making it sound like a joke.

He lets out a burst of laughter. "Nope! I don't *need* your permission to be there, but I'll respect your wishes. We need to talk this through now that you know the truth. Besides, you should know by now you don't have anything to fear from me. How many times have we been alone and I've never hurt you? Not even when you fell asleep on my shoulder watching TV! If I'd *wanted* to hurt you or *turn* you against your will, I'd have done it when you had no idea it was coming."

She relaxes, thinking about his reassurances. *He really could have done whatever he wanted.* She thinks, but says out loud, "I guess it won't hurt to hear you out, but I'm *not* making any promises or decisions before I'm good and ready!"

"I wouldn't expect anything less from you. You need to understand the situation and make an informed decision you can live with, because if I turn you, you're going to live with it a very long time!" He glances at her, smiling, and turns back to watch the road, leaving her to ponder the possibilities.

After picking up enough Chinese food for a party, Phoenix sits quietly, thinking. She asks, "Peder, how does Tess figure in to this? I thought she and Marc were a couple, but she knows about you, and let you drink her blood."

She notices him smile. "Oh, Marc knows, too! There's nothing intimate between Tess and I, never has been. In fact, Marc is like a brother to me!"

Phoenix takes his word for it and feels better knowing Tess and Marc know the truth and trust him. She relaxes into her seat, but comments randomly "It's strange letting someone else drive." She needs to break the silence that's fallen over them in the last few minutes.

"I think if you'd driven tonight, you'd have been wrapped around a tree by now." He jokes, patting her on the leg.

She laughs awkwardly, "You're probably right. This has been one *hell* of a day! First the computer mess, then seeing you bite Tess; now all this!" She sighs, then gets an annoyed look and glares at him. "Did my computer *really* have an issue, or was that part of the setup?"

He shrugs. "Tess suggested the glitch so we could get you someplace private where you could witness me feeding. We knew you were there, watching."

"Remind me to break all of her pencils on Monday." Phoenix snipes.

"Oh, *that'll* really teach her!" He chuckles.

She ponders Tess's helping him set her up, and asks, "Does she know *why* you want me to know?" She's still uncertain how much she can trust Tess after this.

"Yes. She's watched us getting closer. She agrees that before things go any further, I should tell you the truth." He pauses, as he turns into her apartment complex off Hendersonville Road. "We're here."

As they approach her usual parking spot, she mumbles, "Oh *crap!*"

"What? Is something wrong?" He asks, worried she's having second thoughts.

"You mean besides going into my place, alone, *with a vampire* that has designs on me and my future? *Yeah!* Something *really* dangerous! My *nosey* neighbor, Lydia! Ever since I moved in, she's been on me constantly about how a young woman shouldn't be living alone! She's been trying to fix me up with her son, or a 'nice boy from her church'. If she sees you go in with me, I'll get 50 questions from her for the next week!" She complains. "I certainly don't think I want to explain you!"

"I've been to your place before." He reminds her.

"Yeah, but *not* coming in *after* 10 pm! I swear, Lydia has a built-in *bullshit* meter! She knows when something's off, and under the circumstances, I'm not sure I can BS my way through her questions without her 'Spidey-sense' kicking in!" She grumbles.

He sighs. "Do you think you can drive 100 feet without wrapping your car around a lamppost?" He pulls into a parking space around the corner from her apartment.

Her fear of him waning, she barks at him like he's the same old Peder she's been hanging out with for months. "Yeah, I *should* be able to manage that, *smart ass*! What are you going to do, sneak in the back way? She'll have the cops here investigating a peeping Tom in 3 minutes flat!"

He gives her a mischievous grin. "I have *other* skills you don't know about. Remember how I said I don't *need* an invitation?" He raises one eyebrow and vanishes.

Oddly, she's not ruffled by his sudden disappearance, she gripes at thin air, "Couldn't you have taken some of the food in with you?" She hears a disconcerting laugh in her mind as all the bags of Chinese food vanish. "*Show off!*" She shouts out loud but intuitively replies telepathically without realizing it. She slides into the driver's seat, drives her car around the corner, and parks in front of her apartment.

Like clockwork, Lydia comes out her front door to walk her over-groomed and pampered, Yorkshire terrier, Cinnamon, when she hears Phoenix pull up. *I really don't need this crap tonight,* Phoenix thinks.

Lydia makes a show of 'just noticing' Phoenix has gotten home and heads toward her, dragging poor Cinnamon behind her. "Oh, *Phoenix*! You're getting home *awfully* late!" Her deep southern drawl thicker than proverbial molasses!

Phoenix dreads the interaction, so attempts to barrel through to her door, talking without stopping. "I know, Lydia, I had to work late. If you'll excuse me, I'm rather tired. I need to go inside and get off my feet."

Not letting an opportunity to match make her seemingly unattached neighbor, Lydia says, "You know, if you had a nice young man in your life, he could've been inside waiting for you, making sure you come home safe."

"It's *fine*, Lydia. I always lock, and I'm *not* worried about what's waiting for me inside." She snipes.

Lydia doesn't let that stop her. "That *may* well be, *honey-child*, but you should know my son's coming by this weekend for supper! You're *welcome* to join us! I'm fixing my *famous* fried chicken!" She tries to stare Phoenix down and pressure her into coming over for dinner with her son, *a rather portly young man with the IQ of a turnip*, or at least that's how Phoenix sees him.

"Thanks for the invite, Lydia, but I'm involved with something at work that's going to keep me very busy. I doubt I'll have time to socialize in the foreseeable future. Now, if you'll excuse me, I've *really* got to get off my feet!" She fumbles with her keys, unlocks the door, slips in quickly, and closes it behind her, so Lydia doesn't have time to reply. She leans her forehead against the cool door as she locks both locks, letting out a sigh of relief. She feels Peder behind her, gently reaching around her waist and holding her for a minute. *Oh, God! That feels nice!* She thinks, unconsciously leaning into him.

"So, you're not that worried about me, huh?" He whispers in her ear.

"No. I'm not worried about you as much as I am...." She trails off, thinking better about admitting to him she's torn and uncertain she can trust *herself*. "I'm not ready to throw in the towel, but I *am seeing* you more as the old Peder, a friend, whose company I enjoy, more than as a *blood-sucking vampire!*" She turns around to face him. "*However!* That food smells wonderful and my stomach is growling up a storm! If you don't let me get some food *now*, I may have to kick you where even a *vampire* will take time to heal!" She says with a wicked grin.

He lets her go, holding his hands up in surrender, motioning for her to pass him and help herself to the feast of Chinese food he's laid out on her dining room table. She fills her plate and heads for the living room sofa, feeling awkward being alone with him, but so ravenous that the awkwardness fades as she eats.

He follows suit, but grabs a couple of beers from her fridge, and puts them on her coffee table as he sits down.

"Thanks." She says, downing it, knowing it won't get her drunk.

"I thought it might help you relax a little." He strokes her thigh with his hand.

She smiles at his suggestion, then says, "It's weird, you know, being here with you now that I know you're... not human!" She stuffs a fried dumpling in her mouth nervously.

He leans back into the sofa, and sighs. "I *get* it! This wasn't exactly how you'd hoped things would go between us, though, in the long run, I think it can *be* as you *desire*?"

She pauses, chewing slowly, then swallows deliberately. "You mean, as in my fantasies or as an actual relationship?" She looks up at him, holding her breath, waiting for his answer.

"Both? I can tell you need a little time to absorb all of this, so I've got a suggestion." He grabs her remote from a nearby chair. He turns the TV on and chooses one of her online streaming services, skimming through what's available, and puts "The Fifth Element" on. "Let's start off with a more normal activity for us. I know you like this movie, and it might help you relax."

She nods, feeling relieved she doesn't have to jump into the middle of everything with him just yet. He turns the main lights off telekinetically, and a smaller lamp turns on, which startles her, but she realizes that this is how they often watch movies, as though they're in a theater, he just did it without using his hands.

She eats and watches the movie. As has happened far too often before, she dozes off with her head on his shoulder and his arm curled around her.

He can feel the weight of her exhaustion the day's events have wrought. He gently picks her up, carries her to her room, puts her on the bed, and pulls up the covers. He cleans up the popcorn and Chinese food before returning to her room and crawling into the other side of the bed, fully clothed, and falling asleep. There's no way he's going to leave her unprotected, in case they come for her.

GENTLE PERSUASION

Phoenix wakes in the morning, sunlight dancing on her eyelids. She opens her eyes, stretches, and turns away from the brightness, only to notice someone's in bed with her. She's disoriented, and not sure how she even ended up in her bed, so her gut reaction is to think the worst.

She peeks under the covers and is relieved she's still wearing her clothes from the day before. She sighs in relief and gently pulls the blanket down from the person's head, recognizing Peder's sandy blonde, shaggy head. She promptly punches him in the shoulder. "WHAT THE *HELL* ARE YOU DOING IN MY BED?" She demands.

Peder rolls to face her and explain, but falls out of bed, landing with a thud, still tangled in the summer blanket. He pulls himself upright and pops his head out of the end of the blanket and stares at Phoenix, who giggles uncontrollably when she thinks, *Oh God! He looks like a blonde burrito!*

Peder breaks into an ear-to-ear grin, wiggles out of the blanket, and sits on the edge of the bed. "*Sorry!* Didn't mean to upset you, but under the circumstances, I thought I should be nearby in case you woke up and freaked out about everything."

She goes quiet. "So, I wasn't dreaming or imagining things? You're really a...?"

He gives her a quick smile. "I think the word you're looking for is *vampire*. We don't use that term ourselves. My people are called Apara. It's Sanskrit for 'other'. There are so many negative connotations to the term 'vampire' that don't reflect what we truly are." He leans over and puts his hand on one of hers. "How are you holding up this morning? You don't seem *too* freaked out."

She gives him an annoyed stare. "Give me time! I just woke up and have a hell of a lot of questions, so I'm not sure what to think.

I'm still uncertain what is and *isn't* real. Though, I suppose I'll give you the benefit of the doubt on one thing...." She trails off.

"Oh? What's that?" He asks, one eyebrow raised.

"If you'd wanted to, you could have turned me last night. I dozed off on you again, didn't I?" She looks embarrassed.

"I'll give you a pass this time. You had a *very* long day." He laughs.

"Sorry!" She says.

"There's nothing to be sorry about, you were wiped out." He moves back onto the bed and leans against the headboard, legs outstretched on the bed, feet bare.

Her stomach growls hungrily, and he chuckles, "Since it's nearly lunchtime, I'll warm up some leftovers from yesterday, and we can have that talk. I hope you trust me now."

She pauses, then nods. "I'm going to get cleaned up and find clean clothes. I got sweet and sour sauce all over my shirt last night." She trots to the bathroom and shuts the door. She sits on the closed toilet, head in hands, thinking, *why can I only see one ending to this? Why can't I see any way out of this mess? It's not fair! I love the guy, but if I stay with him, I'm going to end up like him. Unless my self-healing thing means I'm also immortal. Maybe that would be good enough for him?* Tears well up, but she forces them back, stands, and splashes her face with ice cold water. After washing up, she checks that he's nowhere nearby, slips back into her bedroom, finds a pair of jeans and a Carolina Panthers hoodie, and heads for the living room. She smells reheated Chinese food, and her stomach growls even louder.

Peder brings out a tray of reheated Chinese food boxes and a plate of oven-warmed Chinese chicken wings and puts them in front of her. He walks away and comes back with plates, silverware, and a couple of bottles of caffeinated soda. "Thought maybe you could use the caffeine this morning." He grins.

"Thanks, but it doesn't affect me lately." She takes a plate and spoons out various food onto it along with five chicken wings.

Peder does the same, settling next to her on the sofa. He leaves a comfortable margin between them, so she doesn't feel crowded or threatened by his nearness. "I hope your fear has subsided by now. We need to sort this out."

She shakes a deep-fried chicken wing at him. "Don't think you can stuff me with Chinese food and fancy words, and I'll just swoon, and give in! I *need* answers. If you want me to consider some kind of relationship with you, then I need to know *everything*. No secrets!" She takes an aggressive bite out of her chicken wing and watches him cautiously.

"I'll tell you what I can, Phoenix, but you can't blame me for being a typical man in some ways." He grins with a hint of fang that sends chills down her spine and distracting fantasies through her mind.

She's annoyed by his comment and flash of fangs. Something's been bothering her ever since he told her about the whole genetic compatibility issue, and she wants to clear those waters before things proceed. "Tell me the truth, did you know I was compatible before we started getting close?"

He pauses to gather his thoughts and figure out how to explain it so she won't get upset. "When we meet a compatible person, it can be like meeting an old friend. A subconscious, telepathic link forms. That person *stands out*, and I felt this connection to you early on. It's like being on a similar frequency. The compatibility usually means heightened psychic abilities, latent or active." Phoenix shifts uncomfortably on the sofa as she listens. "I'll be honest, I confirmed that you're compatible before I allowed myself to get close to you because it's difficult getting close to someone when there's no chance we can turn them, knowing that eventually, they'll grow old or sick, and die! If you hadn't been compatible, I'd have kept things much more business-like. It's painful when someone you really care about has no possibility of being there for more than a drop in the bucket, relative to an Apara lifespan!"

Phoenix is pensive and says, "I suppose I can't blame you. It would be like deciding whether to get involved with someone who's terminally ill. You can be with them for a short time, knowing death is coming soon, or walk away to avoid the pain. I'm not saying one is right or one is wrong. It depends on the person and situation. Of course, the terminally ill person shouldn't be punished for being ill, but now I'm getting off track." She rambles and then goes silent, debating telling him her secret. She decides honesty must go both ways. "What if my aging isn't an issue?"

He gives her a confused look. "Phoenix, you're *human*! Eventually, you're *going* to die!"

She takes a deep breath and lets it out slowly, summoning the will to tell him. "I'm not so sure. You know how I started reading vampire books again after something happened?"

"Yes, but you didn't wish to discuss *what* happened." He reminds her.

She lets out an ironic bark of laughter. "I'm still not sure I do, but you need to know because it might mean you don't need to turn me." She whispers.

He attempts to read her, but she's unconsciously blocking him. "*Well*? I'm waiting!"

"I got very sick after Christmas last year. Everyone was getting it, but just a mild bug, but I got a high fever and ended up in the emergency room." She explains.

When she mentions getting sick, he perks up, wondering if it was the Roulette virus. "You obviously recovered from it. Do they know what you had?"

"They said it was just that weird virus that showed up before Christmas, spread quickly, and then vanished just as suddenly in January." She pauses. "As to recovering, I died with a nearly 107-degree fever, and my organs were failing. I *woke* a few hours later when they jabbed me with a scalpel when they started the autopsy! All my symptoms vanished and there was no sign of any organ damage or brain damage. I was *fine!* They kept me for a few days just to make sure, but it was as though I'd never been sick."

"You must not have been *truly* dead." He suggests.

"EKG and EEG said otherwise. Oddly, they said my temperature never dropped below 96 F, and I developed no signs of rigor. I wrote it off as a fluke. A few days later, I went out with friends and noticed no matter how much I drank, I didn't *feel* any effects. My friends got sloshed. I got bored watching them while I stayed sober, so I made an excuse and left. On the way to my car, someone grabbed me and pulled me into an alley just short of the parking deck. He robbed me at knife-point, and I begged him to let me keep some photos from my purse, but he stabbed me *right here!*" She points to the spot on her abdomen. "It went in deep and I felt my life ebbing away. I *died* again! I woke up the next afternoon, *covered* in dried blood. I couldn't find an open wound, and when I got home, I looked closer, and it was barely a red line with light scabbing. That's just *not* normal!" She says, distraught by the memories. Peder is certain the Roulette virus was the culprit. "When injured, I craved things that were rich in iron, especially red meat, preferably rare. One day, I was watching a cheesy vampire movie on a streaming station when I made the connection. I was craving something to help regenerate my blood! I died and came back twice!"

He shakes his head, realizing, "That's why you identified so much with the heroine in your movie, isn't it? You wondered if you'd become *part* vampire?"

Phoenix nods, holding back tears, relieved that she'd finally found someone she *could* tell. "At first, I thought maybe I was just going crazy, but I couldn't *ignore* the facts! I've been keeping this to myself since January, afraid anyone I tell will think I'm nuts!"

He gives her a grin. "You're not nuts, and I may even know what caused this." He says.

Her eyes go wide. "Like what?" She asks, eager to know the answer.

"The virus that went around was an altered form of the one in my body. Someone tinkered with the virus that makes us what we are. Non-compatible people only got a mild bug. Compatible people got much more, and it often brought out one or more special ability. Some got psychic abilities, while others just got enhanced physical senses. My guess is it gave you our regenerative healing ability." He suggests.

"Does that mean I'm immortal, like you?" She asks.

He chuckles. "I don't know. It may, but only time will tell." He reaches over and strokes her thigh.

"If I am, then my aging shouldn't be a problem and I could stay how I am now, couldn't I?" She asks, hopeful she won't have to choose between becoming like Peder or remaining human.

His eyes are sympathetic, and he says, "The argument can go either way, love. By your own admission, you're already partly turned. Why not *finish* the process? Get the whole package. You'll be able to teleport and have other abilities." He entices her.

"But I'll have to *drink blood* if you change me. Right now, I just want rare hamburgers or steak tar-tar if I'm injured! *That*, I can live with a lot easier than biting people!" She sulks.

"We never hurt the people we feed from, and we pay that debt by protecting humanity." He sighs. "What I mean is we do what we can to make the world a better place. For example, some of us are precognitive and prevent disasters and mitigate others. We depend on humans, so we help them, even if they don't know it."

She shifts uneasily as she ponders this revelation. Her world is turning upside down and sideways, making her *nauseous*. "This keeps getting weirder and weirder." She shakes her head and takes a mouthful of moo-shoo pork. After she swallows her food, she jumps in with both feet. "So, you must drink... feed on blood to *survive*, right? Obviously, you're able to eat regular food, too." She asks.

"I need blood, or I'll grow weak. Avoid feeding too long, even with eating proper food, and I'll go into a type of coma or what we call stasis. It won't kill me, but it will incapacitate me. I can't produce blood cells from raw materials like humans can. I must ingest whole, human blood that my body converts to my own. Only in stasis will my body convert some of my tissue to replenish my blood levels, at least enough for me to come out of it. The biggest issue is if I don't feed regularly, I may become a danger to others."

"You mean you might attack someone?" She asks.

"Yes, but only after not feeding for an extended time." He says, then gives her a goofy look. "I can control my need to nibble on necks!" He says to lighten the mood.

"I guess I should be glad you *snacked* yesterday." She jokes, her face softens, and a wave of sympathy washes over him from her. "I guess that means you don't have any choice, do you?"

"I don't have a choice, that's true. It's a tradeoff. In return, I get a long life, and some cool abilities!" He quips.

"Abilities like telepathy, PK, self-healing, and teleporting?" She wonders if there are others, he hasn't told her about yet.

He catches her curiosity, and answers with a lopsided grin, "Among *others*."

She pauses, thoughtfully, then asks, "What other abilities?"

"It varies from person to person, mostly variations on human, psychic abilities. We can take pain away when we feed and make those we feed upon forget being fed from, and as I showed you earlier, I can control someone when I need to, usually just so I can feed from them." He explains.

She gets a sinking feeling. "Have you ever fed from me and made me forget?" She waits anxiously for his reply.

"No, as tempted as I've been to taste you, I've refrained. It would be too tempting to keep doing it if I had! I hope you'll trust me enough to allow me to do so someday." He says.

Phoenix blushes. "Maybe, someday..." She looks away, but thinks *I can't let him know how tempted I am... I've got to think logically! This is not some stupid fantasy!*

He reaches over and gently touches her knee. "What *else* do you need to know?"

Phoenix's stomach knots, knowing she's running out of questions, *and excuses*. She spaces out trying to process everything, including her feelings for him as a person, as well as her temptation to indulge in her fantasies. Her dilemma is divining what is real, and what are pages out of her fantasy books or mythology.

TEMPTATION

After about three minutes of near-catatonic stillness, Peder interrupts her. "Are you alright, Phoenix? You spaced out so long, I wondered if your mind had broken." He asks, cautiously moving nearer, closing the gap between them. He holds her hand, knowing, even if she isn't ready to let him turn her, she's close to letting him through to her as a man.

She looks him in the eye, glancing away nervously. "This whole thing's crazy. I'm not sure which end is up. I *should* be strong and fight, but part of me cares about you a hell of a lot and wants to let you, needs... you know, to get closer. After years of fantasizing, part of me demands to know what it's like! But that's all based on a bunch of *stupid* romance-book fantasies I thought were safe because none of it was real! Another part of me says *run*! Run fast and far away!" She admits, as a stray tear rolls down her cheek.

He caresses her hand and leans closer to her. "Sounds like it's two against one in my favor in there?" He gives her a charming smile.

She's quiet, neither acquiescing nor pushing him away. She doesn't withdraw from his caress but makes tentative eye contact with him. "Maybe, if it won't hurt too much, you can have that *taste*?" She says, quietly and uncertainly. She's shaking subtly, not with fear, but with anticipation. He takes his other hand and steadies her head, holding her gaze reassuringly. "It *won't* hurt, and you may find you like it."

"That's what *scares* me the most!" Her face turns a deep crimson red, and she giggles anxiously.

He looks at her with sympathy for what she's going through. "Would it be so bad to give in to what you *want*? To indulge this once, or even admit that you want this as much as I want to taste you?" He pulls her closer. She expects him to tip her head back without delay and bite her, still worried he might just turn her.

Instead, he gently pulls her face-to-face and kisses her. She comes out of it breathless. "Don't be afraid. I promise I won't hurt you and I'll only take a little." He tips her head back and to the side gently. He kisses her neck, then pierces her skin and artery painlessly with his fangs. Her blood flows out and into him. There's no pain, but she's overwhelmed by a new need. He senses her rising libido and feeds it back to her empathically, enhancing it. He withdraws his fangs and seals the punctures with a kiss, draws her face-to-face, resting his forehead on hers. "*Well*?" He asks, fangs still in place.

A quiet whimper escapes her lips, "Did you *know* I'd react like *this*?" She gasps; frustration works its way through her system anticipating him taking things further.

"It's not the *usual* response I get, but we share a bond, and you've been feeling this way for a while. Perhaps your heart's trying to tell you something? I can take care of this need, too, if you'll let me; no strings attached!" He says, stroking her hair gently. After a few seconds, she nods, and he picks her up like she weighs nothing, and teleports them both into the bedroom.

"How? Did we just teleport?" She's disoriented, both from porting, and from the wellspring of physical feelings and emotions fighting for dominance inside her.

He puts her down on her bed, kissing her, muffling her questions while getting a grip on her sweatshirt. He breaks the kiss only to pull it over her head, his own need growing with hers. "No more questions; let me take care of you... relax and *trust* me."

"Are you going to bite me again?" She gasps as he kisses her breasts.

"Only if you *ask* me to." He says quickly, coming up briefly for air before further exploration of her body, porting clothing aside in haste, and reserving hands for exploration. Every so often, he senses flares of anxiety, stops, and looks her in the eye. "Phoenix, tell me if you want me to stop."

She doesn't hesitate, saying, "*No! Don't* stop! Just *slow* down a bit. I *want* this! You can even *bite* me again if you want to, just *don't* turn me!"

He leans down and kisses her on the lips. "I'll take you up on that later..." he grins with a hint of fang, "but for now, just see me as plain ol' Peder, the guy you've been falling for, who's very much in love with you!" She nods, and he leans in for a long, deep kiss.

They spend the next couple of hours making love and exploring, intensely at first, followed by more playful, casual exploration. Afterwards, they're lying in bed as late afternoon sun glints through her curtains. He suddenly blurts out, "You know, there are advantages to having me as a lover...." He says, stretching.

"*Oh?*" Phoenix encourages him to elucidate.

He leans over and kisses her stomach, then says, "Yeah, I don't tire easily, and I recover *very* quickly!" He gives her a wicked grin.

"And if I get a yearning in the middle of the night, you can be there in the blink of an eye!" She runs her fingers through his hair casually, realizing, she no longer fears him in the slightest.

His grin widens. "Oh, yes! *Can't* forget that!" He leans over her stomach again, dragging the smooth, curved fronts of his extended fangs along her abdomen and breasts. He props his head up on his arm, knowing he still needs to bring her over as soon as possible.

"Phoenix, I know you're still coming to grips with all this, but *please*, let me change you! There's so much we can share if you're like me that I can't share with a *human*, even a potentially immortal one." He asks, then gently kisses her shoulder, waiting for her answer.

She's quiet for a moment, but admits, "Peder, part of me wants to throw caution to the wind and say yes; but part of me is terrified I may be basing my decision on a *fantasy*. I love you, Peder; even knowing what you are, those feelings remain strong. I have for quite a while. I need time to sort all this through, can you understand that?" She leans over and gives him a light kiss on the lips.

"Yes, I just don't want to wait *too* long. I've been waiting for someone like you for over *800 years!* Now that I've found you, I don't want to risk losing you to a random happenstance!" He exclaims as he looks pleadingly into her eyes.

"Considering I've *died* and come back twice already; I don't think you have too much to worry about! *Give* me the time I need to sort it out in my head and heart, please?" She begs.

He knows the situation is urgent but doesn't want to frighten her by broaching the subject of the *Naqam*. "I suppose I can wait a little longer for an answer. Are you hungry? There are still leftovers, or I can make something fresh." He suggests.

"Whatever you want to do, but I'd like to go soak in a hot bath and process everything." She smirks.

"Go on! I'll take a shower after dinner. I can smell you all over me!" He gives her a lustful grin and walks out of the bedroom.

Phoenix lies in bed, attempting to grasp everything going through her mind and emotions, but it's overwhelming. She grabs a long, knit, floral shirt she often wears around the house, and saunters off to the bathroom, noticing some of her muscles complaining they haven't been used like this in a while.

She runs the water until it's the right temperature and puts out clean towels, pours in fragrant bubble bath, and stares at her reflection in the mirror. The bite wounds have almost healed on their own. She thinks, *I could really get used to this rapid healing thing, as well as the being bitten part,* and her cheeks burn as her blush intensifies. She climbs into the tub and sinks down into the warm bubbles.

Peder's fixing food in the kitchen and senses a sudden surge of energy. He senses a focused and irritated mind just as Liz paths him that someone just tried to port into Phoenix's apartment, but their porting shield rebuffed them. Before he can react, he hears wood splintering as the front door is ripped from its hinges. He ports to the bathroom. Phoenix screams in reaction, the bathroom door is flung open and ripped from its frame. A strange man in fatigues is standing there, fangs bared. Peder acts quickly, fight-or-flight instincts kicking in. He chooses flight, grabbing Phoenix by the wrist and porting them both to his bedroom at Liz's home. Phoenix is lying on his bed, soaking wet, naked, covered in rapidly dissolving bubbles, and still screaming.

"*Hush*, Phoenix! You're *safe!* I ported us out of there." He says, lying down next to her and cradling her in his arms, trying to soothe her. There's urgent banging on his bedroom door, making her flinch and cling tightly to him, but it's not the attacker, it's Liz. "Is she alright, Peder? I sent a team in, but he's fled."

"We're fine. The attack shook her badly, but she'll be okay. Can she borrow some clothes and a towel? She was bathing when it went down." He asks his sister, turning to Phoenix, and reassuring her, "It's Liz, we're at *her* place. He can't get you here." He rocks her gently until her shaking subsides.

She pulls back slightly, looking him in the eye. "That man, he's like you! He had *fangs!* Who is he?" She asks, still trembling.

"That'll take some explanation, but he's the reason I've been pushing you to let me turn you. We had reason to believe you might be in danger from him or one of his compatriots, but you are safe here." He says and looks down at her neck, moving her hair away from her neck where he'd bitten her. "You really do heal *fast* for a human." He says, noting the only thing left of his bite marks from earlier today are pale, pink splotches.

Phoenix is about to demand further explanation when there's a faint knock on the door and Peder hears Kari's calm voice. "I've got some clothes and a towel for her. May I bring them in?"

Peder drags out a quilt and covers Phoenix with it. "Come in, Kari."

"I think these should fit her. I'll ask Amy to grab some of her clothes before they leave there. She and her guys are attempting to track him but are also securing her place. He broke the inner frame on her front door, so they're fixing it first, but will send in a team later to fix the bathroom door. They had to tinker with a rather nosy neighbor's memory, as well. She came out to see what the commotion was." Kari explains, pathing to Peder, *How much does she know? Have you told her about the Naqam yet?*

No, not yet. I was planning to tell her after we ate, kind of hoping it could be a feather to tip the scales, but he attacked before I could. He paths, still rocking Phoenix gently. He feels her slowly relax now that the crisis has passed.

I'd say it'll be more like a lead weight on the scale after this! I don't think you'll have any trouble getting her to understand the danger she's in. Kari paths, but says aloud, "Phoenix, if you need anything, just say so. Liz had to go out, but I'll be here." Kari leaves the room, closing the door to give them privacy.

Peder uses one hand and pulls the towel and clothes closer. He lets the damp quilt drop to the floor and uses the towel to dry any remaining moisture from her skin. Phoenix has entered a state of mental numbness, a protective psychological reaction to trauma. "Let's get you dressed." He helps her, as she's too stunned to make the effort. He gets her settled on his bed and then curls up behind her, holding her close, using his abilities to push her into slumber. They'll have much to talk about when she wakes but now is not the time.

TIPPING POINT

Phoenix sleeps several hours, as she is overwhelmed. When she finally wakes, Peder is lying next to her, reading his tablet. She opens her eyes, yawns, and slowly stretches, looking around her. She knows where she is, and yet, how she got here is a bit of a blur.

Peder reaches down and takes her hand, saying, "How're you feeling?"

"Overwhelmed is the understatement of the century!" She slowly sits up and leans against the headboard, moving lethargically.

"Are you hungry? I can go get...." He asks, but she cuts him off.

"No, not hungry. What the *hell* happened? Who was that guy?" She asks.

"I didn't want to tell you about him until it was necessary. I've been planning to ask you to join me for a while now, but because of him, his people, I had to rush things." He admits, quietly.

"*His* people? Is there another group of vampires out there you *haven't* told me about?" She asks. He senses the strain and fear in her eyes and mind.

He shifts to face her, taking both of her hands in his. "Not exactly. There's a covert, militant group in Israel that recently found out about my people. They think we're 'the bad guys' and have declared war on us. They stole a list of people who are genetically compatible from our computers and have been abducting people on that list for the last week. We assume they are turning them to use as weapons against us."

This revelation makes her question if she can trust him. "Why do they *think* you're the *bad guys?*" She eyes him warily.

"In part, because people automatically fear what they don't understand. Beyond that, they *believe we bombed* Jerusalem. I can tell you, firsthand, that we did not, even though we *were* there." He steels himself to recount the basics of that night; a night he wishes he *could* forget forever!

"You mean you *were* there?" She asks, wide-eyed.

"*Yes...* we, as a people, were there, as was I. About 5000 of us were there. Some of our people who have precognitive abilities foresaw it, though the details were unclear. We spent months trying to determine what they were seeing, where it would be, and how to stop it. Unfortunately, it wasn't until it was imminent that we knew what was going to happen, and we sent our people to search for the bomb, as well as help evacuate, in case we couldn't stop it. We sent others to cities around the world that were targeted, but their bombs were incomplete. Only the one in Jerusalem was complete and armed, with a timer set to go off with the rest of them at a future date." He explains, pausing, as painful memories lash him from their hiding places.

"Can't you tell them you were trying to stop it?" She asks.

"They don't believe us. To them, we're monsters, so, *must* be guilty. They had two of our people in custody. One was a woman who ported into an underground tomb as the bomb blast hit, and the other was Marc." He pauses, giving her time to react.

"*Tess's* Marc?" She asks, eyes wide.

"Yes. He told them the truth, but they didn't believe him and tortured him for what they wanted to hear. To them, we're *demons*."

"You're *not* a demon!" She pauses as something occurs to her. "Marc's one of you? What about *Tess*?"

"*Both* are like me, as are others you know; but the who's who of Aparakind is not important right now, keeping you *safe* is." He swallows anxiously, and she notices him trembling. "The reason I know we were there to help, is that I'm the one who *found* the bomb. I suppose, we were partially to blame, but not because we *intended* to set it off." He says; his eyes haunted by his memories. "*No one* foresaw that the terrorists installed a proximity trigger. As soon as I got within a few feet, a fifteen second countdown began. I warned everyone telepathically to port out, but many didn't react in time. I started to but was partially caught by the blast. Because I wasn't totally there, however, I... I... was thrown clear, but severely injured and went into stasis... what humans would call death, except we recover. About three hundred or so others were in the same boat as me. Phoenix, we lost around 3000 of our people that night trying to save humans, but *these people* insist we are the villains because of *what* we are!"

"How could you survive being at ground zero?" She asks, shocked.

"I know this sounds like a copout, but the how is complicated. I'll explain it when you understand more. Had I not been partially ported out, I would have been vaporized like so many others that night." He pauses, closing his eyes for a second. "I'm sorry, this is still hard for me to talk about, but that's the accident I told you about. That's why I've been staying with Liz and Kari. Being alone in my home is difficult, as I was alone, for weeks, when I revived; slipping in and out of consciousness." He explains.

She leans over and pulls him into an embrace. They spend several minutes that way, just being there for each other. When he regains his composure, he continues.

"The group is called the *Naqam,* and what they want is in their name, *vengeance* against us." He looks up and into her eyes. "It wasn't a gas main explosion that took our building down, it was *them.* They broke in and stole a list of random names of 362 compatible people, worldwide. We recently discovered that compatible people have been disappearing, but it wasn't until yesterday we decoded the encrypted file found on our off-site server. At least half of the first thirty on the list have gone missing." He pauses, then says, "Your name is number 33 on the list. That's why he was there tonight. He was there to take you back to wherever they're hiding, where they would have turned you and psychologically manipulated you into a soldier for their cause."

All the color drains from her face as she realizes how close they came to nabbing her. "So, that's why you were pushing me to decide?" She asks.

"Yes, I didn't want to frighten you with all of this. I wanted you to choose to be with me because you *really want* to be, but now that they came for you, you need to know everything." He says as he caresses her hand slowly.

She sinks back against the headboard, processing it all. "Will turning me make me safe from them?"

"We *believe* so." He says.

"*Just* believe?" She inquires, wondering if he's still holding back.

"We can't be 100% certain; which is why we're doing our best to make *all our people* safe. We must track down all the remaining people on that list and protect them; as you can imagine, you were my personal priority." He explains. "I planned to turn you when you're ready, but this forced my hand."

"Are you going to turn me, even if I don't want to be one of you?" She asks, knowing that he'd promised not to turn her against her will.

He pauses, trying to find the right way to articulate himself. "If it's the only way to save you, I believe, I *would*." He says, and they both turn as the door to his bedroom opens.

Liz is there, looking haggard. "And if he *doesn't*, then I *will*. I can't let anyone else in my care become victims to these people. I'm the one who told Peder he needed to do it *now*. If you want someone to *blame*, blame *me*. He wanted to give you time and let you choose this because you *want* to be *with* him." Liz explains.

Phoenix looks back and forth between the siblings settling her focus on Peder. "I *want* to be with you, and if it has to be done *now*, I'd rather *you* to do it."

He closes his eyes and sighs in relief, then scoops her up in a big hug, finally leaning in and kissing her. She doesn't fight it, but returns the kiss with fervor, finally having decided. Part of her always knew she'd end up with him from the moment she discovered what he is. She just had to be certain she was doing this for the right reasons, and not because she wanted her fantasy life to be real.

FULL ALERT

A COUPLE OF HOURS EARLIER

Now that Phoenix is safe in Sanctuary, Liz returns to coordinate the search-and-protect operation being carried out by her people. Thankfully, the people on the stolen list were from the viable potentials server, including regular potentials, Lost Missioners, and some were from the 'misfiled potential' list. Luckily, Tess, Sue, or Kari have recently reviewed and approved them as psychologically viable. Unfortunately, a few of those on the 'misfiled list' are older and some have families. However, there's a good chance they'll be able to transform most of them and bring them into the fold without too much difficulty.

Assimilating so many at once is the hard part. Amy's teams around the world, together with other Apara operatives, are searching for the potentials on the *Naqam's* list. Tess and Marc are locating them digitally and looking for those who have left no digital footprints in the last week. The number reported as missing persons, worldwide, is up to twenty-two, and they are all in the first forty names on the list. The *Naqam* are using the list as an order of abduction, systematically finding, abducting, and delivering potentials to be transformed. We believe they didn't expect us to discover the list of potentials they stole, as they assumed they'd destroyed the server along with the building.

The Apara must track the potentials and bring them in, creating their own 'missing persons' mess, but the *Naqam* are working quickly, and the only way to ensure the safety of these potentials is to bring them to Sanctuary. There's not enough room in the dorms at Medical, but there are storage buildings nearby. These buildings are used to house various objects and materials that the

Apara have acquired over the years, including art, antiquities, precious metals, stones, and other items of value that can be sold or traded when the Apara need money in the real world.

This is often the source of previously unknown works of art showing up on the market after being stored in Sanctuary for years or even centuries. Proceeds from such liquidations are invested and hidden around the world to provide the funds they need to operate their business fronts, covert operations, and their own personal lives.

They've emptied one of these buildings temporarily; its items are consolidated elsewhere to create an interim shelter for the hundreds of potentials they must bring in. Many of them are fully prepped and can be shown the subliminal images that will bring forth their understanding of what is happening; however, there are around forty Lost Mission potentials on the list, who will be harder to placate after their abductions. Susan Burns and those she's been training as counselors are working to ease these potentials in and deal with this abrupt change in their lives.

Liz calls a meeting with her inner circle to get a status report for this operation. Tess, Marc, Sue, Amy, Colin, and Niall are all there with her in an office within the interim facility. So far, there are about 87 potentials at the facility being settled in as best as possible.

Liz looks and feels exhausted but must get everyone through this. Hers may not be the biggest center by any measurement, but that's by choice. She is part of the upper echelon of all Apara due to her age and early status as a successful recruiter and organizer.

She chose Asheville because the mountains remind her of her home in Norway, and she does not like large metropolitan cities like Los Angeles or New York, except for an occasional visit or shopping trip. Now, not only have her center and people been attacked, but their attempt to stop their enemy was incomplete, and the fanatics are now knocking at their proverbial door once again. As far as she knows, the *Naqam* do not know about their other centers around the world, and she hopes it stays that way. They could only connect Alyona to her and Marc as they'd coordinated the Jerusalem mission to stop the bomb, and by a coincidence, Charlie was the missing link that helped them connect them to Inspiration, Inc.

If the Apara can't stop them permanently, Inspiration, Inc. may need to disappear, and come back somewhere else. She doesn't want to leave the Asheville area. Her true home is in Sanctuary, but she's gotten used to the people, community, feel, and beauty of Asheville. It is as much a home to her as her home in the Nordic region of Sanctuary. She really doesn't want to go dark and relocate, using new identities, as well as a new business front.

She's facing some of her closest family, friends, and confederates among the Apara, knowing there's a chance that they may have to split up and reinvent themselves if they can't eliminate this threat against them.

She sits down with the others and clears her throat. "Alright, let's make this fast. The more time we spend here, the less we're getting done. How are we doing finding and bringing people in?" She asks, her eyes are weary and her voice more subdued than usual.

Tess speaks up. "There are likely more that have been taken than reported. At least eight have been completely silent on their social media this week, when they have otherwise been active regularly. I've made a list for Amy's people to double check, but I'm assuming they've been taken."

"I agree with Tess, which brings us up to thirty-one missing potentials we must assume will be turned by the *Naqam*." Marc says as he holds Tess's hand.

"Amy, what about your teams? I see they've found a fair number so far. Are there any you couldn't trace?" Liz inquires, dreading more bad news.

"Yes, I'm afraid so. We ported into their residences and in one, there were signs of struggle, and in a couple of others, there was either food or lukewarm coffee left out that the subject left behind when taken. Our advantage is that we have images of these people, and more Apara to search for them. I'm hoping we can rescue at least 300 out of the 362, but that still leaves them with a sizeable pool of rogue Apara they can use against us, or even other countries." Amy suggests, knowing that everyone has been so focused on these people being used against them, that they've likely ignored the other possibility. These people could become potent weapons against the enemies of Israel, or even unstoppable assassins should they go that route.

Liz pinches the bridge of her nose as her stress level rises. "Marc, can you coordinate with our precogs to watch for assassination premonitions? Amy's got a very good and distressing point. Apara spies can traverse borders in the blink of an eye, get past security measures, and are stronger and certainly able to kill, especially if their subconscious preconditioning is overridden by militant and fanatical brainwashing. See if we can get any of our field ops to infiltrate the immediate circles of world leaders that may be at risk." She suggests.

Colin and Niall both inform her that there're an additional 43 of the listed potentials already placed in other centers, and they'll push up their planned transformations.

"Niall, how's Callie doing with her portal making ability?" Liz enquires.

He raises one eyebrow and frowns. "It's been a bit wonky since the rescue; harder to control, but we're working on it, why?"

"It's a useful skill to have available, especially if we find their new base and need a quick exit." Liz sighs.

"Liz?" Tess inquires. "How's Phoenix?"

"Sleeping things off for now, but she's safe. I think the attempted abduction was the last straw. She was overwhelmed and distraught when they arrived last night but hopefully will be better when she wakes. Speaking of which, I need to get back there in case Peder needs some backup when she wakes." She nods to everyone and ports out, arriving back home, only to hear Peder and Phoenix talking. She enters the room saying: "And if he doesn't, then I will...."

DEEP INSIDE

THE PERIOD AFTER THE DESTRUCTION
OF THE ORIGINAL NAQAM BASE.

After the *Naqam's* original base in the Judaean Desert was destroyed, The Apara hoped the threat was over. Even if any of the rogue Apara survived the explosion and subsequent collapse of the base, they would not heal unless extricated from the rubble; they would end up in indefinite stasis.

No one knew that when the attack began, Uri Jabarin, two of his scientists, a few human soldiers, and two of their Apara, including Elias, withdrew to a secure, reinforced bunker to direct their own forces in the battle. When the explosives were dropped down the elevator shaft, their bunker was shaken as well, causing a partial collapse. One scientist and two soldiers were killed, while Uri was severely injured. The two rogue Apara ported survivors to safety, and Uri to a military hospital in Tel-Aviv.

They also salvaged an emergency backup drive for the base, including scientific data and plans for various anti-Apara technology, as well as a copy of the purloined database files with lists of potentials they could use to rebuild their vampire army. It, and a good bit of groveling to Mossad, was enough to salvage their operation. Uri spent five weeks making plans for reconstruction from his hospital bed. He lost an eye and one leg because of the cave-in.

During this time, Uri also searched for a new location for their secret base. This time, it will be deep inside Mount Arbel, near the Sea of Galilee. The Caves of Arbela are a historic location where the Jewish people have defended themselves. With the help of modern satellite technology, the *Naqam* locate additional caverns deep inside the mountain no human, or Apara, has ever laid foot in. The two surviving Apara ported in and found an extensive network of stable caverns with freshwater springs. They create access tunnels from near the sea to the caverns. They work as quickly as possible to strike their enemy before they realize they weren't completely obliterated. The mountain and the Caves of Arbela are tourist attractions, giving them cover for the work being done.

Uri believes no one will expect them to rebuild under a tourist destination. Their rogue Apara ported materials and equipment directly into the caverns, hiding much of their operation. Once they had a proper containment center built, they used the list to collect the few remaining regional potentials to increase their numbers, increasing the speed of their progress. Their vampire soldiers are several times stronger than any human, making construction work easier and faster with them taking part.

CURRENT TIME

By mid-July, they're ready for the next stage; increasing the number of vampire soldiers for a new campaign against the Apara. They send their transformees out to collect people on the worldwide list. They work down the list, bringing the abductees back to the base inside Mt. Arbel for transformation and conditioning.

The new base contains buildings inside their caves, as Uri does not like the idea of living in a cold, damp cave with no amenities. They reinforced adjoining caverns with anti-teleportation and anti-ability technology to hold their newly transformed 'guests' until conditioning ensures their obedience and loyalty.

They've recruited additional scientists, as well as more human soldiers, but their primary goal is to create an army of loyal, vampire soldiers to use against the unsuspecting ones in Asheville. After all, they still need to hold a trial for the creatures, as they are certain The Apara were behind the destruction of their holy city, Jerusalem.

Deep inside the mountain, Uri is in his new office. It's a week since they've begun abducting compatible humans from around the world. So far, they've brought in thirty-four, but Uri wants as many as possible, knowing they'll need to overwhelm the Asheville Apara, if they are to capture them. Uri is determined to capture and try Marc Girard and Lissa Pedersen, who he insists are the ringleaders despite Marc's vehement denials while he was their prisoner.

Uri recoils when someone appears without warning in his office. He's terrified the Asheville Apara have found him, but it's only Elias, bristling with agitation. Uri jumps up out of his seat, losing his balance due to his new, prosthetic leg. "Elias! You *know* better than to teleport directly into *my* office!" He bellows, hand on his sidearm in case it was one of the Asheville Apara coming to assassinate him. The gun contains bullets with the special deuterium compound.

"Sorry, sir, but under the circumstances...." He says, but Uri cuts him off.

"What could possibly justify your actions? I *nearly* shot you!" He says, settling back into his chair.

"*Sir*, I apologize, but my last target was *protected*." Elias reports.

"*Protected*? What the Hell do you *mean*, *protected*?" Uri asks as though Elias is spouting nonsense.

"Sir, I tried to teleport in, but was *blocked* from the location. They had some kind of anti-port technology installed on my target's home! So, I *broke* down the front door. I could sense the target, so went for her. She was bathing, sir, but when I broke into the bathroom, one of *them* was there! A tall, blonde man was protecting her. He bared his fangs at me, grabbed the woman by the wrist, and teleported out!" Elias recounts, afraid of retribution by Uri for his failure.

"*Damn!*" Uri says, pounding his fist on the large wooden desk. "That would suggest they know of our plans. Or it could just mean they know compatible humans are *disappearing*. Hmm...." Uri says, leaning back in his chair to think.

Elias relaxes a notch, now that Uri's anger isn't directed at him. Uri has used the deuterium compound their scientists created not only for torture, but punishment, and he does *not* wish to be on the receiving end of that! Elias had been part of the early testing of the compound, before they'd made it more potent and weaponized it. It was bad enough when it was a prototype formula. He has no desire to experience the enhanced formula.

"Tell the others to arm themselves with deuterium darts and increase their efforts to secure the compatible humans! They should report to *you* immediately if they run into any problems! You will report any issues to *me directly*! We must work quickly! They can't possibly protect over 300 of these humans from us! Start choosing randomly as well. Perhaps that will make it harder to prioritize who they protect!" Uri practically snarls as he commands Elias.

Elias nods his head deferentially and vanishes.

LEAVING HUMANITY BEHIND

Liz is overjoyed her brother has finally found someone, and she truly wants to join him. "Peder, take her to Sara first. She needs to map out her altered DNA from Roulette before you turn her." She explains, but paths, *She'll give you a transformation kit for any contingencies.*

"Will do." He nods his head subtly in acknowledgement of her path.

"Who's Sara?" Phoenix asks.

"She's the head of our medical division. She needs to record the changes in your DNA from the Roulette Virus before I change you. It's standard practice with those who caught the virus." He says, making it sound like no big deal.

"Is there any danger?" Phoenix asks.

He smiles gently, pulling her up out of bed to face him. "You'll be fine." They port out and arrive in the large atrium lobby in Medical.

Phoenix looks around her in wonder at the tall windows and the flowering vines draped here and there in the high-ceilinged room. "Wow! Where is this place? Do people know about it?" She asks.

"My people do, but it's not where humans can find it." Peder says, cryptically.

"And where, exactly, would that be?" She asks, confused by his answer.

He guides her up the stairs toward the main floor of Medical and they walk toward Sara's office. "It isn't simple to explain, so if you're still overwhelmed, I'd rather wait until things calm down."

"*Come* on! *Tell* me!" She demands, and he pulls her aside to a bench in the corridor.

"Technically, we're not on your Earth. We're in a parallel reality where humans never evolved." He blurts out, not sure how else to explain it.

"What the *Hell*? How is *that* even possible?" She glares at him as though he has two heads.

"The 'how it's possible' part is going to have to wait, but please accept this much; there are an infinite number of parallel realities. This one was uninhabited by any truly intelligent life, so we made our home where we can get away from the random thoughts and emotions of undisciplined humans." He says, one eyebrow raised, almost daring her to berate him again.

"But *how* did *we* get here?" She asks, reeling in her frustration.

"There are two ways to get here. I can teleport, entering a membrane dimension between realities. I guess you could say this is our nearest neighboring reality. With a little know how, I can slide in from one reality, and re-emerge in the other. We also have technology that creates an inter-dimensional portal, between the two." He explains, taking her hand in his. "That's why *humans* can't find this place."

"Can the *others* come here? The ones you're protecting me from?" She inquires.

"No, not without being *taught* how. You're safe here." He explains and cups her face with one hand. "I'm *still* turning you. You can't just hide out here." He leans in and kisses her, stands, and pulls her up by one hand. "Come on, Sara's waiting."

She follows him quietly pensively. They get to Sara's office, but she comes out of it before they can knock. "About time you two got here! Come with me." She says impatiently and heads down the hall. Peder and Phoenix follow her to an examination room. "Have a seat." Sara says and begins scanning Phoenix with a gadget that transmits data to her tablet. She looks over Phoenix noting she's showing signs of stress. She turns to Peder, saying, "Give me a few minutes alone with her."

Peder nods and leaves despite a pleading look from Phoenix, who's not sure what to make of this strange little woman. Once he's out of the room, Sara looks at a rolling desk chair across the room and brings it to her telekinetically, settling in it, and facing

Phoenix. She lets out a sigh and then graces Phoenix with a large, Cheshire Cat grin. "Sorry for my abrupt behavior. I'm juggling multiple situations at once, including about three different people trying to talk to me telepathically. Having Peder hovering and worrying was *too* much!" She says, as if Phoenix should understand what she's talking about. "Now, I'm going to take a small sample of your blood and tissue so we can compare it to your original DNA and your eventual, fully transformed DNA. We've seen a few of those who had the virus last winter come through transformation with somewhat unexpected or stronger than expected abilities. I'm trying to track how the Roulette virus impacts transformation." Sara explains as she uses a tool like an infuser to withdraw blood. She takes out a small, straw-like device and holds it in front of Phoenix. "This will take a small, tissue sample. I'll numb any pain and then heal you up afterward, okay?"

"Yeah, I guess so." Phoenix says, debating whether to say anything about her own self-healing ability.

Sara puts the tip of the device up against her skin, and it takes a 6 mm circular sample of tissue from her forearm. Sara immediately covers it with a piece of gauze to stop the bleeding, intending to heal it as soon as she's placed the sample in a receptacle. When she pulls the gauze away, however, the wound is already healed, though some dried blood remains. "Huh! Liz told me you'd developed self-healing, but I didn't expect it to be so rapid. It's faster than some of our own!" She comments casually and makes a note in her tablet. "That's all I need from you! Do you have questions for me?" She asks, expectantly.

"Way too many, but I get the feeling Peder wants to get things moving." She says, unconsciously looking toward the door as if Peder might come barging in any second.

Sara chuckles. "He's waited for you for over 800 years, he can wait a few more minutes! He'll come back when I let him! I want to give you a chance to ask any questions you may have been hesitant to ask with him around."

"I guess, most of all, I'm just wondering what comes next? Can you tell me what to expect? Will I change a lot?" Phoenix asks in a rush, like if she doesn't blurt it all out, she won't be able to ask her questions.

"Physically, Peder will drink a large amount of your blood, and you'll feel like you're going to die, but you won't." Sara pauses, then grins. "Of course, in your case, that's not an issue! Then he'll give you his blood, which contains the activated virus in it. Once you're infected, it will spread to every cell in your body, rewriting your DNA. Then you will begin the physical transformation, and your other abilities will emerge, but you will not change as a person. You will still be you! You may experience flu-like symptoms, such as fever, and aches. Occasionally, some will experience seizures, but that's rare. However, none of it will do any *permanent* damage." Sara explains.

"I've been through pretty much all of that with the... what did you call it?" She inquires.

"The Roulette virus—because what ability it brings out in a human might as well be like playing Russian Roulette! It's a shot in the dark!" Sara explains kindly. "Most likely, it is an indicator of where your abilities may blossom once you're fully transformed." She explains.

"But I already heal quickly and come back from the dead! What more is there?" Phoenix asks.

"We'll find *that* out once you're fully transformed!" She grins enigmatically. "A lot depends on the source of your healing ability. We have biological regeneration on a cellular level, but...." She picks up her tablet and pulls up a chart with a wavelike pattern on it. "This is what my sensor picked up when the sampled spot on your arm healed. The pattern is not quite the same as our own, self-healing, but the pattern of the wave is closer to when we heal others. One is biological, the other is psychic based, if that makes sense."

"So, you're saying my mind is healing me, not my body? I'm confused!" She blurts out.

"It's not so important right now, but I suspect your abilities may be strong in the healing field, not just the self-healing field," Sara suggests.

"Are you saying I may be able to heal other people?" She asks, wondering if she understands the implications of what Sara said.

"Sweet child, we all can heal wounds, bites, or small injuries, but only some people are true healers." She says with a quirky smile and a glint in her eye. "Peder is getting anxious. You should go to him now. There is nothing to fear about becoming one of us, child. It is what you are *meant* to be." Sara guides Phoenix out to Peder, who's pacing the hallway impatiently. Sara pulls him aside and gives him a small pouch. "Use only if her fever rises above 102 or lasts longer than 36 hours." Sara instructs and walks away, saying out loud as she paths, "*Quiet*! I can only path with one person at a time!"

***

Peder turns to Phoenix with a smile, extending his arms in an invitation. One she gladly accepts as he enfolds her in his arms, but feeling that odd, queasy sensation, they've ported somewhere. This time, she opens her eyes and is in a darkened home. She sees silhouettes of furniture covered by sheets, the air is stale, and the house is chilly.

Peder says, "Sorry, I haven't been here in quite a while. I should've made it ready for you first, but as you know, it's been chaotic." He closes his eyes and a ceiling lamp with multiple bulbs comes to life over their heads. The lights are set into a ring of antiquatedly carved wood with Celtic-like patterns. Hearing her thoughts, he smiles. "Not Celtic, Viking, and originally, it held oil lamps, not bulbs. We're on the Sanctuary equivalent of the Southern Norwegian Coastline, so it's a lot cooler here than in Asheville." He says and pulls the sheet off a nearby table, shaking the dust out of it. He returns and wraps it around her. "It isn't much, but it will help until I get the fire going." He slips outside and returns a couple of minutes later, carrying a stack of split wood. He descends some steps into a sunken area around a stone fireplace, dumping the firewood in a hammered bronze kettle with intricate patterning all around it. He picks up a few pieces and tosses them in the fireplace, opening the flue with a wrought iron tool. He picks up a silver lighter from the mantle and some small, dry wood shavings, tossing them in the fireplace at the base of the logs, and lights the bone-dry kindling, starting a much-needed fire. "It'll take a while to warm up. This place has been sitting empty since Jerusalem." He explains.

"Is this your home?" She asks, looking around in wonder. The ceilings are high, but the center comes to a peak, with dark wooden beams coming up along the slopes and meeting in the center. The lamp hangs down from where the beams meet in the center.

"Yes, though I've only been back to grab a few things now and again while living with my sister and Kari." He says, looking around. "I'll be right back." He says and runs up a short, slate-covered stairway to a hallway about half a normal floor up. He comes back, arms filled with pillows and a couple of thick, down comforters. He lays out the comforters and pillows on the floor in front of the fire and motions for her to join him. "At least it's warm here." He says, reaching out a hand to her from the floor.

She slowly descends the steps and joins him, dropping the thinner sheet from her body as the warmth builds and radiates from the fireplace. She feels awkward, knowing what's coming, but sits, mesmerized by the popping pinewood and sparks rising up the flue. Still, she is quiet, unsure of what to say. She thinks, *Should I come up with some witty or wise words as the last thing I'll utter as a human, or should I just sit here and contemplate life?*

Peder shifts and puts his arm around her as they sit in front of the fire. "This is your home now, too. You can't go back to your apartment. They know where you live."

"Are you asking me to move in with you?" She asks, not entirely sure what to think.

"You're becoming my partner. I'm responsible for you, your safety, training, and keeping *you* out of *trouble*." He gives her a gentle smile. This has been my home for a very long time, and I've never shared it with anyone else, but you'll be my partner, so what is mine, is yours."

She's quiet, pondering this twist of fate. "I've dreamed about you asking me to move in with you or you with me, but somehow, this feels so final, more like we're getting married." She says as she rests her head on his shoulder.

"In a way, it is. We'll be together for at least ten years, though personally, I'm hoping for a lot longer than that. Taking on a partner is even more than a marriage, it's a responsibility, as well as an *honor* that you'll have me." He gives her a light kiss.

"This is all happening so quickly. Are you sure this is really what you want?" She asks, wondering why an 800-year-old 'vampire' would want someone like her.

"*Yes, this* is what I want. I want you to be part of my life for centuries to come." He insists, scanning her face, worrying she may be having second thoughts, but she just nods, and tips her head back, and to the side, letting him know she's ready.

"I guess we should get on with it?" She says, trying to sound both brave and matter of fact, as though this isn't a major turning point in her life.

He tilts her face so he can kiss her again, and then gently sinks his fangs in, drinking her into him so that the two truly become one. When he finishes, he caresses her cheek gently, then sinks his fangs into his own wrist, quickly moving it to her mouth. She takes it, willingly, and drinks. She's tired and weak but knows this is meant to be. She nods off on the layered, feather comforters with a feather pillow beneath her head.

Once she's sound asleep, Peder ports to his bedroom, strips the covers and sheets off everything, and clears the dust, preparing his bed for Phoenix and himself. He ports back and gently scoops her sleeping form into his arms, porting her to his bedroom, laying her carefully in his bed, and kissing her forehead lovingly. He places the small pouch of infusers and a cent-opal bracelet on his nightstand, ready to use, as needed. He crawls into his bed, exhausted, and falls asleep with his arm across her sleeping form.

SOMETHING NEW

The night passes with no sign of major distress. As the sun rises, Phoenix becomes restless, waking, stretching and yawning—she opens her eyes and feels well-rested. Everything looks brighter, more colorful, and crisper. While she rarely bothers with glasses, her eyesight was slightly blurry, but now, it's sharper than it's ever been. Peder rolled onto his other side during the night and is sleeping heavily, so he hasn't noticed Phoenix is awake. She rolls over and leans up against his back. "Peder, are you awake?" She says cheerily.

He opens his eyes, mind still slow with slumber, but realizes Phoenix is already awake, which seems odd to him. He rolls over and props himself up to look at her. "Are you alright?" He inquires, studying her. He can't see any signs of fever or malaise. She appears almost too well, as usually, transformees are weak until they feed and recover from the changes to their bodies.

"Yeah, I feel great! Sara made it sound like I should feel like I did last winter, but I don't." She says, grinning happily that she avoided a repeat of last December.

He rolls back and looks at his cell, then reaches over, and feels her forehead. "No fever, and it's only been about nine hours! I need to check your teeth."

She rolls her eyes but opens her mouth. He lifts her upper lip and feels around the gums above her teeth. "Your fangs *have* formed. This is quite odd. Everyone else like you took days to transform and had lots of discomfort, but not you...." He ponders.

"You mean others who had that virus?" She asks, being the only thing, she can think of.

"No, not exactly, though perhaps that played in. Are you hungry?" He asks, sitting up in bed.

She shrugs. "I wouldn't mind a little breakfast! Guessing you don't have anything to eat around here with the house being empty so long?"

He chuckles lightly. "No, there isn't, but that's not the *hungry* I meant! You should be feeling a need to feed, but you don't act like you're hungry at all."

Her eyes brighten with comprehension, and she says, *"OH! That* kind of *hungry!* I don't know, what should it feel like?"

His expression shifts from one of mild amusement to more serious. "Are you telling me you don't feel an instinctive need to feed?" He asks, concerned that something may have gone wrong with her transformation.

"I feel like I'm craving something, but it's not overwhelming. Are you saying it should be?" She wonders, picking up on his concern.

"Normally, yes, but you're *not* a normal case." He says without further explanation.

"If it's not because of that virus, maybe you need to fill me in." She gives him a skeptical look, wondering what he hasn't told her.

"You were born during a period where some unusual mutations occurred in children that usually manifest as strong or unique abilities when transformed. However, these transformees also usually have had longer and more difficult transformations than normal potentials." He explains, omitting the whole Benefactors part for the time being.

"I see. Maybe that other virus made it easier? Or maybe it didn't work?" She asks, beginning to wonder herself. *I don't feel very different. I feel good, though, and my senses seem more acute, so something's happened.* She thinks.

"Give me your hand." He says without further explanation. He holds her hand up to his nose and gets an odd expression. "I *need* to taste you." He says and gently bites into her wrist. He pulls back after a few seconds, with a look of consternation.

"*What*? Is something wrong?" She asks, picking up on his anxiety empathically.

"I'm not certain. You don't quite smell or taste right. It's like you're still partly human and your blood levels are much higher than they should be, which is probably why you're *not* hungry." He explains.

"But you said my fangs have formed. Am I or am I not one of you?" She grabs his hand and squeezes it anxiously.

"I think Sara needs to check you over. You're transformed in some ways, but not in others." He says, pathing to Sara, who cuts off conversations with two other people, and ports in with her scanner, startling Phoenix, who lets out a small squeak of a scream.

"One of these days, I'll get used to that!" She gasps out.

"You'll learn to sense when people port in," Sara remarks, then turns to Peder. "So, what's this house call for? Haven't you turned her *yet*?"

"Yes, Sara. I turned her last night, and she woke up on her own this morning, fangs formed, and feeling fine, but things are not quite as they should be." He says, wanting Sara's professional analysis.

"Not quite as they should be?" She eyes him suspiciously, but scans Phoenix again. It doesn't take long before they hear a gruff "Hm...." from Sara. "Very curious, indeed! The virus has finished and gone dormant in her bone marrow, but you are correct, Peder, this is not a *normal* transformation." She says.

"What's wrong with her?" Peder asks.

Phoenix's eyes grow wide, and she stares at him, then asks, "What do you mean, *wrong with me*?"

Sara sits down on the edge of the bed and addresses Phoenix. "Your transformation is atypical, but then again, very few of your generation have had completely normal transformations. However, your specific oddity is a first for me!" She says, pursing her lips. "That doesn't mean anything is *wrong*, but I must take some time to study your variations and understand what is happening." She says, then admonishes Peder. "*Stop* assuming the worst!"

"So, am I *alright*?" Phoenix asks.

"Yes, I believe so, but you are something new to us. While you have transformed, your body still produces some of its own blood, as a human would." She addresses Peder. "Therefore, she smells and tastes partially human. It also explains her higher blood levels and less hunger. However, what I don't know is if this is a transitional or a permanent difference." She focuses on Phoenix again. "Even if you're not hungry, make a habit of feeding every 2-3 days, just in case this is a temporary state."

"Why do you think this happened?" Peder asks.

"I don't know. Could be her LM potential status, could be Roulette! Could be a *combination*. I'll take new DNA and tissue samples and work with Isanda to get you some answers. Otherwise, she seems fine. Let me know if she has any trouble with her abilities or feeding." She says, takes new samples, and notes that she still heals up faster than most Apara. She nods to them and ports out.

Phoenix gets an odd expression and asks, "So, which is it? Am I one of you or not?"

He chuckles. "You're close enough for me!" He pulls her up and against him, kissing her. "However, you need to feed now." He puts his finger up to his mouth and pierces the tip with his fang.

He squeezes some blood out on the tip and waves it under her nose until she suddenly says, "*Ouch!* You made me bite my tongue!" She says with a lisp. She reaches up and feels her fangs with her fingers, making odd faces as she does.

"I guess that should answer your question. You've got the fangs, so you must be one of us!" He chuckles, then holds his wrist, soft side up, out to her. "Follow your instincts, gently bite down, and feed."

She does as he says and instinctively numbs the pain and draws a few mouthfuls before pulling back, saying, "That's all I want." She shrugs.

"Then how about some actual breakfast?" He laughs and pulls her close, porting her to Liz's kitchen.

"*Wow!* I didn't feel like puking this time!" She jokes.

"That's because your senses can cope with the sensory input while porting now. Human senses are slower and get overloaded. It's oddly akin to getting car sick, where your balance center perceives the movement, but your eyes don't, and it causes nausea." He explains. "By the way, we're back at Liz's. I'll go shopping later, now that we'll be living at my home." He pulls out various breakfast foods from the fridge and puts them on a tray.

"Ah, okay, that makes sense." She pauses. "So, I really am *one* of you?" She still needs confirmation, as it still seems unreal.

"Yes, Phoenix; now and *forever*!" He nudges her to go to the dining room.

"This seems so oddly normal that it's strange." She comments.

"What? Eating breakfast?" He chuckles.

"Yeah! So many of the stories have you guys not eating actual food." She says, almost embarrassed to even mention it.

"You'll find we're a lot more like humans than any of your stories, *kjære*. And apparently, *you*, even more so!"

PASSAGES

NIALL AND CALLIE

After leaving the meeting, Niall McFadden ports home to his partner, Callie. Callie is one of the coveted Lost Missioners, whose gifts are often unusually strong or unique. Callie's no exception! In fact, hers is one of the most unique they've seen. While all of them can port from one place to another, and some can even bring objects to them through a similar process, Callie creates physical portals from one place to another, and even between Sanctuary and Human Earth. She's been able to do small portals consciously, but under pressure, has shown greater talent. She created a portal out of a burning music venue that let everyone escape; though minds had to be wiped as she accidentally brought humans to Sanctuary.

When the Apara, including her partner, were trapped in their building in South Asheville, explosives ticking away in the building's basement, Callie created a physical portal, allowing them to escape the building and into her jewelry workshop. Only Marc Girard didn't come through the portal, as he got out of the building through a small access hatch to the roof and was subsequently captured by the *Naqam*.

Callie has been practicing creating larger portals ever since but can't find the energy to create anything larger than a couple of feet in diameter. Like cases of humans exhibiting extreme strength in a crisis, Sara suspects adrenaline acted like a battering ram for her abilities, opening large portals when needed. Both times she created a large, stable portal were high-stress events, which helped her focus, and boosted her energy needed to create and sustain them.

Today, however, Callie has a portal-free day and is working at her jewelry bench, creating some one-of-a-kind pieces. When she isn't working on her special ability, she focuses on her passion for her jewelry art. Niall willing, she's hoping to do a craft show soon, even though she doesn't need to sell her items to make ends meet. Rather, she enjoys the admiration and positive feedback showing off her work gives her, and she's built up a decent inventory.

Niall ports in behind her and begins massaging her shoulders. She doesn't even flinch when he ports in, as she's learned to sense his imminent arrival. "How'd the meeting go?" She asks not even stopping to turn off her torch and put it down.

"Can you stop what you're doing for a second?" He inquires seriously.

She cuts off the gas on her torch and hangs it in a little metal notch. She lets out a quick sigh and swivels to face him. "*Okay!* What's up?" She asks, giving him her attention.

"It's the *Naqam*. They're back and they're abducting potentials from that list they stole." He says.

"Oh, *no!* That's *horrible!* How many are missing?" She asks.

"Over thirty that we know of, which means they're trying to create an army to use against us." He says somberly.

"Does that mean we're in danger?" She asks, shifting anxiously.

"Me, more than you, I'm afraid. Everyone at Inspiration, Inc. is a target. Liz wants to work on tracking down their new headquarters and potentially do a pre-emptive strike." He says in a matter-of-fact way, but she senses he's more concerned than he's letting on.

She narrows her eyes and tries to read what he's hiding from her. She can tell he's holding something back, so is direct. "Okay, Niall, *spill!* What's this have to do with *me?*"

"Liz asked how your portal abilities are progressing. She hopes you'll be able to create an exit for us if we go in and can't port out on our own. She wants us to focus on creating stable portals large enough to send people through." He explains, reaching over and taking her hand.

"I'll try, but I'm not sure what I'm doing wrong! I know they say it has to do with my adrenaline levels, but it's not like I can just flip a switch and make it work!" She says. She's feeling discouraged by her repeated failures.

"I spoke to Sara and some of our trainers. They now think it's not as much the power issue as focus, control, and finesse. Adrenaline helps focus, but we can't always count on that. They suggested focusing on the smaller portals, learning to control them; size, where they go, duration, and so on. Once you can control the small ones and know how much energy you need, you should be able to open the larger ones accordingly. Right now, your adrenalin is like using a battering ram in a crisis, as opposed to unlocking and opening the door intentionally. Does that make sense?" He asks, stroking her back to ease her mood. "As to energy, there are other ways to source energy than adrenaline. For now, focus on control."

"Okay, let me finish up here, get some dinner, and we can work on it some before bed." She suggests.

"Are you up for Thai? I can port out and get some while you finish up." He grins, knowing she's got a soft spot for spicy food.

"Twisting my arm, huh? Go on! I need about an hour to finish." She gives him a soft smile, waves him off, and gets back to her work.

When she's done, she heads back to the house. Niall has put out all the boxes of Thai food on the table with serving spoons and set out two plates for them. When they're finishing up, Callie senses smug amusement coming from Niall.

"*What*?!" She asks emphatically, knowing he's up to something.

He grins mischievously. "I want to do an experiment, that's all!"

She narrows her eyes and glares at him. "Like what?"

He closes all the boxes that aren't empty, setting them in front of her, and puts an old tabletop, stand-alone mirror; the kind that has an ornate frame on a hinged base, in front of her.

"What the *heck* is that for?" She asks.

He gives her an impish grin. "It's a tool to help you focus and control your portal. Imagine the mirror is where the portal is going to be. Think of it like a frame for your portal!" He says.

"Exactly how am I supposed to do that?" She asks.

"Remember that old movie you insisted we watch... *Stargate*? Pretend the mirror is like a stargate. I want you to picture your portal where the mirror is. Keep it self-contained within the frame. No bigger and no smaller." He explains.

"Okay, what about the other end?" She asks.

"The fridge!" He says, as though it should be obvious.

"The *fridge?*" She asks, thinking, *that's a boring destination.*

"*Boring* is what you need right now. We know you can do it when you're stressed. This is about control. You must control the size, location, and destination. Relax and focus on the mirror. Picture the reflective surface starting to shimmer and change into a portal. Take it slowly. You're not in any rush. It's *not* a crisis." He says.

She focuses, staring at the mirror in its frame. She pictures contortions appearing in the reflection, as though it's rippling like physical waves on water, and before long, small contortions appear. Her mind is oddly quiet, thinking without words, as she pictures the ripples and waves spreading out to fill the mirror, but staying within the confines of the frame. As they move to the outer part of the frame, the inner part clears, but instead of the mirror, she sees a dark space that gets lighter as the portal allows light from the dining room in. The top shelf in the refrigerator is right in front of her.

"You've got it! Now hold it open and stable! I'm going to reach through the portal and put the leftovers away. *Don't* let the portal close or I may have to *grow* back my hand!" He snickers as Callie gets annoyed and the portal wavers. "Uh-uh! Hold it steady! Everything else is just a distraction." He says, and the portal stabilizes. The waves and contortions vanish except for a small margin at the edge of the frame. Niall takes each of the closed food boxes and reaches through the portal, putting them away. When he's done, he says, "Now, let it close, smoothly, and evenly."

He watches as the image from the fridge wavers and the mirrored surface returns, contorted and rippled at first, but soon becomes the smooth, silvered glass of the mirror. Callie lets out a long, slow breath before exclaiming, "I did it! I *really* did it!"

"*Yep*! Now, that's *all* we're going to do tonight! We'll try some more tomorrow and work on widening the portal once you have complete control over small ones like this, okay?" He asks. She throws her arms around his neck, elated to finally have some measurable success.

"That was amazing!" She says, exhilarated by her success.

"I've got some other work to do now, so, if you're up to it, you can go back to your jewelry." He says, and she practically skips out the door and back to work.

She feels better than she has in ages, so pulls out some high-end turquoise cabs she cut from material bought at the Tucson gem show in February. Luckily, she went a few days before Inspiration Inc's building was destroyed, or she wouldn't have gotten to go. She'd wanted to go ever since she started making jewelry but could never afford the trip. Niall went with her to keep her from unconsciously porting things she liked home to her studio.

The Apara have few limits on their available funds, so she bought a nice supply of gemstones and rough that she could never have afforded as a struggling, human artist. She's also able to work in mixed metals and gold; something she could never do while human. She makes several asymmetrical earring sets using her turquoise cabs, several in silver and one in gold with opal accents. She takes advantage of her new telekinetic skills to help her fold the silver over the stones to set them.

Niall paths her around midnight that he's going to bed. She acknowledges but lets him know that she's on a roll, and she'll join him in a while. By the time she's done, it's nearly 3 a.m. and she realizes she should get some rest, so heads to bed, but feels jittery and leans against the wall. She thinks, Oh, *crap! I used a lot of energy making that damn portal!* She detours to the kitchen and opens the fridge, noting the neatly stacked boxes of Thai food Niall put away through her portal earlier that night. She opens a crisper drawer in the fridge and pulls out a bag of blood, sighing. She uses a knife to cut off a corner of the bag and downs it quickly, feeling her adrenalin rush from earlier crash and burn. She tosses the empty bag into the trash and trundles off to bed, almost tripping over her own feet on the way.

She quietly crawls into bed, but Niall wakes and checks the time. "Do I have to compete with your stones and jewelry to get some time with my partner?" He jests.

"Sorry, hon, I got into hyper-focus mode and made several pairs of earrings. You know how I get when the creative urge strikes." She yawns and curls up on the bed, facing him. He does likewise and they fall asleep, hands clasped and foreheads touching.

She thinks about her success creating a portal as she drifts off. As sleep overtakes her, and her dream mind takes over, she finds herself sitting in the flower garden outside of their home in Sanctuary, enjoying a beautiful, sunny day. Soon, the sky clouds over with turbulent, dark clouds, and the wind rises, whipping around, keening. The keening becomes a whispering voice calling her name. She focuses on the beckoning voice and follows it, seeking its source.

She enters unfamiliar territory where the grass is high and dry, almost scorched. It comes up to her chest as she wades through it, searching for the mysterious voice. There's no sign of her home, or anything but more tall grass everywhere she looks, blowing in the wind.

She stops and listens again, turning toward a half-heard, whispered siren's song. There's something in the distance and she walks toward it. As she approaches, she can see it's a full-length version of the mirror she'd used earlier in portal practice. She walks toward it, seeing her reflection, but something is off. She sees her own reflection calling to her, practically screaming and banging on the glass as though she's trying to break through the pane from the other side. She gazes in shock as her reflection looks worn and haggard. Her hair is cut short and ragged as opposed to her normal, medium-length, bouncy curls. She looks like she's been in a battle and lost. The sky behind her is dark and foreboding, and the tall grass looks scorched.

Tentatively, she puts her hands on the mirror, her reflection matches her motion, but her mirror-self's fingers emerge from the mirror and interlace with her own, sending her into a panic. The strong fingers of her reflective-self hold her hands in place. In a voice rife with desperation, her reflection says, "Find me, Callie! *Find me!*"

Her panic slips into high gear as the dried grass swirls and rises from the ground into a grass tornado. Her hands slip free, the cyclone thins, and she's back in the garden, alone except for a tuft of singed grass at her feet.

She starts awake with such force that Niall sits bolt upright and turns on the light. "What is it? Are you alright?" He asks.

Callie is soaked in cold sweat, disoriented, and her heart is pounding. She's breathing rapidly and shallowly, almost unaware of what's happening around her.

Niall moves in front of her and grasps her shoulders, shaking her. "Callie! *Callie!*"

Her eyes focus on his, her body crumples in his arms in exhaustion, and her breathing slows. He pats her back and rocks her, knowing something upset her. "What is it, *mo chridhe*"

She doesn't speak immediately, but eventually looks him in the eye. "I had a *horrific* nightmare!" She says and recounts it to him in detail.

"Any idea what it might mean?" He asks.

"I don't know, hon, I just don't know! It felt like I met some nightmare version of myself." She says, visualizing it as clearly as she had in her dream.

"Well, I doubt it was precognitive. That's your weakest ability." He admits. "But it certainly is an odd dream. Think you can get back to sleep?"

"Maybe, I don't know...." She says, sounding anxious.

He scoots back over to his side of the bed, lies down, and motions for her to join him. "Put your head on my chest." He suggests, and she curls up against him, clinging to him like the contact can ward off some ghost of herself. He holds her, sending soothing energy, willing her to sleep, and not to dream. It takes nearly half an hour, but she sleeps again, and Niall has the oddest feeling her dream is more than a nightmare.

INSIDE INFORMATION

Liz is in her office, stressed over the latest turn of events. She needs first-hand information on the inner workings of the *Naqam*, so calls in Dr. Hannah Zelkind, Charlie, and Janna for a meeting. Hannah and Charlie are the only two humans privy to the inner circle of the Apara, and both have proven themselves trustworthy.

Liz is wary of Janna, as she was with the *Naqam* quite a while, and there's a slim chance she could be a sleeper agent, conditioned to blend in and feed them information, so has held her at a distance from any Apara business, and has not allowed her to be trained more than necessary. However, Liz needs to know all she can about the *Naqam* and what they may be up to.

Amy ports in with the three of them in tow, motioning them into the office. Liz sits at the head of the meeting table. There's a large tray of Norwegian-style, open-faced sandwiches on the table with plates for each of them.

A few seconds after they close the door, Tess and Marc port in. "Sorry we're late! I've been updating the missing potentials list. They've gone random on us now, so we're spread thin trying to protect the remaining ones." Tess says, sitting down, and snagging a couple of gravlaks sandwiches before they all disappear. Marc settles in beside her, nodding to Liz in acknowledgement.

Liz looks from person to person around the table, then says, "As you may have gathered from Tess's comments, we have a problem. The *Naqam* are not as vanquished as we believed. We don't know where they are now, but we do know they've been abducting potentials from the list they stole from our server. Charlie, Janna, and Hannah, I *need* your help. I need you to tell us everything you can about the *Naqam*, especially about Uri Jabarin." She asks Hannah, "I know you've been working with our people on the weapons and tools they've developed to use against us, and I appreciate that, but anything you can tell us about Jabarin and Elias could give us insight into what they may be planning." She pulls up a sketch on her tablet. "This is the man who tried to abduct one of our potentials that got away. We believe it's Elias?" She hands it to Hanna Zelkind, who gets a rather disgusted expression.

"Yes, that's him. He was the first we were able to transform, and Uri's personal protector. They must have been together when you attacked and gotten him out." Hannah suggests handing the tablet back to Liz.

"I get the impression you're not particularly fond of this man?" Liz asks.

"No, he and Uri are quite similar. Both are egocentric and enjoy having power over others. He lacks any sign of genuine compassion. In fact, I would say that both men lean toward fanaticism with a streak of sadism and paranoia!" She says emphatically.

Liz makes notes and says, "Yes, that's problematic. Had *we* been evaluating Elias for transformation, he would never have made the cut. We only select those who will use their abilities responsibly and ethically. Do they do any kind of psychological screening before they transform someone?" Liz asks, concerned, and suspects Hannah will confirm her fears.

"The only thing important to Uri and the other scientists is finding people who are compatible. They put everyone they transform through an intense program of conditioning. To Uri, their psychological suitability is a moot point. They break them and turn them into weapons to be wielded by those in charge. They obey and act as ordered." She explains.

Tess is upset by this and motions to speak. When Liz nods to her, she says, "Liz, I know we left the ones from the other base behind, but we're talking at least thirty or more potentials, and all *promising* ones. I don't feel comfortable writing them off as casualties of war! This isn't their fault! There must be some way we can bring them in and give them the chance they deserve."

Liz nods subtly to herself and replies, "I agree, Tess. I've been considering sending a team in to recover any of the viable ones from the Judean Desert base. However, before we do that, we need to know what we're dealing with. Hannah, do you know anything about the process they use to condition them?"

"I know some of their techniques. With human subjects, they use a combination of drugs and more traditional stimulus/response conditioning. They tried to condition early transformees while still human but transforming them broke the conditioning. They switched to transformation first, and then conditioning, but the usual drugs don't work, so they use a variant of the deuterium compound to induce pain in the process, relieving the pain when they comply. Uri has been known to use other forms of pain induction, including electricity, heat, and sonic, since Apara hearing is quite sensitive. I heard him discussing how they could use such stimuli without worrying about doing permanent damage since your people regenerate and heal quickly but still feel pain." Hannah explains.

Liz sits back in her chair, controlling the anger raging inside her for what Uri and his people are doing to her potentials, but after a minute, speaks in controlled tones. "Alright, I'll get Sara to make up neutralizer darts. We'll need a lot of them, and some kind of dart gun if possible. Amy? Can you work with Sara on adapting them to use with a tranq gun?"

"Yeah, I can do that, though we're going to have to do some practice. I'd suggest aiming twice. Once when you see them, but they'll likely port out, so we should be ready to reorient, and shoot as soon as they port back in. It's like what Tess and I worked on with aiming her blasts." Amy explains.

Liz nods, "We may also want to look into other delivery methods, as it will be hard to hit them all with individual darts." She says, then turns back to Tess. "Inform Sue so she and her team will be ready. We'll need to deprogram any we capture. See if any of them have experience with that sort of thing, and if not, they should do the research. We must be sure we can trust them before we allow them into our society." She sighs, then looks at Janna and Charlie. "I'll need you two to make a report of any routines or observations you can give me about Uri, Elias, and the old base." She pauses. "Janna, how are you holding up in the dorms?"

"Okay, Ma'am. I've mostly been hanging out with Charlie there or working out at the rehab gym in Medical. They've been providing me with bagged blood, though Charlie's offered as well, but I just feel weird about that. I'm still adjusting, I guess." She explains, still nervous with so many 'vampires' around her, even though she is one herself now.

Liz spoke with Hannah earlier about Janna. Hannah explained that Uri didn't condition Janna once turned but mentioned that Janna was the one that informed Uri Charlie was having doubts about his mission, and whether the Apara, and specifically, Amy, were a danger or not.

Liz finishes up the meeting by saying, "Alright everyone, you have your tasks to do, so I'll wrap things up for now. Janna, could you stay?"

Janna looks awkward at being singled out, but says, "Yes, Ma'am." And tells Charlie. "I'll be along shortly."

Everyone else leaves and Liz closes her door so she can speak with Janna privately. Liz sits and smiles kindly at the young Apara woman. "I wanted to talk to you privately, as what I need to ask you about would be difficult for Charlie to hear." Liz says and pours herself a fresh cup of tea, then motions with the pot to inquire if Janna would like any, but she just shakes her head. "I understand you were the one who told Jabarin Charlie was having some second thoughts about us?"

Janna's face blanches and her heart rate speeds up, but she answers Liz truthfully. "You're wondering what kind of hold Uri has on me, aren't you?" Liz nods. "They never *conditioned* me like the other transformees, nor when I was human, though he planted a seed in my mind that Amy might be bewitching him. I thought I was *protecting* him from Amy and your people, Ma'am."

Liz nods, saying, "First, call me Liz, *not* ma'am. We're informal here, and I'm old enough that calling me ma'am makes me feel my *real age!*" She chuckles and takes a sip of her tea. Liz can tell from reading Janna that she's speaking the truth. "And how do you feel about us now?" She inquires.

"Fine, I guess. You've been kind to me, and to Charlie, despite everything." She pauses and Liz senses lingering anger in her mind. "I told Uri I didn't consent to being transformed, and that as a US Citizen, he didn't have the right to force that on me, but he did it *anyway*. That was when he informed me both Charlie and I were listed as deceased after the cave in, so our nationality didn't matter, as we were dead as far as the US Government was concerned! I had a horrible transformation, though I understand Marc told Hanna how to deal with that. I have *no* reason to see any of you as my enemy, especially after I learned the true story behind Jerusalem." She admits.

"*Good!* Then, I think it's time we get you up to speed! Are you okay with working with Amy on combat skills?" Liz asks.

"I guess so, though I was a medic more than a soldier." She reminds Liz.

"I get that, and I'll make sure you get some healing training and how to use our medications. When we go in, it'll be helpful to have you there in case any of us get hurt in the skirmish." Liz pats her on the arm. "I'd like you to visit Sara at Medical and see if she can analyze your DNA. You're one of the Lost Missioners. You were born with mutations which will eventually give you some enhanced abilities, though we need to figure out what they are. The easiest will be to start with a DNA mapping and analysis."

"I can do that. I'll get Amy to help me set that up." She says, relieved it wasn't something more dramatic Liz wanted to talk about.

"You'd better catch up with Charlie out in the lobby. I can feel him getting anxious from here." Liz smirks, guiding Janna to the door. "By the way, if I haven't said it before now, welcome to our world." Liz opens the door, and Janna hastens over to Charlie, knowing he's worried about her.

Liz returns to her desk, picks up her tablet and sets things in motion from her end, thinking, *Now, if I can just figure out where their new base is!*

STRANGER IN THE MIRROR

The next day, Amy takes Janna to Medical to meet Sara. "Heads up! Sara can be quirky. She's crazy about Star Wars and likes to think she's the Apara equivalent of Yoda!" Amy jokes.

Janna smirks. "My little brother's obsessed with it, too! Especially the newer ones." She comments, but her gait falters as she thinks about never seeing her younger brother again.

"Are you alright?" Amy asks.

"Yeah, guess so... I just realized that I'll never see my brother again. My whole family believes I'm dead." She sighs.

"That's the hard part of all of this, isn't it? I'm not looking forward to the day I 'die' to the world because I'm not aging." Amy says.

"Do you still have contact with your family?" Janna asks.

"Mostly my mom and she keeps asking me if I'm going to take up my martial arts competitions again now that I'm out of the Army. I don't have the heart to tell her I can't...." She smirks. "Unfair advantage now, girl!"

"I guess you would have an advantage over any humans you'd compete against." Janna says, letting out a long sigh. "There's so much to figure out, though I guess I should be thankful I'm still alive and not under all the rubble in the base."

"We looked for you. Charlie insisted we try to find you, but you weren't in your room." Amy remarks.

"I know. I just keep thinking how close I came to being one of the casualties." Janna remarks.

They arrive at Sara's very cluttered office and Janna must stifle an amused giggle when she sees the office filled with Star Wars memorabilia. Sara catches her thoughts and raises an eyebrow as she looks at the two women in her doorway. She says, "Let's go down the hall and check you out, Janna." They follow Sara a short distance to an examination room. Sara commands, "Well! Don't just stand there gawking, have a seat so we can get this done!"

Janna isn't sure how to take Sara but sits down in the proffered chair. "What do you need me to do?" She asks.

"For now, just sit there. I need blood and tissue samples, and some scans of your energy levels. Nothing for you to do, just me." She says, short-tempered from all that's been going on of late. She takes the samples and runs her scans, looking pensive as she tries to make sense of the results. "Hm...."

"Hm?" Janna asks.

"I'm mapping your energy levels relative to the skills we typically have, but you've got one area..." She pauses and turns the tablet toward Janna, showing what looks like a 3D rendering of brain activity. "right here," She points to a spot on the tablet. "I've not seen *that* before. Have you experienced anything unusual since your transformation?"

Janna gives her an incredulous look and says, "Yeah, everything!" and shakes her head.

Sara glances at Amy, who has an apologetic expression. Amy says, "Nobody's really had time to bring her up to speed. That's why Liz sent her over to you. We need to know where to start with her, so anything you can tell us about her potential skill set would be helpful."

"I see. I'll get this into the analyzer and compare it to her original print from the database. In the meantime, if she has any difficulties with her abilities, I'm working on a gradual course of psi-amp for people like her." Sara tells Amy.

"Psiamp?" Janna inquires.

"Yes, it's a drug that opens latent psychic synapses and brings out your abilities. Do you know who's going to train you?" Sara inquires.

"Amy's supposed to train me in combat, and they said you all will help me with medical stuff. I was a medic in the Army, but other than that, I don't know." Janna admits.

"Hm... I'll get Vanessa Manheim to handle your training. She can give you the basics here, and some 'field' training on humans where she volunteers. Once we have some idea of where your talents lie, I'll set up a course of psiamp for you." Sara says, patting her on the back.

***

Two days later, Janna returns to Medical for a crash course in healing and using her expanded senses to see within someone's body to diagnose what's wrong, such as broken bones, bleeding, and other illnesses from Vanessa. They go on a field trip to the hospital where Vanessa volunteers so she can do some practical diagnoses and basic healing. Where a person's illness is too far advanced, they work on palliative care, reducing pain and easing the minds of patients. Janna's amazed she's able to make a difference and returns home to Charlie in the dorms that night more energetic than usual.

Charlie looks up from a book he's reading as she comes in. "Went well today, did it?" He inquires, noting she's in a better mood.

"Yep! I think I can get used to this, after all!" She says and plops down on the sofa beside him. "I want to show you something." She says and carefully unwraps a bandage on his hand where he'd spilled hot coffee on himself, burning his hand.

"What are you doing? It's not time to change the bandage yet." He gripes.

She leans forward and kisses him, saying, "Trust me, you big baby!" Once unwrapped, she takes his hand gently in her left hand and covers the burn with her right. He flinches, expecting pain, but is surprised when there's none. She closes her eyes, and a grin spreads across her face. Charlie feels an odd warmth around his hand. She opens her eyes and gives him a sly look as she removes her right hand from his and the burn has completely healed.

"*Whoa!* What the...? Did *you* do that?" He asks, incredulously.

"Pretty cool, isn't it? They taught me basic healing and diagnosing psychically, as well as pain suppression today! I'm so *psyched!*" She exclaims and snuggles up against him on the sofa.

"That's great! Congrats, sweetie!" He says, leaning over and kissing her again. "What else are they going to teach you?" He asks, genuinely interested in her progress.

"Amy's going to work with me on a few combat tricks tomorrow, and that disappearing thing we can do... *porting*? She showed me the basics today but said in combat I must learn to anticipate when others are porting in or out. And they're going to teach me the general stuff too. The stuff *everyone* has, but they're still not sure what all my abilities will be." She says, picking up the remote, turning on the TV, and searching for a movie to watch.

"Oh? I thought these guys knew *everything!*" He chides her sarcastically.

She glares at him. "Nope, I've got something they haven't seen before, but no one's figured it out yet." She flips through the movie listings and finds a recent comedy she's been wanting to see. The lead actress is a leggy blonde with stunning, blue eyes. She rests her head on Charlie's shoulder. "How do you think I'd look as a blonde?" She asks out of the blue.

"Huh? I don't know. Does it really matter?" He asks, focused on the movie.

"Yeah, it does! With being dead to the world, I've been thinking of changing my look. You know, dying my hair, getting colored contacts, so maybe I can go out in public and not be recognized. I've been dying to go back home and get some pizza from this one local place, but if I show up in that podunk town, someone's gonna recognize me!" She explains.

"Well, we could always ask Amy or someone if they could pop down there and get carryout. Then you wouldn't *have* to worry about being seen at all!" He says gruffly and picks up the remote to rewind the movie a couple of minutes back, as he's lost track of what they said. "If we don't go back to where you'll be recognized, you shouldn't need to change your appearance." He grumbles.

"Yeah, but sometimes, I feel like I *need* to go back there, even for a quick trip. Kind of a reality check." She says.

"Doubt they'll let us do that anytime soon. I'm not even sure when they'll let us leave this Sanctuary place! To be honest, I'm still not entirely sure they trust us, or at least me." He gripes.

"They do, or they wouldn't be teaching me to use my abilities or training me in combat! I mean, I could use that against them if I wanted to." She insists.

He reaches around her with his arm and pulls her close. "Let it go. I want to see the movie, okay?" He says impatiently.

Men! She thinks. "Alright, Charlie, but we'll talk more about it later." She relents.

They watch the movie, taking a break to fix some food and popcorn, then finish that movie and watch part of another. Janna's wiped out from using so much psychic energy. They made her feed before she left medical, but she's still exhausted, so they go to sleep.

In the morning, Janna wakes up when Charlie exclaims, "What the *hell*?"

"*What*?" She stretches and yawns.

"I can't believe you snuck out in the middle of the night and bleached your hair!" He exclaims.

She opens her eyes and hears him gasp. "Did you get *contacts,* too?" He queries, surprised she'd go out and do that in the middle of the night when she was the one complaining how exhausted she was.

"What are you going on about?" She asks, sitting up, then grabs a spray of hair that falls in front of her eyes. "I'm blonde?" She asks, surprised.

"Yeah, and your eyes are blue, too! But you *know* that! You did it while I slept!" He says accusingly.

"I did *no* such thing! I've been sleeping here the whole time!" She argues, getting out of bed, and going to the bathroom to stare at her appearance. "Holy cow!" She squeaks, shocked by her appearance, then comes back and stares at Charlie. "How'd this happen?" She asks, confused by this sudden turn of events.

"Beats me! If you didn't dye it, maybe you've got some kind of shapeshifter thing going on!" He laughs, knowing she's into werewolves.

"Don't joke! I *didn't* do this! I don't know how it...." She trails off when she notices him staring at her, mouth agape. "What now?"

"Your hair just went dark again and your eyes went back to normal." He says, stunned by this strange turn of events.

She sits next to him, silent in thought. "I wonder... we talked last night about how I'd look as a blonde and with blue contacts, remember?"

"That's why I thought you'd snuck out on me and did it but now it's back to normal." He says, confused by the whole situation.

"Let me try something, okay? Tell me if anything changes!" She closes her eyes. After a minute, she can hear his heart rate go up and Charlie gasps. Eyes still shut, she asks, "Did something change?"

"Hell yes! You've got bright red hair now!" He exclaims, weirded out by the change.

"And my eyes?" She opens them.

"Green! *Stark* green! How the *hell* are you doing this?" He demands.

"I'm not sure, but maybe this is what Sara was talking about. None of them has mentioned this as one of their normal abilities, so maybe it's something *only I* can do!" She says with glee. "Back in a few!" She says. She dresses, and ports out in front of Charlie, catching him off guard, and leaving him alone in their bedroom.

When she ports out, she focuses on finding Sara, and appears half a foot in front of her, colliding with the petite doctor.

"Oh, my God! I'm so sorry!" Janna says, realizing her error.

Sara glares at her, annoyed, but knows Janna's new to her abilities. "Look *before* you port, young one! Focusing on the person you're looking for is only half the process! You must learn to use your clairvoyance to see ahead. This time it was only me, but in the future, you may *pop* in before of a bunch of humans if you aren't careful!" Sara gives Janna an odd look as she realizes Janna's hair and eye color have changed. She can tell Janna isn't wearing contacts and can't smell any dye chemicals. "What have you done, child?"

Janna gives her an ear-to-ear grin. "I think I found my special talent! I can change my eye and hair color at will!"

Sara grabs her by the arm and drags her off to an examination room, snagging a tablet and scanner. "Sit down and change something!" She commands.

Janna switches her hair back to blonde and her eyes to blue and Sara's grin widens, as her scanner confirms the activity in Janna's brain corresponds to the earlier, mystery activity. "I believe you have! Can you change anything else?" She inquires curiously.

Janna is taken aback, but replies, "I haven't really tried anything else. What else should I try?"

"Try giving yourself a tan." Sara suggests enthusiastically.

It takes a few minutes, and the change is more gradual, but eventually, her skin tone darkens a few shades over her entire body. Janna looks down at her hands and arms in excitement. "Wow! I can't believe that worked!" She exclaims.

"Useful gift if you want to change your appearance and not be recognized, don't you think?" Sara grins at her enthusiastically.

"That's how it started. I was thinking about dying my hair and getting contacts so I could sneak back to my hometown some time without being recognized." Janna explains.

"Hm, impressive gift, indeed! We'll have to test its limits. I'd like to give you a dose of psiamp under supervision. I'll need to prepare for that. Can you come back later today? Perhaps at 3 pm?" Sara suggests, curious to test Janna's new skill and limits.

"*Cool!* I'll be back!" She exclaims excitedly, deciding being Apara might be a lot better fate than she'd ever imagined.

She ports in at home and Charlie has gone out to give Liz his report about the *Naqam*, Uri, and Elias. She flips on the TV and a superhero movie with Charlize Theron is on. She experiments with matching her hair and eye color with a mirror handy to watch the changes. Charlie returns home and stares at her, wide-eyed, not believing his eyes. He thinks *Charlize Theron is in my living room? What the hell?*

Janna asks, "Hey, Charlie, want to see something cool?"

He realizes the voice coming out of the woman in front of him is Janna's, not Charlize Theron's. "*Janna?*" He asks, uncertainly.

"Who *else* would I be?" She laughs at his odd reaction.

"Let's just say you don't *look* like yourself!" He says, sitting beside her, scrutinizing her face.

"I'm just playing with my hair and eye color, but it turns out I can do more! Watch!" She says, turning her skin a deep bronze as if she'd been in a tanning booth for hours.

"Okay, but *how* did you make yourself look like *that*?" He inquires, still feeling weirded out because Janna's voice and face don't match.

"Like what? I'm just doing what I did this morning! Playing with my hair and eye color." She says, confused by his odd reaction.

"But you *really look* like Charlize Theron! Can't you *see* that in your mirror?" He asks, frantically.

She stares at her reflection again before replying. "My hair and eye color are like hers, but I still look *like me*! I'm nowhere *near* as gorgeous as she is." Janna remarks.

"You really *don't* see it? You look *just* like her! I thought you *were* her for a second!" He exclaims, and takes out his cell and snaps a picture, but when he looks at it, she doesn't look like Theron at all, at least not beyond hair and eye color. "Now I'm *really* confused! My camera shows you one way, but I see you as Charlize Theron!" He insists.

"You're *not* kidding, are you?" She asks, seriously. "I'm going to try to see what you're seeing, okay? You know, *telepathically*." She says. He nods and relaxes so she can touch his mind as they've practiced. "*Holy cow!* You really *are* seeing me as her! But why don't I see that when I look in the mirror?"

"I don't know, but whatever it is, it's pretty cool!" Charlie thinks about what it would be like to make love to Charlize Theron, or at least Janna when she looks like her.

Still in light mental contact, Janna picks up on his daydream, grabs a throw pillow from the sofa, and smacks him with it. "Stop that!" She insists!

"*What*?" He asks, dodging a second swing when he doesn't drop his daydream fast enough.

"You and your *fantasies*! That's what!" She sulks.

He realizes she read his mind and caught him in the mental act. "Oh! *Sorry*! What do you expect? I show up with you looking all super-modelish! What do you expect my mind to do! Of course, it went *there*!" He says, feeling both justified and ashamed.

Janna shakes her head in annoyance. "*This* is not something to help you live your fantasies, Charlie! *Grow up!*" She snipes at him, then focuses on her appearance, and fades back to her normal self. "You're *with me*, not Charlize Theron!" She says and leans closer to him. "Are we *clear*?"

He looks away and then says, "Yeah, yeah! I get it!"

Later, Janna returns to Medical and excitedly tells Sara about the latest development. After a little experimentation, Sara discovers that Janna's gift is two-fold. While she can physically change the color of her eyes, hair, skin, and other things, she can project a telepathic illusion to the minds of those around her, making them see her as she wants to be seen, be it Charlize Theron or someone she knows, like Amy.

Sara makes her stay the night, and she gives her a first dilute dose of psiamp. The next day, she's able to make her physical changes more rapidly. She learns to change her hair from straight to curly, her illusions come more quickly and are more convincing.

Sara says, "We'll try another dose in a few days, but update Liz and Amy about your progress. I'm sure they'll be able to put your gifts to *good* use!"

WINS AND LOSSES

About a week has passed since the Apara began searching for the potentials on the list. Amy sends Liz a path that they've done all they can. Liz calls a meeting. This time, it's herself, Kari, Tess, Marc, and Amy. Liz has barely slept in the last week, and she looks worn out. Kari isn't much better as she's been worrying about Liz. Everyone gathers in Liz's office. Over the last few months, Liz's hair has grown out from the neat, short haircut she had when Tess first began at Inspiration, Inc. Tess notices not only has it gotten long, but Liz hasn't bothered to style it with her usual immaculate precision.

Tess paths privately to Marc, *I'm worried about Liz.*

Marc replies, *I know. The last couple of years have been more than anyone should have to deal with, and it's hit her harder than most.*

Liz settles into her chair, slouching, reflecting her physical and psychological exhaustion. She sighs deeply. "So, where do we stand with the endangered potentials?" She asks, looking from one face to another around the table.

Amy chimes in first. "My guys have brought in 307, and I doubt we'll find more than that. I had Tess double check the remaining ones' social media..." She motions for Tess to continue.

"All their pages have been inactive for at least three days and some as long as two weeks. I'm guessing they got to them first. I'll keep monitoring, but it doesn't look good. On the bright side, our wins are far greater than our losses. Assuming they have the ones we don't, then they have around fifty-five of our potentials. In the end, we prioritized the Lost Mission potentials, so they only got five of them, while we got thirty-three." Tess sums up.

Marc motions he has something to add. "Those are the potentials from the random list of 362 potentials. In addition, we'll have to assume they've turned the ones on their list of local potentials in and around Israel and the Middle East. Our people in Tel Aviv found a few of them and brought them in, but most have not been accounted for."

"So, assuming they had two survivors from the Judean Base, plus fifty-five and then most of their original list, we're talking as many as 75-100 rogue Apara on *their* side?" Liz asks, checking her math.

"Yeah, that's our estimate. Assuming none of the missing are still out there, on the run, or were killed in the abduction attempts." Kari says stroking Liz's arm.

"How are those we've brought in responding?" Liz asks Tess, knowing she and Sue have been working on that aspect of the situation.

"It varies. Luckily, most of them were prepped, so we've been able to use subliminals on those potentials, and they understand what's going on, however, some of them have had life changes since they were evaluated, including relationship status and two pregnancies I didn't know about when I reviewed their files." Tess explains.

Liz closes her eyes and sighs. "What about the non-prepped LM potentials?" She asks, lethargically opening them again. Tess senses Liz's frustration about their disrupted lives, especially the two pregnant women.

"They won't transform pregnant women, so, they'll be allowed to remain human to raise their children. They may have to remain in Sanctuary until the danger passes, or new identities can be created, and they can relocate them. They'll know about the Apara, but Sara can create a mental block to prevent them from divulging our secret, as she did with you, Tess. The hard part is what to do about their families. We may have to consider bringing them in, which expands our already growing problem." Kari suggests, dropping her pen on the table in frustration.

"As you can imagine, the non-prepped ones are having the hardest time. They aren't sure who to trust because they have no reason to believe we are better than the *Naqam*. To them, we're all *vampires;* mythological *monsters* who've *abducted* them. Sue and I are doing what we can, and she's got several others trained to deal with situations like this, but some people are having more difficulties than others." Tess explains.

"Marc, have you been able to convince any of our unattached members to volunteer as partners for our unplanned transformees?" She asks wearily.

"A few, but most want to meet them and choose someone they get along with. So, we're coming up short. I've asked some of our partnered members to consider taking on some as apprentice Apara, meaning the partners would *adopt* them and train them together, but after a few years, they'll be on their own again." He explains.

"Any takers?" She asks; her tone less than optimistic.

"Some are considering it, though my focus has been on some of those who lost partners in Jerusalem. It's been nearly two years for them, and while our grieving process is complicated, some will take on a new partner, if it's someone they feel comfortable with." He says.

"Amy, I need you to talk to Charlie, Janna, and Hannah and see if they have any idea how long it will take Uri to transform and condition the ones they've taken. We need a working time frame, so we have some idea when we might be on the receiving end of their new army. That many Apara would overwhelm us here in Asheville, so we must make sure we have as many of your people on standby in case they come to us before we can get to them." Liz says.

"Will do, Liz. I've got training with Janna later today. Hannah is working with Sara and Isanda on countermeasures for Uri's weapons." She remarks.

"Oh? Anything promising?" Liz asks, perking up at possible positive news.

"Yeah, a few things, but the most promising so far is that a green variant of Cent-opal creates a protective field that counteracts the anti-ability field they use. Hannah recreated an anti-ability unit, so we've been testing that. In fact, it converts the anti-ability wavelengths and boosts some abilities higher than usual, which should be helpful." Amy explains.

"Let's call that one a win!" Liz almost smiles when she says that, but everyone can see she's still very stressed.

"Speaking of Janna, Sara's giving her another dose of psiamp tonight. Hopefully, it will help her hone those appearance-changing skills she's developing. If she gets good enough, Liz, I'd like you to consider letting us take her with us when we go into the base. Once there, she could blend in by making herself look like one of their people. She'd be perfect for doing reconnaissance." Amy suggests.

Liz is uneasy, saying, "I'm concerned she's too new to all of this. You've got to get her up to speed, so she can fight her way out if necessary. Can you introduce her to Callie? Callie should get to know her so she can home in on her and pull her out if we send her in."

"I'll give her and Niall a call after the meeting and see how everything's going. Last I heard, she's been making progress with smaller portals, but nothing big enough for an escape route yet." Amy hopes what little good news they've given will help Liz snap out of the personal black cloud she's been in lately.

Liz addresses the group. "Thank you for your efforts and keep up the good work. We need to be ready if they come for us and equally ready to move if we find them first." Liz says and goes back to her desk without formally dismissing everyone. It's clear the meeting is over, and everyone except for Kari leaves. She sits on the edge of Liz's desk.

"Love, you *need* a break. Remember our deal? I tell you when I think you're nearing your limits, and you *listen* to me." Kari says, covering one of Liz's hands with hers.

"How can I take a break with all of this?" Liz looks her partner of several centuries in the eye, waiting for a response.

"Because if you don't take a break, you'll *break* for real when the stress is on! Come on, our cabin near Lindesnes is still nice this time of year. Take the weekend with me. If something happens, we're just a port away, but you need this break, *elskling*! We can take the boat out and fish on the fjord like we used to." Kari does her best to convince Liz to take care of herself.

"Alright! *Kjæresten min*! but only for the weekend! I'll leave Marc in charge in the meantime." Liz gives in, knowing Kari won't let her avoid taking care of herself. She also knows Kari's right. If she doesn't rest, and they attack, her decision-making ability in a crisis will be impaired.

Kari makes a list of what they need with them for the weekend. She arranges for a gathering Saturday night with some of their Norwegian Apara friends, knowing it would be good for Liz.

Liz sits at her desk, looking at her notes on her tablet, saying out loud, "I guess it's as they say, you win some and you lose some, but at least our losses are significantly less than our wins."

RAISING EXPECTATIONS

Phoenix has been stuck at home in Sanctuary, or at work since her attempted abduction. Today, she's working at home on some of her psychic skills, as well as a book project for a client, while Peder is at the office in downtown Asheville. She's having difficulty focusing on her book formatting, so she takes a lunch break and checks her social media. Her old cell phone rings, and she recognizes the caller ID.

While all the Apara got new cells with proprietary security technology, she kept her old cell in case family or friends call her old number. The caller is an old friend from Charlotte who she hasn't heard from in some time. She picks up the phone, excited to hear from Devyn. "Hey! Devyn, what's up?"

"*Phoenix*? Oh, thank God! I went by your apartment but you weren't there!" Devyn says, sounding anxious.

"I'm moving in with... my boyfriend, Peder." She says, realizing how banal that sounds compared to reality.

"Oh, that's great!" She says, distracted, then changes the subject abruptly. "Do you still have that envelope I asked you to hang onto for me?" Devyn asks, sounding anxious.

"Yeah, it's at my old apartment. Do you need it immediately?" She asks, wondering what's going on with her old friend.

"Yes! Is there any way you can meet me there soon?" She asks, sounding desperate.

Phoenix pauses for a second, but thinks, *by now, they should have given up on grabbing me. I'll be okay running over there briefly. I'll keep it quick.* She tells her friend, "Yeah, I'll be there in about twenty minutes, *okay*?"

"Oh! *Bless* you! I really need that envelope! I'll see you soon!" She says and hangs up.

Twenty-two minutes later, Phoenix pulls up in her car, and Devyn is sitting on her front porch, rocking anxiously. "Devyn, *what's going on*? I can tell you're upset." She asks.

Devyn stands, crosses her arms in front of her protectively, and paces. "Remember when my brother was involved in that gang crap in Charlotte?" She looks anxiously around as if she expects someone to jump out and attack.

"Yeah, but didn't they put those guys in jail?" Phoenix asks, passing her friend, unlocking the front door, and guiding her inside.

"Yeah, but the gang leader got out on a technicality! Now, he's harassing my family, calling all of us, and making threats!" Devyn explains, noticing Phoenix didn't lock the front door, so she does it herself.

"So, where's the envelope come in?" Phoenix asks, as she pulls it out of the bottom of a drawer. She hands Devyn a sealed, manilla envelope, thick with something in it. She never knew what, but Devyn asked her to keep it safe and she did.

"It's photos my brother took that implicate the gang leader in a series of execution-style murders. It's leverage against him, and he's threatening to hurt us if we don't give it to him." She explains, almost hyperventilating.

"*Jesus! Devyn!* Why *didn't* you tell me? What if someone had come looking for it *here*?" Phoenix asks, realizing her friend may have inadvertently put her in danger.

"I'm the *only* one who *knew* you had it. I've got to get this back home to my brother. We're going to turn it over to the police! If we hand it over to him, there's nothing to stop him from killing my brother, or any of us! Hopefully, they'll lock him up again." Devyn says.

"Devyn, sit down for a second and talk to me." Phoenix says, but as they settle on the sofa, Phoenix senses someone porting in. She thinks, *It must be Peder coming to drag me home*, but when she turns around, it's the guy who'd come for her before.

Devyn sees Elias port in and screams, so Elias shoots her without so much as a second thought. Devyn collapses onto the sofa, blood draining out and soaking into the light green floral upholstery.

"*Devyn!*" Phoenix screams but her mind hollers instinctively for Peder, who ports in next to her just as Elias is lunging toward Phoenix. Peder pushes Phoenix out of the way toward her friend on the sofa and engages Elias. Peder uses his PK to disrupt Elias's porting ability, but in the end, Elias uses all his power and ports away, so Peder turns his attention back to Phoenix.

"What in *all the gods' names* made you come back *here*?" He asks, but his tone softens as he sees her sobbing over the other woman's lifeless body. He can tell she's dead, as he can only hear Phoenix's heart beating. He approaches Phoenix and crouches down next to the sofa. "Was she a friend of yours?" He asks, soothing Phoenix's grief.

Phoenix gasps through her tears, "Yeah... a friend... from... Charlotte. She...." Phoenix's sobs increase and she can't get the words out but paths the situation wordlessly to Peder.

"*Damn*, I'm *sorry*, *elskling*. I'm so sorry, I know you're upset, but I must get a team over here to clean things up." He says as he hears an urgent knock on the door and a tiny dog yipping furiously outside.

"*Shit*, That's Lydia, she must have heard the gunshot or my scream." Phoenix says.

Peder opens the door, easily snaring Lydia's mind with his own, as Lydia is not a particularly complex-minded woman. After a few seconds, she scoops up Cinnamon, hushes the dog, and returns to her apartment wearing her fuzzy, pink day slippers as though nothing's the matter.

When Peder comes back in and locks the door, he senses an almost physical wave of energy hit him from Phoenix's direction. He turns and stares at her. Her aura is a super bright mix of gold and green, as he's only seen on a few people, like Sara, when she's healing someone who's seriously injured. He whispers, "*Phoenix*?" He hears an odd, gurgling coughing from the woman on the sofa, and the radiant energy of Phoenix's aura dims rapidly. She slouches down against the sofa in exhaustion, breathing slowly and labored.

He hastens over to her and is shocked to see that the woman on the sofa, still unconscious, is breathing, and her heart is beating regularly. He moves the woman's shirt to look at the wound, and it's healed as if she'd never been shot, though the hole in her shirt and blood everywhere, says otherwise. "*Dear God!* You not only *healed* her; you brought her back from the *dead!* How?" He reaches over to Phoenix and pulls her close. Her hands are soaked with her friend's blood and they're trembling uncontrollably. Devyn's blood covers the sought-after envelope of photos, as well.

Phoenix finds it hard to remain coherent, like she's on the edge of passing out. "You need to feed. Whatever you did used a tremendous amount of energy." He pulls her to him and guides her head toward his neck until he feels her instinctively feed. While she does so, he paths Liz requesting a clean-up crew, and Sara for her medical expertise. The two women port in, followed by a team of Apara specialists who will clean up the blood, dispose of the sofa, and make sure none of the other neighbors remember hearing anything. Liz pulls up her tablet and checks to see if any 911 calls were made, but they were lucky this time.

Sara checks the human woman first, noting the odd energy around her feels more like an Apara, but the woman is clearly human. Phoenix transferred much of her energy to her friend to save her. By the time Phoenix finishes feeding, she's nearly asleep. Peder holds her in his arms and ports her to Medical. Sara ports the human woman there as well, so the clean-up crew can do their job. Liz ports into Medical five minutes later, pathing to Peder. *Hva i alle verden skjed?* She paths rapidly in Norwegian, as until five minutes ago, she was hanging out with friends at a dinner party in Lindesnes, Norway.

Long story, sis, sorry to bother you. I should have called Marc, but I think it's under control now. I'll fill you in later. Go on back to Kari

and our friends in Norway and give them my regards. He paths, regretting adding to his sister's burden.

Javel, broren min?" Liz shakes her head and sighs, saying, "I want a *full* report tomorrow, *got it?*"

"Will do, Lissa, as soon as I figure out *what* happened!" He says and she ports back to Kari, knowing Kari's ready to port in and drag her back herself.

Peder sits in a chair next to Phoenix's bed in medical. Sara joins him, saying, "She's fine, just weak after a nearly herculean act of healing. Normally, it's nearly impossible to heal someone *and* bring them back from the dead without also using technology to restart the heart and lungs anew. As far as I can tell, she temporarily transferred her self-healing ability to her friend and forced it to heal her nearly instantaneously. What she did rivals what our best healers can do when augmented by Benefactor technology. It's amazing! Unfortunately, the amount of energy she needed has left her weak, but she'll recover. Just let her rest."

"Do you think this is what her Lost Mission talent is?" Peder asks, reaching over and holding Phoenix's hand.

"Without a doubt, though, she could have more than one, you know! I suspected it would be healing related; in fact, I'm pretty sure her own rising from the dead and self-healing was a combination of biological regeneration and psychic healing." Sara explains as she hangs up an IV of blood for Phoenix. "Now, I need to check on her friend. She didn't have any ID on her. Do you know her name?"

"I think I heard Phoenix call her Dillon or something. Odd name for a woman." He comments, thinking out loud.

"The good news is, either Phoenix got to her early enough, or her abilities undid any brain damage because everything looks normal on her brain scan." Sara explains, fascinated by this latest, unique ability.

"If this is her big ability, what good is it if it takes so much out of her?" Peder inquires, worried about her resulting condition.

"I think this young woman would argue with you on that point!" Sara says, motioning to Phoenix's friend. "She'd be dead if it hadn't been for her."

"Okay, I'll concede that, but how do we know the next time she *raises the dead,* it won't put *her* in stasis?" He asks, exaggerating to make his point.

"We don't, but this was the first time she's done this, and she did it *intuitively.* If she wants to use it consciously, she'll have to learn to draw in energy to prepare for healing someone, drawing it from the earth, the sun, nature, or even other people. I suspect she could have done this without the huge expenditure of energy, but she just put everything into saving her friend." Sara explains. "Now, go on home! She'll probably sleep for a couple of days and your anxiety is starting to get *to me!* I'll take *good* care of her, Peder!"

He leans over and kisses Phoenix on the forehead, straightens up, and tells Sara, "Call me if there's *anything!* I mean absolutely *anything!*"

Sara rolls her eyes as Peder ports home. He gets there, expecting not to be able to sleep, but lies down to catch his breath, and is out before he knows it.

DISTANT VOICES

Callie's been having weird, turbulent dreams, ever since she and Niall began working with the mirror to make portals. Sometimes she dreams about people gathering in a field, and other times, she sees dark, cloudy skies over ruined cities, much like the pictures of Jerusalem after the bomb. One night, she wakes in a cold sweat, screaming because she dreams that she's in the shockwave's path from a nuclear explosion, and knows she's about to be vaporized. She feels herself dissolving into nothingness and wakes up screaming herself hoarse. Yet, in every dream, she hears a voice calling to her by name, begging her to find her. The catch is, it's her own voice she hears.

She and Niall continue to practice, at first using the small mirror and then trying a larger wall mirror or a framed painting. They're working up larger portals, but having something with a defined edge or framework helps her control the size and location.

Today, Callie's waiting for Niall in the living room. He ports in with something as tall as he is, covered by cloth. Niall's grinning. "Today, we're going to create a portal you can step through! And tomorrow, we're going to meet up with a new girl, Janna. She may go on some missions where she'll need you to open a portal to get her out if she can't port herself, so Liz wants you two to hang out, so you'll be able to locate her by mental signature, okay?" He explains.

"I guess so." She says, yawning uncontrollably.

"Remind me, and I'll see if Sara has something to help you sleep better. You need to be at your best if we go into the new base and must rely on you to get us out." He says, gently rubbing her back reassuringly.

"Talk about pressure! I'll do my *best* no matter what, but these dreams are getting to me. I don't know if they're symbolic or what! I mean, I keep hearing myself demanding I *find myself!* Literally! Geez! Talk about cryptic." She gripes. "If it isn't figurative 'finding myself', then how can I do it? How can there be two of me?" She sounds exasperated.

Niall leans up against the wall and says, "The only thing I can think of is a twin of some kind?" He suggests.

"But I'm not a twin! I've seen my birth certificate, and it lists me a single birth." She says.

"Hm... there is one other 'literal' possibility... though I'd also say it is literally impossible! In theory, there are an infinite number of realities, and therefore, you exist in some of those, but we can't travel to anywhere but here and Sanctuary." Niall suggests.

"I hadn't thought about that. Why can we only go between Sanctuary and our Earth?" She asks.

"I know this is going to come across like a parental answer, but because our Benefactors made it that way." He says.

"*Huh*?" She gives him a confused stare.

"Sanctuary is based in a technology our Benefactors use when their population becomes too large for their planet. Instead of going out, finding a habitable world, or terraforming one to their specs, they developed the technology to find these other realities. My understanding is they had a few missteps when they first developed the technique. One of the realities they visited was very much like their own, except that the beings there survived and became immune to a horrible plague but still carried it in their systems. Those who visited that reality fell ill, and many did not survive. For beings that normally live indefinitely, don't get sick, and self-heal, this was quite a shock. Luckily, they didn't bring it back with them to their original world or the plague may have destroyed them all. In another case, they were seen as invaders, even though they were of the same race. After that, they made a rule that all parallel worlds with intelligent civilizations on them were off-limits. They created a technology that can bind the usable realities together, and separate them from the infinite number of others, preventing anyone from accidentally traveling to an off-limits world. Earth and Sanctuary Earth are *bound*, so we may only travel between the two, and not the others. We'd need their advanced technology to even look for other realities, let alone travel to them." He explains.

"I guess that makes sense, but what if, somehow, I'm in touch with another reality?" She asks stubbornly.

"If you are, then we have a *big* problem. It's *forbidden*! When all of this is over, and we've done what we must end this conflict with the *Naqam*, we'll talk with Liz, and she can talk to our Benefactors or some of the hybrids. My guess is that it's just your subconscious or imagination." He reassures her.

She lets out an ironic laugh. "Let's hope so, or you might have to deal with *two* of me!" She grins.

"Oh! Heaven *forbids!*" He says in a snarky tone. "Let's get back to practice, okay?"

Callie rolls her eyes and sighs. "Alright." He walks over to the covered object with her behind him.

"Now, we're going to do this just like we did the other exercises; use this to confine your portal to the size of the framework. I want you to picture the portal going to our bedroom." He suggests, pulls the cloth that's draped over the object away, and Callie gasps dramatically. He looks at her, trying to get a read on her, and senses fear and confusion. He takes her gently by the chin, forcing her to look at him. "What's wrong?" He asks.

Callie pulls free from his grasp and focuses on the object before her. It's the *mirror* from her first *calling* dream, down to the intricate scrollwork on the gilt frame. "*Where'd* you get *that* mirror." She asks, her voice trembling.

"I've had it stored in the attic. It's Katie's, but she doesn't use it much. She asked me to store it for her; why?" He watches as she walks forward, touches the framework tentatively, tracing the patterning and feeling the coolness of the metal frame. She faces him, looking haunted.

"Remember that nightmare I had after our first night working with the tabletop mirror?" She asks, halfway glancing back at the full-length one, expecting to see herself as she was in the dream; emotionally worn, and physically ragged, but only sees her own, normal reflection.

"Yes, but that was *only a dream*, my sweet." He reassures her.

She swallows anxiously. "I'm not so sure it was; not *now*, at least. That..." And she motions to the full-length mirror. "*Is* the mirror from my dream, down to the finest detail!" She says.

"Callie, even if it is, maybe your clairvoyance just grabbed the image from the Attic. It's *just* a mirror; not something to be afraid of." He says, but she's not buying it.

She turns around and stares at it, but nothing changes. "I'll try, but if some creepy version of me comes out the other side, in the bedroom, don't say I didn't *warn* you!" She admonishes him

"Don't worry! Just do as we've done the other times. Use the mirror to make your portal, except *this* time, I want you to step through it. You're only going as far as the bedroom, so it's not like you're going to get lost on the way." He grins and gives her a gentle kiss on the back of her neck.

She tries to put the nightmare out of her mind and begins spinning the energy that will create the portal. The mirror ripples like someone threw a pebble in a pond, and it spreads, filling the entire mirror. As the center of the mirror calms, she sees their bedroom on the other side.

"*Go* on! Step through and close it when you're on the other side." He instructs.

She hesitates briefly, then strides toward the now open portal, closing her eyes right as she steps through it. She doesn't immediately step into the bedroom, but becomes disoriented, hears her name all around her, and can swear she feels fingers grab at her arm just as she emerges from a bare portal on the other side. She's frantic, trips as she steps through, and lands with a thud on the bedroom floor. The portal sputters and closes chaotically with a flash and a pop of energy, cracking the full-length mirror in the living room.

Seeing her fall, Niall ports straight to the bedroom, and finds her curled up on the floor, shaking. "Are you okay?" He says as he crouches down beside her on the floor, running a hand along her back, soothingly.

"I'm *NOT* doing that again!" She mutters at the floor.

"Did something *happen*?" He asks, concerned about her reaction.

She rolls on her back and looks up at him. "Didn't you see? The *hand*! Someone *grabbed* my arm! I was afraid I wasn't going to get out of there!" She's hyperventilating and sobbing.

"I didn't see anything but you going through, losing your balance, and landing with a thud. The portal snapped shut! That's all I saw." He helps her up into a seated position on the floor while dropping from crouching to sitting cross-legged in front of her.

"I *heard* my name being called like in that dream, only more distorted. Then I felt a hand grab me and nails dug into my skin! *Wait*! That's it!" She says, examining her arm for any signs of damage from the fingernails she felt. However, if there had been any real damage, it's already healed, leaving her with no evidence of anything having gone awry.

She faces him. "*I know what I felt, Niall*! It was like someone desperately latching on to me as I went *through* the portal!"

"*Okay*! We're going to take a break for the rest of tonight, and I'm going to get Sara to fix up something to help you sleep through the night! You're so worked up over everything you were expecting something crazy like this!" He suggests rubbing her forearm lovingly.

She glares at him. "*I AM NOT CRAZY!*" She shouts.

"I didn't mean you're crazy, just that what you experienced was strange, but it could easily have been the power of suggestion because of your dreams." He says, trying to soothe her frustration and anger. "We're already in the bedroom, get some sleep. I'll see if Sara can throw something together to help you, okay?"

She lets him help her to the bed, feeling somewhat unstable in her gait, and sits down on the edge of the bed. "Go on! *Call* Sara! I need a break from these *dumbass* dreams!" She gripes and slides under the blanket, rolls on her side, halfway curled up with the blanket almost covering her head.

Niall contacts Sara and gets a wave generator that should ease Callie's dream mind, as well as prevent any outside influences from waking her in case something external is triggering the dreams. He sets it on her nightstand and turns it on. He can feel her muscles unknot and her mind become less frantic. He gives her a few minutes, then joins her in bed, sleeping heavily.

He lets her sleep late in the morning. She had a night without nightmares, but he climbs out of bed to get ready for their guests. Amy is bringing Janna by in a couple of hours, but Niall wants to be sure Callie is well-rested before the noon meeting. He wakes her at 11 am with a tray of food and a bag of blood, which she needs after her psychic activity the night before.

He sits carefully on the edge of the bed, tray in hand, and dangles a strip of bacon in front of her nose. After a few seconds, she opens one eye and glares at him. "That's *not* fair! How am I to get any sleep if you tempt me with bacon?" She scowls.

"Oh! You had plenty of sleep! Look at your nightstand!" He demands, his Scottish accent slipping out stronger than usual in his amusement.

"What's that?" She asks and notices the time. "Wait! I slept over fourteen hours?"

Niall chuckles. "Yes, that gadget is courtesy of Sara. It's a wave generator, and helped settle your mind into a deep sleep without nightmares. Feel any better after a good night's rest?" He inquires with a lopsided grin.

She sits upright in bed and reaches for the tray with her breakfast on it. "Yeah, I do. First night in a week that I didn't have any bad dreams, though that trip through the literal looking-glass was bad enough for ten of them!" She grumbles and gnaws on a crispy piece of bacon.

"I am concerned about that. Sara says she'll have to check the psychic energy logs, but she's stressed today with all the new, human potentials that were brought in, and are being transformed, so it may take a while until she has time to check the logs and analyze them." He explains.

"I keep forgetting she's got those things set up. Probably just as well, or they'd make me feel paranoid being constantly monitored." She admits, sopping up some runny egg yolk with a slice of bread.

"We must monitor all the Lost Missioners. Their abilities are unpredictable and unknown because of the mutations." He explains, swiping a small piece of bacon from her plate, eliciting a glare, and a raised eyebrow from her. "Yours, more than most, must be monitored because it is completely unique and uses a lot of energy. But don't worry. I'm sure Sara will get back to us soon. Right now, you need to get ready for guests." He grins.

"Guests?" She asks, trying to remember what he's talking about.

"Yes, remember me mentioning the new gal, *Janna*? Amy's bringing her by in about forty-five minutes." He reminds her.

"Oh, crap!" She utters and puts the tray aside, kicks off the blanket, and stumbles toward the bathroom to get ready. Niall chuckles and heads back out to make sure everything's ready.

BAITING THE TRAP

Liz feels better, though still not her normal, confident, and capable self. She sits in her office, going over the report about Phoenix and her friend, Devyn St. Clair. She's engrossed in the details of her new sister-in-law's doings. Liz has met many healers over the centuries, but none of them could pull someone back from death without additional tools or technology. Phoenix did so by sheer willpower alone.

Yet something concerns her even more. Why did Elias attempt to grab her now that she's one of them? *Doesn't it matter that's she's already Apara, or did he not realize she'd been turned?* She ponders, considering Phoenix still has a partially human scent and taste because of her unique transformation, but they couldn't have known from afar. A light rap on her doorframe interrupts Liz's focus. She looks up to see Peder looking like he needs the same 'vacation' she just had forced upon her by Kari.

"Come in, Peder. I'm just going over the reports about Phoenix and her friend. Quite a feat your partner pulled off." She says as she watches him settle in the nearest chair.

"That's an *understatement!* Sara's still trying to figure out *how* she did it." He comments.

"Yes, I know; I just finished reading Sara's preliminary analysis. Why didn't you go with her to her old apartment?" She asks.

Peder glares at his sister in annoyance. "She went without telling me! Her friend needed an envelope she'd entrusted to Phoenix a couple of years back. It was an urgent matter." He says.

"I would *think* so if she risked going back there *without* you. Speaking of which, we need to figure out why they went after her when she's already one of us! They must have realized that we'd turn her after their last attempt, and yet, Elias was waiting in the wings." She sighs in frustration.

There's another knock, and it's Amy, holding a gadget that looks like an oversized forehead thermometer in khaki green. "I think I can shine a light on that!" She says, looking like she hasn't slept in a couple of days. She flops down on the sofa, putting her feet up on it. "This is a thermal scanner. It's a variant of a military unit I've used before. We used it to detect possible soldiers or other people hiding, so we could avoid ambush. They use similar ones in search and rescue missions to find people under the rubble. It scans for infrared heat sources. The thing is this one is hyper-sensitive. They've made it possible to separate humans, who show up as more orangish-red, from Apara, who show up in the bright yellow range, as our bodies average temperature is slightly *higher* than humans. Ironic, considering vampire mythology, don't ya think?" She says and turns to Peder. "Your partner doesn't just smell and taste partly human, her body temperature, according to the history in this device, *shows up as human* on this scanner." She turns back to Liz. "They had this wedged up in a tree, aimed at her place. It had a remote link until I disabled it." Amy explains. "It probably set off some kind of signal when she arrived."

"So, as far as they know, she's still human... interesting...." Liz says, contemplating the possibilities.

Peder gets a distraught look and objects before Liz can even air her thoughts. "Oh, *Hell NO!* We're not using my partner as *bait!*" Peder erupts.

"I know that she's new to our life, but we *can prepare* her. I'm betting, with some of Sara's masking agents and her own mixed readings, that they'd never know she's one of us. If they take her to their base, we can *track* her." She suggests.

A clearly agitated Peder stands and paces in front of Liz's desk. "*NO!* I won't *risk* her!"

"There won't be much risk! Yes, they'll *try* to transform her, but she's already one of us! I want you to see if you can get Sara to let her out of Medical. Bring her to Niall's place at noon. I have an idea, and I want you two to hear me out. Got it?" She stares her brother down, as she's done many times over their preternaturally long lifetimes, knowing he'll eventually back down. He scowls, but doesn't argue, and ports to Medical to retrieve Phoenix.

Liz turns to Amy. "Thank you; I think you may have just given us an opportunity to find their base. I know you need to go get Janna over to meet Callie, but could you also get Hannah Zelkind? I need her input on this as well."

"Sure thing, but are you sure Phoenix is *ready* for this?" Amy asks.

"We'll *make* her ready. Can you fit her into your training sessions?" Liz asks.

Amy nods. "Of course, whatever you need." She slips her shoes back on and ports out, leaving Liz to ponder her plan.

MEETING OF MINDS

A little before noon, Callie, freshly showered and dressed, enters the living room carrying the rest of her breakfast, nibbling the last specks of crispy bacon as she takes it to the kitchen. "Thanks for breakfast!" She tells Niall and leans over and kisses him on the cheek.

"What are partners for?" He gives her a roguish, lopsided grin.

"Oh, *lots* of things! But this morning, it was breakfast!" She laughs lightly.

"Did you take care of your *other* breakfast?" He asks, noticing she's only brought her food plate down.

"Yeah, drank it down before I grabbed the plate. Tossed the bag in the bathroom trash." She says, rinsing off her plate and putting it in the rack. "So, this Janna you mentioned, she's new?"

"Yes. She was the last one turned by the *Naqam* at the old base. Seems she's developed an interesting skill. Like you, she's Lost Mission, but she's got the ability to disguise her appearance through a combination of physical changes and telepathic projection of illusions." Niall explains as he puts out some snacks on a tray for their visitors.

"Wow! That's a mouthful. Telepathic projection of illusions? What's that?" She asks, sneaking a cookie off one tray. He gives her a scowl when he notices she's munching in his ear.

"It means that if she knows what someone looks like, she can project that image into the minds of people around her, and that's who they'll see. Quite a handy skill if you need to infiltrate somewhere everyone is known." He explains, carrying out trays to the living room coffee table.

Callie follows him out. "Is that what she's going to do? Infiltrate the *Naqam*?"

"That's the plan, at least eventually. Liz wants you to get to know her so you can open a portal on the fly and pull her out if she gets into trouble." He clarifies as he brings out coffee cups, a thermal coffee carafe with coffee, and another with hot water for tea. While caffeine doesn't do anything for Apara, the social habit is still strong as they must fit in when in mixed, social situations, so coffee, tea, and alcohol become social props, though some drink them for the taste rather than their effects. Niall gets a distant expression and lets out a sigh. "*Heads* up! Here they come!" He says as he senses someone porting in. However, it's not who he expects.

"*Liz?* Peder? What are you two doing here?" Niall inquires, somewhat confused by their appearance.

Liz gives him an impish smile. "Slight change of plans! Meeting's *expanding.* Besides Amy, Janna, Peder, and I, Phoenix and Hannah Zelkind will be coming." She explains, settling in and fixing herself a cup of tea. "Got any honey?" She inquires.

Before Niall can go get it, Callie closes her eyes, and it appears out of thin air on the table in front of Liz. Niall paths an amused, **Show off!** to her as he goes back into the kitchen and sees what else he has for snacks since there will be extra guests.

When he comes back, Phoenix is sitting on the sofa next to Peder, looking uneasy, and Amy ports in with Janna and Hanna Zelkind.

Liz looks at everyone one by one and says, "That's everyone, at least for today." She waits for them to settle around the living room coffee table. Niall must bring in extra chairs to accommodate everyone, but they all get settled and wait for Liz to begin. "As everyone knows, these last few weeks, we've been dealing with the unfortunate fact that we did not fully eliminate the *Naqam* as a threat. In fact, like bacteria, our incomplete attempt to wipe out their threat created a stronger, more resilient strain of adversary."

Hannah Zelkind clears her throat. "Yes, that is consistent with Uri's psychology, I'm afraid. What doesn't kill him, strengthens him, and makes him more fanatical. The same for Elias. They are quite alike." She explains.

Niall appears confused. "I know you want Callie on standby to pull Janna out if things get dicey, but what do Peder and Phoenix have to do with that?" He inquires.

Liz smiles. "Patience, Niall. Callie will be important in this mission, but the mission is expanding. Peder's new partner, Phoenix, has an important role to play in finding and infiltrating their base." Liz nods toward the young, redheaded woman, emanating anxious vibes. "Phoenix is also Lost Mission, but she was infected by the Roulette virus, as well. We're not sure if that affected her transformation, but if you try to sense if Phoenix is one of us or not, you may get a mixed reading." Liz suggests, one corner of her mouth turned up in a quirky smile.

Niall focuses on Phoenix, noting she feels and smells almost human, but *not quite*. Liz reads his reaction and says, "As you see, it's not clear if she's human or Apara. She is Apara, but her body still produces some red blood cells on its own. We've discovered that our foes have been placing infrared heat sensors to monitor some potentials they haven't acquired, including at Phoenix's apartment. Ironically, we Apara are warmer than humans by about a degree, so when Phoenix returned to her human dwelling, they came for her because the heat sensor flagged her as human." Liz explains.

Niall perceives Peder's and Phoenix's anxiety almost palpably. "Are you considering using her as bait, Liz? That seems rather risky."

"In some ways, but it's riskier to leave them to build an Apara-based army to send after us, don't you think? Besides, Phoenix has *extraordinary* healing abilities, and Sara believes they'll protect her even against injuries we would consider severe." Liz explains and Phoenix gawks at her, surprised, as she hasn't heard this tidbit about her abilities. "Nothing is set in stone, but I want us to brainstorm. If we use some of Sara's masking agent on Phoenix, she should be indistinguishable from a human, even close-up;

however, she'll have her Apara strength, and we're working on counteracting their anti-ability tech."

Peder puts his arm protectively around Phoenix and pulls her close, reassuring her he'll protect her. "Don't you think they've given up on me yet?" Phoenix tries to articulate her thoughts, but they come out a bit awkward.

Liz motions to Amy to explain. "I discovered a thermal scanner set up to screen your apartment. It alerted them you were still human because your body temperature is *lower* than normal for an Apara. Sara believes it goes hand-in-hand with your body's ability to produce some of its own red blood cells. I checked the homes of a couple of others we've already brought in and discovered active scanners as well, so they haven't given up on those they haven't found or brought in, at least not all of them."

"So, how did they know it was me and not Devyn, or the mail carrier at my door?" Phoenix wonders.

"How did Devyn get in touch with you?" Amy asks.

"How else? She called me!" Phoenix says, sounding annoyed and defensive.

"You're old cell, right? Not the *new, encrypted* one?" Amy inquires with a knowing look.

Phoenix looks slightly deflated and closes her eyes, giving a curt nod. "*Yeah,* my regular, *non-encrypted* cell phone. Are you suggesting they have my phone bugged?"

"Something like that. We suspect they have some sort of eavesdropping algorithm in the telephone network itself, and your old phone is vulnerable to that." Amy explains.

"Sorry, I hadn't thought of that! Can we switch my old number to an Apara phone?" She asks, embarrassed by her oversight.

"Yes, but we're planning to take advantage of the *insecurity* of your *old* phone." Amy grins. "When we're ready, or when *you're ready,* you're going to make a call from that phone that will let them know you'll be going back to your apartment to pack. We're hoping that will bring them out of hiding to grab you." Amy suggests.

"I don't want to get grabbed!" Phoenix exclaims, comprehending how the worm on the fishing hook feels.

"We'll do everything we can to protect you and prepare you for this. I'll train you in self-defense and other practical skills. Sara wants to work on your healing abilities and see what they need to do to make you pass as fully human." Amy elucidates.

"Wait, a *damn* minute! I don't really feel like letting some asshole bite me and try to 'turn me'! What if they decide to take things further and... I've heard stories about that *jackass*, Jason! What if these guys are just as *nasty*?" She blurts out, worried they might try to rape her in the process of turning her.

Hannah raises her hand tentatively to get Liz's attention. "If I may, that shouldn't be an issue. Uri does not want there to be shared bonds between those whose blood is used to transform someone and the transformees. At least when I was there, everything was done by syringe. Blood was drawn from the person to be transformed and given to one of the already transformed soldiers. After ten minutes, blood was then withdrawn from them, and given to the person to be changed, all done without either party knowing who the other was. Uri wants no firsthand or intimate interactions in case things go wrong and someone has to be put down. He doesn't want to risk emotional bonds between their Apara. Honestly, I think he fears that if they bond with each other, they might mutiny against him. Better to keep them all distant from each other but subservient to him." She hypothesizes.

Phoenix is somewhat mollified, but says, "Ugh, I *hate* needles, but I guess that's better than the alternative."

Liz addresses Phoenix. "I wouldn't be asking you to do this if there were a better way. We need to find their base as soon as possible, not only to prevent them from creating and using their own

Apara against us, but to rescue them from the *Naqam*. After all, they were *meant* to be *with* us, not *against* us."

Phoenix shrugs and shifts awkwardly.

Liz continues "While our finders are working on this, as well as others searching for clues to where their new base is, I believe you will give us our best and timeliest hope of finding them. Hannah's been working with our people to counteract their anti-ability measures, so you'll be able to contact us even if they place you in a cell or area with anti-ability measures. If things go awry, Callie can get you out if you can't port out yourself."

Peder keeps his arm around Phoenix, knowing this is an enormous responsibility to put on her young, Apara shoulders. He senses when her resolve shifts and she acquiesces. "*Alright*, I'll do it, but I want Peder to be there whenever I'm training. If he doesn't think I'm ready when the time comes, I'll go with *his* judgement." She tells them and feels him give her a side hug for her courage.

Liz looks relieved. "*Deal!* Though we're going to make sure you're ready for this, both you and Janna. I think it will do you, Janna, and Callie good to work together. Even though Callie won't be going into combat, she should get some combat training, as well as work on her portal skills. Having the three of you work together will make it easier for you to locate each other psychically in a crisis."

Liz breathes deeply and looks around the table; her eyes lingering on her brother's face. She senses his earlier frustration with her and her idea has diffused somewhat, though he's still clearly skeptical. She smiles softly to her brother and says, "Peder, Amy, and Hannah, if you could come with me to the center, we can do some brainstorming on the other aspects of our mission. I think it might be best to let these three have some time to themselves. Niall, perhaps you should come as well?" Liz suggests.

At that, everyone but the three, young Apara women port out, leaving them sitting awkwardly in silence.

That doesn't last long. By the time Niall and Peder port back nearly three hours later, the three young women are talking and laughing as if they're old friends.

Peder paths Niall, *That's what Liz was hoping for. The three of them have bonded with each other.*

Niall replies, *It seems like they've all hit it off, doesn't it? That'll be good for Callie. She's been working at home on her jewelry, so doesn't get out among others of our kind that much, nor humans, for that matter!*

It takes a couple of minutes, but Callie notices Niall leaning against the wall, watching them. She runs over to him and hugs him. "Didn't notice you two port in!"

"You three are getting along, I see?" He inquires, returning her affection.

"Yeah, and I think I needed this! Things have been so crazy lately, it's been good to just sit around, and prattle on about *shit*!" Callie slips loose from Niall and edges back to her new friends.

"So, what have you three been talking about?" Peder asks.

Phoenix blushes to match her ginger hair. "*Mostly* you guys!" She glances at Janna. "and *Charlie*! And how our lives got turned upside-down and backward since we met you all!"

Peder rolls his eyes. "Is *that* all?" He shakes his head, raising one eyebrow and addressing Phoenix, "So, do you all need more time to chew the fat, or can we go *home*? You and I need to work on some things, too."

Phoenix looks at her new friends with fondness. "I guess I can pull myself away, but I want to get together with you guys again soon!" She exclaims.

Peder lets out a gregarious laugh. "Don't worry! You *will*! If Liz has her way, you three are going to be meeting daily with Amy to train. You'll see so much of each other you may get sick of each other!" He chuckles again. "Janna, I'm to take you back to Charlie. Amy's busy with some errands for Liz." He explains and Janna joins Phoenix and Peder. The three of them port out, leaving Niall and Callie alone.

"How about I fix some *proper food*?" He says, glancing at the living room table covered in cookies and junk food remains. "And then we can try some portal practice while your mood is better?" He gives her a pleading look, knowing that Liz's plans depend on her unique ability.

"I guess so." She says and cleans up the mess from her visitors, while Niall fixes some dinner.

ON THE DEFENSIVE

During the next couple of weeks, everyone's on high alert. Until they can set their plan in motion, they can only prepare for attacks. Being downtown may protect them from a frontal assault, but if the *Naqam* attack, their only option is to retreat to Sanctuary and disconnect the linkage between their building in Sanctuary and its twin in downtown Asheville.

They've arranged sensors within a half a mile radius to alert them if any unknown Apara approaches or ports in nearby, and they've strengthened their anti-porting shields. An emergency 'detach' is created so separating the two versions of their building will take seconds should the *Naqam* attack, and anyone inside the offices will be safe in Sanctuary.

They create a temporary training center in Sanctuary, much like an emergency shelter FEMA might set up after a natural disaster. Amy will train the new Apara in combat and self-defense, while others will train them to use their abilities.

Amy recruits Tess to help with the combat training as she's already jumped through most of Amy's hoops before they rescued Marc. Liz hopes Tess can teach others with strong PK to do something similar to her PK blasts.

They bring in a few other new Apara, such as Teresa Mendoza, whose EMP ability will be useful, if not crucial. Alice also joins them. Dimitrios, their longtime, and previously retired, *Invenir*, or finder, took Alice in as an apprentice, but they have since become partners. Her finding skills will come in handy, though Dimi, as she calls him, insists they will work *only* as a team.

Peder works as a PK instructor. Marc and Amy work with them on precognitive and intuitive skills they can use to predict an opponent's attack. Marc teaches them to use telempathy similarly.

Sara, Isanda, and the hybrid science team create a protective field that counteracts the anti-ability field the *Naqam* use. A rare, green, Centauri-opal creates an interference bubble that neutralizes the effects of their anti-ability field, allowing them to use some of their skills such as telepathy, clairvoyance, PK, and precognition with ease, though porting remains partially hindered by the anti-ability field.

Rendering the *Naqam's* Deuterium dart solution inert is more complex. In the end, the hybrids create a compound that converts the deuterium in the heavy water to normal hydrogen, rendering it inert. The compound is injected immediately prior to battle, so it's already in an Apara's system before exposure. There will be a brief episode of weakness, usually just a couple minutes before the compound strips the deuterium's extra proton and neutron and converts it to standard hydrogen. Without the deuterium, the quartz infusion in the serum becomes harmless and the particulates pass naturally from the body. Unfortunately, the compound doesn't last more than an hour at a time, so all combat Apara must have rapid-infuser ampoules on any mission that may last longer than that. If multiple darts hit someone, they will need a booster infusion immediately.

One of the most important preparations for the young, Apara women is teaching Callie to home in on her new friends and open a portal to them.

The next few days, Callie, Phoenix, Janna, and several others play clairvoyant hide-and seek. Callie remains at the training center, while the others port out to various locations in Sanctuary, at first, and then the human-world Earth. Callie must locate each of them quickly, using her clairvoyance. Normally, she could locate them through telepathy, but should they be neutralized, unconscious, or blocked, Callie must be able to locate and create a portal to them using clairvoyance.

The last day, Sara knocks each of them out, in turn, and has someone take them to an unknown location, leaving them there. Callie must locate them and create a portal big enough to walk through so they can be retrieved. The added focus and energy usage leaves her exhausted by the end of the day.

"Niall! *Time-out!* For *God's* sake! My head's all frazzled, and I feel like I'm gonna fall over if I do more!" Callie complains.

"Niall laughs and comes up behind her, hugging her. "You lasted longer than I expected, *mo chridhe*. All right everyone, that's it for now. Go home and get some rest!"

Callie sags into him and he grabs her to keep her from sinking to the ground in exhaustion. He turns her to face him, holding her close, both in affection, and to prevent her legs from giving out. He leans in and gently kisses her. "You did an *amazing* job! You've really come a long way." He pauses. "Have you *heard* any more *voices*?" He inquires, hoping that has finally stopped.

"Not really. Occasionally, it was like I could sense something, but I didn't *hear* anything. I think I was too focused on my friends." She explains, as he pulls her near and ports her home, releasing her onto the sofa, and heading to the kitchen for food and blood. However, when he comes back out, her exhaustion has won out, and she's sound asleep. He ports her up to bed and puts the blood and food into a mini-fridge in the bedroom in case she awakens starving.

Niall paths Liz, *Hey! Callie's doing great locating the others and creating a portal for them. She's getting faster at closing the portals with no backlash, as well.*

Good! Let me know when you think she's ready to do it on the fly. If Phoenix or Janna get in a bind, she must be able to portal them home as quickly as possible and close it to keep any potential pursuers from passing through the portal and into Sanctuary, at least unless we WANT them to. Liz paths.

Niall sends a confused vibe to Liz, followed by pathing, **Who, exactly, would we want to come here? If any of them come here and then escape, it's entirely possible they could teach the others how to get here.**

He can sense the equivalent of a lopsided grin from Liz. *I'm not planning on letting any of their Apara through, at least not until they're all neutralized and preferably knocked out, but I am considering bringing Jabarin here. We need to find out just how extensive their organization has become, and if he is out of commission, I suspect the organization may collapse in chaos. His fanaticism drives them. His and Elias', at least.*

There's a momentary, mental silence from Niall, followed by, *As you wish, Liz, but I'm not sure he'll be very forthcoming.*

He won't have to be! If he won't talk, we have powerful telepaths who'll dig the info out once his anti-path implant is removed. This isn't a diplomatic mission; it's nigh unto war with the Naqam! If we can, I want to create an understanding with this man, but I'm not sure that's an achievable goal. Liz paths.

So, the goal is to repatriate as many of their Apara, deprogram them, and then what? He inquires, curiously.

She pauses, gathering her thoughts. *If we can, we'll mentally condition the humans involved, including Uri. If we can't, we'll have to consider other solutions.* She paths cryptically with overtones of regret and sadness, knowing what any war sometimes requires.

He goes to bed, curling his body around Callie, who is so exhausted and deep in sleep that she doesn't even stir.

The next day is a rest day, except for Callie. There's one new thing he needs to work on with her -- creating multiple, small portals simultaneously. They practice in the larger room at the training center. When they arrive, Callie notices X's made of tape in a grid on the floor. She asks, "What're those for?"

"They're spots for you to open your portals. Start with the one closest to us and use the window as an exit portal." He suggests.

She opens a small, one foot in diameter portal above the X, and the window across the room shimmers. He picks up a ball and tosses it into the portal nearby and it pops out from the window and rolls across the floor. The marks are numbered, and he randomly calls them out, having her open portals rapid-fire and close them before opening a new one.

They pause to eat, and she feeds from him, as her psychic energy expenditure was great. Then Niall moves on to the next, and perhaps most difficult task.

"Ready to get back at it?" He asks.

"Guess so...." She says, facing the field of numbered X's.

He calls out the number 8 and less than a second later, a portal opens above it, again exiting at the window.

"Now, hold that one open and open one at number 3, with an exit to the right of the first one." He commands.

"What? *Two at once?*" She asks, confused, as she's never done more than one at a time.

"Yes, and I'll explain why when we're done." He says.

It takes more effort but soon there are two energy portals over the number 8 and 3 locations.

"Now add number 13!" He says.

She glances at him briefly, shaking her head, and opens a third portal, but can only hold all three briefly before the first one collapses with a small backlash, making her stagger backward, and lose the other two. "*Damn it!*" She exclaims in frustration.

"Don't worry, my love! Take your time with this part. We'll work on speed after you master having multiple portals open." He says, reassuringly. By the end of the day, she can manage up to seven, 1 foot in diameter portals at one time.

"That's it for today, but we'll practice more tomorrow." He says.

"Niall, are you going to *freaking tell me* what this is all about?" She asks emphatically.

He pulls her over to the side of the room where they settle on a long bench. "Sara's developed a neutralizer that can be delivered in gaseous form. If we can find where most of their Apara are located in the base, you can open portals to multiple locations simultaneously, and Peder, who's one of our strongest kinetics, can hurl neutralizer canisters through to take their Apara down. Think of it as tear gas for Apara. The problem is, you may have to open them rapid fire or even simultaneously; hence, this exercise."

"*Hell!* I'm exhausted just *thinking* about it!" She gripes.

"I realize this is overwhelming, but you're doing *great!*" He encourages.

They practice more with the X's for two days, increasing the speed at which she can create a network of portals, as well as focusing on making them one way so the gas cannot come back and overwhelm them.

Last, they focus on widening the portals so multiple people can be evacuated at once, as she did at the concert venue, and to save everyone at Inspiration Inc.

DEFCON 3

The Asheville Apara have been on a heightened alert level for some time, so Liz calls a meeting with the three couples and Amy. "Sorry to drag you in on your rest day. I hear your training is going well." She compliments them with a smile, but her expression grows more serious. "However, I need you to be honest with me. How ready are you?"

Niall glances at Callie and says, "I'm not sure there's much more we can do to prepare. The only thing we haven't been able to test is how she'll function under pressure." He explains, putting an arm around her and squeezing her reassuringly.

Liz addresses Amy next. "And what about combat and self-defense training?"

"It's going well. In fact, Tess taught Teresa to do a variation of her energy blasts. Since Terri can manipulate electrical energy by absorbing and creating EMPs, it wasn't difficult for her to adapt it on a more controlled, smaller scale to do something like what Tess does. I plan to bring in a few of my guys with high PK ratings and see if she can train them to do something similar." Amy suggests with a questioning expression.

"Yes, do that. The reason I called this meeting is that our sensors detected unidentified Apara near our center *twice* this week. There have been no attacks, but I believe they must be doing reconnaissance and information gathering; searching for weaknesses prior to an eventual attack." Liz sighs in exasperation. "We must set things in motion soon. If they're getting bold enough to do reconnaissance, then they must believe they're strong enough to have an advantage, if not now, then soon." She says, concerned that time is running out.

Peder interjects, "So, you're saying it's time to *bait* the trap?" His voice is riddled with anxiety and worry, as he knows Phoenix will be the proverbial cheese.

"I'm afraid so." She turns toward Phoenix. "How are you feeling about all this? Are you ready?"

"As ready as I can be. Sara's been coaching me, and I can alter my body temperature to Apara levels. Sara implanted a variation of the masking agent in me subcutaneously. Once they try to turn me, I'll break it, and it will mask the human scent I normally have, making me seem fully Apara, or so Sara says." Phoenix explains as confidently as she can.

Liz looks around the room at everyone, wishing she didn't have to force this on such new Apara, but their skills are all vital to the mission. "Set things in motion. Assuming they take the bait and abduct Phoenix, Janna will be next to go in, but not until Phoenix has been 'turned' by them."

Peder's expression is filled with concern. "Does Hannah know how quickly they go from turning to conditioning?"

"When she was there, they took about a week, but that may have changed." Liz says with deep concern in her eyes.

"How do we protect her from whatever that conditioning entails?" He asks, worried they may break Phoenix, and jeopardize not only the mission, but harm her psychologically.

Phoenix reaches over and puts her hand reassuringly on Peder's leg. "Sara's been working with me on a few things that should help, shielding, and being able to withdraw my mind into a psychologically protective state while letting them think the conditioning is working. It's not foolproof, but ...." She trails off, looking Peder in the eye.

Liz nods, then says, "No, nothing's foolproof or certain with this situation. Other than individual rogues over the years, we've never faced an enemy with equal abilities and strengths to our own. We must beat them to the punch and catch them off guard." She addresses Amy, "Get your people ready. I want to set things in motion with Phoenix by Friday. You'll have a few more days to prepare, but we can't put it off much longer or we'll be the ones caught with our psychic pants down."

Amy looks unusually serious, "Got it, Liz." She ports off to set things in motion.

Liz turns back to the others. "Practice but get some rest as well. I need you at your best." She looks at each of them, lingering on Charlie. "Charlie, you're human, so perhaps have the greatest risk in this endeavor. If you aren't up to this, I'm sure we can find a less dangerous part for you to play."

"No, Ma'am. I'm a soldier. I know what I'm getting into. I've always known there's a chance I'll go into a fight and not come out. The only thing different this time is that I'm fighting for someone I care about and not some random war in another country. If I can take the risk defending someone else's country, I can *damn well* do it to protect Janna and... her people." He tells Liz, maintaining eye contact as an equal, not a mere human among the Apara.

"Very well. I wish there were some way we could bring you over to join us, officially, but consider yourself one of *our* people, even as a human." Liz says.

Charlie nods and takes Janna's hand. Janna ports the two of them home to spend some time together and get some much-needed rest before the big event.

Liz faces Niall and Callie. "Callie, you've perhaps got the least personal risk, but one of the most important roles. I don't want to put any more pressure on you than necessary, but you must understand your place in all of this."

Callie sighs and nods. "I get it, really. I know I can do this, especially with Niall's help."

Niall gives her a side hug. "I'll make sure she's ready." And they port out, leaving Liz, Peder, and Phoenix.

Liz's expression shifts to one of emotional conflict. "I really wish I didn't have to put you two in this situation. In some ways, you'll be at the greatest risk, Phoenix. Peder's been alone for a long time, and I don't want to jeopardize that, but...." She sighs.

"I get it, and so does Peder. We'll get through this. We must!" Phoenix says with a nervous smile.

Liz's expression shifts as though she's forgotten a cake in the oven. "*Oh!* We've got one more trick up our proverbial sleeves that may help."

"Like what?" Peder asks, confused by her sudden admission.

"Tess came up with the idea of making our own variant of the artificial telepathy implants the terrorists used before Jerusalem. They should be at a frequency that can bypass both their EM shield and their anti-path technology. All of you will be implanted with them, just in case their anti-path tech has improved. The terrorists' implants automatically connected everyone who had them within a certain range, so was chaotic to use. We've upgraded the tech so you can direct your messages to individual users. It's a backup, but it will also be on a frequency their Apara can't pick up on."

Peder relaxes slightly. "*Good!* I'll feel better knowing we have a backup form of communication. I've been dreading losing touch with Phoenix once she's in their base."

"That's still a possibility, but this should decrease the risk significantly," Liz says, clapping her brother on the arm reassuringly. "Get some rest, you two. I'll arrange for Sara to do the implants tomorrow so you all can get used to them." she says. Peder and Phoenix port out, leaving Liz alone in the room, but only briefly.

As soon as everyone is gone, her stamina wanes, and Kari ports in as she senses Liz falter. "I'm here, *love*. We'll get through this, as will they."

"I know, there's just been so much the last two years. Every time I feel like I'm getting back on top of things, some new crisis pops up.

"When this is over, I think you should let Peder or Marc take over for a while, then we can have some time to recover from everything," Kari says as she massages Liz's taught shoulders.

"I'm not sure I *can*! I'll just *worry* even more." She says.

"If you don't, you won't be any good to anyone! You haven't had a break since you became Apara, at least according to Peder, and certainly not since *we* met centuries ago! Promise me you'll take a break when this crisis is over!" Kari begs her.

After a minute, Liz relents. "Alright! I'll *consider* it!"

"No, *Lissa*, not consider, *promise!*" Kari says as she clamps down a little rougher on Liz's rock-hard shoulders.

"*Ouch! Alright!* I'll take a break, but only if this situation resolves completely. I won't leave my people in danger!" She says, putting a hand on her partner's, getting her to stop torturing her tendons. "I *promise*."

COME AND GET ME!

Peder and Phoenix are home Thursday evening, spending time together, knowing tomorrow they'll be separated several days for the first time since he transformed her. Their mood is somber, and Peder is anxious. They're sitting together on the sofa, leaning into one another, Peder's arm around Phoenix protectively.

Peder faces her and asks, "Are you *sure* you're ready for this? Maybe we can get a couple more days to prepare.

"You *heard* Liz! They've been lurking around the new center. They won't give up on us just because you all went in and beat their *asses* a few months ago! It sounds like they're more determined than ever to paint us as the villains and put a target on our backs!" She sighs. "I *can do this!* And Callie will pull me out in a flash if *anything* goes awry."

"I know, but with over 800 years under my belt, one thing I've learned is things rarely go as smoothly as you expect. I can't stand the thought of you getting hurt or even killed. They know more about us than any other enemy we've faced. They've studied us and know our weaknesses." He says and cups her cheek with his hand.

"As far as they'll be concerned, I'll just be another human potential they're bringing into the fold. And besides..." She pauses and focuses, triggering their newly implanted synthetic telepathy chips. *I've always got this thing in my head for backup! I promise! I'll contact you every night through it. That way, they won't know I'm communicating with you!* She reassures him through the synpath chip.

"That thing's going to take some getting used to. Almost feels like my skull is vibrating my brain like a blender!" Peder jokes and draws her close again. "You *better* come back in one piece!" He says emotionally.

They get up the next morning and run through her mission. There's no guarantee the *Naqam* will even take the bait, but they must try.

Phoenix will use her old phone to call her friend Devyn to check up on her, assuming the *Naqam* are still monitoring it.

"Now, remember, when they take you, you're *supposed* to be human. Fight them but watch your strength. If you fight them too hard, they'll realize something's off." Peder reminds her.

"I *know*. Amy and I talked about that, and I sparred with Charlie until I got it about right for him." She pauses, then says, "It's time." She fishes her old cell phone out and calls Devyn. It rings about four times before she picks up.

"Hey, Phoenix! How goes?" She says, having checked the caller ID out of habit.

"Oh, pretty good. Remember, I told you I was moving?" She asks.

"Yeah, something about your new boyfriend. I still think you should have let me give him the once over before I went home!" Devyn ribs her.

"Next time! Anyway, I've gotta go over to my old place to pack stuff, which made me think of you, so I just wanted to check-in. I'm going to be pretty *tied-up* after I move, so figured I'd better call now. Did you get everything sorted out?"

"Oh, yeah! Guy's back in jail and we're all moving. We're heading out of state just in case. Besides, I've got a job waiting for me in San Diego as soon as I can get out there." Devyn says excitedly.

"*Cool!* I know you've wanted to move back for a while. Anyway, I'm on my way out now to my old apartment but I'll holler when things calm down." Phoenix says, hoping the *Naqam* are listening and get the idea Peder is finally going to change her and they must grab her now, or never.

She tells Devyn goodbye and faces Peder, hands on hips. "Well, if that didn't get their attention, nothing will! It'll be okay." She reassures him,

He takes out an infuser from a small pouch and injects her with it, then gives her a good sniff after a couple of minutes. "Hmm, you smell so human now, I'm almost tempted to have a snack!" He grins with a flash of fangs and fishes her car keys out of his pocket. "Here, you'll need these." He says and tosses them to her. There's a flat-pack of moving boxes in your back seat to make it look legit." He says and pulls her into one last, long embrace.

"Peder's portal home isn't far from his sister's, so it's a short drive to her old apartment. She pulls into her old parking spot and sits there briefly. She sees Lydia peek out of her curtains and can hear her call for Cinnamon, to take her for a walk. Phoenix rolls her eyes and paths Peder. *Make sure they've got a team on standby! Lydia's home and will no doubt need yet another memory adjustment if this works!*

His reply is wordless, mental amusement at Lydia and anxiety that Phoenix has made it to her place.

She grabs the thick bundle of packing boxes and her old apartment key and heads for the door. Lydia comes out with Cinnamon.

"Oh, *my Lord!* I haven't seen you in *forever*, Phoenix! Where've you *ever* been hiding yourself!" She says with an overly embellished, southern drawl.

"Nothing to worry about, Lydia. I met someone at work, and I'm moving in with him. Just came home to pack up some of my stuff." Phoenix says and can feel Lydia's disappointment that she's missed an opportunity to pawn her son off on some unsuspecting young woman.

"Oh, well, I hope you'll be happy. But if things don't work out, I know my son would *love* to see you again!" She slips in.

"Well, tell him hello from me, but I'm sure this is a long-term relationship." She says, unlocking her front door and awkwardly squeezing in with the boxes, tossing them down on the floor. She mentally scans the apartment for energy signatures, but there's nothing.

After half an hour, she thinks, *Guess I might as well do some packing, as all this needs to go to Peder's eventually!* She puts the moving boxes together so she can fill them. She packs some of her books and then grabs a bunch of her clothes. She finds a stray stuffed toy from her childhood and packs it in with her clothing.

She loses track of time as she packs. As she sorts through some of her DVDs and CDs, the hair on the back of her neck stands on end, because someone is porting in. She plays human, ignoring the sensation until someone puts their hand over her mouth and pulls her up against him, then struggles for show.

Phoenix uses the synpath chip to send Peder a quick message: *GAME ON!* She feels a jab to her arm, and touches her assailant's public mind, finding out he dosed her with a tranquilizer. She slumps in his arms and withdraws her active mind into a mental shell, as Sara and Tess taught her. From there, they won't be able to sense she's awake or any of her mental activity, but she can observe everything, at least audibly and psychically.

She feels the unmistakable sensation of slipping into the membrane and out again somewhere warmer, where the air is clearly recirculated. They lay her on a bed, and she hears a door open, close, and lock.

Phoenix waits a few minutes and then uses the synpath chip to reach out to Peder again. *Peder? Can you hear me?* She paths.

Yes! Thank God! Did they finally come for you? Peder asks anxiously.

Yeah, they must believe I'm still human as they dosed me with Ketamine. That was the name in his mind. It didn't do anything, but I faked it. They just dumped me in a cell or something. I heard them lock the door. Not sure how long I should pretend to be knocked out, though.... She paths, while feigning unconsciousness.

They didn't hurt you, did they? Sara says without knowing the dose, she can't say how long you would normally be out, but at least an hour or two seems reasonable. Peder paths.

I'm fine, though my nose itches like hell, and I want to scratch it, but I'm supposed to be FREAKING unconscious! She paths in frustration.

Can you sense anything around you? Any others? He paths, as Liz listens telepathically.

I think so. She listens with her hypersensitive hearing and hears someone pacing nearby and a woman crying. In the opposite direction, she hears someone turning pages in a book. *There are others nearby. I think they're still human, possibly in cells like mine. So, I'm guessing they may not have turned all the abducted potentials yet.* She paths.

Hannah's here with Liz and me. She says Uri would only have one transformed at a time and condition them before turning another. Uri is paranoid about his 'vampires' ganging up on him in a mutiny. Peder paths.

Hmm, we assumed they'd try to turn me quickly, but if they still have others ahead of me, you may have to send Janna in before they do it. She paths.

Noted! Liz says we'll play it by ear. Do you know where you are? Were you able to get a sense of it when they ported you there? He inquires.

Not exactly. I sense we're underground, or at least there's a lot of rock all around... and water! Every so often, I get a whiff of moisture, like I might be near water—possibly salt water. The air's recirculated. Despite the walls being regular walls, there's an odd echo, like you might get in an enormous cavern. I used to go spelunking with a club in college, and that's what it reminds me of.

That's good to know. Liz says she'll have people do some research on cave systems over there. I'm so glad the synpath chips work! I was afraid they'd take you and you wouldn't be able to reach me! Peder paths, relieved, yet still worried about his beloved partner.

Hey! I hear voices and footsteps in the hallway. Don't know if they're coming here, or dealing with others, but I'm gonna focus on that! Will holler again soon! She paths sending waves of love to Peder, hoping to ease his mind.

Phoenix lies there, eyes closed, listening to the sounds nearby. She hears a door open, and the sobbing woman she heard earlier wails in panic. Someone speaks to the woman in another language, and she believes it's French. Even though she's never studied French, she intuitively understands what's being said. She hears, "*Quiet* woman! Did we hurt you earlier when we took a blood sample? I promise you will feel much better when we're done." The person's language shifts to Hebrew, and Phoenix is amazed when she understands what's said. The man tells another man: "Hold her! And for Jehovah's sake, keep her *quiet!*"

The woman's panicked crying becomes muffled as the assistant grabs her and puts a hand over her mouth. The first man says, "Just a little prick, and in a few hours, you'll feel better than you've *ever* felt." He says, in French. Phoenix hears the woman's muffled squeals and senses her terror as the man injects her with a large syringe full of blood, no doubt infected with the active virus.

The woman cries in shock and fear as they release her and leave the room, slamming the security door. The first man speaks to the second, again in Hebrew. "It'll probably take her about a day to change, so post a guard outside her door. There are sensors in her cell that'll tell us when the fever sets in and breaks. As soon as it breaks, the anti-ability measures for her cell will turn on. We don't want her accidentally porting out like the *last* one! Luckily, he didn't get too far before we recovered him, but Uri had a *fit!*"

Peder had explained how Apara can understand and speak other languages by tapping into people's speech centers. Aside from him speaking a little old Norse and understanding him, this is the first time she's experienced it spontaneously, and the effort is exhausting. She reaches out to Peder through the synpath chip. ***Pretty sure they just started the transformation on a woman down the hall; the one that was sobbing. I can hear them walking away, but I'll let you know if anyone comes to see me.*** She paths, then drifts off to sleep for real because of her psychic expenditure.

Luckily, since her body produces some of its own blood, she doesn't need to feed as frequently as others. She'll have time before she must feed, and as she falls asleep, wonders what she'll do if she needs blood before they "turn" her.

After a couple of hours, she wakes when she hears two sets of footsteps coming down the hall. She thinks, hm, sounds like two women. Though one has a more delicate a step than the other. She hears one woman say to the other, this time in English, "Her sedative should be wearing off by now. Uri wants us to question her and see what we can get out of her before she's transformed. She's been living with one of them, so may have some useful information."

Phoenix hears fingertips pressing numbers on a keypad and the lock for the door releases. It swings open with a squeak and a thud as the door handle hits the wall. Phoenix reacts to the thud but acts groggy. She raises her head, looks toward the door, and squints like her vision's blurry. As she thought, two women. One in military fatigues, holding a stun gun, and the other dressed professionally, in slacks and a blouse, with a clipboard in hand.

"Phoenix Johnsen?" The more properly dressed woman asks in heavily accented English.

Phoenix stares at her and makes a show of pulling herself up, acting as if it's difficult. The professional woman motions for the other to assist her. 'Military gal', as Phoenix thinks of her until she gets a proper name, comes over and helps Phoenix sit up, pulling a lever that raises the back of the hospital bed.

Phoenix acts like she's clearing her head, but says, "Who the *hell* are you and where... *where* am I?" She closes her eyes and shakes her head.

The woman pulls up a chair, making a grating sound as it slides along the floor. She gives Phoenix a lopsided grin. "Let's cut through the *bullshit*. I'm sure you have a good idea *who* we are, and why we've taken you. You've been living with one of them for a while, and considering he rescued you from earlier abduction attempts, I'm certain you have some concept of what's going on?" She raises one eyebrow and waits for her reply.

"You're the same ones who tried to take me before? Your guy *shot* my friend! What the *Hell*?" Phoenix says with indignation.

The woman shifts in her seat uncomfortably. "Yes, I will admit that was an unnecessary move on his part, but it was and is vital we have you on our side."

"And why is that?" Phoenix spits out, shivering as though she's both angry and afraid wrapped up in one.

"Surely, you know what your *boyfriend* is, yes?" She asks.

Phoenix sits quietly, seething and staring the woman in the eye.

"Well, we know what he is...." She drawls out and grins, showing her fangs. It takes Phoenix a second to realize she should have recoiled if she wants the woman to believe she doesn't know what Peder and the others are, and she'll have to acknowledge her awareness to make her reaction fit.

"*Yes*. I know what he is and what you are as well. What I don't get is *why* you sent those thugs in, drugged me, and brought me to wherever *here* is! I'm not going to fight my friends, if that's what you think!" Phoenix feigns a sulk.

The woman gives her a haunting smile that makes chills go down Phoenix's spine. "I'm assuming, if you were packing up to move in with your boyfriend, the decision has been made for him to change you?"

"What *business* is it of yours? That's between Peder and me!" She snaps. She wasn't expecting an interrogation, so she's winging it and hoping it sounds natural.

"We couldn't let you get away from us! Not if there was any *chance* we could acquire you first. Compatible humans are a rare commodity, and they've certainly done their best to deprive us of most of those on our list. So, when we picked up your call to your *friend*, we knew we had to move before you could be changed and brought into their fold." The woman says in an almost sickeningly sweet, mother-like tone, as if trying to convince her they were protecting her from a much worse fate.

"You had *no right* to take me! I *want* to be with *him*, not you!" Phoenix exclaims angrily.

"Be that as it may, you are *needed* here, and here is where you will be transformed. However, we can make it easier on you should you make it worth our while." She says with a sly grin.

"What do you *mean*?" Phoenix asks, wondering if she's in over her head.

"No doubt your *lover* has told you about his people to convince you to turn away from humanity and join them. You must have some useful information you could trade for, let's say, an *easier* transformation, or perhaps a more comfortable position than front-line, foot soldier when the time comes to engage them. You've already said you *don't wish* to fight your *friends* or your *lover*." She sneers.

"I won't fight for you! Even if you change me, I won't do it!" Phoenix says obstinately.

"My dear girl, you'll do *whatever* we say! At least, after you're *conditioned* to be loyal to us." She explains threateningly, staring her down like a hawk eyeing a meal. "If you help us with some information, *perhaps* we can find you a job among us that will not require you to fight, at least not *right* away."

"Why do you hate them so much? They're not the *bad guys!*" Phoenix insists, looking increasingly agitated. She thinks, *Thank God I took a year of theater in college! Those acting classes are coming in handy!*

The woman looks aghast. "*Not* the bad guys? Is *that* what he *told* you? My *dear* child! They're responsible for the destruction of Jerusalem and many, many deaths! I'm guessing they left that part out, perhaps?"

Phoenix thinks, *Maybe I should tell them what Peder told me?* She gets a determined expression, saying, "I think it's you all that don't have the *entire story*. My 'boyfriend', as you call him, was there, he was the one who *found* the bomb! They were trying to stop it, but when he got close to it, hoping to diffuse it, it had a proximity trigger that started a 15-second countdown. The best he could do was warn everyone to evacuate, and his delay resulted in him being severely injured. They lost many people too. You aren't the only ones who were victims that night." Phoenix says, fighting tears as she remembers flashes she'd gotten from Peder's mind when he recounted that horrible night.

"How convenient a story that is! *Foolish* girl! Of course, he told you they were the *heroes* trying to *stop* the bomb! If they'd told you the *truth*, would you have agreed to join them?" She spits out vehemently. Uri has transferred much of his own paranoia and hate to his subordinates when he had them conditioned.

"I believe him. He's a *good* man, and so are the others I've met! All good people. If it weren't for them, the death toll would have been even higher and would have included other cities around the world!" Phoenix is on the verge of tears, wishing she could convince this woman, or any of them, that the Apara are the good guys and avoid the coming confrontation. Unfortunately, she's dealt with people like this before, in high school, and her early years of college. People who get some conspiracy madness in their heads and nothing, not even hard evidence, can dissuade them from their ideas of who is 'really' to blame for whatever upsets them. There is no way she'll convince *this* woman, or *any* of them, of the truth.

"Ms. Johnsen, take some time to think it over. There are still thirteen others before you in the transformation queue. Should you *decide* to take us up on our offer, all you must do is say so before it's your turn. Transformation can be quite traumatic, you see, though we are finding ways to ameliorate the experience. Cooperating means less intense conditioning for you if you provide us with something of value, *proving* we can trust you." She says with a curt nod, then continues. "A meal will be brought to you soon. Pay close attention to those in the cells around you as they're brought over. I think it may encourage you to see things our way." She grins, showing her fangs, then leaves the room with her bodyguard pulling up the rear.

Phoenix waits until she's certain they're both a good distance away and is about to synpath to Peder with an update when she notices a slight whirring sound from the ceiling. She looks around, trying not to be obvious, and notices a tiny camera lens in one of the ceiling panels. She thinks, *Damn it! I must be careful! Of course, they're watching new potentials, especially one who is a known associate of their enemy.*

She puts the back down on the bed, and lies down, rolling away from the intrusive camera. She thinks, *I certainly don't need them seeing any odd facial expressions while I path Peder! Hope they didn't see any earlier!*

She activates the synpath chip and paths, **Running into a bit of a situation here. They know I've been living with you, and assume I have valuable information. They want me to tell them stuff in exchange for an easier turning or a non-combat position afterward. What do you want me to do?** She inquires.

Let me talk to my sister. Maybe we can work this to our advantage and feed them some misinformation. He suggests.

Okay, let me know what to tell them. Oh, there are about thirteen in line ahead of me to be transformed, so it may be a while. They've given me until it's my turn to give them something to make things easier on me. Phoenix paths, feeling uneasy about being locked up that long. **Peder, what do I do if I get hungry? I know I don't need to feed as often as most of us, but if I need to feed, that'll blow my cover for sure!**

We assumed you'd be in and out quickly, or at least 'turned' by them so you could feed normally. I'll see what Sara and Liz suggest. He pauses. **How're you holding up?** He paths.

Okay, I guess. They've got a camera on me, so I'm going to have to be very careful about anything non-human I do in here. She paths anxiously.

Be careful, love! I want you back here in one piece and of sound mind! If they figure you out, things could get messy! He paths with overtones of love and concern.

Don't I know it! Gotta go, they said food will come, and I hear someone pushing a cart in the hallway. Love you, Peder! She paths and cuts the synpath chip connection.

The door opens and a middle-aged human man comes in with a tray of food. "Here, it's not much, but it's food." He says, putting it on a table next to the bed.

Phoenix sighs and says, "Thank you." In a slow, depressed voice.

The man leaves, and she smells her food before eating it, but can't detect any medicinal overtones that suggest they've drugged it, so eats it, and lies back down in bed.

Phoenix senses the mind of the earlier guard, walking up and down the hallway. The guard is doing her best to ignore the sounds and feelings of sorrow and fear around her, but Phoenix senses it's getting to her. She knows there's nothing she can do but wait for Peder to get back to her, so she rolls over and sleeps.

MISDIRECTION

Peder rouses Phoenix from her rest in the middle of the night, Israeli time and gives her a few things she can tell the *Naqam* to misdirect them. He suggests she wait a couple of days to tell them, or it may seem like she's giving in too easily, so she bides her time. She doesn't see anyone except the person who delivers her food and fresh clothing; however, she can hear others nearby, and thanks to her Apara abilities, senses their emotions and thoughts as well. The day after she's brought in, they turn another potential. This time, it's a man. Phoenix gets a sense of him. He's older than her, possibly in his forties. Once the transformation begins, she can hear him moan in pain and anguish. A couple of hours later, she can tell he's hallucinating, both from his vocalizations and from the images his newly budding telepathy is projecting. As opposed to transformation by the Apara themselves, the treatment by the *Naqam* is nigh unto negligence and abuse. Granted, they don't have the drugs the Apara have, but they leave them alone to transform in terror. She thinks, *Granted, I had an easy transition, at least compared to Sue and some of the other Lost Missioners, but they were taken care of while changing. I can't imagine this does any of them any good psychologically.*

She tells Peder how they are treating the potentials, knowing Sue and her team need to understand what these people have gone through if they're going to help them adjust later.

Another two days and they're down to 9 people ahead of her to be transformed. Despite already being Apara, she's obviously unnerved by what's happening around her. Her need for blood is becoming more pronounced. It will be another two or three days until it becomes urgent, but it adds to her unease. She paces her cell frequently, especially when someone is having a rough transformation, as she can sense their discomfort and fear of what is happening to them.

She gets an idea which will give her a legitimate reason to 'share' her information with them, and give her a means to feed, but she'll have to do it quickly or her need may out her first. She fills Peder in on her plans and paths him, *I think Janna should impersonate this guard.* She sends the image to Peder of the guard she met the first day and who has routinely been walking the halls. *She's a similar size and build as Janna, though she'll have to work on coloring and mannerisms. I'll path her the images directly.*

Do that and be careful! Are you sure you can fake the transformation symptoms? Peder paths.

Yeah, Sara went over those with me, and I've had examples around here to go on! The main thing will be forcing my core temp to go up and then back down, but be higher than my normal temp, then I'll break the other masking agent to mask my semi-human scent, and hopefully, I'll be able to feed before I lose control! She paths, irritation piggy-backing on her words.

Think you can multitask during the transformation part of it? He inquires.

Depends on what you have in mind! She replies, curious.

Since you're not sure where you are other than near water with lots of rock around you, Alice and Dimitrios want to come by, along with Callie. We're hoping if we link the three of you gals, with him to guide Alice, we might get a map location on the base, then Callie will be able to do her thing much easier. He explains.

I heard you all did that before, and Tess went astral as well? Phoenix asks.

True, she did. Perhaps I should get her in as well. She also went astral to find Marc, and that gave us details about the place. Let me know when they're going to 'turn' you, again! He mentally laughs, *and I'll get everyone together.* He suggests, wishing he could be there to comfort her. This separation would be completely unbearable if not for their ability to communicate telepathically.

Will do! I hear the meal guy coming this way. I'll ask him to get me someone to talk to about all this. Wish me luck! She paths, preparing to go through with their plan.

The door opens and the usual man brings in a tray with a hamburger and fries on it. "Here you go, Ms. Phoenix. Are you doing well this evening?" He inquires nonchalantly.

"No, I'm not. I've been hearing all the others going through what sounds like hell for the last few days. It's hard to listen to. Could you do me a favor?" She asks.

"What would that be?" He looks at her quizzically with one eyebrow raised.

"The woman who was here the first night; I never got her name, but she's the one going around with a clipboard and was trying to get me to tell her stuff. Do you know who I mean?" She asks, trying to sound anxious and desperate.

"Yes, Ma'am, I do, indeed." He says, straightening up and facing her.

"I need you to give her a message. I have some things to tell her, but I want them to move me up in the queue. If it's going to happen eventually, I'd rather get it over with! All those people! Their reactions give me nightmares! I'd rather get it over with than listen to several more nights of that!" She says, doing her best to look haunted and anxious.

The man stares at her for a minute, as though he's deciding if she's serious or not. He says, "I'll inform her." He says and leaves the room.

Half an hour later, Phoenix hears those same two sets of footsteps she heard from the first night. She takes a deep breath and does her best to prepare herself, using an internal shield to hide her mind from the Apara women coming in. She'll intentionally leak certain things through the shield but must hide other things or they'll know that she is not only a plant but already turned. She lies in bed and waits until she hears the woman punch the unlock code and the heavy bolt lock slide back. Phoenix sits up as they come in and acts anxious.

The woman eyes her warily and Phoenix can feel that prickly scan sensation graze over her public mind. "Raphael said you wished to speak with me?" She asks, standing next to Phoenix's bed, broadcasting impatience.

Phoenix intentionally hesitates for a minute, as if she's trying to decide if she really wants to take some momentous leap or not, then says, "What kind of information do you want from me?"

A cautious smile spreads from ear to ear on the woman's face as she reaches out, and a chair slides toward her from a few feet away. She moves it into place and sits, facing Phoenix. "Have you reconsidered?" She asks.

"Kind of. As you suggested, I've been paying attention to those around me. Every time you change someone, I hear their tears, groans, and screams during the transformation. I don't think I can go through that, and it doesn't seem like my friends are going to rescue me. You're going to change me whether or not I cooperate, so I'd rather get it over with if you can make it easier on me. I guess you could say I'm willing to trade some information for that." Phoenix says, intentionally emanating fear, anxiety, and guilt to the woman, as she'd likely feel if she were really betraying the Apara and Peder to save herself.

"Some information? This is not for you to decide. You will provide the information we want, or no deal." The woman says bluntly.

"I don't want Peder to get hurt! I still care about him." She says and projects the proper emotions to go with her statement.

"Let's see what you can give us, and if it is enough, I will see about moving up your transformation and making it easier on you." She says, warily. "Let's start with how many people are there associated with Inspiration, Inc., and how many of them are vampires?

Phoenix looks at her uneasily. "I'm not sure. I'd guess there are at least thirty employees there, including humans, but they're in the middle of expanding, and after the kidnapping attempt, I haven't been at the office. They haven't told me who is and who isn't a vampire. I know Peder, Liz, Kari, and Marc. I suppose Tess is as well, but until they change me, they haven't introduced me to everyone on the who's who of *vampires* list." Phoenix says, improvising.

"Are they local or are there others out there besides those in Asheville?" The woman inquires.

Phoenix looks like she's trying to remember something. "Peder told me there are others but scattered all over the place. Asheville is a place where some of them banded together to create a community. Otherwise, the rest are solitary or loosely networked around the world."

"So, the others are unlikely an organized threat, *no*?" The woman says without looking at Phoenix as she takes notes.

"I've told you before, the people in Asheville *aren't* bad guys either. *You* all came after *them*. They *defended* themselves against a threat." She tells the woman, annoyed that these people can't accept the truth.

"You'll soon understand that your friends are not as *harmless* as you believe. What they've told you about the events in Jerusalem are lies to get you to join them!" She berates her as though she's a gullible child. "Tell me, do you know why we cannot scan their new building? When we use our sensors, it shows an empty building, even though we can see people through the windows."

"How the *hell* would I know that? I guess maybe they have some kind of technology, but I don't know stuff like that! All I know is what they've *told* me and the few of them Peder's introduced me to." She says, exasperated.

The woman narrows her eyes and asks Phoenix. "Why has this Peder waited so long to change you? I would have expected him to do so right away after we attempted to abduct you the first time, and certainly after the second."

"*I* wasn't ready yet. Maybe it's just Peder, but he told me it needs to be *my* decision." She sighs. "But now that it *seems* inevitable, I just want to get it *over* with...." She trails off and forces tears to flow.

"Hm, I will see what I can arrange. I'd hoped you had more information, but it's clear they did not give you any more than necessary while you're still human." She clicks her pen under the clip of the clipboard and motions to the guard that they're leaving.

They leave the room, but this time, Phoenix hears a telepathic communication between the woman and the guard. She hears *I'm going to have her transformed ASAP. We may have more use for her as one of us than any information we can get from her. Perhaps this Peder has a soft spot for her? We can lure him in, and get information directly from him to save her from us?* The guard doesn't react but stands quietly outside the door and nods.

ONE GOOD TURN
DESERVES ANOTHER

An hour later, the woman and guard return, along with a medical technician pushing a cart. There are empty blood bags, tubing, and a needle. The woman says, "We have discovered that the more blood taken and, in turn, given, the easier the transformation goes. Normally, we've been doing a minimal exchange, which prolongs the transformation and the body's fight against the virus. Since you've provided us with *some* information, we will do our best to speed things up.

The medic approaches with a syringe full of liquid. Phoenix touches his mind and discovers it's a sedative with a human immunosuppressant, and thinks, *a lot of good that would do!* However, she knows she must act accordingly. He injects her with the drug cocktail. After a few minutes, Phoenix acts very relaxed and groggy. The technician inserts a needle into a vein in her arm and connects it to thin tubing running into a collection bag.

Phoenix lets out a small 'ouch' from the needle for show and then slumps back down on the bed, sinking heavily into the pillow. There's a small gauge on the tube that controls the flow. The MedTech slows it down, so Phoenix doesn't go into shock. When one bag is full, they swap it for another, filling four 450ml transfusion bags with her blood.

Phoenix acts weak and loopy. The Med tech wheels the cart out with the bags of blood and a few minutes later, comes back with four equivalent bags, and sets up an IV, this time setting up a central line into one of the larger veins in Phoenix's left shoulder.

He sets up the first bag and allows it to flow rapidly into her body, swapping each one out as soon as it's run dry, until all four are drained. Phoenix already feels better even though she will still need to feed soon but closes her eyes and pulls her mind tightly behind an internal shield, as Tess taught her, and uses a form of Apara biofeedback. She forces her body temperature to rise to fever levels and acts restless. "I'm achy all over." She tells them an hour into her second 'transformation', shivering from her self-induced fever.

The woman in charge has long since left, but the MedTech and guard remain. The MedTech is human, so she relaxes a little, knowing he can't read her, focusing on making sure the guard doesn't see beyond her inner shell. The MedTech says, "I'm sorry, we don't have anything that works on the fever, and other symptoms. Once the virus really takes hold, human medications don't do any good. That's why we dosed you beforehand, so you'll at least go into it with a weakened immune system and relaxed." He explains, and she feels waves of sympathy coming from him. She tries to touch his mind ever-so-gently and finds that he was conscripted for this duty and hates doing this to people, but some sort of debt or punishment would be waived if he did his duty here, though she gets no details.

Phoenix senses Peder via the synpath chip, but says, **this is taking all my focus. Tell Alice and everyone we'll have to wait.** She feels his non-verbal acknowledgment and his presence supporting her through her whole act.

After a couple of hours of playing 'fever', she lets her temperature slide slowly down and acts like the discomfort is lessening as well. The MedTech checks her temperature and other vitals. "Looks like you've turned the corner on the transformation. The worst is over, but now, your body will change. Don't be afraid. You're not in any *danger*. *Sleep* if you can." He says as he draws a cool cloth over her forehead and face.

She complies and pretends to sleep, but ends up dozing for real, but not before remembering to break the subcutaneous bubble Sara implanted. It will keep her temperature slightly elevated to Apara normal and mask any remaining human scent.

She sleeps about four hours, largely due to weakness from hunger, and wakes to the voice of the woman from earlier. "Time to get up, Phoenix. Your transformation is complete." She says, nudging her until she opens her eyes. She doesn't have to feign hunger as it has been growing for a couple of days now, so she gives into it and lets the need show in her eyes.

"You're feeling your hunger for blood. Nothing to worry about." The woman says, tone mollified now that Phoenix has joined the ranks of their 'vampires'. "Here, drink this. Close your eyes if it helps." She says and hands her a tall cup of warm blood.

Phoenix takes it, trying to feign a little disgust as anyone forced into this situation might, at their first feed. She sniffs it, then closes her eyes, and raises it to her lips, slowly, at first, but once the first bit crosses her lips, she downs it quickly as though she's ravenous, which she doesn't need to fake. When it's empty, she lets the cup drop from her hands, and it clatters to the floor as if in shock at what she just drank.

"You'll feel better soon." The woman says.

Phoenix notices something odd. She feels a pins and needles numbness starting with her scalp and enfolding her entire body, and realizes she can't read anyone around her. She thinks *They must have turned on the anti-ability tech. Well, at least, that means they can't read me either!*

The MedTech is gone, but the guard is there, and the familiar voice of the man who served her meals is in the background, saying "Yes, Ma'am. I'll see to a room and a warm meal for her right away." Then he leaves the cell.

"You'll likely feel a bit odd for a while as you adapt to your new senses and the changes to your body. You'll probably sleep for the next day or so, so make sure you eat your meal when Raphael brings it to you." The woman insists and Phoenix notices that the woman's attitude toward her has softened. "Oh! Welcome to the family, Phoenix." She says with a knowing grin. "There's a change of clothing for you in the bathroom. Ester will help you over there so you can clean up and change. We'll be moving you out of this cell to more comfortable quarters now that you're one of us."

BULLSEYE

Once she's settled into her new quarters, still securely locked and fitted with anti-ability tech, she lies on her bed. It's a twin bed like you might find in a college dorm. Not the most comfortable, but better than the hospital bed. She glances around surreptitiously and locates three cameras in the ceiling and walls. *Damn, still no privacy!* She thinks.

She pulls the covers up over her and focuses on Peder, once again opening the synpath chip. **Can you hear me, hon?** She paths

He replies, though she can sense mental static from the anti-ability tech. **Yes! Are you alright?** He inquires desperately. **You've been out of touch for a while.**

I had people around me during the transformation. They think they've transformed me, and I've fed, so I'm over that hurdle. They've given me private quarters somewhere, but it's locked, and anti-ability protected. There are cameras here too! THREE of them! Remind me not to change clothes anywhere but the bathroom! She paths with the mental equivalent of an overly dramatic eye-roll.

I hate to tell you this, love, but that could tip them off you know you're being observed. He paths, sensing her discomfort.

Damn! That sucks! Who knows what kind of creep is manning the cameras? She pouts. *I guess I could stand to get undressed down to my underwear and bra, but that's it!*

How are you feeling now that you've fed? Are you up to trying a linkup with the Invenirs? He paths.

You mean Alice and Dimitrios? She paths.

Yeah, and Tess is on standby once they have a location. Last time, we had Charlie, who knew some of the layout from experience, but not this time. The EM field keeps clairvoyants out, but Tess can bypass that with her Astral travel. He explains.

Let's try it tonight when things are quiet. Damn! I just realized I have no idea what time it is! There aren't any windows or clocks. She paths.

My guess is they want you disoriented. Give me a heads up when you're ready and activity around you slows. He suggests.

Will do! She sends him an emotional, telempathic embrace before disconnecting the synpath chip.

She explores her new quarters and finds a tablet with information on accessing e-books or their video library and settles in to read The Lord of the Ring's Trilogy for the fourth time in her life.

Raphael brings her evening meal in as usual. She makes a mental note to get some information out of him later, but asks him, "Do you know what time it is? I have no idea how long I've been here or anything. Even the damn tablet has the time and date disabled!" She gripes.

He gives her a sympathetic look. "All I can tell you is it's the evening meal, Miss. Afterwards, they expect you to rest. In fact, I'm surprised you haven't been sleeping all day." He admits, reminding her they expect her to sleep off the transformation.

"I'm tired, but I'm anxious about everything. I miss... I miss Peder. No matter what that woman thinks, I care about him and worry about what may happen to him." She admits. She's not fully playing a part, as she's sincere in her concern for all her Apara friends.

"You should rest tonight. No one will bother you for the next day or so. I'll bring your meals by and can relay any messages for you, but you should let your transformation finish up and get your rest." He advises.

"I guess you're right. I've been fighting my exhaustion." She says, sitting on the bed and pulling over a lap tray with her food and picking at it.

"I'll bring you your other sustenance tomorrow morning, Miss Phoenix. You'll need to drink blood often in the first weeks." He says. She notices a visible uneasiness in him as he remembers another transformee who pounced on him rather than taking the proffered, donated blood one time. "If you don't, you could lose control and *hurt* someone." He says, nervously looking her in the eye. He leaves her alone to eat.

After she eats, she stands and makes a show of stretching, yawning, and feeling in her mouth for her fangs. She acts like she's trying to bring them down and skewers the end of her finger with a sharp point, scowling as a novice might do, knowing they are watching her.

She pulls off her institutional t-shirt and heads into the bathroom, coming back and undressing down to her underwear. She's uncomfortable but knows it will help convince her observers that they have the advantage over her. She crawls into bed, rolls toward the wall, and pulls the blanket up over her. She waits a few minutes until the lights dim and go out due to lack of motion. She reaches out to Peder. *Any time now, love!* She paths.

Twenty minutes later, she feels the synpath chips of Alice and Callie clicking in, and it makes her feel less alone to have so many minds touching hers. She hears Alice path, *Just relax. I'm working with Dimi to locate you. He'll be able to pinpoint you on a map.*

Phoenix relaxes and keeps her synpath connection wide open. After a while, she hears a path from Alice, *BULLSEYE! We know where the base is! Good going! Now Callie wants to try something.*

Callie chimes in. *I'm going to send you something. I'm going to place it in your hand, okay?* She paths.

A few seconds later, Phoenix feels something small and soft, almost rubbery. She pulls her hand up where she can see it with her enhanced, Apara night vision, and it's a small, gel pill. *What's this?* She paths.

Sara sent it. Since you may be there a while. It's the same masking agent from the subcutaneous bubble, but this one is time released and will last longer. Just swallow it. It should keep you from smelling semi-human for a while! Callie paths.

How long is a while? Phoenix inquires, wondering how long she'll be stuck there.

She senses unease and uncertainty from Callie but hears, *It'll last up to a month, not that she thinks you'll be there that long, but better safe than sorry!*

Ugh! I hope I'm outta here LONG before that! The food sucks and so does the company! She jokes.

Sara says get some rest. They finally got the green-cent-opal dosage figured out, so that also contains some of the dust. It should relieve some of the anti-ability measures once it diffuses into your body. Callie explains. *Just hang tight!*

TREASURED MAP

Once they have the location of the base, Sue and Tess work together using the wave generator Sara modified to help her enter a psychic state conducive to out-of-body travel. Combined with Sue's ability to go into dreams and guide Tess on her travels, Tess finds the base and explores it. As before, her astral body passes through the EM barrier, and she meanders through several connected buildings constructed inside a series of caverns under the Caves of Arbel, near the Sea of Galilee.

She travels systematically through several levels of caverns and buildings memorizing the layout with great effort. When she passes through the cavern where new Apara are kept, she finds Phoenix and gives her a mental hug.

Not too much longer and we'll get you out of here, Phoenix! Peder really misses you. Tess paths her by touching Phoenix's arm with her astral hand.

I miss him too, but don't rush pulling me out if I can do some good here. I've met some people here that have been forced into working here, and not just those being turned. I'm here and they think they've won me over. Phoenix paths.

I'll tell Liz, but it's up to her in the end. I've got to finish exploring this place and get back before I get so tired, I slip back with a bang. Tess paths. She disconnects from Phoenix and continues her exploration.

Tess methodically traverses the entire base and all the sub-caverns, then returns to her body, waking with a start. "*Ugh!* I'm gonna have a hell of a psychic hangover after this one!" She exclaims, sitting up and grabbing paper and a pencil. She tries to draw the layout of the base, but she just can't remember it all consciously. She reaches out to Liz telepathically. *Liz! I need your HELP!* She paths and gets a wordless grumble followed by *COMING!*

Liz ports in and stares down at Tess on the bed. "Didn't you get anything?" She asks impatiently.

"Yes, and no. I went through the whole place and even touched base with Phoenix. I thought I had it all memorized, but when I try to put it down on paper, it's like some funky dream! None of it makes any sense now, like the layout is all jumbled." She whines in frustration. She sits on the edge of the bed.

Sue ports in from home, where she was directing Tess's astral trip. "Tess, what's wrong? I felt you disconnect abruptly."

"Sorry, my astral body collided with my physical one, and everything got jumbled. What good is this gift if the information I get is unusable?" She says, balling up one of her drawings and throwing it across the room.

Marc paths Tess, *Do you need me up there, love?*

She replies telepathically, *No! There's already three of us up here!* And he can feel her seething that things didn't work out the way she hoped.

Liz settles in a nearby chair and Sue on the edge of the bed, sending soothing energy to calm Tess's frazzled nerves.

Liz suggests, "Send it to me and I'll try to make sense of it." Tess tries, but it comes in more jumbled than a Rubik's Cube. "Damn, I see what you mean. Must have something to do with the shifting states of consciousness." Liz considers the problem. "It's too bad you don't have a touch of Val's newest gift." She ponders aloud.

"You mean directly creating digital images?" Tess asks, perking up at the thought.

"Yeah, that might work better than trying to draw it out." Liz suggests.

"The problem *isn't* the drawing. It's that when I wake up, my random-access brain scrambles the blocks on my mental hard drive, and I can't put it back together." She says, frustrated.

Sue is lost in thought. "There's something called 'state dependent memory'. It means you remember best when you're trying to recall within the same mental and physical state when you experienced or learned something. For example, if you have a student studying for a test while in an altered state because of smoking pot, then it's harder for them to remember the information when they aren't high. However, if they're high again, they may retrieve the memories correctly. I wonder if we can put you back in a dream state to fix the broken memories?"

"What good will that do? I can't draw them in my sleep!" Tess grumbles, her head throbbing from effort and her extended astral travel.

Liz's face lights up with an idea. "Sue, what would happen if you took Tess into a dream state and she could remember the layout, but then tie in Val? Maybe when Val wakes, she could either draw the layout or even put it down digitally?"

"That could work! Val clearly has an ability to bring her dreams and visions to a conscious level. I'd suggest we get her over here, so she and Tess are near one another." Sue suggests.

Before either of them can suggest it, Tess crosses her arms and looks at them both. "Don't even think about giving me psiamp!" She sulks.

The two women laugh at her reaction. Sue reassures her. "I don't think we'll need that if the three of us are together. I'll pull you into a theradream and take you back to the base and then pull Val in and you can give her a tour! Hopefully, when you're done, she'll be able to bring the memories with her and put them down in a usable form."

Tess rolls her eyes, and capitulates, "*Whatever*! Let's just get this done so I can... (yawn) get a real nap! I'm already tired, and now I've got to give a *freaking* tour!" She glowers.

Val arrives a few minutes later. Ty visits with Marc while 'the girls' do their thing upstairs.

Sue touches Tess's mind and drags her into a dream state. ***Tess, you're in the new base, starting at the top.*** She says. Tess is in the middle of a large hub, as vividly as if she were physically there.

Sue reaches out and pulls Val in. Val appears next to Tess. Val speaks to Tess in the dream, "Well, this is funky! I have vivid dreams, as you know, but not this vivid!" She says, taps her foot on the floor, and listens to the sound echo as if she were physically there.

Tess takes her on a walking tour through the base, from top to bottom, and all the chambers. When they're done, Sue breaks the connection and allows Val to come out of it at her own pace.

Val opens her eyes and tries to speak, but nothing comes out. Liz smiles, knowing this is a good sign Val's ability is kicking in, and hands her the well-used sketchbook and pencils. Val shakes her head and points to her tablet on the dresser across the room. Liz hands it to Val, who holds it and it lights up as images flow rapidly across the screen. They shift quickly until Liz realizes that the sequential images are creating a stop-motion walk-through of the base from her memories. When Val's done, she hands Liz the tablet and flops back on the bed. She whispers, "Oh, *hell!* That one took it out of me for real!" Her heart is beating rapidly, and she lies there trying to recover.

Liz reviews the sequential drawings of the walk-through and smiles. "You outdid yourself, Val! I've got people who can convert this into a 3D map of the base, but this is amazing work, all three of you!" She grins and ports out with the tablet.

Tess paths Marc, ***Don't suppose you're willing to fix some dinner for five? We're famished!***

She senses Marc chuckling to himself. ***I'll see what I can scrounge up. In the meantime, I'm sending Ty up with some blood for the three of you. Can't have three grumpy gals at dinner, can I?***

Marc makes extra food and Colin joins them. They have a good evening together and the three women feel like they've accomplished something important

TRADING PLACES

Janna's sitting in her dorm room with Charlie. He's crashed on the sofa reading comic books, and she's sitting in front of a mirror, practicing changing her hair, eyes, and skin color. Earlier that day, she got a synchip path from Phoenix from inside the *Naqam* base with images, memories, and information Phoenix could glean from their target, a female Apara soldier for the *Naqam*, named Esther. She's Israeli-American, which makes things easier as she'd lived in the US most of her life and speaks English without an accent. She's a similar size and build to Janna, so it's a matter of adjusting her hair, eye, and skin tones and projecting her actual image to surrounding minds. Right now, she's working on adjusting her coloration.

Charlie peers over his comic book at her and shakes his head. "If you can make everyone around you see what you want them to, why bother changing anything physically?" He inquires, as though she's wasting her time.

She turns around and stares at him as if he's overly obtuse. "Charlie, I may be able to project those images into minds, but I can't make the security cameras see what I want them to! The only way to do that is to have the same hair, eye, and skin tone. You know those images are grainy as hell, so if I look and move similarly, the ones watching the cameras are unlikely to realize I'm *not* her!" She explains.

"What if you run into her while you're there?" He asks, laying his comic on his chest and halfway sitting up to stare at her.

"She *won't* be there! I guess you could say she'll be the first one we 'rescue'. She often escorts Phoenix around the base, so we're going to wait until she takes Phoenix back to her room and do a *swap*." Janna says as if it's so obvious, anyone should get it.

"What about the cameras in Phoenix's room? Won't they see the portal and the swap?" He inquires, thinking Janna is ignoring the obvious.

"Already taken that into consideration. In the next couple of days, Phoenix is going to create disruptions in the feed to make it look like a technical issue. The green cent-opal in her system is neutralizing the psi-dampeners they've set up, so she can mess with the electronics with impunity. They won't think she could possibly be doing it if their measures are turned on." She explains and looks back in the mirror trying to fine-tune the color and flecks in her eyes.

"So, then what?" Charlie asks, sitting up to watch Janna shift her hair color through several shades of dirty blonde.

"Phoenix will let us know when Esther is taking her back to her room, and when she's in there, will start a video disruption and Callie will literally send me in and I'll push Esther back through, where they'll be waiting with neutralizer!" Janna says, realizing that she really is getting the hang of not being human. She focuses on what Esther looks like and turns to face Charlie. "What d'ya think?" She asks, projecting the image into his mind.

"*Whoa!* You really do look like a totally different person!" He says with a wide grin. "You know, this could be a lot of fun if you use it right!" He says with a lustful grin.

"Sorry, Charlie! If you want me, you're gonna *get me*, not some centerfold model from one of your magazines you've got stashed under the bed!" She snipes, giving him a nasty look as she picks up on some of his more creative daydreams. "Go take a cold shower!" She quips and ports out to let him cool down.

Hot Swap

Janna is on standby to go in a couple of days later. She's learned to maintain her guise for hours at a time and can project to multiple minds, but it takes a lot out of her. She's memorized the layout Tess and Val created, so knows her way around. However, her primary goal, once she's there, is simple; locate Uri and bring him in. Without him, the *Naqam* may collapse, or at least be weakened significantly.

She arrives at the training center with Charlie in tow. Niall, Callie, Liz, Peder, Amy, and some of Amy's team are waiting, neutralizer darts ready. "I'm here!" She says, mimicking the tone from the movie Poltergeist.

Liz nods and puts one hand on her shoulder. "*Ready?*"

"As ready as I can be, Ma'am!" She says, using the honorific out of habit.

"Now, Janna...." Liz trails off.

"*Sorry!* So used to using Ma'am and Sir in the military, *Liz*. I think I'm ready but won't know for certain until I'm in there. I memorized the base layout. I've got Esther's movements down and can imitate her voice." Janna says.

Liz pats her on the arm and turns to the rest of her people in the room. "Alright, everyone. We're just waiting for Phoenix to give Peder the go-ahead when she and Esther are in position. Amy, remember, she's *not* the enemy, she's a victim of the *Naqam*. We want to neutralize and tranq her without hurting or frightening her too much, then we'll ease her through this."

They wait. Charlie holds Janna's hand anxiously, and she senses how worried he is about her empathically. She squeezes his hand and whispers, "I'll be *fine!* I went through the same military training as you guys before I opted to be a medic. I *know* how to handle myself! Besides," She reassures him. **They fitted you with a chip as well, so I can keep you in the loop!** She paths

He looks a bit disconcerted at her voice in his head but sighs and leans against her. "I know, but I still worry." He says.

After a couple of hours, Phoenix paths Peder. Get ready. **Esther just arrived to escort me back to my room after 'training'**, but she thinks to herself, *More like a prison cell even if they call it my room and claim the lock on it is for my protection!*

Esther is more relaxed around Phoenix now that she's been there and complying for several days. She feels a certain kinship with her, considering they were both forced into this crazy life. However, she keeps her thoughts to herself even though she'd really love to have someone to talk to about everything. Most of her other fellow transformees have fallen in line since Elias and Uri ran them through the 'loyalty' program, as they call it euphemistically. They make it sound like shopping at your favorite grocery store, more than what it really is, conditioning and brainwashing to make you obedient.

For some unknown reason, it didn't work on her as it did the others, but she plays the game she's expected to play and acts like the others, doing what she's told, but hoping she can escape this hell someday. She's lost in thought as she escorts Phoenix back to her cell, and doesn't notice Phoenix's mood is one of cautious anticipation the closer they get to her room. She also misses the building up of psychic energy behind a mental shield in Phoenix's mind.

They get to Phoenix's cell, and Esther opens it for her, motioning her in. Before she can close it, Phoenix says, "Could you come in for a second? I think something's wrong with the entertainment tablet they gave me, but maybe I'm just using it wrong." Phoenix says as though she's embarrassed to admit she might not know how to use it.

Distracted, Esther says, "Sure, I can look at it. Sometimes they lock up if you try reading a big e-book." She says and comes in, the security key back in her pocket as the door slides shut behind her.

Phoenix leads her over toward her bed and focuses on disrupting the camera feeds again. She also focuses on the key in Esther's pocket, as Callie had taught her, until she feels something metallic in her hand. "Here you go. It's been driving me crazy." She says and hands her the tablet.

Esther takes it absentmindedly and turns it on, tapping on the screen, and pulling up an eBook. "Seems to be working fine at the moment." She says and looks at Phoenix, who has an odd expression. Before she can react, there's an odd, silverish swirling around her. Phoenix is gone and there are several people around her in a large room. There's a jab in her arm and she becomes disoriented, as all her heightened senses snuff out to human levels. She drops to the floor as her legs feel too weak to hold her upright. "What the...?" She says and looks around at the faces, settling on one she has ingrained in her mind from various briefings with the other transformees. It's the woman she's been told repeatedly is a fanatical terrorist, Lissa Pedersen.

Liz crouches down beside her on the floor as Amy's team pulls back. Liz extends a hand to Esther cautiously. "Esther, my name is Liz. Don't worry, no one here is going to hurt you. We want to *help* you. You're *safe* here with us." She reassures her and is relieved when Esther tentatively takes her hand.

Esther realizes that even without her special abilities, she can tell from the woman's demeanor and tone that she's not the 'rabid vampire' Uri and Elias insist she is. She stands as Liz pulls her up and reaches to Esther to support her, guiding her over to Sara and Annie, who are waiting to take her to Medical.

On the other side of the portal, Janna reappears as Esther, nodding to Phoenix when she comes through. Before the portal closes, Phoenix's reading tablet skitters across the floor and lands at her feet. Phoenix gets a path from Callie. **Thought you might need that!** And the portal snaps closed.

Phoenix slips the security key and tablet to Janna before slowly stopping the interference on the camera, and when it comes on again, the only thing the people manning it see is Esther, from behind, holding Phoenix's tablet. There's no sound on the cameras, but since all seems well, they assume nothing more than a glitch in the system is at fault.

As both Janna and Phoenix have the synpath chip, they can safely communicate telepathically.

Phoenix paths, *You ready for this?*

Janna replies, *I haven't been ready for much this last year or so has thrown at me, but if it means stopping Uri and his band of crazies, then yeah, I'm ready for that! Just remember, when I've got him, Callie's got to pull us both out fast, cause all hell will break loose when they realize he's gone!*

I want to stay and help here! Phoenix complains.

You'll get your shot! But they want us both out of here for phase 2. It should mean far fewer battle casualties! Wish me luck! She paths and uses the key to leave the cell.

OFF WITH ITS HEAD!

Janna walks down the hallway and does her best to make note of where any cameras are. If she's lucky, her projection will reach those in the surveillance room too, but she can't be certain her ability will reach that far. The cameras themselves will not be 'fooled' by her telepathic projections and will record her as she physically appears, so it's best to keep her face turned away from them. She must move like Esther, which isn't easy. A subtle difference could make someone observant suspicious.

She makes her way down the hallway and turns right, into another hallway that will lead her to a central hub for the base. From there, she plans to make her way toward the administrative wing where Uri's office should be. She spies a group of others like herself and shores up her projection. She doesn't have to visualize anything; she just sends the thought to those around her to see her as Esther. If she were dealing with people who don't know Esther, then she'd have to project the image to their minds.

As she gets closer to the two women and one man heading her way, a woman waves at her. "Hey, Esther! Want to get together and practice sparring tonight?" She asks with an eastern accent. The woman is from either India, Pakistan, or somewhere in that region.

Janna reaches out with a featherlight touch and finds the woman's name in her mind, "Sure, Satya. What time?"

"I get off at 1900 hours. Meet you at the gym." She says and walks away with the others.

Janna breathes a surreptitious sigh of relief, knowing her new abilities just passed their first real test with flying colors.

Feeling less anxious now, she enters the hub and tries to remember which corridor will take her to the administrative offices. She watches those coming and going in the hub and sees the woman Phoenix described as 'Clipboard Gal' to her and follows her down the hallway to the left, hoping it will lead her to Uri. She follows at a distance, doing her best to look nonchalant like she belongs there. The corridor turns about three times as it follows a natural tunnel in the cave system to a chamber used for the administrative division of the *Naqam*. She follows a hallway down a ramp and into a smaller hub. There are several security cameras, so she keeps her head down to avoid showing her face. She sees 'Clipboard gal' talking to a woman in a small office. She walks slowly and listens in.

"We're down to the last few compatible humans, but Uri's people are behind with their 'conditioning' efforts. Several of the new ones are rather stubborn and taking longer than expected to break." Clipboard Gal says.

The other woman looks thoughtful. "I don't know what to tell you, Naomi. Personally, I think having so many of you people around makes him more and more paranoid every day! He spends increasing time with each new one to make sure the conditioning sticks!"

Janna makes a note that Clipboard Gal's name is Naomi, and finds a bench to sit down on, observing what she can without looking obvious.

Naomi looks annoyed and sits down in a chair next to the woman's desk. "If he's got anything to be paranoid about, it's his *own* doing! He treats us more like animals than people sometimes, and the conditioning is like cracking a whip to keep the lions at bay! He doesn't realize that we don't have anywhere else to go. We can't go back to our old lives, can we? I miss my family; I was forty-two when they dragged me in here and changed me. My children are over fifteen, so they don't really *need* me, and I'd have a hard time explaining what happened to me without frightening them. Besides, they'd see me as some sort of monster or demon. I'm better off here, where I can do something to help bring the ones who bombed Jerusalem to justice. Maybe you can drop some hints that he needs to remember we're all people, too?"

The other woman sighs and says, "I'll try, my friend, but the only one of you he trusts without question is Elias."

Naomi rolls her eyes. "I suspect he's the one he should worry about the most! That man has ambitions and I wouldn't put it past him to do whatever he needs to achieve them."

A man pushing a cart with covered trays of food comes cautiously down the ramp into the hub and pulls up to the office where the two women are talking.

"Meal time again, Raphael?" The office woman asks.

"Yes, ma'am. I'm running behind, though." He says.

Hearing this, Janna sees an opportunity, gets up, wandering over to the room, projecting that the others should see Esther. She comes up behind Raphael and lays a hand on his shoulder. "I can deliver them for you, Raphael."

He turns to her and smiles. "That would be a *blessing*! I still need to do the compatible wing. and the human soldiers as well." He says, looking relieved. Janna can tell, besides being able to get caught up, that Raphael doesn't particularly enjoy this part of his rounds. She can sense that many of the higher-ups look down on him as an indentured servant, not worthy of their time or respect, especially Uri. The man bows slightly and turns, scurrying up the ramp and on to his next delivery.

Naomi gives Janna an odd look, saying. "Have you changed your hair or something, Esther?"

Janna thinks quickly, realizing something in her guise must not be right. "I fell asleep after my shower last night, Ma'am. My hair was still wet, and it wouldn't behave this morning." She rambles out. She senses that her response has satisfied Naomi, so says, "I'll deliver the meals, Ma'am. Have a good evening." She grips the handle on the cart and pushes it down the hallway.

She goes door to door and various human subordinates to Uri come out and pick out their meals. Luckily, it is like on an airplane. There are four choices: meat, chicken, fish, and vegetarian, including kosher, of course, except for one, which she finds labeled 'Uri', and it's sealed shut with red security tape. Janna assumes his paranoia extends to a fear that someone may adulterate his food with drugs or toxins. She shakes her head as she realizes the level of his mental imbalance and paranoia, and her resolve to remove this dangerous man from power solidifies.

As she continues down the corridor, she gets an odd, familiar feeling, like someone she knows is nearby. As she turns the corner, she faces a door with a symbol on it, and no doorknob. The symbol is green, white, and red, with inverse colors on the left as compared to the right. The pattern is an abstract outline of the Star of David, inside a circle. In the center is a shape resembling a spearhead from some old, heraldic design. One side is mostly white with green, and the other side is primarily green with white, except for the right side of the spearhead, which is blood red. Janna knows that symbol from before. She'd seen it on papers lying on Uri's desk at the old base. It's the symbol for Israeli, military intelligence, or would be if it were just green and white. She thinks, *I'll bet the red is specific to Uri's operation, being blood red to represent either the Apara he's conscribed, or his targets, the Apara in Asheville. God! This is so fucked up!*

There is a small panel with a button beside a speaker. She lets out a nervous breath and pushes the button. A gruff voice speaks in Hebrew, which she is unnerved to understand without effort, and instinctively answers in the same language, saying, "Sir, it's Esther. Raphael was running late, so I'm delivering meals." She hears a gruff sound, like the clearing of Uri's throat, and there's a click as the door unlocks and pops slightly ajar as the lock releases. She reaches forward and pushes the knob-less door open, picking up the meal meant for Uri. She carries it in. He's very difficult to read, but she gets some emotional overtones. Charlie told her he habitually uses the same implant they'd fitted him with be-fore meeting Amy, though he suspects Uri's is more advanced and powerful as his paranoia demands no less.

"Your meal, Sir." She says and approaches him cautiously, damping down her own emotions as she nears her goal. She stands beside him and puts down his meal. An alarm goes off and she hears Naomi's voice bellowing from the hallway, warning Uri that something is amiss. Naomi dashes toward his office, seeing that the door is ajar. Uri turns around and scrutinizes 'Esther', wondering why Naomi would be shouting a warning, when Janna uses an infuser on his arm. Before he can open his mouth to shout for help, he collapses onto his sealed food tray.

Janna uses her telekinesis to close the office door, and after some initial resistance, it shuts and locks. She reaches out to Callie with her synpath chip. *NOW! CALLIE! NOW!* She paths, mentally shouting. Five seconds later, a shimmering portal opens in front of her and Janna drops her guise, grabs Uri, and drags him through the portal. A second portal opens a few feet away from Phoenix in her quarters and she joins Janna in the Training Center seconds later.

NEUTRALIZING THE PROBLEM

As soon as Janna portals through with Uri, two of Amy's people take him in hand and port him away to a secure location. Charlie is there and pulls Janna close, but she pulls away as her fangs come down due to hunger from the amount of psychic expenditure her mission required. She signals someone to get her a bag of blood, but Charlie stops her. "Janna, it's okay, *really!* I trust you!" He insists and bares his neck to her.

Janna's tempted, but keeps her distance, and says, "Next time, Charlie! You can't afford to be weakened, even a little, not if you're going in with us!" She says, as someone shoves a bag of blood into her hand. She bites down on the plastic and drains it quickly, staggering backward in exhaustion and relief. She can rest while stage two plays out but must be ready soon.

Liz sends a telepathic **NOW** to a team in place as tourists on Mt. Arbel who have placed their own anti-porting net over the base, inactive until needed. They also worked to turn away all real tourists so that few, if any, civilians will be on the mountain during the operation.

Now that Uri has been extracted, and Janna and Phoenix are both safely back in Sanctuary, the net is activated, preventing any of the enemy Apara from porting out of the base. This security net is unlike the earlier one used with Jason in Hot Springs. This time, it's far too important to make sure that no one escapes, so their hybrids and Benefactors have provided the technology to ensnare the entire base with the suppression field penetrating deep into the mountain.

Liz clears her throat. "Alright, everyone! Let's clear this space of everyone but Callie, Niall, and Peder for stage two! Amy! Get your teams ready to go for stage three!" She commands, looking around to see if the others she'll need for the operation have arrived yet. Tess is talking to

Teresa Mendoza across the room and breathes a sigh of relief. She thinks, *Good! We'll need those two for any stragglers after stage two.*

Niall gives Callie blood and a quick pep-talk as she's anxious about her role in the mission. Opening two portals at once is hard enough. This time, she'll have to open even more, albeit smaller ones.

Peder and Phoenix are in a tight embrace after being separated for well over a week, and it's all Peder can do to keep himself from grabbing her and porting home with her. However, *his job* has just begun. He hugs her close and gives her a long overdue kiss then releases her. "*My* turn, *hjerte mitt*! Sara wants to check you over." He says, releases her and heads over toward Callie and Niall, reluctantly.

Phoenix lingers, watching Peder walk away, but turns and searches for Sara. She locates her in a corner of the training center that's been converted into a triage center. Not that they're expecting that many of their own to be injured or need treatment if their plan goes well, but their eventual captives, human and enemy-Apara alike, are another matter. Phoenix approaches her, feeling a little giddy now that the ability suppression field is gone. It didn't stop her, thanks to the green Cent-opal in her system, but it still felt like a constant, wet blanket weighing down her mind.

Despite Callie's successful practice, she still feels anxious. Niall won't be fighting but will support her in her mission. He makes her feed from him to replenish her blood levels, but also to improve her mental state with the intimacy of feeding from someone she shares a bond with. Peder waits at a respectful distance until Callie's finished feeding and approaches them. "Ready for our mission, Callie?" He asks, giving her a mischievous grin.

She laughs nervously. "Not really! But that hasn't *stopped* me yet!" She grins.

The three of them walk over to a staging area walled off by plexiglass-like walls. Inside the walls are a pile of greenish-silver balls. Peder walks over to inspect them. Alright. We've been inoculated against this stuff ourselves, but not everyone here has; hence, the protective encasement around us. Phoenix, we've narrowed down our targets thanks to the map Tess and Val created." He walks over to her with a tablet that projects a 3D map of the base. "However, we initially planned to target the Apara living quarters, here...." He says, pointing out the lower-level cavern where the transformed sleep and spend their free time. "Their training center, mess hall, transformation wing, and their administration cavern." He points and each section lights up in yellow with a red ring somewhere in the space. "The red ring is our target for your portals. This is where our tactical specialists believe the aerosolized, neutralizing gas will be most effective. Unfortunately, Liz just informed me our plan may have some holes in it... no pun intended! Janna could not port out with Uri unnoticed. Something clued them in that things were amiss, and Janna had to portal out with alarms going off and others descending on her location in the admin cavern, about here." He explains. "We must assume the entire base is on high alert now. We're still going to hit most of the planned spots, but we're adding the main hub here. We assume their forces will all be mobilized and the hub will probably be their ideal staging point." He says and the hub lights up with a new, red ring in the center. "And I'll be distributing the neutralizer spheres a bit differently." He explains. Niall's standing behind Callie, arms around her, concern in his eyes at the last-minute changes.

"Just how many simultaneous portals will she have to maintain?" Niall asks, concerned for his partner's wellbeing with such a large, energy expenditure.

"Six, all-together, as we'd planned, but we're dropping the residential chambers, and adding in the Hub. He says, understanding Niall's concern for his novice partner. "I'm sure she can do it, though. Just help her stay calm and focused and I'll literally do all the lifting!" He says with a fanged, lopsided grin.

Niall turns Callie around to face him. "Are you sure you're ready?" He asks.

She gives him an odd grin. "Kinda late to be asking that now, isn't it? I'll do my best, that's all I can promise." She says aloud, but paths him privately. *So long as I don't start hearing voices calling me, I'll be fine!* Even though he can sense some uncertainty in her voice, he can sense her resolve to do her part.

Niall won't have much to do other than guide her, like they've practiced, if she gets disoriented or flustered. Otherwise, his presence reassures her. Callie gets settled in a comfortable chair on one side of the enclosed chamber. They find it's easier for her to maintain multiple portals if she doesn't have to focus on staying upright at the same time.

Peder and Niall stand behind her chair. The tablet is on the floor, docked into a machine, which creates a larger projection of the 3D map of the base in front of them, to help Callie target each location. It's vital she opens them simultaneously so they can target as much of the base at once as possible.

Besides neutralizers, the spheres contain a sedative that will take down most of the humans. Originally, they planned to open a portal to the human barracks as well, but with their base on alert, the military residents will probably be spread across the entire area.

Their goal, with this attack, unlike with the Judean Base, is to preemptively disable people, humans and Apara alike, prior to going in with their forces. They plan to take as many alive as possible, rather than destroying the base with them in it, as they did before. Since the element of surprise has been lost, the ground team has blasted any physical exits, trapping everyone inside.

The lights dim in the chamber, and Callie focuses on the large, 3D representation of the base. She focuses on the red rings in each target chamber and a small portal, no larger than a soccer ball opens at each location. On the other end, each portal will open in the actual location in the base. Once the portals are stable, Peder uses his PK to lob the gas-filled spheres through the portals to their targets. Most of them are sent to the Administration chamber and the Hub, with the assumption enemy forces have been mobilized because of Uri's kidnapping. A substantial number, albeit fewer than originally planned, are sent to the mess hall, the training center, and the transformation wing.

Once 80% of the spheres have been deployed, Callie releases the portals and allows them to close. Wisps of gas leak back into their chamber, but a counter mist, which neutralizes any of the blow-back gases, is deployed. Once all is clear, Peder leaves the chamber, but Niall and Callie remain there so Callie can rest and feed before stage three.

CLEANING UP THE MESS

Tess and Teresa Mendoza are waiting with Amy's security teams. Charlie and Janna have joined them in the staging area for stage three, but Phoenix is just outside, arguing with Peder.

She demands, "I want to be part of this! Besides, I've been inside, I know some of the people there, and if necessary, I can use my healing thing if any of their humans get badly injured!" She pauses. "Besides, there's this nice man, Raphael; I want to make sure he gets out of there safely. He's human and a servant there, but he's a kind soul and I don't want to see him get hurt." She insists.

Peder shakes his head and rolls his eyes, but says, "Then I'm going in with you!"

She opens her mouth to tell him he doesn't need to, but before she can even utter a single word, he puts a finger to her lips. "I've been sitting idle long enough, Phoenix. It's time I rise from my own ashes and do my part." He explains and her resolve softens as she realizes this is important to him. It's more than a need to protect her, it's a need to take back his own life as an Apara now that he's physically and emotionally healed after Jerusalem. She nods and says, "*Deal.* We'll *both* go in." She concurs and the two of them join the rest in the staging area after a brief detour to the armory room to change into protective gear, as well as grab neutralizer, and tranq dart guns. If they're going in, they're going in prepared.

Liz is in a small office with Kari with the door shut, trying to calm her anxiety. "Lissa, this is happening way too often! You've had to use that medication for blood pressure, of all things, every day lately! The very idea that one of us would have high blood pressure is weird enough, but your anxiety levels are becoming a serious issue." Kari berates her as she works on unknotting the muscles in Liz's shoulders.

"I know, but after today, the *Naqam* will no longer be a problem. Our numbers are increasing again, though not through our normal vetting and transformation routines, but our numbers are inching back up toward pre-Jerusalem levels." Liz says, trying to convince herself, more than Kari, that things are going in the right direction.

Kari stands in front of Liz and squats down to look her in the eye. "*Lissa Pedersen!* Just because the pressure may ease doesn't mean everything is going to be fine and dandy with *you* again! *YOU. NEED. A. BREAK!*" Kari says assertively, pausing between each word for emphasis.

"I *can't afford* to take a break!" Liz says in a huff.

"Yes, you can. Let Marc take over for a while. At least for a few months, if not a year or two! Surely you deserve that much after over *800 years* of service! You need some *real* down-time, Lissa! *Hell*, you haven't taken a break since before you turned me, if ever! Marc's your second in command, let him take up the slack for a while. I'm sure he'll step aside when you're ready to return." Kari insists, holding her partner's chin, forcing her to make eye contact.

"How about I take a two-week vacation? Will *that* satisfy you?" Liz snipes, knowing what her partner says is true, but hates to admit any weakness on her part.

Kari stares at her, not speaking, as though her eyes alone can drill through Liz's thick skull and make her see sense.

After a three-minute stare-off, Liz slumps down in her chair and relents. "*All right! You win!* If we get through this successfully, I *promise* to take a break!"

Kari looks at her, mouth quirked up skeptically. "At least three months and preferably a year, *elskling!*" Kari insists, never breaking eye contact with her overwrought partner.

Liz stares at her and knows Kari won't back down. "I *promise*. *Three* months!" Liz agrees.

Kari raises one eyebrow skeptically. "Three months, *then* we re-evaluate. If, I, Sara, and Sue agree that you're ready to return to work, will you do so. If not, it's more *vacation* time, as well as *continued* therapy with Sue! *YES!* I said, *continued!* You will not recover from this by hibernating for three months. You must *work* through *everything!* The anger, depression, and outright grief you've been dealing with since Jerusalem!"

Liz's eyes appear shadowed with exhaustion. She knows there's no arguing with her partner. No matter how much Liz is a leader among the Apara, the strong one in their partnership has always been Kari. Kari asked Liz to bring her over to the Apara when she found out what Liz was. No hesitation and no lust for power. She just wanted to spend an endless life with Liz, and do her part for humanity, with no reservations. That's what ultimately convinced the Benefactors to make her compatible and allow Liz to bring her over as her partner. Liz has always admired Kari's strength and tenacity, but it makes her feel like her own outer strength is but a fragile facade.

Liz has hidden her struggles since long before Kari entered her life, but she's always persevered. Liz admits, "I get it, the incessant stress of the last couple of years has taken its toll. It's time to step back and let those I've brought over take the reins for a while." Her face softens as she finally acknowledges the need to release her burden of 800-plus years and take a break. "I promise, *elskling.* I'll do this as soon as this crisis is over." She says and Kari knows she means it this time.

Nearly an hour passes while they wait for the gases to permeate as much of the *Naqam* base as possible and do its work. It won't reach everyone, but the security net and collapsed exits will keep them inside where the Apara can deal with the remaining humans and enemy Apara. Facilities have been prepared to receive everyone they can get out of the base alive, and they can process the *Naqam's* people. The hybrids will attempt some form of memory redaction in the hope that some of the humans can eventually be set free. Otherwise, the enemy Apara can hopefully be deprogrammed and integrated with their own as productive, Apara citizens. That is Liz's goal that can give her enough peace of mind to take the time she needs to recover from the burnout that's eating her soul from the inside-out. She joins the rest of the team in the staging area. Niall and Callie have joined, as well as Marc and Tess, ready to do their part.

Liz regards everyone, realizing that she has a fantastic team of people at her command. Even Charlie, the lone human in this mission, is willing to give his all for Janna and their cause. She takes a deep breath and addresses her flock. There's enough background chatter among her people that her initial call to attention goes out both verbally, and telepathically, making all chatter cease without delay.

"Now that I have everyone's attention, I want to thank you for your efforts and perseverance through everything over the last couple of years. Some of you have been with us for centuries, while others are barely getting your 'teething fangs'!" She jokes. "But every, single one of you is necessary and doing your part. I know some of you have come to think of our fight with The *Naqam* as a holy war, but I need everyone to reframe their focus. This is a *rescue mission*. Most of those we'll be facing were dragged into this by a paranoid zealot with power. They've coerced, compelled, and converted both humans and Apara alike to their cause, but none of that is indissoluble, my friends. No, *my family!* We removed the tumor that was the mind of the *Naqam*, Uri Jabarin. He's in custody and we will do what we can to cure him of his delusions and paranoia. Now, we must cure the body of the *Naqam* itself. I know it will be difficult, especially with some of the human soldiers, but I want you to avoid ending their lives. Capture and retrieve everyone you can. You'll each be armed with additional neutralizer darts, as well as sedative-gas grenades to use on humans. Once someone is down, bring them to the central hub, extraction teams will bring them back here."

Liz turns to Callie and smiles. "Callie, you've done an *amazing* job so far, but now may be the greatest task we ask of you. You'll need to do as we discussed. Open a portal to the central hub of the base, similar in size to the one you created at the concert venue. Our people will enter the base through it. We'll need you to be on standby to open smaller portals for retrieval of captives, as well as another large one for evacuation."

She addresses everyone once again. "Once the base is empty, our Benefactors have provided an expanding filler compound. It's essentially synthetic granite; something they use for building when they colonize parallel worlds. It will flow through the entire complex as an expanding foam-like material, but will solidify indistinguishable from granite, permanently filling and sealing the base." Liz scans her teams, eyes glancing at each face in turn, memorizing them all. "Good luck, everyone! I'm proud of every, single, one of you!" She says and nods to Amy to start the mission.

Amy acknowledges Liz's unspoken instruction and orders everyone into formation. Once everyone's ready, Niall and Callie step forward. Niall holds her gently, feeding her extra energy from himself, and supporting her physically as well. Teresa Mendoza joins them, drawing small amounts of energy from everyone around them, as well as from electrical sources nearby, converting it into usable energy for Callie, and channeling it to her through Niall. Once Callie feels the energy flow into her, she feels euphoric, like she could take on the world, but Niall pulls her back into focus. "Open the portal, love. Central hub and make it big." He whispers in her ear.

Callie focuses easily this time and the portal forms in front of her, growing rapidly into an archway straight into the heart of the base. They can see bodies lying all around, unconscious, but some who are not, staring in surprise at the portal. Some run, but some of their still active Apara, and military soldiers approach the ever-widening doorway, preparing to do battle with whatever might emerge. Callie smiles as she realizes a suggestion Amy made has worked. While they can see into the hub from their side, those facing the portal see only an opaque, swirling mass of energy.

Amy motions her guys to line up on this side of the portal, pathing to them to have their neutralizers and tranq gas at the ready. They take aim and fire the darts, neutralizing seven active Apara on the other side. They send through the sedative gas and watch as the few human soldiers crumple to the ground. It's only then that they pass through the threshold and enter the central hub, fanning out through all the tunnels in smaller teams.

Charlie and Janna pass through the portal as well, Charlie uses a gas mask until the gas disperses, making certain the sedative doesn't take him out of action. The two of them, as well as about a dozen of Amy's team stay in the hub and drag bodies together in the center so they can bring as many as possible back with them to Sanctuary through one of Callie's portals.

One of Amy's teams goes with Theresa to the Apara quarters. They, too, encounter many unconscious bodies, but continue to the residential chamber. As they approach, four Apara launch themselves in an attempted ambush, but Theresa has readied herself with stored energy and does as Tess taught her, sending out a controlled blast that knocks them back across the room and against the walls. Amy's guys quickly neutralize those few active Apara, and they begin the tedious task of carrying bodies back to the central hub, as their Benefactors security net disables their porting ability, but not their other gifts, so they must carry or drag the unconscious Apara and humans to the hub's portal.

Tess, Marc, Amy, and her usual team proceed down a twisting tunnel and down the ramp into the Administration section. They're prepared to meet resistance but aren't prepared for what awaits them. There are unconscious bodies everywhere, both human and a few, converted Apara. Those who are still conscious and not neutralized stare in dismay as the team of 'enemy' Apara descends the ramp. The soldiers don't even pick up their weapons, but sit there in shock, demoralized.

Marc reaches out with his empathy to read the situation, afraid it might be a ruse to lure them into complacency before an actual ambush, but he senses a mixture of confusion, dismay, and even relief from some. The unexpected abduction of Uri, as well as the gas attack, caught them off guard. Most are uncertain what to do without Uri or Elias commanding them.

Marc touches a mind, learning that their other leader, Elias, told them to hold the line while he and a group of other 'vampire' soldiers took off down an otherwise off-limits passageway and have not been seen since. The minds that feel relief are those whose conditioning has failed, and are glad that their nightmare may be ending, even if it means being 'killed' by their enemy. Marc is dismayed by the state of things and paths the others in his team, *It's what it seems. They're not in any shape to fight. Be firm, but show them compassion and kindness, then get them to the central hub. Tess, Amy, and I will check the offices and see what we find, but I can't sense anyone here with a will to fight.*

Amy calls in Dave and his team to go down the 'off-limits' tunnel they saw in the one person's mind, to see if they can find Elias. Amy, Marc, and Tess go office to office, extending their telempathic and clairvoyant senses to find people, conscious or not, including a few doing their best to hide. As they're found, Amy paths the location so the next, available member of her team can come collect them and evacuate them to the Hub. Any enemy Apara are given the neutralizer, but told they will not be harmed so long as they wait there to be evacuated.

As the three of them near the end of the hallway, they find almost no one in the remaining offices, but Marc can sense a loud, terrified mind ahead. As they turn a corner, they reach a dead end. A door with no doorknob lies in front of them, closed, and locked from inside, they assume. There's a green, white, and red logo on the door and they hear quiet simpering beyond the door. Marc reaches out mentally and tells Tess and Amy, "There's a woman in there. Apara, but partially neutralized. If she were completely neutralized, she wouldn't be broadcasting. She's terrified."

Tess nods with understanding. She moves toward the door, and runs her hand over it, seeking whatever locking mechanism might be in use. She closes her eyes and focuses. After a minute, they hear three clicks as three separate bolts retract and unlock the door. Tess motions to Marc and Amy that she's going to go in alone and they should wait in the hallway.

She pushes the door open slowly, keeping a mental eye on the terrified woman to make sure she doesn't fight instead of giving up quietly as the others had. When the door is barely ajar, she clears her throat and says, "My name's Tess. I'm not going to hurt you. I'm coming in, but you don't need to be afraid of me." She says while oozing mental overtones of compassion and calming energy toward the terrified woman.

Tess hears the woman grab something and drag it, heavily along the floor. She realizes she's likely armed herself with something handy as a last-ditch effort to defend herself. She stifles a sigh and reaches out to touch the woman's mind. She can feel the terror the *Naqam* have instilled in this woman about the 'evil vampires from America, who wantonly destroyed Jerusalem', and so on. Tess is saddened as she thinks about how many others in history have had a similar fear of her people. She thinks, *Yes, my people. How long have we been the subject of nightmares, when the reality is quite the opposite? Hell, this woman is like us, and she fears us as if we were demon-spawn from hell!* She digs a little deeper and plucks a name out of the woman's mind.

"Naomi, you've got nothing to fear from me. I'm here to *help* you, *really*. I know what they told you about me and my people, and it's just *not* true! I realize your conditioning makes it hard for you to accept, but it's true. We *didn't bomb* Jerusalem. My people were trying to *find and stop* the bomb. We were trying to help, just as I want to help you." Tess says and feels the woman's wariness waiver slightly, so she slowly opens the door a little more so that her face is visible to the woman cowering behind a large, mahogany desk. The woman sneaks a peek from behind the desk and Tess smiles kindly. "You realize, don't you, that if I wanted to hurt you, I could have by now, *right*?" Tess asks.

Naomi's holding an ancient stone statue, wielding it like a weapon, but unconsciously loosens her grip and readiness as she sees Tess's face. Her dilemma is that's all she can see. She can no longer sense the stranger's thoughts or feelings, so must rely on more human cues, such as body language and vocal intonations. Even so, she feels her defensiveness wane as her exhaustion sets in. The statue in her hands feels like an ever-heavier burden until she lets the artifact slip from her fingers to the carpeted floor with a dull thud.

Tess senses Naomi has come to grips with her predicament. Naomi's still not certain she trusts Tess, but she realizes fighting is pointless. Tess smiles and says, "I'm coming in, *okay*? I'm not armed." She says, pathing to Marc, *Take my weapons please. I need to gain this woman's trust. If she comes at me, I can handle her without those!* She feels Marc ease the dart gun off her belt.

Tess cautiously opens the door, maintaining eye contact with Naomi the entire time. She moves slowly, so as not to startle the terrified woman. She takes a few slow, methodical steps toward the desk and gives the woman a sympathetic smile, extending a hand down to her to help her up off the floor.

Naomi's resistance breaks completely, she takes Tess's hand, and tries to stand, but is too weak to do so without help. Tess pulls her upright slowly and eases her into the large, swiveling, office chair. Tess releases her grip on Naomi's hand and sits on the edge of the desk. She looks at the disheveled woman, who was dressed professionally for work, but her clothes are now rumpled, the tails of her formerly neat blouse are halfway out of her skirt, and there's a rip in her matching jacket where she snagged it on something. "Are you okay?" Tess asks, eying the woman with concern.

Naomi stares at Tess warily, but nods, saying nothing. Tess sighs in relief and smiles. "Good! With all the fear I was getting from you, I was afraid you may have been hurt." She pauses and extends her hand again, this time for a handshake. "As I said, I'm Tess, and like you, I haven't been like this for all that long. In fact, I became like this the night of the bomb, but that's a *long* story. My point is, I know my people didn't intend any harm that night because I was part of the whole mess. I helped, while still human, to figure out what was going on. In fact, I nearly *lost* my partner in the explosion. He was here, in Israel, helping with evacuations when the bomb went off. He barely escaped and was not unscathed by the firestorm that followed." Tess explains, pausing to let the woman process everything.

After about half a minute, Naomi says, "My grandparents were in Jerusalem. They said there were people who helped guide them out of the city, but I assumed they were other Israelis."

"There were plenty of them as well, but we had about 5000 of our people here that night. Many were searching for the bomb, but quite a few were helping with the evacuations, either guiding people to escape routes or the buses that took people outside the city limits and into the desert. Many of my people were driving those buses or working triage to help with injuries, as people fought their way along the escape routes. I promise you we were not here to harm your people. We saved those we could, but in the end, there was no way to stop the bomb from going off." Tess assures her.

Naomi relaxes her guard slightly, both from exhaustion and starting to trust Tess. She looks at Tess and asks, "Why did your people kidnap Uri? Is he *dead*?"

"He's *unharmed*, but he's been telling you and the others that we're the bad guys when nothing is *farther* from the *truth*! We've been working behind the scenes for millennia to *help* humanity. After all, we *depend* on humans for blood, so we do what we can to pay it forward by safe-guarding humanity... mostly from itself! Sometimes it's through being teachers or diplomats, while other times, it's through those of us with strong, precognitive abilities. That was the case with Jerusalem. A lot of my people, including my partner, foresaw something catastrophic coming, but it was unclear what. By the time they figured it out, it was too late for Jerusalem, but we stopped nearly a dozen bombs in other cities worldwide. Unfortunately, as the terrorists sourced the radioactive material for the bombs in the Middle East, they completed the Jerusalem bomb long before the other ones around the world. It was already armed and booby-trapped with a proximity trigger. Not even the most gifted of us could have stopped that thing in the 15 seconds it took to count down and explode." Tess explains. She pauses, waiting to see how Naomi reacts.

Naomi sits quietly, not quite sure what to say, then nervously says, "He told us you destroyed the old base, *killing* many people! Is that true?"

Tess swallows visibly, not sure how to handle this part of it. "Our leadership felt it was necessary. Uri sent Elias and others to our center in Asheville. They rigged the building to blow and tried to lock us in so that the explosion would take us all out. Luckily, we escaped, but our building was destroyed. We saw your organization as an enormous threat and the relatively few deaths as acceptable casualties. But now, we're doing our best to get everyone out of here. Many of you, at least those they've changed, were meant to potentially *join* us in working to protect this planet. Not everyone is called, however." Tess touches her mind when she feels sadness and longing coming from Naomi, and sees that she has a family, including children. "For example, you have a family, right?" Tess asks.

She's startled by Tess's knowledge, but answers, "Yes. I... I had a husband and three, teenagers." She says, her voice audibly quavering as she thinks of them.

"We would *never* take someone away from their children. We wouldn't even have taken you away from your husband. We evaluate every person we consider bringing into our fold carefully, and taking a mother away from her children, even adult children, is not acceptable." Tess explains, hoping that will make her see the difference between the *Naqam* and the Apara.

Naomi sits quietly, torn between what she's had instilled in her, and what Tess is telling her. After a minute, she looks up and studies Tess's face. "Can I go back to them now?" She asks, as if begging for her very life.

Tess looks at her with genuine sympathy. "No, I'm afraid that's *not* possible. We don't have any way to make you human again, nor make you your original age. However, we can offer you a place in our world where you can be productive and help safeguard this world *for* your children, and for *their* children." Tess explains.

Naomi looks like she's going to cry, but asks, "Why would you *want* me? Or any of us? We're your *enemies*." She asks, finding it hard to believe Tess.

"But you were *meant* to be *friends*. However, we wouldn't have brought you over because of your family, but now that you're one of us, you're very much what we are! We won't get rid of you just because *we didn't change* you! We're certainly not going to turn you loose on your own, either! We'd like to ease you and the others Uri had turned into our fold, if possible. *Frankly*, we can use all of you! Just as Israel suffered many losses that night, so did we. We lost nearly 15% of our people to the bomb, and some of those who survived are impaired."

"Will you trust us not to turn on you after everything that's happened?" She asks, skeptically.

"Perhaps not right away, but we'll give you the opportunity to earn our trust. In the meantime, we'll work with you to help you adjust and learn to use your skills. However, it would help the others if one of their own works with us as a liaison. Perhaps you'd do well in that capacity, Naomi." Tess suggests, hoping that offering her a higher level of trust, might return to them several-fold, and help bring the others in more easily.

"If what you say is true, then yes, I will work with you. Many won't trust you at first, and some, like Elias, *never* will!" She tells Tess.

Tess gets an 'about that...' expression and says, "Speaking of Elias, he's a problem. We don't plan to hurt him, but we can't let him run around, change others, and start this insanity over again. Do you have any idea where he might be?" Tess inquires.

Naomi shifts uncomfortably, but answers Tess. "There's a secret cavern somewhere along a long tunnel. It was built as a safe room in case we get attacked again. Most don't know about it as it's too small to hold everyone. Uri, Elias, a few elite scientists, and elite soldiers would have escaped there if you hadn't hit us all at once, and taken Uri before we raised the alarm." She explains.

"Can you tell us where the cavern is and how to get into it? We've had people searching the tunnel but haven't found a cavern." Tess admits.

"No. I was not *elite* enough! I only heard some of the others speak of it. It is somewhere between the beginning and the end of that tunnel, but not at the end. The entrance is carefully hidden, so if they've gotten in there, they're set for at least three months with food, water, and blood." Naomi explains, irritated at the thought of Elias sitting safe somewhere, while the rest of them have been left exposed.

"We'll find them, but if you'll come with me, I'll take you to be evacuated from here. You'll be taken to a safe location and not harmed; I promise." Tess says and extends her hand to Naomi.

Naomi takes it, and they enter the hallway, but she hesitates when she sees Marc because she recognizes him from Uri's rants about the enemy. Amy has left to help Dave and the others.

"Naomi, I *know* what you were told, but this is Marc, my *partner*." Tess explains.

Naomi replies nervously. "Uri said he was *behind* the bombing." She says, unconscious conditioning makes her afraid in Marc's presence.

"Remember what I told you, Naomi, he was working with the evacuations that night. If he were behind the bomb, he wouldn't have helped people get out, would he? He wouldn't have let himself get caught in the wake of the explosion. He barely escaped, appearing burnt and bloody in our home. I watched him die, by human standards. I honestly thought I'd lost him. It took weeks for him to revive, and longer to fully recover." Tess says and senses the wheels turning as Naomi processes the incongruity of what Uri told them and what Tess has told her about that evening. Naomi nods and takes Tess's hand anxiously, letting Tess lead her out and back to the others in the Hub.

SEALING FATE

Tess's talk with Naomi took precious time, and about a third of the humans and enemy Apara have already been evacuated by the time Tess and Marc return with her. Tess hands Naomi off to some of Amy's people who have been ferrying them through the portals, and to a temporary holding facility where registration, de-programming, and other treatment can be done.

Tess is standing with Marc when she spies Amy loping toward them, out of breath. Amy stops by Tess, halfway bent over and breathing heavily. "*Damn*, girl! I think I've gotten too used to port-ing! All this physical traveling is harder than I remember!" She says, looking up at Tess, and grinning.

"Any sign of Elias and his cohorts?" Marc asks, knowing it's imperative they don't let anyone slip through unaccounted for.

"I could sense them somewhere down that corridor, but they've got some kind of tech that makes it *damn* hard to pinpoint! We'll find them eventually, but I don't think Liz wants to give us days to do so." Amy explains, still breathing heavily.

"No, I'm sure of that." Marc says, pointing at the woman being escorted through the portal as they speak. "Naomi is one of the few Apara in the administration. She's the one who told us where to look. She told us they have supplies, including blood, to last them at least three months. I know Liz wants us to rescue as many as we can, but honestly, after what *they* did to us, I say seal them in and leave the anti-port net turned on! We can always dig them out once they've gone into stasis!" Marc snaps bitterly.

Amy glances at Tess, gives her a slight eye roll, and a private path, *He really doesn't like those assholes, does he?*

Tess gives her friend an understanding glance and says, "He *does* have a point, though! We can't waste time trying to coax them out, the granite-fill won't get them, and they'll go into stasis eventually. We can always deal with them then! Let's get the rest of them out of here and see what Liz wants to do." Tess suggests.

***

Callie brings Apara and human refugees from the base through in small groups, but she must pause frequently as exhaustion sets in, until Niall has to put his foot down. He speaks with Kari, who's overseeing the evacuation in Sanctuary while Liz takes a needed break.

"Kari, I know Callie won't say anything, but she's exhausted! She's draining more quickly with every new portal. She needs some downtime to recover." Niall says.

Kari glances back at Callie, who's sunken into her reclining chair and can sense the heavy weight of exhaustion pressing down on her. "I can give her two hours, will that do? Send Dave back through to let everyone know to sit tight, okay?" Kari suggests as she gently puts a hand on Niall's arm. "*You* should rest, too! And feed! She needs your strength! Get Theresa back here, too. She may be able to leech some additional energy and feed it to Callie when she's ready to continue.

Niall does as suggested, then helps Callie into a side room used for treating injuries during practice. There's a bed, and the room is soundproofed, so she can sleep and recharge. He gives her food and two bags of blood before she sleeps. She crawls into bed under a light blanket and is asleep seconds after her head hits the pillow.

***

Back in Israel, under Mount Arbel, nearly everyone has been moved to the Hub and is waiting to be evacuated. While Tess was talking Naomi into being the liaison to her people for the Apara, Phoenix and Peder searched the human quarters, where all nonmilitary humans were sent after Uri was abducted. They emerge into the Hub with the last batch of evacuees, including Raphael. Most of them are walking under their own power, but a few are still weak or groggy from the sedative and are leaning on others.

Tess approaches Phoenix when she sees her emerge from the tunnel. "Looks like you might as well make yourself comfortable, we're going to be here a while." Tess explains and helps Phoenix with a man she's supporting. He isn't sedated but has a sprained ankle.

"*Oh*? I thought this was an in and out operation?" Peder asks.

"It would be, but Callie ran out of steam! They're giving her two hours to recuperate." Tess explains, helping the man settle on a bench in the hub.

"Tess, this is Raphael. He's the one who always brought me my meals." Phoenix explains.

"Hello." Tess says with a polite nod of her head, "Speaking of which, it might help ease some of these people's minds, if we could get some food for them in the interim."

Phoenix says to Rafael, "If you can tell me where I can get food, Peder and I will go get it." She lays her hand gently on his leg, unconsciously easing the pain and swelling in his ankle.

Raphael's foot stops aching and he glances down as the swelling visibly recedes. He looks up at Phoenix, asking, "Are *you* doing that?" and points to his foot.

She looks down and chuckles. "I guess I am! I wasn't trying to, but one of my strengths is healing." She explains and crouches down, laying her hands on his sprained ankle, focusing, and causing the healing to complete.

He puts his foot down and pushes down with it, but there's no pain, so he carefully stands and puts his weight on it. "That's amazing! *Thank you!*" He hugs her without thinking. At first, she feels awkward, but then hugs him back.

"Least I can do for all your kindness! Now, about that food?" She inquires.

He tests his foot a little more and then tells Phoenix and Peder, "Follow me!" They go off in search of food, returning with three large carts laden with food from the base galley, distributing what they have before returning for more. This puts the so-called prisoners more at ease. If their captors feed them, and treat them well, they're less likely planning to kill them.

EXODUS!

It's been about an hour since Callie started her break, and the mood in the hub, while anxious, has calmed significantly as people realize the so-called monsters aren't acting like monsters. Some of the transformed feel a sense of relief peeking through their conditioning as they grasp the true nightmare that Uri and his people have put them through. Not only were they kidnapped, violated by changing them into blood-drinking creatures, and tortured into submission, but the beings whom they were told to fear are acting with compassion and kindness.

Unfortunately, it's not only those from the *Naqam's* fold who've let their guards drop, but some of the Apara themselves. Instead of being vigilant, they relax their watchfulness, and miss danger approaching.

Near the opening of one tunnel, there's a whizzing sound as something flies and lands with a thud and the sound of erratic rolling. People turn toward the tunnel but are caught off-guard by a loud bang and a bright flash. Smoke billows from the explosion, and then two more whizzes, thuds, bangs, and more smoke.

Panic erupts from their prisoners, who try to move away from the smoke, some of them temporarily blinded by the flashes. Amy's voice cuts through the din and smoke. "*AMBUSH!*" She shouts and several of her teams stand, ready to fight, but as the gas billows and roils, the Apara soldier nearest to it is stricken by uncontrolled coughing, and screams, doubling over in anguish as his lungs take in the gas. The other Apara back away from the toxic clouds, and Dave shouts, "The gas is laced with the deuterium compound!" All the Apara inch back from the clouds, knowing they'll be vulnerable if they breathe the gas. It would sting and then numb their skin from contact but getting it in their lungs is far worse!

The antidote would eventually work, but the minutes they'd be down could be all the enemy needs to turn the tables.

The remaining Apara whip out lightweight gas masks, and Amy shouts, "Someone get Callie up! Get that *Goddamn* portal open *now!*"

The Apara, their human prisoners, and their rescued kin move away from the smoke toward the other end of the chamber, where the portal was earlier.

Amy and Dave search the billowing smoke and see dark shapes moving through it. Several rogue Apara wearing protective gear emerge into the hub. They're all armed with high-capacity combat rifles and more grenades; both gas-bearing and concussive.

Dave shouts, "Where's that portal? Get it open *NOW!*"

A few seconds later, the energy swells, swirls, and sputters. The crowd stops moving in that direction, wedged between the *Naqam* soldiers and the sputtering energy of the nascent portal. No one dares approach it until it's stable, as getting trapped halfway through a portal means severe injury or even death.

Dave's watching the enemy soldiers move closer, while Amy keeps an eye on the unstable portal; keeping everyone at a safe distance from it but turns around when she hears the distinct sound of the safeties being switched off on weapons; likely some variant of AK-47's, and ammo sliding into chambers. She paths Kari, **Light a fucking fire under Callie's Ass! We're under attack and about to be under fire!**

Kari paths in reply, **Working on it!**

***

Back in Sanctuary, at the training center, Kari receives a path from Tess, saying, **Kari! We can't wait another hour! We're under attack and need the portal open NOW! We can't protect all the humans or the neutralized if things get crazy!**

Kari's heart rate rises, and she's glad Liz isn't there to face the stress. She replies **I'll get Callie up, but it may take a few minutes to get her going. She was absolutely drained!**

Tess holds her telepathic tongue and thinks better of letting loose a string of curses, as it would not make the situation any better. ***Do what you must as fast as you can! Find some way to get the damn portal back online! We need a big one! We've got at least eighty or more people to evacuate!***

Kari replies, ***GOT IT!*** And ports off to find Niall, who's sitting outside the infirmary making sure Callie gets her rest. "Niall! *Wake* her! It's an emergency." She demands.

He senses waves of frantic energy rolling off her. "What's wrong?" He asks.

She paths the situation to save time, making him dash into the room to wake Callie.

He hates to rouse her, but lives are at stake. "Callie, love! You've got to get up!" He says, sounding firm but not so frantic that it freaks her out, and makes her too nervous to do her job.

She groans and rolls away from him. "Wanna sleep more...." She trails off, pulling the blanket over her head.

"I know you're exhausted, but this is urgent! You must get up *now!*" He says firmly.

She rolls back over to face him, squinting. "Not sure I've got anything left to give." She says, sluggishly.

He grabs another bag of blood, saying, "Feed! I know you're beyond tired, but this can't wait!" He helps her up and shoves the blood into her hands. "You *need* it! Now, drink quickly!" He insists, desperation permeates his words, and she gulps as waves of urgency hit her like a slap to the face. She bites the corner the bag, downs it, oddly wishing she had a second, but wipes her face and stands.

He steadies her as the blood needs time to get into her system, scoops her up, and ports her out to the staging area, laying her in the recliner. "I know you're not ready yet, but you've got to try!" He insists, taking one of her hands and feeding her some of his own energy.

Callie hears Kari in the background, demanding, "Where the Hell is Teresa? We need her to channel energy! This portal needs to be a big one!" The thought of another mega-portal makes Callie groan with exhaustion, but she focuses on creating the rift between spaces and worlds.

At first, there's a weak wavering in the air in front of her, but it doesn't connect with the other end in the Hub. She persists, and the portal grows, but looks like moth-eaten cloth, with small clear zones in the larger fabric of energy where she can see masses of people heading toward the nascent portal. She flinches physically as their terror and panic blast through the honeycombed openings in the portal and hears Amy commanding everyone to keep their distance until it's stable, while she hears gunfire in the background, giving her a much-needed adrenalin boost, enough to stabilize the portal, but only about the width of a car.

Amy instructs people to go through four at a time and not to shove. Humans first. There are more gunshots, screams, and an angry voice demanding, "Halt! No more warning shots!" but prisoners and refugees continue to stream slowly but steadily through the narrow portal, being helped through, and off to the periphery of the staging area to make room for others as they come through. A human woman trips as she comes through, and is nearly trampled by the others, but is pulled clear by Theresa as she's heading over to help Callie.

Kari says, "Callie needs an energy boost!"

"I see that, but it will take me a few minutes to build it up. If I draw too quickly, you'll have people passing out all over the place!" She shouts as her Latino dialect comes through heavier under pressure.

***

In the Hub, Amy puts through groups of four, and then eight at a time to push people through. The panic in the crowd rises, especially among the humans, but also from the neutralized subjects, who feel vulnerable without their abilities and strength.

Amy sends a team to defend the crowd, shooting back at the rogue Apara soldiers, including Elias. They fire at them, but they retreat into the dark tunnel behind the gas and smoke, taking aim at the line of resistance.

Slowly, the portal grows as Callie's strength increases. Unfortunately, it's still small enough to create a dangerous bottleneck, especially as the soldiers shoot back at the resistance. A stray bullet hits a human woman in the shoulder as she approaches the portal, and Marc runs over, pulls her off the ground, instinctively heals the surface wound to stop the bleeding, and rushes her through the portal. He monitors the crowd as it pushes forward. Charlie helps a couple of young, neutralized, enemy Apara toward the portal. He suspects the youngest isn't even seventeen yet, while the other is likely around twenty.

Several shots ring out from the tunnel and Charlie's body lurches forward as if shoved. His face momentarily shows the shock of the impact, followed by his eyes going blank. Janna's nearby, helping others through the portal. She feels the mind of her lover dwindle and fade to barely an ember. Her eyes go wide, and she dives through the throng of people to his body, protecting him from being trampled by the terror-stricken crowd.

She was pathing with Phoenix to check on her and the humans she's bringing forward, when Charlie fell. Phoenix feels like she's been gut-punched by Janna's distraught panic. She looks at Peder and he nods. "Get over there! I'll manage these people!"

Phoenix runs through the crowd, zig-zagging between them until she gets to Janna and Charlie. Janna has stopped fighting the crowd and lies over Charlie's lifeless body, not caring if anyone steps on her. She feels energy swelling behind her and turns to see Phoenix. There's a visible, golden, and greenish glow around her as she approaches them.

She paths Janna, *I think I can bring him back.* She motions for Janna to move aside. The crowd instinctively parts and goes around the three people as Phoenix's energy swells, drawn from the crowd on this side of the portal. She leans over Charlie, who's lying on his stomach, wounds still oozing blood out of three bullet holes in his back. She puts her hands on his back and reaches out, finding some remaining twinkle of his essence or soul, and pulls it back with a mental yank, while healing the damage to his body. Less than a minute later, his body jerks as if struck by a jolt of electricity, and he groans audibly.

Janna puts her hands to her mouth in shock as Phoenix has again raised the dead. He was barely dead, but with little hope of revival without her intervention. Janna lunges forward and hugs his back, then rolls him over. He opens his eyes. "What the *hell*?" He mutters, not fully coherent.

Phoenix says, "Take him! Get through the portal!" She senses waves of exhaustion coming from Callie and wishes she could help. Before she can think about how to help, the remaining energy she's built up to heal Charlie flies through the portal and suffuses Callie, giving her a needed burst of energy. The portal flares to life, and the remaining refugees move quickly through it.

Amy paths for her guys to fall back, grab any wounded, including those who may appear dead, and bring them through the glowing gateway.

As the exodus continues and the resistance retreats, Elias and several of his most elite team members move forward, determined to follow their prey to wherever the energy portal takes them, retrieve their people, and unravel this secret weapon that's allowing their enemies to escape for a second time.

***

More people are now in the training center than in the Hub. The healing energy from Phoenix helped Callie immeasurably, though she still feels exhaustion nipping at her heels. She sees Peder scoop up a now weakened Phoenix and support her as they come through the portal.

Only a few groups of stragglers are left, but there's a malevolent wave of anger and hate from beyond them. Eight to ten enemy soldiers run toward the portal. She knows she can't close it with people still passing through but must stop them from entering the portal. She remembers someone saying that if they ever came to Sanctuary, they may be able to make it back there on their own, threatening the safety of all the Apara and their new charges. They're gaining on the stragglers, narrowing the gap. She thinks, *If they get too close, I might not be able to close down the portal quickly enough!*

She becomes disoriented and hears a thought in the back of her mind. It sounds like her own internal thought but is strangely separate from her mind. She hears, *Use your gift! SEND them away!*

She realizes if she has enough energy, she could open a secondary portal and send them away, but the boost Phoenix gave her is fading by the second. She focuses on energy, and the next thing she knows, instead of Theresa sending her energy, as she isn't quite ready yet, Callie latches on to whatever energy Theresa's built up.

A sudden burst of light flares on the other side of the portal. It's like a glowing orb of plasma, moving toward the enemy Apara, who retreat, but the ball lashes tendrils of energy out and grabs them, one by one and they disappear. The last of the evacuees pass the threshold of the portal and Callie lets it close when the other, glowing orb swells and then shrinks, flaring like a supernova. It knocks several people over who were close to the portal, but Callie snaps it shut in time to avoid any serious injuries and passes out.

Sara runs over and checks her, but quickly turns around after a cursory examination, telling Niall, "Lots of rest! And plenty of blood! I'll send Annie over to set up an IV and give her a sedative so her synapses can heal in peace. She'll be fine, but what she did is nothing short of amazing, and used a tremendous amount of energy. Plus, she's got a wee bit of psychic burn, probably from the backlash. It appears, in the process of closing it to protect everyone, she absorbed the energy herself. I've people to check over! Port her home and to bed!" She says, scurrying off to check on people who were wounded in the exodus.

Niall scoops Callie up in his arms and holds her against his chest. He ports straight to their bedroom, settling her under the blanket. He's a little unnerved by how heavily she's sleeping, as she doesn't rouse in the slightest, but he trusts Sara's medical opinion. He turns out the lights and settles beside her in bed, exhausted in his own right, from giving her a lot of his own energy to shore up the portal.

AFTERMATH

A few days have passed, and all the refugees have been processed, both human and Apara. Teams are sent back into the base to secure whatever they can of weapons and information they have about the Apara. All their computers and backups are collected and delivered to Ty, Val, and a team of experts to go through. It's imperative they eliminate any traces they can of the *Naqam's* knowledge of them.

They have a substantial job finding out who else knows of Uri's secret organization and the Apara, besides those directly involved. Clearly, the Mossad must know something, and possibly others. Hannah volunteers to help them with her uncle in Mossad. They will find and interrogate him about the project, then make him forget everything about it with the help of the hybrids. With Uri in their custody, they hope this will be the end.

They search until they find the hidden safe room where Elias and his soldiers hid, leaving it wide open so it will be filled when they use the synthetic granite compound.

Once the Apara are done with the base, barrels of the expanding, granite compound are loaded into the base in strategic locations, and the process of filling the entire complex with solid stone is set in motion. When it's done, no one will be able to access the base or ever use it again.

Now that the crisis is over, Liz has some unfinished business that can no longer be put off. She calls in Marc, Tess, Colin, Sue, and Amy for a meeting. Naturally, Peder and Kari are also there, if for no other reason than moral support for Liz.

Once everyone arrives for the meeting, she begins. "As you know, the last couple of years have taken a toll on all of us, but it's hit me particularly hard. After a lot of thought, and *encouragement* from Kari," She motions to her partner. "I've decided to step back from my responsibilities for a while.

Other than Kari and Peder, who both knew this was coming, the others shift in their seats, clearly concerned by this news. Liz lightly touches the minds in the room and senses reactions from concern for her wellbeing, the wellbeing of their center without her, and finally, Tess and Sue thinking, *it's about damn time she took a break!*

Liz sips her sassafras tea to hide her subtle smirk at Tess and Sue's reaction, then continues. "For now, it will only be three months, and then we'll see how it goes. If Kari has her way, it will be at least a year. Whatever the case, I've asked you here because you will have to take on additional responsibilities while I'm away. Kari, naturally, will also be taking some free time, but will be in from time to time as my liaison."

Kari grin sarcastically, saying, "It was the *only* way I could get her to agree! She's been running things so long, it's hard for her to go cold-turkey. I'll primarily be with her at home or in one of our cabins in Norway, but will check in, and I'm on call if needed."

Liz stares at her partner with a mixture of amusement and annoyance. "The truth is, unless I feel this place is in good hands, I won't be able to rest." She takes another sip of tea, then says, "Marc, I'd like you to take over for me. You've been second in command for a long time. Peder and Colin will assist you, but with Phoenix so new, Peder's going to have his own hands full." She grins knowingly.

Marc looks at her, surprised. "I'll do my best, Liz." He says, knowing the size of the shoes he must fill.

Liz turns to Tess and Sue, who are sitting together with their partners flanking them. "Tess and Sue, you two will have to take up the slack for Kari. She'll meet with you periodically, but you're going to have a lot to do now. Not only finding new potentials to turn, but you must coordinate the refugees from the *Naqam*, as well as those that may turn up with Roulette virus abilities."

Liz nods, saying. "Now, regarding the human *Naqam* refugees, I've been meeting with the leaders of the other centers and other senior Apara, as well as the hybrid leader, Isanda, Sara, and even the representative Benefactor who came with the hybrids. We've come up with a plan for what to do with so many humans who know of our existence. It's one thing when it's one or two, or even a handful. We can make it so they can't tell anyone about us, but we must monitor those people. We've got more than enough on our plates as it is! Dedicating people to monitor a bunch of humans we can't make forget is not a practical option. Considering most of the humans working there are from Israel, we've decided to use the Sanctuary equivalent of Corsica to create a human settlement."

There are looks of surprise from Marc and Colin as the idea of having a large group of humans permanently in Sanctuary seems wrong but wait for Liz to finish.

"I realize we've always seen Sanctuary as *exclusively* our world, but it's the best option we have. Besides them, some of the 300 or so that we rescued before they could be taken by the *Naqam* may also end up there, plus some of those hit with Roulette that know of us, or whose abilities are not possible to suppress but are not psychologically suited to join us. We're giving some of them the opportunity to bring their immediate families here. They will all be mentored, such that in the future, they, or their descendants can be helpful when our Benefactors decide it's time to go public. Some of their offspring may also be gene-tagged to join us in the future. This way, they'll be raised to join us. Not all will, but if they are promising potentials, psychically, and intellectually, training them consciously during their formative years should provide us with some high-grade Apara in the future. Mostly, they'll be limited to the island, but if their population expands substantially, or we bring more humans in, we can expand onto our version of Sardinia. Those among them that are able-bodied, for example, their soldiers, will be involved in building housing and infrastructure there." She explains.

Colin asks, "Are there any Apara living there now?"

"There were, pre-Jerusalem. The two that were living on Corsica and three on Sardinia were all in Jerusalem when the bomb went off. We'll be using their former residences as Apara centers to monitor the humans until they get on their feet and become self-sufficient." Liz explains.

Marc asks, "What about all the people they turned? Has any decision been made about them?"

Liz's mouth and eyes tighten with hints of stress. "They are one of the bigger issues you'll be dealing with. We can't change them back, and we can't let them loose on humanity without supervision. Tess and Sue will be working on this. Sue, I assume you've got a good crop of budding shrinks to call on by now?" Liz asks with an amused expression.

"Yes, they're all coming along nicely and have helped us get several of the long-termers out of rehab housing and back home," Sue explains.

"That's great. Put them to work with those who were turned by Uri's Apara. Most have been subjected to rather extensive conditioning, as well as the shock of being plucked out of their lives and forced into becoming one of us. You will need to use whatever resources are necessary to get these people treated, acclimated, and eased into life with us. For now, they'll be confined to Sanctuary until they can prove themselves trustworthy. Isanda has also offered the services of her hybrids with some advanced, psychic-based treatments for the more difficult cases. They may be able to suppress some of the conditioning that way, but it's trial and error." Liz explains.

Amy clears her throat. "Liz, what do you need from me? Obviously, you have something in mind if you asked me here."

She gives Amy a slight smile and a nod. "We'll need some of your teams to monitor the human settlement for a while. I want you to keep training your teams to deal with enemy Apara. We must be prepared in case the *Naqam* Callie sent away return. Marc tried to sense Elias, since he's familiar with his mind, but couldn't, but we cannot assume Callie got rid of them for good." She sighs and turns to Tess. "Continue teaching others to do some variation of your psychic blasts. Hopefully, we won't ever need to use it, but we can't afford to be caught off-guard again."

Amy nods and says, "I'll do my best. I assume I can bring Dave in on all this?"

"*Naturally*! And anyone else you deem necessary." Liz replies. She pauses and looks around the room. She closes her eyes for a minute, willing the burgeoning tears to stay at bay. She opens her eyes and tells them, "You've all become a part of my Apara family. I turned Kari, Peder, Marc, and Colin, but I feel the rest of you belong in my closest circle as well. Amy, just as Marc has been my right hand to me in these troubling times, you have been my left. Sue, Tess, even though I did not turn you, you are like daughters to me as well. I know I can trust every one of you to do what needs to be done, no matter how long I'm away. I'll stay on for the next couple of weeks while you adjust to your additional responsibilities, and then I'm leaving Inspiration, Inc., and my other responsibilities in your capable hands." Liz can no longer hold the tears at bay, but everyone in the room is there for her, taking turns comforting her, and reassuring her they will do what she needs them to do.

WAKING DREAM

Sara keeps Callie under sedation and on a blood IV for five days while she recovers from her first official Apara mission. They couldn't have done it without her. It's agreed Callie should continue working on her special abilities because they will come in handy in the future. She must learn to do it without draining herself to the point of dropping or giving herself psychic burn.

At the end of the fifth day, Sara stops the sedative and turns off the wave generator that has kept her under. She removes the IV and turns to a rather anxious Niall. "*Stop* hovering! She's fine, but I'd rather she come out of it on her own!" She snaps and makes a shooing motion to make him back up. "Come, we need to have a talk about your partner." She says and heads to the living room.

Niall follows her. "What can I do for her?" He asks.

"Have patience, Niall, have patience! As with all the Lost Missioners, as well as some of those that will come *after* them, their abilities go well beyond our usual limits. What she did during the mission to Israel was momentous, and yet, we don't know if she's reached the limits of her abilities, just that she reached her limit at that moment." Sara explains cryptically.

"Are you suggesting she may have other gifts or that she could do even more?" He inquires.

"I'm saying *expect* the unexpected! You've been around long enough that your life could certainly use a shake up!" She chuckles. "Be patient and listen to her. Is she still having those nightmares?"

"I'm not sure. I think she's been too pre-occupied with the mission. Why?" Niall asks, leaning against the wall as Sara settles into a comfortable chair.

"I reviewed the logs from when she had those incidents. They were *psychic*, not psychological. Something happened there, but, for the life of me, I can't make sense of the waves in the logs, other than that...." She trails off.

"Other than what?" Niall asks, sitting down in a chair near Sara, concern rolling through his soul like an incoming tide.

"Sometimes, I'd swear her wave patterns were almost doubled. Like there were two of the same mind generating slightly different patterns. It's quite puzzling. I just don't want you to write it off to stress or imagination. I don't know what's happening to her, except it's *real!*" Sara says with an unusually candid expression. "Don't ignore *anything* and keep me in the loop." She says, standing and walking past him, clapping him on the shoulder reassuringly as she ports out.

Callie sleeps another three hours before stirring. She wakes alone in the bedroom, disoriented. She's been dreaming but can't remember what. No matter how hard she tries, she can't remember what she knows were hyper-vivid dreams. Dreams that feel important. After a few minutes of wracking her brain, she gives up and sits on the side of the bed.

The world around her feels unreal, as though this is the dream, but she knows it's not when she puts her foot down and steps on a small, but jagged chunk of raw turquoise on the floor, and it hurts. She had it in her pocket for good luck during the mission. She thinks, *Niall must have put me in bed. I bet that fell out of my pocket when he undressed me.*

She reaches out and the chunk of turquoise flies into her hand. She stares at it and the small bloodstain on it from the already healed wound on her foot. She puts it on her nightstand and stands, careful to look where she puts her feet this time. She still feels ungainly, so she moves slowly, but gets dressed. She grabs the Starship T-shirt Niall gave her after the concert. She slips on a pair of purple leggings and goes in search of Niall. She finds him in his home office, on the computer, hyper-focused on something, but his mind seems closed off.

She stands in his doorway, unnoticed, until she clears her throat.

"Callie! You're awake!" He says, embracing her, relieved she's finally awakened.

"Yeah, I guess you could say that!" She laughs lightly. "How long have I been out and what happened? Did we get everyone out? Did we *stop* them?" She asks as her memory is fuzzy from her psychically singed synapses.

He lets her out of the embrace, but holds her by the shoulders, grinning at her with a lopsided smile. "Yes! We got everyone out of there, though we still don't know where you sent those last soldiers, including Elias. Marc searched for his mental, but he couldn't locate him anywhere, but we will find him." He says. "The base has been filled in and we've got teams working to find anyone else who knows about us."

"What are they going to do when they find them?" She asks, concerned about what might happen to those people.

"No need to worry, love. The hybrids have agreed to step in this time and do some tinkering with their minds. Ty, Val, and a cyber team are using the computers we retrieved to propagate a selective virus that will worm its way through their networks looking for information about us and delete it. Other teams will check for backups and deal with them accordingly." He puts his arm around her shoulder and walks her over to the sofa in the living room. "How're *you* feeling?" He asks, trying to peruse her aura, energy, and mood.

"Okay. Just a bit disoriented when I got up." She says, but thinks, *I won't bother mentioning the dreams since I can't remember them....*

He smiles. "I'm guessing you're hungry?"

"For food, yes! Oddly, I'm craving pizza." She says with a smirk.

"Your wish is my command!" He says and ports out with a flourish, returning later with three large pizzas for her to gorge on.

EMERGENCY EXIT

Callie spends a few days taking it easy as she regains her strength. She spends time in her studio, hoping for a creative recharge. The first thing she does is cut the piece of turquoise she stepped on when she woke up. It's a piece she's been saving for something special; a piece of rare, Bisbee turquoise. Somehow, the brilliant blue turquoise with dark, blood-red matrix seems appropriate for her new life, so she cuts it to make herself a piece of jewelry. She thinks, *I'm not putting this one up for sale!* She finishes polishing the gold and turquoise necklace with a ruby to accent the red matrix, cleans it, and puts it on a chain around her neck. She looks at it in the mirror in her studio to see how the pendant looks and smiles as she shifts around to see it from different angles.

As she gazes at herself in the mirror, she feels disoriented and puts her hand on a nearby chair to stabilize herself. The mirror ripples by itself as if she's invoked one of her portals. The view clears, and a hand reaches through the mirror, wearing a ring with the exact same piece of Bisbee Turquoise in it. Her heart pounds when she realizes she knows that hand all too well! It's her own, down to a small, heart-shaped birthmark under her ring finger.

She gasps, lets out a small scream, and steps away from the hand grasping at thin air through the mirror. She audibly hears her own voice saying, "Callie! You *must* find us soon! We can't stay here much longer!" then slides back into the portal, but not before the ring slips off her finger onto the floor in front of her, giving her physical evidence that it's not her imagination.

Niall senses her panic as she lets out a blood-curdling scream. He ports in behind her as the portal is in the last stages of closing.

Callie is hyperventilating, so he reaches around her, whispering in her ear, "Callie! What's *wrong*? What happened?"

She can't get the words out, focused on controlling her breathing and getting her wits back in order. She leans against him, letting him support her, and closes her eyes, concentrating on slowing her breathing and her heart. After a minute, she relaxes into him like she doesn't have the strength to stay upright, so he carefully lowers her to the floor and moves to sit with her, face to face. "What's wrong?" He demands and tries to calm his own anxiety about her well-being.

She takes a couple of slow, deep breaths, looking him in the eye. She looks like she's seen a ghost and stammers, "I... I made this pendant tonight. I went to look at it in the mirror and... I swear I didn't do it, *but* a portal opened right there, in *that* mirror! Next thing I knew, a hand reached out of the *goddamn* mirror and... it was *my* hand! Down to the *freaking* birthmark right here!" She exclaims, pointing to the heart-shaped birthmark on her right hand.

She stares at the floor under the mirror and lunges forward, grabbing the ring and scrambling back to where she was sitting with Niall. She sticks it up in his face. "*This*! The hand dropped *this*! Niall, I just cut that stone *tonight* and put it in *this* necklace!" She says, holding the two pieces of jewelry side-by-side. "No two pieces of matrix turquoise are identical, even if cut to match, but these two stones are identical, down to the tiny, copper inclusions on one end of the stone. That's impossible! There's no way these stones can be identical!" She turns and searches his face for answers she knows he's unlikely to have.

"Okay, Callie. I *get* it. Something *real* happened, but I honestly don't know what! We'll figure this out, I *promise*! I'll get Sara to check the psychic logs for tonight, and see if you made the portal, or if it came from somewhere else. She's concerned about you. She told me the day she brought you out of your induced rest that something real was going on when you heard those voices. She could see it in the logs. She just doesn't know what."

She looks at him, annoyed. "And you *didn't* think you should tell me what she said?"

"I didn't want to make you any more unnerved than you've been. I thought it best just to wait and see if it happened again." He explains, gently caressing her hand in his.

"Well, I know now, and I have hard, as in *rock* hard evidence, it's real!" She looks off in the distance for a second, unfocused, trying to remember something.

"What is it? Did you figure something out?" He asks.

"Not figured out, no. I just remembered what the message from the mirror, from me, I guess. The other me said 'I need to find them soon because they can't stay there much longer'. But how can I *find* myself? *Oh, God!* I'm getting a headache just thinking about it!"

He helps her up. "Rest. I'll get in touch with Sara so she can check on her end." He says.

She crawls off to bed and lies down, thinking through it repeatedly. By the time Niall comes in to check on her half an hour later, she's sound asleep. He paths Sara, ***She's asleep. I'm sure it can wait until tomorrow, right?***

Sara replies hesitantly, ***I suppose. I'll talk to Liz as well. I want to see Callie here tomorrow.***

Niall says, ***Thanks, I'll make sure she comes in.***

They break contact and he joins Callie for the night.

***

Callie is back in the strange field, skies dark and lightning flashing around her. She hears, "Follow my voice! We *need* you!" but can't see anyone around her. She follows that voice—no, *her* voice through the wind and storm, through a wooded area, across a small river, past a house that looks familiar, but she can't place it as she's moving too quickly to focus on details. She enters a dense, wooded area and fights her way through it until it opens into a clearing. She hears,

"We're here! Come find us!" Lightning flashes, and she wakes up, sitting bolt upright and smacking Niall with one hand to wake him, because she knows where she needs to go.

"Niall! Get up! We've got to go! I *know* where now!" She insists and gets out of bed. Luckily, she fell asleep in her clothes or she might have ported out in next to nothing. Before she can port out, Niall reaches out and grabs her by the wrist.

"*Stop!* Slow down! Tell me what's up." He insists as he drags her back to the bedside.

"I had another dream. *Same* place, I think. I followed the voice, and I know where I *need to go*." She says, certain in her need to get there as soon as she can.

"*Wait!* I'm not letting you go by yourself! You have no idea what you'll face, if anything!" He insists, trying to calm her down and talk sense into her.

"If you're coming, get ready, because *I'm going!* I don't know what's going to happen, but it's urgent I get there and get *there soon!*" She insists.

He knows how stubborn she is. He gets up and hurriedly pulls on his pants and shirt from the day before. He grabs a pair of shoes and looks at her expectantly. "Well?"

She takes his hand impatiently, and the two of them port into a clearing somewhere, surrounded by woods, in the dark. There's a weird feeling in the air, like there's a giant, Van der Graaf Generator under their feet. They both feel the fine hairs on their bodies stand on end. There's energy here, and a lot of it. She turns and says, "Stay here. I must do whatever it is alone, and if it involves a portal, I don't want you too close in case it opens on top of you." She senses his hesitation in letting her do what she must do, so leans closer to him and gives him a kiss, saying "*Trust* me." She holds his hand and continues to do so as she edges away toward the center of the clearing, only letting it go when their fingertips can no longer touch. She turns around and walks until her intuition says stop. It's darkest night, but there's so much energy building the field almost glows.

Niall reaches out to Liz, Sara, and others to get them to join him in case things go badly, but he can't get his message through the growing, chaotic, energy field. He watches her move toward a stone in the center of the field. She kneels in front of it and puts her hands up in the air as if she were a mime pretending to feel a wall in front of her.

Something tells her the stone marks the spot where she needs to be. She hears that strange, yet all too familiar voice in her mind, but there's more. It sounds like a cacophony of hundreds of minds biding their time, waiting for something momentous to happen. She shakes her head and focuses on the one voice, not on the cacophonic chorus.

She moves her hands in front of her, fingers up and flat as though she were feeling a wall. She seeks the peak point of the energy, possibly the source. As she gets closer to it, she slows her movement until she feels invisible, but physical resistance, as if she were pushing against another set of hands that aren't there. She swallows anxiously but knows she must do this. She calms her mind and summons a portal to open. She doesn't know where it's going, just that she must open one *here*. The air vibrates with energy, as random ripples form before her, making a giant wall of fluctuating energy.

It's difficult for Niall to stand by, watching helplessly, but knows she's right. With the energy flying around, a portal could randomly open and cut him in two if unstable. He settles on a fallen tree at the edge of the clearing, willing himself to watch. The only thing he can do is what they've practiced so many times before her mission. He opens his mind and feels her take the energy he offers. As she does, a flare of light flashes and nearly blinds him. He worries about her but knows she's okay. He can feel her consciousness and she's become oddly calm.

Callie welcomes Niall's proffered energy feed and draws on the other energy around her in the clearing, from the plants and earth around her. When the light flares, another set of fingers interlace with her own through the invisible wall. She opens her eyes and sees her own face, eyes hollow and expression worn. Her hair is cut short, and she seems off, but the intertwined hands cause the portal to spread out until it's enormous. It's larger than the one at the concert venue or during the exodus from the Israeli base. It shimmers, ripples, flutters, and slowly clears, so she sees where the mental cacophony is coming from.

Hundreds of people are behind the other Callie, many of them looking far worse for wear. The other Callie draws in energy given willingly from the crowd to create the portal from her side. Other Callie locks eyes with her and their minds become one. The giant portal stabilizes and the people from the other side move through and spread out in the field to make room for those who follow.

Niall bolts up from the log as he watches the exodus from another world, and into his Sanctuary, quickly but orderly, like the portal could close at any time. The crowd spreads out, edging around the sides of the portal to the other side of the field, making room for the hundreds crossing the threshold.

When the last of them come through, Callie nods to her counterpart and stands, pulling the other Callie up and through the portal until they stand side-by-side, like a pair of identical twins from some warped Prince and the Pauper story. Niall's Callie with her longish, curly black hair, neatly cut, and healthy, and her counterpart who looks as if she's not eaten or fed in weeks, hair cropped short, face drawn, but at peace now that her mission is complete.

***

Nearby, Marc and Tess are curled up together in bed in their home in Sanctuary. Marc wakes with a start and a gasp. He shakes Tess until she swats him with one hand. "Tess! *Wake* up! Can't you *feel* that?" Marc asks urgently.

"Feel what? Exhaustion? You know I worked out with Amy and Co. today! I want to sleep!" She mutters and rolls away and back to sleep.

"I *know* you're tired! But seriously, can't you *feel that*." He asks.

She turns around and asks "Feel wha...." She trails off as an incredible surge of energy grows nearby. "What the *fuck* is that?" Tess asks, sitting up and staring inquisitively at Marc.

"I don't know, but I've never felt anything like it! Get dressed, we need to check this out. I'll holler at Kari and get some of the others to join us."

They get dressed and three minutes later, Liz, Kari, Peder, and a very grumpy Phoenix are in their living room. They quickly react to the increasing energy levels. Sara ports in shortly thereafter and her eyes go wide. She looks at Tess and demands, "What did you do now?"

"It's *not* me, Sara! I *swear*! Marc woke *me* up because of this."

They go outside and instinctively know which way to go. The energy surge is coming from behind the house, away from the river. They try to port but can't; something is disrupting their ability to slip into the membrane, so they hasten through the woods toward the energy. Ten minutes later, they emerge into a field full of people, and the source of all the energy. As the portal closes, they stand there, stunned at the sight.

Marc mutters, "*Merde! Mon Dieu!* What the *hell*?" as he looks at the crowd of people that resemble refugees from a war zone.

Liz looks at the crowd and asks, "Who the *hell* are they and *why* are they in Sanctuary?"

Kari gasps, "They're *all Apara!* Every last one of them!"

They can see a figure moving through the darkness toward them. Cautiously at first, then picking up speed. Marc can sense something oddly familiar about the person... the woman. He knows the figure is a woman now, as his soul floods with confusion and disbelief as the figure emerges from the darkness and her face becomes visible as the moonlight shines upon her. Marc is practically in shock with disbelief as the woman comes up to him and wraps her arms around him, kissing him.

She pauses briefly to say, "*Mon amour!* I thought I'd lost you forever!"

Marc takes a step back, in shock. He grasps Tess's hand tightly and utters, "Collette?"

FOREIGN WORD LIST

FRENCH

Merde! Mon Dieu!	Shit! My God!
Mon amour!	My love

ITALIAN

Amore mia	My love
Merda	Shit

GAELIC

Mo Chridhe	My heart

HEBREW

Naqam	Vengeance

NORWEGIAN

Blåbær saft	Blueberry (Bilberry) juice, often made from bottled concentrate
Bror	Brother
Brunost	Brown Cheese-a caramelized goat/cow cheese. Taste is somewhere between peanut butter and caramel.
Du må spise noe!	You need to eat something!
Elskling	My love
Faen, Faen i hel-vete!	Damn, Hell, literally: The devil in
Jævla drittsekker!	Damn shitbag (scumbag)
Fyttirakkern!	Bloody hell
Gravlaks	Salmon cured in sugar, salt, and dill
Hnefatafl	A Viking era game that uses a board similar to chess
Hei	Hi
Helvete	Hell

Herre Gud!	Dear lord! Oh, God!
Hjerte mitt	My heart
Hytte	Cabin
Hva i helvete driver han med?	What is he going on about?
Hva i alle verden skjed?	What in the world happened?
Ja	Yes
Javel	Southern Norwegian expression that has several meanings, include 'Well?"
Kjære	Dear
Ostehøvel	A Cheese Plane-invented in Norway
Piffi	Popular Scandinavian spice blend
Risgrøt	Rice Porridge
Takk for maten	Thanks for the food (traditional saying after meals)
Tusen Takk	Thank you
Utrolig!	Unbelievable

www.ingramcontent.com/pod-product-compliance
Lightning Source LLC
Chambersburg PA
CBHW070307040726
47501CB00018B/312